DIMINISHED GODS *of* PREVAIL

Diminished Gods of Prevail

KYLA GALINDO

Charleston, SC
www.PalmettoPublishing.com

Copyright © 2023 by Kyla Galindo

All rights reserved.

No portion of this book may be reproduced, stored in a retrieval system, or transmitted in any form by any means—electronic, mechanical, photocopy, recording, or other—except for brief quotations in printed reviews, without prior permission of the author.

First Edition

Paperback ISBN: 979-8-8229-1599-2
eBook ISBN: 979-8-8229-1600-5

Table of Contents

Part I · vi

Part II - Serpent Realm · 22

Part III - Fire Realm · 74

Part IV - Winter Realm · 105

Part V - Water Realm · 181

Part VI - Light Realm · 245

Part VII - Dark Realm · 291

Part VIII - Nature Realm · 356

Part I

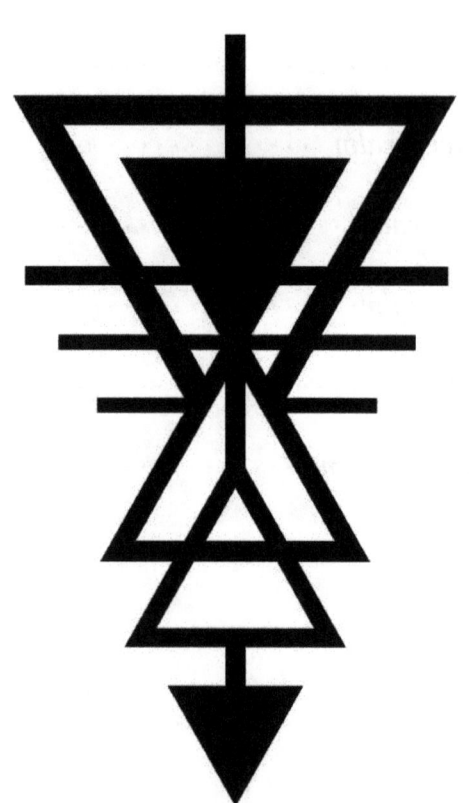

Chapter 1

The Art of War

The supreme art of war is to subdue the enemy without fighting.

—Sun Tzu

The world was covered in blood. And they called this time Tumultus Bellum Sacrum, Latin for Upheaval Holy War.

The mortal beings had no justice and no laws; all they had was their religion, and in this time, that was all they needed.

But since there were so many gods, it caused great conflict between the mortals. The human race was coming to an end as they continued to slaughter each other to prove that their god was stronger than all the rest.

The gods could not take it anymore as they watched and did nothing as innocent women, children, and men died for their faith.

So one night when the moon was full and the air was hot, Orifiel the God of Light came down to meet the other Elemental Gods.

Glycon the Serpent God was very puzzled about why he had conjured up this meeting. As was Armetha the Goddess of Water, so she asked him, "Orifiel, why have you brought us here?"

Orifiel said, "When there are no more humans, we cease to exist, and that is rapidly approaching as the mortal beings continue to rip each other apart trying to put one of us at the top of the pyramid."

But Hermia the Goddess of Nature knew that the last time they intervened, it was bad.

When they tried to come together to tell their believers that they needed to worship all the gods, it made the mortals angry.

Hermia said, "But, Orifiel, when we tried to send signals to the mortals to praise all of us, it caused them to kill themselves."

The mortals would rather die than think of their god as weak. Believing that the god you were worshipping was the only true right way, then to find that you needed another god would make you feel like you had been lied to and that you had wasted your devotion on a false prophet.

But what their believers didn't understand was that the Elemental Gods all played a significant role to create life and it's existence.

Proving this to the humans caused the Upheaval Holy War.

Balor the Demon God laughed at all of this. He did not care that the mortals were killing each other. He preferred dead humans to live ones anyway since he was the ruler of death.

Before Orifiel could respond to Hermia's concerns, Balor began to chuckle. The gods all looked in his direction.

Balor said, "Let the mortals kill themselves. After all, the more souls I consume, the stronger I become in the underworld. I kind of like the sound of being the only god left to inhabit the world."

Vulcas the God of Fire was very happy to make it clear to the God of Death that, whether he liked it or not, he was in the same situation as them.

Vulcas said, "If humans no longer existed, then there would be no more souls for you to consume."

Balor looked at Vulcas with narrowed eyes.

He hadn't realized that he had just as much to lose as the other gods.

Balor said with anger, "OK fine, then what does the God of Light have in mind?"

Orifiel responded, "I'm going to create a Predominat one, who will be made of flesh and blood."

Bormack the God of Winter had his doubts about this, as did his sister Zephira the Goddess of Snow, who could only be summoned by her brother Bormack.

Zephira said, "Orifiel, I don't want to cause an argument, but I don't see how this predominat one can help."

Orifiel responded, "We are going to give this mortal champion one of our godlike powers."

All the gods looked at each other with mixed feelings.

Boramck said, "Orifiel, humans are very fragile beings."

Egrass the God of Cold Wind felt that the God of Light was not looking at this the right way.

He said, "Bormack is right: mortals and power do not mix well. Usually what happens is that humans let power go to their head, and that's when they stop listening to their heart."

Orifiel said, "Then we will fine a mortal with a pure heart."

"How will we do that?" asked Hermia.

The gods were all eager to hear the God of Light's response.

Orifiel said, "We shall put them to a test."

"What kind of test?" Glycon asked.

"We shall pick three beings, and we will give them each a box of treasure of some sort. Whoever does the most unselfish thing with their treasure will be our champion.

Balor responded, "Are you out of your mind? That is the stupidest thing I have ever heard of. I'm out raged that you would think I would stoop so low as to give a mortal any of my power."

The Demon God felt very strongly about the mortals being beneath him and would never stoop to endeavoring on such a thing.

The God of Fire was getting very agitated watching the God of Darkness yell and scream in anger about how the humans were less than worthy of his power.

Vulcas shouted, "Enough!"

The God of Fire burst into flames.

Armetha said, "That's right, enough is enough."

She put her hand on Vulcas's back so he would calm down.

After Vulcas extinguished his flame, the God of Darkness smiled 'cause he knew he had struck a nerve with the God of fire.

Balor said, "I just don't see how this is going to fix everything."

In order to have world peace, the gods would have to agree on everything. That was not going to happen since they were all so different and were worshipped differently.

Balor continued, "Let's take Vulcas, for instance. Your worshippers are called 'torches,' are they not?"

Vulcas just looked at the God of Death without giving him an answer.

Balor said, "And they call them torches because they burn anything and everyone that doesn't convert."

The God of Fire just shook his head; he did not want the God of Death to see that he was upset.

But it was true his followers had become something he was not about.

Balor went on, "Glycon, your worshippers are all men because they have no respect for women."

Glycon, too, was ashamed that his believers raped women and used children as slaves and, to his dismay, had done nothing to stop it.

Glycon said, "You know very well that's not what I preach to my people."

Balor responded, "It doesn't matter because that's how they see you."

Orifiel added, "Stop it, Balor; we have all had a hand in this."

Balor said, "Orifiel, I think it's safe to say that if any of the gods are going to be diminished, it is going to be you since your worshippers are dropping like flies."

The God of Light's people were forbidden from causing harm to one another. They tried to spread peace and love.

Balor continued, "This makes you the weaker God."

The Demon God was tickled to see the God of Light upset.

The God of Light was frustrated.

He said, "Yes, my people don't fight back; they openly walk into battle, hoping that the love they speak of will have some effect on their executioners."

Balor responded, "But it always ends in bloodshed."

"You know, Balor, you have no right to past judgment," said the God of Light. "After all, you have no people and your followers don't love you; in fact, they fear you and try to avoid you."

The God of Death didn't have any worshippers; he preyed on other gods' followers. They did everything they could in hopes that their souls would go somewhere else.

Orifiel and Balor got into each other's faces. As they continued to stare down each other, you could feel the pure tension and antipathy they had for one another.

Armetha shouted, "Stop it, both of you!"

The Goddess of Water got in between them so that they wouldn't do anything foolish.

The God of Darkness had an evil grin upon his face as he moved in on the Goddess of Water.

He said, "Armetha, your people are called the water hoarders because they guard and stake a claim on all the water resources. The only way you can get any water is by paying a hefty price; in fact, your followers sell it by the pound."

Because of this, a lot of innocent people died. The water hoarders didn't care that they deprived lots of families of water.

Balor continued, "The Goddess of Greed is what they call you now."

Armetha said, "I take full responsibility for what my people have become."

The Goddess of Water knew where she had gone wrong with her people. Instead of helping them by guiding them the right way like she should have been doing, she had turned her back on her people, hoping they would find their way on their own.

All of the gods were guilty of this. They did not mentor their people. They were so wrapped up in their own world that they forgot about securing their believers in their own faith.

And they are all now facing the consequences.

Armetha went on, "I have no one to blame but myself, and if I had had a chance to fix it, I would have."

The Goddess of Water looked at the God of Light, signaling that she agreed with him on this.

Hermia said, "You know, Balor, calling out our faults isn't helping the situation."

Balor responded, "Hermia, I'm so sick of you acting all high and mighty when you have nothing to be proud of."

"At least my people aren't killing anyone."

The God of Darkness laughed.

He said, "Oh no, your people are too busy doing nothing as they look the other way when it comes to helping anyone out."

The Goddess of Nature's people turned their backs on their own kind. They ignored the screams of innocent people crying out for help and they continued to do nothing, just watch them die while hiding out in the trees that she so graciously provided for them.

Her followers stayed hidden and kept away from confrontation.

Balor went on, "Hermia, you are the Cowardly Goddess, and your people are spineless."

The Goddess of Nature began to cry. As she was sobbing, the Goddess of Water comforted her.

Bormack said, "Balor, you are such a bully."

Balor responded, "Bormack, last but not least. Now, the gods of winter are the most barbaric of them all."

These gods' believers ate the flesh of humans and drank their blood. They were known to eat their own kind, making them the most uncivilized savages of them all.

Balor went on, "The Winter Gods of Carnage is what they call you now."

North the God of Ice was the youngest winter god. He was not afraid of the Demon God passing judgment.

North said, "I'm gravely upset by how our followers see us, but can you blame them?"

Zephira said," He's right—we made them this way."

It was in a human's nature to want to feel loved, feared, respected. They all longed to be needed and wanted. That is what power did for them. That was why human hearts needed to believe in something. They wanted to feel what they felt was real.

Egrass said, "We made the humans so delicate so that they can choose to believe that what they worship is a true and noble cause."

North added, "Whether it be for good or bad."

Bormack said, "I agree with the God of Light that we must help."

Glycon said, "I, too, agree that this superior being can help us relate to the humans."

Armetha said, "You can count me in."

Hermia said, "I am with you as well."

Vulcas said, "What do we have to lose?"

All the gods look at the God of Darkness, waiting for his response. After all, they couldn't do this without him.

Orifiel said, "Balor, we don't have much of a choice; this is our only hope."

The God of Death looked at all the other gods and reluctantly agreed with the God of Light's decision.

He said, "Fine, but I still feel it is a big mistake."

The God of Light told the other gods to pick three contestants quickly but carefully. And without delay, the gods were off. Hermia the Goddess of Nature stayed behind to talk to the God of Light.

She cautioned, "I hope you understand the risk you are taking."

Orifiel responded, "Of course I know what's at stake."

"Good, 'cause you are putting a lot of trust into the mortal beings."

"And why not? They put so much trust in us."

"It's about time we put our faith in them 'cause they need us just as much as we need them.

Chapter 2

Mortal Champion

*A just person is one who is conformed
and transformed into justice.*

—Meister Eckhart

The gods looked high and low, but it was hard in a world filled with hate and greed. So much selfishness spread throughout the land.

The goddess picked a forty-one-year-old man named Buran, who was a blacksmith. He had a wife and three sons who were very vain and selfish. Buran was one of Vulcas's believers. Since he worshipped the God of Fire, he was known as a torch.

But the reason why Buran was so appealing was he would make toys for kids. He did this out of the generosity of his heart and wanted nothing in return.

So the goddess gave Buran a chest full of gold. And without concern for where it came from, he took it.

He built a big house with his money and gave his ungrateful wife all the jewelry she could wear.

His sons, on the other hand, became extremely jealous of his new wealth. So they killed Buran in his sleep and took his fortune. Before they could squander what was left of their father's fortune, they ended up killing each other for it.

The goddess thought they had picked the right man, but they were wrong.

The gods had come to a man called Gibbous. He was a thirty-six-year-old man who loved the nightlife. Gibbous had no family but was always willing to invite anyone to join him. He worshipped the God of Light.

He was a good candidate because he got along with everyone. He was very good at making sad people happy and always preached about love.

Gibbous took his newfound fortune from the gods and threw a party the likes of which no one had seen before.

Gibbous evidently died from drinking too much liquor at his party.

Another minor setback for the gods.

Balor the Demon God was very happy that the gods were not finding their so-called champion. He hoped they would never find him.

He said, "You do realize that we are supposed to be helping the humans, not killing them."

Orifiel responded, "Yes, I am aware of that."

Balor said, "It just seems that this new fortune you have been handing out has caused more problems."

Glycon said, "You know, Balor, you could help by looking for another candidate."

Balor responded, "No way. This was your guys' idea, not mine.

Hermia said, "I think I have found one."

"Really? Who?" Armetha asked.

Hermia said, "He's one of my followers; he's a little young, but he has a good nature."

Balor commented, "They all appeared to be good-natured."

Hermia responded, "I feel this one is different. I don't know why."

Orifiel asked, "How young?"

"Nineteen," responded Hermia.

Balor commented, "Jeez, he's practically a baby."

Vulcas said, "Well, it can't be much worse than what we have been picking."

Bormack said, "That's true."

"Show him to us," said Orifiel.

The third candidate was a nineteen-year-old young man named Saul. He tamed horses and was very good to them. He prayed to Hermia every day, thanking her for his many horses.

Saul had a little sister name Jenny and a mother who was gravely sick. He looked after both of them. He spent most of his time in the field with his horses and sister Jenny, who loved riding them.

As the gods watched him from afar, they noticed that he was very different from the other men they had chosen.

Balor said, "I don't think he is the one."

"Why not?" Hermia asked.

"Well, for staters, he is one of yours, so he's probably a coward."

"Does he look like a coward to you?"

"No, but looks can be deceiving."

Orifiel added, "This is our last chance. If we don't get it right this time, we never well."

Balor responded, "Yeah, we have been wrong so far. What's one more?"

Hermia said, "He might surprise you."

Balor concluded, "Highly doubtful."

The gods decided to give Saul a try. They left his treasure out on the field where his horses were grazing and waited for him to find it.

When Saul found his new riches, he was dumbfounded and puzzled. What should I do with it? he thought to himself.

He figured that someone must have lost it and he should go and return it. But how would he learn who was the rightful owner of this loot? Saul stayed away from crowded areas; he was not big on confrontation. But he had to do the right thing.

The next day he went into town with the treasure in his satchel. As he was getting ready to walk into the main gate, someone pulled gently on his hand.

When he looked down, he saw a woman and her child. They looked like they hadn't eaten in days. Saul wanted to help her, but how?

As he looked at his satchel, he thought, Is it wrong to give away something that doesn't belong to you? Saul also knew that he would probably never find the true owner of this fortune, especially since he lived in a world where honesty was nonexistent.

Saul decided that if he was not going to find the owner, then he would rather give it to someone who needed it. He did just that. He gave the woman some of his gold, and she looked at him like he was a miracle.

The feeling Saul felt in that moment kindled his heart, so he gave the rest of his money to all those that were suffering. He never spent any of it on himself.

As you well know, the Gods were very pleased with this; they had found their new messiah. Of course the Demon God was very upset. He felt that Saul was still no better than the men they had chosen before.

Now it was time to give Saul his real gift, the one that was going to change mankind forever.

It was evening. The sun was getting ready to set, but it was still a very hot day. Saul was rounding up his horses. Then a sudden chill came upon him.

Flurries filled the sky, then fell to the ground.

Saul couldn't understand the drastic change in the weather.

The gods showed themselves to Saul. As they appeared, Saul didn't know what to do but kneel.

Orifiel said, "Rise, my son."

"But how? What?" Saul responded.

Hermia said, "This is real, Saul; we are standing in front of you."

"Wait, you're Hermia, the Goddess of Nature."

"Correct."

"And the rest of you are the Elemental Gods?"

Vulcas said, "Correct again."

"But I thought Hermia was the rightful way to life," said Saul.

Orifiel explained, "That's why we are here, Saul."

"I don't understand," said Saul.

"Join the club," said Balor.

Orifiel said, "We are here 'cause we need your help."

Saul asked, "But how can I help you? I'm a nobody."

Balor responded, "Well, I won't argue with you there."

Vulcas said, "Balor, will you stop? You're not helping."

"Whatever," responded Balor.

Orifiel said, "Saul, you are going to be the person that is going to bring all our people together."

"I think you have the wrong person. I'm no God—just a horse tamer."

Orifiel continued, "No, but with our help, you will bring peace and justice to the land. Saul, I give you the gift of immortality against any mortal weapons."

Armetha added, "Saul, I give you the gift of healing all mortal wounds with water."

Glycon said, "Saul, I give you the gift of sight throughout the mortal world."

The Serpent God entrusted Saul with one of his favorite snakes, called Omens Videntes, also known as the All-Seeing Snake. Saul would be able to see everything that was going on in the mortal world without having to go anywhere.

Hermia said, "Saul, I give you the gift of growing food so that the humans will never know starvation."

Vulcas said, "Saul, I give you the gift of a true and noble pet dragon that will only be loyal to you."

Bormack said, "Saul, my brother and I would like to give you the gift of ice so that you can freeze hatred forever."

Balor the God of Death did not want to give this mortal anything. He looked at the other gods with disgust as he was less than eager to go at all.

He walked up to Saul, growling under his breath so that Saul could see he didn't want to do this. Saul could feel the animosity the God of Death had for him.

Balor said, "Mortal, I give you, much to my displeasure, the gift of my dark army, the Arathagore."

Vulcas said, "Wow, Balor, I'm surprised you would give him such an extravagant power."

Bormack added, "Especially when you're not a generous god."

Balor responded, "Who knows, maybe this will benefit me more than him."

The gods of winter did not like the sound of that. But what was done was done. Orifiel told Saul that with his new gifts, he had to cleanse the world from evil.

Saul was very grateful for his new powers, and he did just that.

He brought the people together to worship all the gods, to love them and praise them equally. This new religion was called Prevail.

Saul did such a good job spreading Prevail that it ended all the wars, and they made Saul King of the World.

Saul was a great king; everyone loved him. He was very good to his people, and their love for him was so strong they made a beautiful kingdom in Saul's name.

The Kingdom of Prevail was full of kindness and love; there was no more hatred or anger. The human life was now longer and more prosperous.

Saul married a beautiful woman named Oriana, and they had a son named Odin. Oriana was just as kind and generous as her king, making their legacy even greater.

The Elemental Gods were rejoicing that their peace-bringer had ended the Upheaval Holy War. Saul created laws to prevent this from ever happening again.

But there was one god that wasn't rejoicing. Balor was not embracing the new change; he was suffering due to it.

The Demon God was sick with envy listening to the mortals praising Saul as their new King of the World. He was also disgusted with the mortals singing and preaching about love and kindness; it was making him physically ill.

His anger was past the boiling point, and his rage had become so strong that he couldn't take it anymore, so he called the other gods for a meeting.

Orifiel asked, "All right, Balor, what do you want?"

"I want things to go back to the way they were," Balor responded.

Armetha asked, "Why would we want that?"

Balor said, "Because I need souls."

"But you are getting souls," said Bormack.

"Not anymore. I used to get them by the boatload; now I get one every once in a while. And the souls I do get are happy and really old."

Hermia said, "I still don't see the problem."

"They don't fear me anymore. They come to me willingly."

Hermia asked, "Isn't that a good thing?"

"No. It's a terrible thing," he responded.

The difference between a happy soul and a sad soul was that one could be manipulated and the other couldn't. In the underworld a pure soul is claimed by the God of Death, but he could not consume it. The Demon God preferred corrupt souls because they could be consumed and easily enslaved, all the while making him stronger.

Balor said, "And I'm so tried of them talking about how great their life was."

Orifiel asked, "So you are upset 'cause you're not getting enough souls?"

Balor responded, "Don't you get it? If I don't get enough bad souls, then I get weak."

Vulcas chimed in, "But when the Arathagore cleaned the land, you got lost of corrupt souls."

"That war is over; now there is no more bloodshed," said Balor.

Armetha said, "Balor, I sympathize with you, but you have to look at the greater good."

Glycon added, "That's right—the greater good is to save the mortal world; that's all that matters."

Balor laughed. "Ha ha. I don't give a *damn* about the greater good! I want this world to go back to being covered in blood, now!"

Bormack advised, "Calm down, Balor."

"No, I will not. I'm sick to death of how your so-called beloved mortals are worshipping this King of the World."

Orifiel said, "Oh, I see. That's what this is really about—you're jealous."

"What!" Balor exclaimed. "Why should they praise him? He is nothing more than a human. So what should I be jealous of? He is no God; *I am*."

Hermia said, "Balor, Saul isn't being worshipped as a god but as a king; that's all.

"I gave him his power, and I can take it back. Let's see how many followers he'll have after that," responded Balor. "Then you will all see how weak and insignificant he is."

Orifiel said, "Balor, if you take Saul's gift away, it won't just be bad for him but us as well."

"I don't care. I'm raging war with this so-called King of the World."

Hermia pleaded, "Balor, please don't do this; it won't end well for anyone."

"If you are not with me, then you are against me," Balor said.

The Demon God stepped back into the underworld where he continued to pace back and forth. He tried to call back his army, the Arathagore, but they would not listen to him; they had become completely loyal to Saul because he was so good to them. He treated them better than the God of Death ever had, making them no longer evil.

So Balor needed a new army if he was going to rage a war against the King of the World.

CHAPTER 3

The Jealous God

Religious wars are not caused by the fact that there is more than one religion, but by the spirit of intolerance…the spread of which can only be regarded as the total eclipse of human reason.

—Charles de Montesquieu

The Elemental Gods were trying to figure out away to stop Balor from unloading his wrath of evil. But it was hard since they couldn't use their powers against each other.

The gods all agreed that they needed to warn Saul about what the God of Darkness was up to so that he could be prepared.

Hermia the Goddess of Nature could not help but feel guilty for putting the humans at risk again.

"Orifiel," she called.

He responded, "Hermia, I know what you're going to say, and I believe we made the right decision."

Glycon added, "Well, there is good news, if you can even call it that."

Vulcas asked, "And what's that?"

"Balor doesn't have an army," said Glycon.

"Yet he will make one," Vulcas responded.

Glycon said, "So a mere distraction is some kind of good news."

Armetha asked, "Who's going to be the one to break the bad news to Saul?"

All the gods looked at the God of Light.

Orifiel said, "I guess that's my cue."

"Is there anything we can do to stop this?" Bormack asked.

Orifiel said, "It's all up to Saul now."

Saul was very happy to see the God of Light. So happy that he gave him a tour of his kingdom.

"See, there isn't one part of this kingdom that doesn't have a statue of the gods," he said.

"I see that," responded Orifiel.

"Look, even Balor's statue gets an honorable mention."

"You have done good, Saul."

The God of Light wanted to be happy for all of Saul's good work, but he couldn't be when he knew what was coming. He really didn't have the heart to tell him, but he knew what had to be done.

Saul could feel the change in the God of Light's behavior as he was showing him around.

"What's wrong?" he asked.

Orifiel said, "What makes you think there is something wrong?"

"It's all over your face."

"Is it that obvious?"

"It is to me. Have I done something wrong?"

"No, Saul. You have done more than we could have ever imagined and then some."

"Really?" Saul said with a smile.

"Saul, we are very proud of you. But a war is coming."

"But I ended all the wars."

"You did, and there shouldn't be any more. But this one is different."

"How so?"

"You will be going up against a higher power."

"I see. Does the God of Death hate me that much?"

"Saul, you never cease to amaze me."

"Can I win this war?"

"I'm sorry, my friend, but no."

"So then what should I do?"

"You must fight for what you believe in, even if you know the outcome."

"Can you help me?"

"I'm going to try."

The God of Light went to the underworld to plead with Balor one more time. He knew it was a long shot, but he had to try.

In the underworld, the God of Death was creating his new army; they were made of his blood, and they looked like men, only much taller and stronger. The God of Evil knew they would be a good match against the Arathagore.

He said, "Oh, the stench of light—how it disgusts me."

"You always were the charmer, Balor," mocked Orifiel.

"Whatever you have come here for, forget it."

"Balor, you have to listen to me: this is not going to end the way you want."

"What I want is to be rid of all of you."

"You might just get your wish if you keep on."

"Good."

"Balor, there has to be away we can coexist; we must make this work."

"Orifiel, I don't care about the human race or you, for that matter."

"Balor, if you kill Saul, it will be the end of us as well."

"No, just you, God of Light."

"Balor, you've got to listen to reason."

"I'm listing to reason; my reason is all that matters."

"Do you really want to be known as the god that destroyed everything?"

"As long as I'm the only god—that's all that matters."

"It's a shame you have to learn that the hard way."

"Leave, Orifiel, and never bother me again. It's over."

Chapter 4

God vs King

When you kill a king, you don't stab him in the dark.
You kill him where the entire court can watch him die.

—Amsterdam Vallon

The God of Death's new army was called the Arattus. They had no remorse for human life. They had black wings and two black horns that came out of their heads.

The Arathagores' entire bodies were red, including their wings and horns. They also had a tail and hooves.

Balor wasted no time and unleashed the Arattus on the Kingdom of Prevail. The King of the World did the same with the Arathagore.

And because both armies could fly, their fight took place in the sky. Blood rained down on the Prevail Kingdom for days. What once was a beautiful city had now become the scene of a massacre.

As tired as both armies became, they did not give up.

The gods were struck with grief for having to put the humans again in danger.

As the war continued on, days turned into weeks and then months.

The God of Darkness was getting very impatient. He thought that this would be easy. But the fact that he wasn't getting what he wanted fast enough caused him to turn to drastic measures.

The God of Death kidnapped Saul's wife Oriana to the underworld. There he raped her, and she died giving birth to a half-demon baby.

When Saul heard this awful news, he became overwhelmed with sorrow. Suffering from heartbreak, he surrendered to the God of Death.

The God of Light took one last look at the world below as he could feel it coming to an end. The Goddess of Nature hugged the Goddess of Water tight. They did not want to be alone in their final moments.

The God of Death was happy in his victory. He growled with pleasure in his triumph.

Balor sat on Saul's throne admiring the view of all his subjects; those who hadn't died in the war were crying and suffering as the Arattus had them chained up to do what they wanted with them.

As they brought Saul out, the God of Death told his army to bring Saul to his knees.

Saul complied. Saul was not afraid of the God of Death. He wanted to die; he was ready for it.

Saul took one look at his sister Jenny and his son Odin. Jenny was crying so heavily, and she couldn't look away. Odin was very young, but he knew deep down that he was never going to see his father again.

The God of Darkness held up his mighty axe to Saul's neck, and with great force, he slashed Saul's head clean off his body. Saul's blood spilled out onto his loyal subjects, including his son and sister.

The Arattus growled with excitement. His lifeless body lay there, bleeding out.

Balor picked up the King of the World's head.

Before the God of Death could say anything, he started to feel very funny, not well. His body felt weak. The feeling was getting stronger. He dropped Saul's head as his hands were disappearing. He had a look of panic on his face as fear set in. After his hands were gone, his arms followed, along with his legs. His body was vanishing right before his eyes, and he was powerless to stop it.

He looked up at the sky and screamed. The God of Light name, and then Balor the Demon God was no more.

The Arattus and the Arathagore went back into the underworld, where they continued their fight in hating each other.

Jenny crawled over to her brother's dead body, praying that by some miracle he would come back.

With her brother's blood all over her and Odin, they both sprouted white wings and took to the sky.

The rest of the king's loyal subjects, who where also covered in Saul's blood, changed as well.

Some grew snake eyes, and their hair went black; they took to the east. While others' hair turned white as snow, and they took to the north.

A couple others' hair turned green, along with their eyes, and they took to the south.

The hair of another group of people who had the mortal champion's blood on them turned red, and so did their eyes. They took to the west. The eyes and hair of the rest turned blue. They took to the water.

The rest of the gods were never seen or heard from again; they all vanished. The Kingdom of Prevail, along with Saul's body, began to wither into dust. The Prevail religion was never heard of again.

The kingdom was sucked down by the earth as it lay there decaying away. There was nothing left but ruins in the hollow lands, as they called it now. Swampland it had become.

The legendary King of the World became nothing more than a fairy tale that no one believed in. What existed now was seven different realms that went back to worshipping their own individual god.

To avoid war, they all kept to themselves. Even though the gods were being worshipped individually, it wasn't enough to bring them back since each realm was suffering in some way.

But like all great legends, which never really die, there was a prophecy, a foretelling here: if someone could possess all traits of all seven realms, he or she would bring back the Elemental Gods.

Part II

THE SERPENT REALM

Introduction

The Serpent Realm is to the east. Nothing but an endless desert. Blazing rolling hills of sand dunes. The temperature is always scorching. There are five kingdoms in the Serpent Realm and one very old empire.

The Ja-bar Empire used to be the sole ruler and owner of the Serpent Realm. But as faith shows us, an empire is only strong as long as it has believers.

The Ja-bar empire is the kingdom and protector of snakes. They are true believers in Glycon the Serpent God.

Those who believe in Glycon are called the Shyam. The Shyam all have fair skin, black hair, and snake eyes. The Shyam have many enemies; their biggest one is called the Solifugids.

The Solifugids hate Glycon and everything he stands for.

The king of Ja-bar is Tyrant Ouroboros. The Ouroboros family has a very strong royal bloodline. So strong that they have a gift by which they can turn into very big snakes.

Tyrant Ouroboros has the power to change into the genus *Ophiophagus*, also known as the upscale king cobra. He weighs in at 10,000 tons and is 1,083 feet long from head to tail; he can lift his head 541 feet off the ground.

His son, Prince Tyga Ouroboros, who is nineteen, can transform into Nosferatu Aku, also known as the vampire snake. This particular snake is a very rare breed because it feeds only on blood. When Tyga is in snake form, he is 2,073 feet tall and weighs in at 850,000 tons. He can lift his head 1,036.5 feet off the ground.

Now his daughter, Princess Eden Ouroboros, who is seventeen, can transform into the Narcotize Allele, also known as the hypnosis snake. She is 1,018 feet long from head to tail and weighs in at 46,000 tons; her head can reach 509 feet off the ground.

The Ja-bar Kingdom doesn't have an army; they don't need one because they have snakes to defend them.

The problem that the Ja-bar Empire is facing now is that no one believes in Glycon anymore.

And because of this, the snakes have died off. There were once millions of snakes in the Kingdom of Ja-bar, but now there are only three full-blooded snakes left.

The biggest and oldest of them all is called Golden Rose. Golden Rose is an Aurum Nathair, also known as a gold-plated snake.

She is the last female snake left, and she is 6,000 feet long from head to tail. And she weighs in at 100,000 tons. She can lift her head 3,000 feet off the ground.

Even though they are not gold, Aurum snakes are covered in metallic scales, and when the sun hits their skin just right, they send off a shiny glare, luring people to their deaths. They are nontoxic but extremely dangerous.

The second snake is Drachma. He is a Cerberus Fidi, also known as a three-headed snake.

His name says it all: three heads and one powerful, strong body. Cerberi have four arms, two on each side of their body, to counterbalance their heads.

Their scales are prone to changing color in response to humidity and light. So they are very good at camouflaging themselves in their surroundings.

Drachma is 1,981 feet long from tail to head, and he weighs in at 16,000 tons. Each one of his heads is 350 feet wide. He is also nontoxic but, again, extremely dangerous.

The youngest of them all is Set. He is a Hymenoptera, also known as a fire-breather snake. Set is 1,063 feet long from head to tail and weighs in at 2,000 pounds. Set is a baby and still has a lot of growing to do. He is nontoxic but extremely dangerous.

This is all the Ja-bar Kingdom has left to defend against its enemies. And since this empire is no longer favorable, it has lost all its credibility. The Kingdom of Ja-bar is almost completely deserted. There are now fifteen thousand people, including the royal family, left in the kingdom. A kingdom that had been built to support over two hundred thousand people. The other five kingdoms are lucrative and doing great, while the Ja-bar Kingdom is slowly on its way to depletion.

One of the kingdoms that is the most prosperous is Sand Cry City. It is now the ruler of the Serpent Realm and buying everything it can get its hands on. The king of Sand Cry is Tzar, who is trying to get rid of the Ouroboros family once and for all. He wants the Ja-bar Kingdom since his kingdom is overpopulated.

Then there are three other kingdoms and one temple. Boa City is the third-biggest kingdom, and it is the second most powerful kingdom in the Serpent Realm. The ruler of this city is King Nefud. He is a young king.

The fourth kingdom is Etoch City. King Phlox rules that one, and it is the third most powerful. Chaya City is the last kingdom; it has the highest profits but is fourth in power. King Ezamir rules this one, and he is Tzar's younger brother.

Then there is the Temple of Naga, which has now become a safe haven for the Shyam; that are hiding there.

Glycon symbolizes empowerment. Their religion is Naagasree.

Chapter 5

Prince Tyga Ouroboros

My father gave me one job to do, and I screwed that up horribly. There was no getting out of it this time. Usually there isn't much he can do to me, but this time I can feel what is coming my way, and it isn't going to be good.

I was climbing the steps to his office in a brisk walk. I got to the top floor, where I could see the door to my father's office and I could see my father's bodyguards hovering by the door. Tacitus is my father's head bodyguard, and his father is Exodus, who is my father's trusted adviser. Tacitus and I are the same age. We used to be best friends, a long time ago. But now we can't stand each other. And I just knew he was going to rub this in my face.

Tacitus said, "Well, well, the prodigal fuckup returns."

I responded, "Fuck you, Tac."

"You couldn't handle this."

All the other bodyguards laughed.

I continued, "I can take you any time, any place."

"Well, let's go, sweetheart."

"You think you are supercilious, but you aren't shit."

"Well, there is only one way to prove that theory."

Exodus interjected, "Shut the fuck up, the both of you."

He walked out of my father's office and got in between us. He continued, "You two can fight over who has the biggest penis later."

I have no doubt I have the biggest one.

Exodus said, "But for now, Prince Tyga, your father is waiting to talk to you."

Tacitus added, "I guess we will finish this fight after your father tears you a new one."

I gave Tac the finger as I was walking into my father's office. I could hear him and his father laughing behind my back. Fuck all of them, literally.

My father had a very calming face when he looked up at me from his desk. Maybe it won't be so bad, I thought. Yet he said nothing to me. Just stared at me. Now I felt the awkward, distraught silence in his eyes.

I was panicking; I didn't know quite what to say. He still said nothing. I felt like him not saying anything to me was punishment enough.

I had to say something. His quietness was suffocating me. I wiped the sweat off my head, which was pounding with pain on both sides. I knew he could see me freaking out.

I admitted, "I fucked up."

My father leaned back in his seat as he got comfortable watching me sink in failure. He still said nothing.

I continued, "I'm very sorry."

"Do you have any idea how long it took me to save that much gold?" my father responded.

"I know, and I'm so very sorry."

"I don't want your excuses; I want my gold back."

"I'll get it back."

"How?"

The truth was I had no idea how I was going to get his gold back. My father trusted me to make sure his gold made it safely to King Phlox to pay off our debt to him. I couldn't even do that right.

"I know it was the Solifugids who took it," I explained.

He responded, "How do you know that?"

I didn't know for sure who took it, but I had a hunch it was the Solifugids. They are sand pirates—it's what they do—and they are the only ones stupid enough to pull this off. Plus, whoever did this took everything and didn't leave any witnesses. That's the Solifugids' signature.

I thought my father could tell I had no idea how I was going to get his gold back, but I knew I had to or King Phlox would be beating down our door.

We owed money to everyone, including King Tzar. But I was promised to his daughter. My father hoped that our marriage would somehow wipe out the debt we owed him.

I said, "You need not worry, Father—I will get your gold back."

"Good, 'cause there are two people in this world: the ones who do it, and the ones who think about doing it."

"I will do it."

"If you don't do it, you will be disinherited. No throne, no king, nothing—do you hear me?"

"I understand, Father. I will not let you down."

"Tyga, a king becomes a king when he can take effective action, so show me you have what it takes."

"I'll show you, Father, that I have what it takes."

I don't even know where to start. No one knows who leads the Solifugids. They wear masks and turbans. These underground marauders didn't leave any clues to work with. I might as well just get banished from the kingdom now and get it over with, I thought.

The only person who could help me was my sister, and I hoped to Glycon she had a plan.

CHAPTER 6

Princess Eden Ouroboros

I love playing snakes and ladders with my grandfather. He makes the game more exciting. He tries to cheat, and he thinks I don't notice.

My grandfather wasn't the nicest man. When he was king, he was ruthless. They say Thaddeus Ouroboros is the reason why we went into further debt. If he hadn't past the crown down to my father when he did, the Ouroboros family would be living in a cave somewhere being hunted down by our enemies.

But now that he's no longer king, he's much more calm and restful.

I rolled the dice and got eleven.

I said, "Ten, eleven. I win."

My grandfather replied, "You are cheating."

"I am not."

"Really? Let me see your eyes."

I looked straight into my grandfather's eyes with confidence.

"See, snake eyes," he commented.

I laughed, then said, "We all have snake eyes, and we can't help that; we were all born with them."

"That's my point: you don't play games with someone who has snake eyes."

"Especially when he loses while he's cheating."

My grandfather smiled at me with narrow eyes.

As my grandfather started a new game, Tyga burst in having a panic attack.

"Hey, Granddad, I need to barrow Eden for a minute," he said.

My grandfather responded, "Sure thing."

My brother grabbed my hand and led me into another room, then shut the door.

He was walking back and forth. Seeing him like this kinda turned me on. My brother is a very handsome and determined man. He will never admit to anyone that he needs help. But seeing as he came to me, he must have not had a choice. Watching him squirm got me wet.

I smiled as my eyes followed him pacing back and forth.

"I fucked up, E," he said.

"Wouldn't be the first time," I responded.

"Yeah, but this time I really screwed up."

"What is Father threatening now?"

"Exile, banishment, my head on a spike—take your pick!"

"So nothing he hasn't threatened you with before."

"No! He means it this time; these threats aren't empty!"

"Would you calm down, please?"

"How can I calm down? I just told our father that I was going to get his gold back, and I haven't the foggiest of how I'm going to do that."

"It's going to be all right."

"All right, there is no more gold; do you realize what that means? I'll tell you it means: we can't pay King Phlox what we owe him. If we can't pay him, he will come down with his massive army and kill each one of us."

My brother's face was turning red. He started punching a hole in the wall. And I still couldn't help but smile at him.

"You might want to stop before you completely destroy this room," I said.

"This is turning you on, isn't it?" he asked.

"A little."

"I'm so glad that my failure is making you horny."

"I have a solution to your problem."

My brother's eyes got wide, then he got down on his knees and begged me to help him. I love seeing him grovel at my feet, I thought.

"Tell me, I'm begging," he said.

"You will send another shipment of gold to King Phlox," I explained.

My brother got back to his feet and looked at me like I was crazy. "Have you been listening to anything I have said? There is no more gold, none!"

"Will you let me finish before you dismiss my idea!" I shouted.

"Fine!"

"Thank you. As I was saying, you will send another shipment of gold tonight, and when this one gets robbed, which it will, instead of obtaining the gold, you will have vigilante assassins waiting to catch prisoners."

My brother looked at me like I had just brought someone back from the grave. He gave me that smile that made me weak in the knees. He grabbed me and kissed me like I was his oxygen. I was more than happy to accept that kiss since he is such a great kisser.

"Eden, you're brilliant," he said. "Of course—a trap."

"That will definitely get you some Solifugids," I said.

"I love you more than anything."

"Yeah, I love you too."

My brother was now on his way to put his plan in motion with haste. I love seeing him grovel, but I love it more when he's happy. My sexual desire for my brother has become more of an addiction. One that is not my fault.

Of course my happiness was put on hold when Tuck came in and told me that Golden Rose was very sick. I wasted no time and hurried down to the snake pit with him.

Tuck is the family doctor, or as we call him, the snake healer and charmer. He's been with our family for many years. He helped my mother as much as he could when she got sick.

Golden Rose looked awful; her eyes were droopy. She looked weak, and her scales were very drab.

It hurt me a lot to see her in pain. I laid my hand on her head as she lay there suffering. I gently petted her so that she knew I was going to help her. Her scales felt brittle and dry.

"Tuck, what is wrong with her?" I asked.

He responded, "I'm not sure, princess. Her symptoms don't make any sense."

"How do you mean?"

"Her vitals are fine, but she stopped eating and she's throwing up bile."

Tuck came over to her side and brought out some device to listen to her heart.

"See, her heart is reading at normal," he commented.

I responded, "But she is having massive abdominal aches."

"Yes, and she is lethargic."

"Tuck, can you help her?"

"I have some remedies, but it doesn't look good."

"What do you need from me?"

"To pray to the Serpent God."

"I can do that, and if you need anything, please don't hesitate to ask."

"I won't, princess, but if I could get some of her feces, I could find out more."

"I see, and since she in not eating, there is none."

"That's right. Usually a stomach bug is brought on by something you eat, and since she doesn't eat anything…"

"You're right; it doesn't make sense."

"She started being like this a few months ago; her appetite was decreasing and decreasing, and I thought it was lack of sun, so I opened the rooftop, letting in more sunlight. But it didn't work."

"Tuck, listen to me, tell no one about Golden Rose's condition, except the royal family, and do whatever you can to save her."

"Yes, Your Highness."

I then got word that my father wanted to see me immediately. Before I could leave the snake pit, I about tripped over a boy who was no more than eleven years old.

"Hey, watch where you're going!" I said.

"I'm so sorry, Your Highness."

He got on his knees and pleaded for his life.

"Relax. It's OK, and stand up," I said. "What's your name?"

"Raj."

"Well, Raj, this in not a playground, and it's no place for children."

"I know that; I work here."

This boy was filthy, covered in shit. And smelled horrible. I had to plug my nose so I wouldn't puke from the smell.

"What exactly do you do here?" I asked.

"I clean the snake pits."

"Aren't you afraid of the snakes?"

"What good is fear? It doesn't help you get your job done."

"I'll take that as a no, then."

"I'm sorry I tripped you. I'm not used to this many people being around."

"Why is that?"

"I usually work at night, when there is no one around and the snakes are asleep."

"But you're on days now?"

"Now that they hired a new crew to feed Golden Rose."

"Well, just be careful, OK?"

"You got it, Your Highness."

Raj picked up his shovel and went back to work. I had to admire his courage for not being afraid of snakes. Even though we are all Shyam, it's not every day a kid sees a snake bigger than anything he has ever seen before. I hope my son is as brave as him when he's his age.

I shut the door to my father's office. My father is nothing like my grandfather, which is why they don't get along with each other.

"You sent for me," I said.

My father explained, "Your bother is in hot water, and I don't want you helping him."

Too late.

I asked, "Why not?"

"'Cause he is going to have to learn how to do things by himself, and he can't always run to his baby sister when things go bad."

"But I like helping him; I'm good at it."

"That reminds me—you are going to be married."

I had been dreading this my whole life. I knew I would have an arranged marriage just like my brother. But I hoped that I wouldn't have to go through with it.

"And whom am I marrying?"

"That I'm leaving up to you."

"I don't understand."

"You have two days to choose between King Nefud and King Ezamir."

"Great. One is a pervert, and the other is an adolescent asshole."

"It's slim pickings for a family that is barely hanging on to their title."

"And my children?"

"They well stay here with me."

"No, I won't do that."

"I assure you that they will be well taken care of."

"Great, so now it will look like I have abandoned them. They won't understand that."

"You're telling me that they won't understand this but they will understand who their father is?"

I hate when he brings this up; it made me mad. It was none of his business, especially when he was the cause of it.

"Don't go there," I said.

"Thaiah is only one, so she won't understand right now, but Tallamay, he is almost four."

"What's your point?"

"My point is that Tall is going to figure out that Tyga is your brother, and what are you going to do?"

My brother and I have been having a sexual relationship since I was fourteen. We didn't mean for it to happen, but it did. I was thirteen when my mother died. After that, my father locked us up in the west wing of the palace. While grieving for my mother, he couldn't bear to look at us. We reminded him too much of her. My brother was all I had, and I was all he had. We thought we would never meet anyone new. I had two children as a result of my affair with my brother. And as I said before, I don't feel guilty about it at all.

"What do want me to do? Apologize? 'Cause I won't."

"No. I want you to understand that you and your brother can never be."

I fought very hard to stop my feelings for my brother, but they got so strong, I couldn't do it anymore. I knew my father felt guilty about what he had done and was now trying to fix it. But he can't; I will always love Tyga more than I should.

"I get it, but that doesn't mean I have to accept it," I said.

"Then you are going to have an even harder time letting go."

"It is what it is. That's all I can say to you."

"Then you must understand that you have to marry and leave your children here. That is how it is now."

"Fine. Then in two days, you will have your answer."

"Thank you."

"You know about Golden Rose?"

"Yes, of course I know."

"And how are you dealing with that?"

"I told Tuck to do everything he can."

"And what happens if he can't save her?"

"Then we have an even bigger problem than paying back our debt."

My father was right—Golden Rose was the only thing keeping our enemies at bay. He wanted us secured in marriages so if our kingdom fell, we would be safe.

Chapter 7

Prince Tyga Ouroboros

Night snuck up on me before I knew it. Every minute counted. I hired Zelts. They were the only ones I knew who could handle a job like this. The Zelts are not men of religion but men of gold. I told them if they pulled this off, they would have so much gold, they wouldn't have to work again. The Zelts consist of five men. The leader is Baka; he is very good with a dagger or should I say, daggers. The second-in-command is his brother Tavi, who is very deadly with a scimitar sword; he carries two. Left Ear and Right Foot are the trackers; they are very good at finding anything. Last but not least is Kabir. He is the expert in inflicting severe physical and psychological pain to get what he wants.

My grandfather couldn't believe I hired them, but I didn't have much of a choice; I needed results, and fast. I didn't care how I was going to get them. Even though this was my sister's plan, I was the one executing it.

I watched as they loaded the wagon up. My grandfather was standing right next to me. I could feel him saying this was a bad idea. But I ignored it. Everything was in place, and as the wagon left the palace, I was on pins and needles.

Grandfather Thaddeus asked, "So what did you promise them?"

I explained, "Gold, of course."

"And what are you going to do when you can't pay them?"

"Grandad, I have every means to pay them."

"With what!"

"Will you just trust me?"

"You know your great-grandfather had to let the Zelts go because—"

"Yeah, I know. 'Cause they caused more trouble than they were worth; I know the story."

"I just want to make sure you understand what you got yourself into."

"I know, believe me."

There I was, pacing again. I was a bottle of nerves. I was definitely freaking out, but I maintained my composure. I couldn't possibly sleep right now, even if I wanted to.

"How long do you think?" I asked.

"Not long. The Zelts are considered good for a reason," my grandfather answered.

That was comforting. Made me feel a little better. I had no idea how I was going to pay them, but if this went right, then everything would work out, right?

Two hours had gone by. I felt I should have heard something by now. So something had gone wrong. I was trying to come up with reasons why it was taking so long. Just think positive, I told myself.

I was just about to jump out of my skin when I heard the guards yelling out, "Open the gate!" My nerves calmed down a little bit when I saw the Zelts coming, not empty-handed. They had been able to catch five Solifugids. Now we were getting somewhere.

Let the torture begin, I thought.

I was standing in the dungeon waiting for one of these thieves to give me what I wanted. But it was taking forever. I didn't have much longer. I knew my dad could only delay King Phlox for another day. My head felt like it was going to explode, and I was slowly unraveling. I watched Kabir put his final touch on one of the Solifugids, and before we knew it, he was singing like a canary. He kept saying the word

"Ba-lie." I should have been happy about this, but I was not. That was not much to go on. I had no idea what that meant.

I told Baka to keep going with the torture. "Don't stop till we get more out of them." I had way too much tension in me, and I needed to release it, and I knew just how to do it.

I found Eden on her way out of her bedroom. I grabbed her by the hand and pulled her back into the room and shut the door behind me.

She looked at me with surprise and wanting. I slammed her up against the wall. I needed her so bad right then. She smelled so good. I took over her mouth; she melted into me. My body pressed up against hers, which was beginning to let loose. I had to feel her skin on mine. I ripped her clothes off; she did the same to me. I cupped her sex; she moaned. She whispered in my ear, "Don't stop." I had no intention of stopping. She grabbed my rock-hard penis and shoved the tip into the entrance of her yoni. She was so wet; I loved it. I grabbed both her legs. She wrapped them around my waist.

Before I knew it, I had slammed all the way inside her. She arched her back. I groaned into her neck. I fucked her slow and hard and let out all my frustration inside her.

After we had calmed down from our excitement, I couldn't help but look at Eden. She's so beautiful. She's got a great body and creamy skin, as well as beautiful long black hair that I'm obsessed with. I love everything about her.

Eden said, "Well, that was amazing!"

"Yeah, I can tell by the way your body was shaking up against mine."

I love making her blush. She tried to hide it as she rolled her eyes.

"I take it from this that you found Father's gold?" she asked.

"Not exactly."

"What happened?"

"I have a couple of Solifugids being interrogated, but so far all I have gotten out of them is 'Ba-lie.'"

"That sounds so familiar."

"You have heard it before?"

"I think so, but I can't remember where."

"Oh think, E. I'm running out of time."

"I want to say I heard Mom say it once."

"The only thing I remember Mom telling us is where all the watering holes are on maps."

"Yeah, 'cause she wanted us to be safe if we ever found ourselves stranded."

"She was a smart woman," I commented.

"So that puts you back at square one then, right?" Eden asked.

"Unfortunately, yes."

"Hmm."

"What are you thinking about?"

"The Solifugids took our wagonful of gold; something like that would be noticed, right?"

"Yeah, but they must have stayed off the main roads."

"I see."

"What?"

"Nothing. You go back to the dungeon and see if the Solifugids have talked anymore."

"OK."

Chapter 8

Princess Eden Ouroboros

I needed a map. Something about this off-road thing was bothering me. There are not too many back roads around that area where the gold went missing. The scouts my brother sent looking for the wagon never found anything.

There was only one person I knew who had the map I was looking for, and I knew that it would come with a price. I couldn't tell Tyga what I was doing 'cause he and Tacitus didn't get along very well. Plus, if Tac knew I was doing this for Tyga, he'd say no.

Tac is a big flirt. He loves to toy with me when he has something I want. He's handsome, don't get me wrong, but my heart belongs to another. Ty and Tac are very similar. They both have great bodies and are physically fit. But Tac is leaner, whereas Ty has more muscle. They both are very headstrong; there's no getting around that.

They used to be best friends but had a falling out after my dad took power. I have never known why, and every time I ask, they say I wouldn't understand.

When I was twelve, I had the hugest crush on Tac. I never told anyone about it, not even my brother.

I stopped at his door. I hesitated before knocking. I feel guilt doing this sometimes. Because if I'm honest, I love flirting with him back.

He opened the door and leaned up against the doorjamb.

"I love when the most beautiful woman knocks on my door," he said.

I responded, "Hello, Tac."

"E, to what do I owe this pleasure?"

"I was wondering if I could have a look at some of your maps."

He grabbed his chin and said, "Hmm, what's in it for me?"

"What do you want?"

"What do I want?"

He crossed his arms and crooked his neck up at the ceiling. There he goes, toying with me, I thought. And I can't help but smile a little at this.

"Dinner," he said.

"Dinner?"

"Yep, you and me, dinner, tomorrow night."

"You know I can't do that."

"Well, if you don't want my maps…"

He goes to shut the door on me.

"OK, wait," I said.

"I'm listening."

"You do know Tyga won't like this?"

"So don't tell him."

I didn't want to lie to my brother, but I really needed these maps. My bother had to get this gold back. These maps better tell me what I need to know 'cause I'm risking a lot, I thought.

"OK, you have a deal," I said.

"Great. You won't regret it."

"Just dinner, Tac. Nothing else."

"I know. I'll be the perfect gentleman."

That's what I was afraid of.

Tac led me to his study. It looked a lot like a library. He climbed the staircase to get to the top shelf and brought down a wide book.

He said, "OK, where on the map are you wanting to look?"

"Along the road to Etoch City."

"Then that would put you here, on Dune Road."

Tac pointed to the road on the map. I leaned in to get a closer look at it. Tac was so close behind me, I could feel him smelling my hair. And I knew he liked it so much, he was doing it with his eyes closed. I should have felt weirded out by this, but I liked it. I think it's because of the female snake in me. After all, female snakes do not know the word "monogamy."

"OK, are there any back roads that lead to that road?" I asked.

"I'm sorry, what?"

I turned around and could see I had just broken him out of his fantasy.

"Back roads," I repeated.

"Umm, yeah, I think so, but why do you wanna know that?"

"Well, if I stole a wagonful of gold, I would want to go undetected."

Tac pulled out another map. He said, "Here, there are only two back roads that lead from Dune Road."

"And what are these markings on them?"

"Oh, those are watering holes. One is called Yuri, and this one is Ba-lie."

"Ba-lie!"

"Yeah, it's a watering hole; most roads have them."

"What is the name of the road Ba-lie is on?"

"Abul."

"Tac, you're a genius."

"Yeah, I know."

"I have to go."

"Don't forget dinner tomorrow night—say, six thirty?"

"Yeah, yeah, I'll be there."

I couldn't wait there any longer; I had to go tell Ty what I had found out. After I explained it to him, he and the Zelts, with a few other guards, went to Abul Road to find Ba-lie.

I felt so good helping Ty. The look on his face when he understood I had gotten more information than he had gotten from torturing the Solifugids was priceless.

While my brother was off getting his redemption, I headed down to the snake pit to check on Golden Rose.

"Tuck, what's the update?" I asked.

"It still doesn't look good, Your Highness. I'm afraid she could go at any minute."

"What about the new feeding crew? Have they said anything about her eating?"

"What new feeding crew?"

"The one Raj said moved him to days."

Tuck looked at me like I had worms coming out of my nose.

"There's no new feeding crew, at least there is not supposed to be," he explained.

"Are you sure?"

"Yes, and Raj told you that?"

"That's what he said."

Tuck and I went in search of Raj and found him washing up Set's pit. Set is the youngest snake we have and is still having trouble producing fire. As a fire-breather, he sometimes has trouble with his surroundings.

"Your Highness," Raj said.

"Raj, tell Tuck what you told me about this new crew."

"Gladly."

Raj told Tuck about the new crew that came a few months ago. Then he told him how they said they were now changing Golden Rose's feeding time from days to nights. Tuck looked so confused.

"Raj, what happened to the old crew?" he asked.

"I'm not sure, doc. They just didn't show up one day, and then the next day—new crew."

"And you had never seen them before, right?"

"Nope, but they are really mean. I told them Golden Rose likes to eat in the day, not at night. But they don't care; they even told me to make sure I keep her droppings out of sight."

"What droppings?"

"Her poop droppings. Here, I'll show you."

Raj led me and Tuck into the furnace, where we saw a couple piles of Golden Rose's droppings.

He explained, "The new crew says I have to burn her droppings straightaway and I can't have any lying out."

Tuck and I looked at each other.

Tuck wasted no time. He took a sample of Golden Rose's feces and starts testing it. I sat next to Golden Rose while Raj helped peel some of the skin she was shedding to make her feel a little more comfortable. She looked so awful, and I was going to do whatever I could to help her.

"I have the answer," Tuck announced.

I stood up immediately when Tuck entered the pit.

"What's wrong with her?" I asked.

"She's being poisoned."

Raj and I both said, "Poisoned?"

"That explains why her vitals are fine but she's always so sick," Tuck said.

"Who would want to poison her?" I asked.

"I don't know, but we have to stop it now."

"Tuck, can you still save her now that you know?"

"Yes, I can. Whoever is poisoning her isn't very smart."

"How do you mean?"

"Either they are slowly trying to kill her or they don't know how much to give her to die."

I said, "Raj, from now on, you are in charge of her feeding."

"Really? That is a huge honor; I won't let you down," he responded.

"I know you won't," I said. "Now, we need to deal with this new crew."

"First I'm going to administer the remedy," explained Tuck.

He took out a jar with a thick green liquid in it. He then administered it into her mouth. She was too weak to fight, so she swallowed it all. Thank Glycon she did, 'cause if she hadn't, we would have had to go into her cloaca.

"Tuck, how long till she's back to normal?" I asked.

"Two days at the most. She's going to need lots of rest and sunlight."

"But she will be OK after this, right?"

"Oh yes, she will be back to her old self."

I planned to deal with this so-called new crew personally. Golden Rose is my family, and when you mess with her, you mess with all of us. I was going to make sure that whoever hurt her was very sorry.

Chapter 9

Prince Tyga Ouroboros

I strolled into the throne room with my head held high and a gold bar in my hand to show my dad I got his gold back and then some. I was the man and was feeling overly confident about it too. Because not only had I gotten my father's gold back, but I had also gotten back all the money and treasure the Solifugids had ever stolen. From the looks of the loot, it looked like we would never be in debt again.

It turned out that Ba-lie was not just a watering hole but a secret passageway to an underground cave filled with treasure. The Solifugids didn't even have it guarded because they thought it was well hidden.

My father was sitting on the throne with what looked like a small smile on his face. The guards unloaded all the loot from the wagon into the throne room to do the final count of just how much we had. Hamza is the family's treasurer. He was going around the piles of wealth tallying everything up.

"Well?" I asked.

"Well what?" my father responded.

"Aren't you going to say something?"

"What do you want me to say?"

"Oh, I don't know. How about 'Good job, son. Way to go. I guess you have what it takes to be a king after all.'"

"Good job, son. Of course I would have congratulated you if you had done this on your own."

"I did do this on my own."

"*Really?* Your sister didn't help you at all?"

"So what if she did help me? I got the gold back."

"Then I guess you don't have what it takes to be king."

"Wow! There is just no pleasing you, is there?"

"If you want to please me, then stop going to your sister every time you are in trouble."

"But she had a great idea that led me to the gold."

"Tyga, what kind of king will you be when you are always relying on your sister? You have to figure things out for yourself if you want to lead and make this kingdom great."

"Eden is one of us, Dad. She's there to help all of us, not just me."

"It doesn't matter, because your sister is going to be married."

"What! To whom?"

"She has a choice between King Nefud and King Ezamir."

"You can't be serious."

"I'm very serious. It's time you learn that she is your sister and not your lover and she won't always be there to catch you."

Well, my father might as well have ripped my heart out and stomped on it a bunch of times.

Hamza interjected, "I don't mean to interrupt this conversation, Your Grace, but I think you should look at this."

"What is it?" my father asked.

"While doing my analysis, I came across this."

Hamza pointed to a footlocker chest that had King Tzar's symbol on it.

"You think they stole from King Tzar?" my father asked.

"I didn't realize they were that stupid," I chimed in.

"Well, open it. Let's find out," said my father.

When the chest was opened, my father and I looked at each other. I leaned down and grabbed something from the chest and held it out in font of me. Everyone was stunned at the object in my hand.

Tzar rubies are bright red and bigger than an ostrich egg. Theses rubies do not get handed out to just anyone. One of the reasons King Tzar took over the Serpent Realm was that he built his kingdom over a private diamond mine. The mine was sealed up so tight, and he was the only one allowed in it. I used to hear rumors that this mine was so big that you could get lost forever in it.

"How the hell did the Solifugids get their hands on these?" I asked.

"They didn't," my father said.

"What are you thinking?" I asked.

I knew that the Solifugids were thieves, but masterminds they were not. You would have to be a genius to get into King Tzar's diamond mine undetected and back out alive.

My father responded, "That King Tzar is the one who is funding the Solifugids."

That made sense. The Solifugids had been trying to wipe my people off the face of the planet. King Tzar was not our biggest fan. But then why did he agree to me marrying his daughter? That I didn't get.

Eden walked into the throne room. She told us that Golden Rose was being poisoned by the Solifugids. King Tzar is smart. He was going to take out the only thing protecting us from his army coming in and slaughtering us all right then.

"Is Golden Rose going to make it?" I asked.

Eden responded, "Yes, Tuck says she will be back to normal in two days."

Our father added, "Well, apparently King Tzar will stop at nothing."

I handed Eden a Tzar ruby. It about took her breath away. Then I explained to her that King Tzar was the leader of the Solifugids.

She said, "Father, this can't go unpunished. We have to do something, or they are going to keep coming."

Our father said, "And what would you like me to do?"

"Send Golden Rose out to Sand Cry City to create havoc. When she's feeling better, of course."

"Even if we do that, she is still not a match for his entire army, even on her best day."

"Then we send the rest of the snakes."

I interjected, "E, Set is still a baby; he's never been in combat before. And Drachma got out of his snake pit and escaped underneath the palace. Nobody has seen him in two years. Yeah, he's most likely dead."

"What about us?" Eden asked.

Our father answered, "Your grandfather is too old to fight in battle. He has a hard time transforming. And you and Ty have never been in battle before; you don't know what to do."

"Excuse me, but I just ate the new crew that was poisoning Golden Rose. I think I can handle it," Eden declared.

"Eden, we are only half-breed snakes. We are more vulnerable than Golden Rose," our father cautioned.

"What good is our power if we can't use it to protect the ones we love?"

"We are not gods."

"Why not? We have power from a god."

"Eden, I feel where you are coming from; I really do. But the way to handle this is with your bother; he will marry King Tzar's daughter, and then we will have a foot in the door."

"So we just play nice? That's your plan?"

"For now."

Eden stormed off. She had every right to be upset. We were being picked off one by one and were powerless to do anything about it. I didn't know if my father was right, but I knew that if all the other kingdoms' armies came together to fight us, we didn't stand a chance. We had no army, just a snake.

My father asked, "Hamza, how are we doing so far?"

"After paying the Zelts and King Phlox's cut, we are looking at two hundred million, and I'm still counting."

"Well, that will definitely help this kingdom get back to the top."

I went to search for Eden; I knew she was upset. This wasn't going the way I wanted it to either. Coming into this room, I had felt like the man; now I felt less like a man.

Chapter 10

Princess Eden Ouroboros

I was in my room trying to calm myself down. I couldn't believe how blind my father was. If King Tzar was going to great lengths to obliterate us, then why would my brother marry his daughter? This sounded more like a plot to get rid of us.

We are the last of our kind. I remember when I was little, we had so many family members around us. And one by one, they died off. My mother included. Not to mention all the snakes that used to be here. Of course that was before my time. It must have been beautiful to see this kingdom thrive. I wish I could have seen it.

They say the reason our kingdom is dying off is that everyone believes in spiritual power without a god . Ietsism is more favorable among the people. I don't get why when there is so much hurt in the world. That a godless faith can just allow that to happen. But then again, look at my god. Here we were dying off, and yet he does nothing.

I stood out on my balcony and looked down at the kingdom, which had been deserted for centuries. Only the Aryan Castle, which sat in the middle of Ja-bar City, held life and everything I cared about. Even the Aryan Castle was falling apart. I looked around my bedroom, feeling helpless. Then my brother walked in, giving me that look that makes me feel warm inside.

"Have I ever told you that you are the most beautiful woman I have ever seen?" he said.

"Maybe once or twice, but I like hearing it all the time."

"Good, 'cause I love saying it to you all the time."

Tyga moved closer to me, making my heart flutter. He's so damn sexy, I can't get over it. His body sets my body on fire every time. He doesn't even have to touch me, and I get excited.

"Do you agree with father about doing nothing?" I asked.

"No, but he is right, E."

"How is he right?"

My brother let out a big sigh. He responded, "Because we don't have much of a leg to sand on."

"We have Golden Rose; that's better than a leg."

"Eden, it's not enough."

"Then we need more snakes."

"That would be great, but there aren't any. Hell, there are barely enough of us."

"Then we make more snakes."

"How do we do that?"

"Dad could mate with Golden Rose."

"Oh, E, don't start this again. You know it doesn't work that way. Granddad tried doing that when he was king. Remember Uncle Thorn?"

"Yes, I remember, but maybe Uncle Thorn wasn't up for the challenge."

"That's not what Tuck said. He said, and I quote, 'It won't work because it's against our religion.' That's kind of why Grandad lost his credibility; he was going against Naagasree."

"He was trying to save our species."

"That's not what it says in the Serpent Book. That half-breeds cannot breed with full-breeds."

"Yes, I know the story. Aryan the serpent was transformed into a human and will never return back to his original form."

"E, I know you want to save our people. I want that too, but we have to face the facts."

"What, that we are a dying breed?"

"Well, look around you. There's us, Dad, Granddad, Tall, and Thaiah. Exodus, Hamza, Tuck, a handful of guards, including Tac. A couple of servants and the snake pit crew. That's it. That's all that's left."

"What about that rumor that the Shyam monks have a snake?"

"E, that's just a rumor."

"I think we should check it out."

"First of all, that would be impossible; they don't like us very much."

"And don't you want to find out why?"

"Not really. Besides, there hasn't been a Shyam monk in Ja-Bar since the first dynasty."

"Naga Temple is a home for all Shyam, and we are Shyam."

"I think we should forget all of this and make love now."

"I'm being serious."

"So am I."

"I'm going to Naga Temple tomorrow morning."

"E, that's crazy. Besides, you don't even speak Serpent; they won't understand you."

"I have spoken it before."

"Yeah, back when we were little."

My grandmother taught me and my brother how to speak Serpent when we were little; it was our first language. And the Ouroboros family's native tongue. But my Grandmother died when I was nine, and my mother only spoke the common tongue, so we stopped speaking it. Ty and I were a little rusty. No one spoke it anymore, anyways. Except the Shyam monks; that's all they speak, I think.

"I'll study it tonight," I said.

"It won't matter. Dad will not let you go."

"I'm not asking him. Besides, I'm not going to sit here and watch us slowly disappear."

"You do realize you're doing this over a rumor?"

"Ty, go with me, please."

"Why? There is no reason to go."

"Well, just humor me. Besides, the sooner you agree with me, the sooner we can screw each other's brains out."

My brother looked at me with narrow eyes and a smirk. I sat down on my bed and spread my legs apart just enough so he could see I was wet.

Tyga grabbed me by the nape of my neck, rough, and put his mouth to my ear and said, "You fucking drive me crazy." I smiled and then closed my eyes as he bit my ear and moved down to my neck. Kissing and biting me. He slipped two fingers inside me, and I threw my head back and let out an eager moan. It feels so damn good when he pushes in and out of me.

He started kissing my inner thigh. Goose bumps covered my body as he spread my legs farther apart. The anticipation was building as I knew where he was headed. He spread my yoni lips apart and slowly licked my clit. My God, is there nothing this man can't do perfectly? I thought. I dug my nails into his hair as he took over my vagina with his mouth and his fingers. My climax was getting stronger the closer I got to my relief. He gripped my thighs as he pushed his face farther inside me, and that was all I needed. Before I knew it, my body as shaking so hard I about fell off the bed.

It wasn't over. Ty flipped me around and took me from behind. Both of his hands squeezed my neck as his huge erection rammed me. I shook with pleasure as my body took him all the way in. No matter how many times I make love to Ty, I can never get used to how huge he is. I feel like he is in my throat sometimes.

But he always manages to get me off, no matter what. When pain becomes pleasure, I am the most enraptured.

Chapter 11

Prince Tyga Ouroboros

I woke up to the sunlight beaming through the window. Now that I had gotten my dad's gold back, I was not an erratic mess. Now I could relax. I lay on my side to see Eden was lying right next to me. Her back was facing me. So I spooned her. I wrapped my arms around her to feel her naked skin, which felt like silk.

I spent the whole night making love to her, so my body felt refreshed. I started kissing her neck as she was waking up.

She rolled over on her back and looked up at me.

"Do you want more?" she asked.

"Yeah, I could probably do this all day."

"People might worry we have gone missing."

"Let them worry."

I kissed her lips, and she shoved her tongue in my mouth. I was getting hard. Then all of a sudden, she stopped me.

"What's wrong?" I asked.

"I don't know; I just started feeling sick."

"Well, is it something you ate?"

"I don't think so."

Eden pushed me completely off. Then rushed off to the bathroom. I could hear her puking up her guts. I got up to see if she was OK.

I asked, "Are you sure it's not something you ate, 'cause you did eat a couple guys last night?"

"I was a snake when I ate them, so no, it's not something I ate."

She got up from the floor and walked over to the bed and sat down.

"I'm going to get Tuck," I said.

"Why? I'm fine."

"You don't look fine. You look sick."

"Don't think this is an excuse to not go to Naga Temple."

"I have no idea what you are talking about."

"Yeah, right."

"I'm going with you, I promise."

"Yes, you are."

After I got dressed, I kissed her on the forehead.

"I love you. I'll be back," I said.

Before my sister could get words out, she headed back to the bathroom to puke some more.

I was going to find Tuck when I ran into Exodus. He told me my father wanted to see me. Of course he does; I can't wait to see what he has to say now, I thought. Probably he wants to remind me what a failure I am to him.

My father was in his office with my grandfather.

I said, "You wanted to see me, Father?"

"Yes, I have invited King Tzar for dinner tonight."

"Why would you do that?"

"Because you are about to marry his daughter, we need to get to know each other."

"But he is our enemy. I don't think this is a good idea."

"He won't be your enemy for long. He will be your father-in-law."

"That's not my choice."

"Ty, this is for the best, trust me."

"Do I have a choice?"

"No."

"Then what does it matter?"

My father looked at me with narrow eyes.

How is this the best for my life? Being married to a woman I'm not in love with, I thought.

Then my grandfather looked at me like I should be grateful, but really I wanted to tell him to go suck it.

I was getting ready to leave his office when my dad yelled at me to no be late for dinner. I said absolutely nothing as I left.

I met King Tzar's daughter once. It was about three years ago. It was very brief, but what I got from her was that she was pretty. Not as pretty as Eden. Aramaya is the same age as Eden, and I can tell she doesn't care much for her father, and I think he feels the same way about her. Marrying her has never been something I cared about or even though about.

But now that I was getting closer to the consummation of this arrangement, I couldn't help but wonder what kind of husband I would be or what kind of relationship this would be, for that matter. The fact that I'm half snake and have to change into that form every once in a while is probably not what a normal girl considers sexy, not that I care what she thinks.

Eden would be marrying soon. I don't like another man touching what belongs to me. She's mine, and she always will be mine.

I really didn't want to go to Naga Temple. It was a big waste of time. But I knew my sister was on a mission. A mission that was never going to work out.

After I told Tuck what was up, I ran back up to check on Eden. Then the one person I can't stand walked right up to me.

Tacitus said, "Ty."

"Tac," I responded.

"I thought you were going to kick my ass."

"It's still early."

He laughed. I would have loved to smack that smug smile off his face.

"Well, I told you to name the time and the place," he said.

"What are you doing here?"

"My dad wanted to know how Golden Rose is feeling."

"Better, now that Eden has taken care of the situation."
"Well, that's great."
"Isn't it, though?"
"Eden is an amazing woman."
"Your point being?"
"Just stating the obvious."
"I don't have time for you right now."
"What does that mean?"
"It means I know what you are doing."
"What am I doing?"
"She chose me, Tac, OK? Get the fuck over it."
Tacitus's jaw ticks told me I had hit a sore spot. He moved closer to me. I didn't move; I held my ground. I was not afraid of him at all.
"Who says she chose?" he asked.
"Trust me, she did," I responded.
"We shall see."
He walked away from me. That last comment really pissed me off. "We shall see." Whatever the fuck that meant. He was sorely mistaken if he thought he could get with Eden. Not going to happen.

Chapter 12

Princess Eden Ouroboros

I said, "I'm telling you, I'm fine."

Tuck asked, "How long have you been throwing up?"

"It just stared this morning."

Tuck put his hand on my forehead. He then listened to my heart. "Well, that's interesting," he commented.

"What?"

"You're pregnant."

"Are you absolutely sure?"

"With out a doubt."

"How did this happen?"

"Well, you see, when two people love each other…"

"Tuck, I know how it happens. I'm just saying."

"What are you saying?"

"Nothing, Tuck. You can't tell anyone about this."

"Your Highness, you know I have to tell your dad."

"I will tell my dad. Just give me some time, please."

"Fine, but don't wait too long."

"I won't, I promise."

Hearing you're pregnant catches you off guard even when you know or suspect it. When you get that final answer and it is confirmed that you are with child, then and only then, it sets in. I was not sure how to feel about having another baby. Now that I thought about it, I was kind of happy. I couldn't help but wonder what Ty was going to think about this.

Tuck said, "You know I gave you stuff to stop this from happening."

"I know. I guess I just forget to take it sometimes."

"Well, it only works when you take it."

"Yes, I know. I had a lot on my mind."

"Your Highness, you are putting yourself and your baby at risk."

Tuck told me that it was best that I didn't have any kids with my brother because of our genetics. Since we are both half-breeds, there is a good chance our babies will come out more like serpents than humans. He thought my babies would have a hard time functioning in the real world. Tuck also said I was very lucky that my son and daughter came out the way they did. But pushing it a third time, I was taking a big risk.

Chapter 13

Princess Eden Ouroboros

I kissed my son and daughter goodbye for the day since I was headed to Naga Temple with Ty. I told my father we were going to the market. He didn't say anything. Ty told me that father had invited Kind Tzar for dinner tonight. That reminded me that I had a dinner date with Tac that night. I was trying to come up with an excuse to see Tac without letting Ty know. But this dinner date with King Tzar would help keep Ty busy.

Naga Temple is far away. It would be dark by the time we got back home. King Tzar would have already arrived at Ja-Bar Kingdom before we got back. I agreed with my brother that inviting King Tzar to our home was a bad idea. He would definitely see how vulnerable we were. That we had a skeleton crew helping the Ouroboros family.

The Naga Temple was falling apart, much like the Ja-bar Empire. The temple was surrounded by very high walls that kept enemies from getting in. I was not even sure they would let us in. The Shyam Monks don't take kindly to strangers, even if you are royalty.

My mom told me when I was little that snakes were always misjudged by the way they looked. Sure, they look scary and mean, can even be construed as evil, but the truth is, they have a heart just like everyone else.

We got to the massive doors of the temple and stood there looking up at them.

"Should we knock?" Ty asked.

"Well, I don't know how else to get their attention."

Ty was getting ready to knock when the doors opened up. They creaked as they were opening, sending a little bit of sand swoosh into our faces.

I could tell Ty was annoyed with the sand in his face as he was dusting it off him.

Shyam Monks wear black and gold robes with the symbol of Glycon on them. They say it's a vow of chastity.

Three monks came walking down the stairs to greet us.

I was really nervous. I hoped that I would greet them right.

When speaking Serpent, you have to get the hissing just perfect.

As I was speaking Serpent, I could tell the way I was saying it was not right at all.

One of the monks put his hand up, signaling me to stop.

"I don't think that will be necessary," the monk said.

Oh, thank Glycon they speak the common tongue, I thought.

"You speak English?" Tyga asked.

"One must do what they can in these modern times if they want to survive," said the monk.

Another chimed in, "Besides, you just said you were going to eat our face."

"Then it's a good thing you stopped her," commented Tyga.

"I'm so sorry," I said. "We are—"

The first monk said, "We know who you are, Your Highness. What do you want?"

"We were hoping we could have a little talk with the head monk."

"Come with us."

That was really easy. I wasn't expecting them to let us in so willingly.

They led us to a room with a huge round table and lots of chairs around it. One monk was already standing in the room. His robe was different than the others, more elaborate.

He signaled for me and my brother to have a seat, and we did.

Tyga leaned over to me. "You still think this is a good idea?" he said.

"They let us in, didn't they?"

"I don't know if that's a good thing."

"Just relax, will you?"

I felt some kind of warmth inside me all of a sudden. Something telling me that it was OK. A feeling that felt safe.

The monks stopped talking among themselves and sat down.

"I'm Nathair, the head monk," one said.

I responded, "It's a pleasure to meet you. I'm—"

Nathair interrupted, "Eden Belinda Ouroboros, the Serpent Princess, and Tyga Thuggee Ouroboros, the Serpent Prince."

I wasn't shocked that they already knew who we were.

"What I don't know is why you are here," continued Nathair.

"I hear you are in possession of a really big snake," I said.

Nathair squinted his eyes as he crossed his arms. He responded, "I'm happy to tell you that there is no snake; you are mistaken."

"See, I told you," Tyga said.

"I think there is," I said.

I could feel the snake. Its presence gave me intuition. Golden Rose did the same thing when I communicated with her, and Set did too, for that matter.

Nathair knew I could feel the snake.

"Even if we did, what's it two you?" he asked.

I responded, "We could use it to breed with one of our snakes to make more."

"I see. Well, the answer is no."

"Wait, why not?"

"Why should we help the Ouroboros family?"

"'Cause we are both Shyam."

"No, *we* are Shyam. What you are is a disgrace to Naagasree."

I looked at him with confusion. Nathair got up and walked over to the statue of Glycon.

He said, "The Ouroboros royal family has a gift that they have squandered away on greed and lust. You don't even know what Glycon means or stands for."

"Actually, I do." I stood up and faced him. Tyga tried to grab my hand to calm me down, but I pulled it away from him. I continued, "Glycon means 'strong spirit,' and it stands for the seed of empowerment."

"I see your tutors taught you the basics, but you have no idea what it really means."

"I don't understand. We both want the same thing."

"No, the only king who knew what we wanted and what we are all about was the first king of the Ja-Bar empire, your ancestor Thyme Ouroboros. You don't even know why or how you got the power you have. You are less than worthy of the power you have obtained."

"I'm tying to save my people."

"No, you are tying to regain ownership of the Serpent Realm."

"Is that so wrong?"

"Yes, because that's not what we want at all and that's not what we are about. You don't even practice what you preach, Serpent Princess. The symbol on your neck behind your ear is gold for a reason, but you don't know that reason."

All the Shyam have a tattoo of the serpent symbol on their neck, behind their ear. The symbol is black. The Ouroboros family has the same tattoo, but ours is outlined in black with gold scales.

"We are very sorry; we will show ourselves out," Tyga said.

He grabbed my hand and led me to the door. But I was not going to let this go; I couldn't. I ripped my hand away from him.

"So that's it, we just give up and become no more?" I asked.

Nathair responded, "We are ready to leave this world to be with the Serpent God if he sees fit. Extinction is not our fear, Your Highness; it's yours."

Tyga interjected, "E, come on—they can't help us."

"They can help us; they just choose not to."

Nathair asked, "Do you know the only reason why King Tzar has not outlawed the Shyam?"

I shook my head no.

He continued, "It's because we keep to ourselves. But your family continues to cause problems, and you need to stop."

"It's over, E. Let's go home," Tyga said.

I let my bother lead me to the door to leave again. But before I did, I had something to say.

"Glycon wanted a child, but he did not want a lover. So he created one with his own power. A boy. He named his son Aryan. Aryan was different from all the other snakes Glycon made. He was special because he was the most beautiful snake anyone had ever seen. His scales were gold-plated. He had red rubies for eyes. He shined everywhere he went.

"Everyone loved Aryan. They would shower him with gifts and compliments. Telling him over and over how perfect he was. How beautiful he was. Till one day he decided he was better than his father and anyone else, for that matter.

"Aryan's pridefulness caused him to be so vain and selfish that he played games on the humans. He would hurt them with confusion, deceitfulness, pain.

"Glycon was so tired of fixing Aryan's mess when it came to human hearts that he decided to punish him.

"So he turned him into a human. Constricted and bound by human form. Aryan was vengeful and hateful toward his father.

"But his hatred melted away when he fell in love with a woman. Their love was so strong that they had a child. A half-breed that was my ancestor. That's how we got the power we have today. The gold scales on our symbol are reminders that beauty is a gift, that it can be taken as fast as it is given."

The monks looked at me, impressed.

Nathair said, "Very good, princess."

"I know that my devotion to my religion is lacking. I would like to be closer to Glycon. But right now I'm scared because I have two kids who are everything to me and I want so much for them. I don't know how to give it to them when our world is falling apart."

One of the monks who was sitting down looked at Nathair.

I turned around to head out with my brother.

"Wait," Nathair said.

"What is it?" I asked.

"The snake you are looking for is this way."

"That was awesome," Tyga said to me.

"Thank you."

Nathair and the other monks took us down a flight of stairs leading to a door. When they opened the door, the biggest snake we had ever seen was waiting for us.

Our mouths dropped open we were so astonished. It had turquoise scales. And the biggest set of wings we had ever seen.

"Holy shit, it's a *Chrysopelea*," Tyga commented.

Nathair responded, "Yes, also know as the flying snake."

"Where did he come from?" I asked.

Nathair said, "We believe Ja-Bar Palace; it must have wandered underneath the castle and made its way here."

"But how?" I asked.

"When we were remodeling the floor here, so that we could make him feel more comfortable, we found a honeycomb of tunnels that led everywhere."

"How old is he?"

"He came here when he was a baby, during the third dynasty. At least that's what I was told."

"Oh wow, so he's older than Golden Rose."

Tyga went into the pit, and the snake warmed right up to him.

"Can he fly yet?" I asked.

Nathair responded, "He has gotten off the ground completely, if that's what you mean. But because this temple is not meant for snakes his size, he has no room to fly. That's why he belongs at Ja-Bar Palace."

The Ja-Bar Place had more than enough room for this snake to spread his wings and fly. The *Chrysopelea* breed was another rare breed. I wanted to know everything about him.

"What's his diet like?" I asked.

"Ravenous," Nathair responded. "He feeds mostly on dogs, small animals."

"I see. How big is he?"

"He weighs in at five hundred thousand tons, and he's five thousand feet long. His wingspan is ninety-eight feet."

"Tuck is going to love this one," Tyga commented.

I added, "I think he's magnificent."

Nathair asked, "You are going to take good care of him?"

"Yes, of course," I said.

"Good, because he's become very sentimentally attached to the monks here."

"Trust me, we will take very good care of him."

I walked into the snake pit and brought my hand out to him. He slowly lowered his head down to me so that he could feel me. As we made contact, I could feel us communicating with each other.

"How are we going to get him out of here?" Tyga asked.

"That's a good question," I responded.

"We can't fly him out of here; he's not trained yet."

"Yeah, I know."

"We will have to figure it out later. We've got to leave now if we are going to make it home on time."

Tyga was right. I didn't want to leave this snake here, but we both had dinner dates and we were going to be late. The monks reassured us that the snake wasn't going anywhere. On our way out, I asked one more question.

"Does he have a name?"

"Lcarus," Nathair responded.

"I love it."

Chapter 14

Princess Eden Ouroboros

We made it back just in time. Tyga was eating dinner with Father and King Tzar, allowing me to eat with Tac. I was so happy that we found a male snake. He was older and bigger than Golden Rose. That meant he could help protect us as well.

I told Tac all about it. He was very impressed. I felt like I had accomplished something. Tac was staring at me from across the table. He pulled out all the stops too. Candles, flowers. It was nice, but I still felt guilty being there with him.

I hadn't even told Ty I was pregnant yet. I was waiting for the right time.

Tac said, "So you found this snake at Naga Temple."

"Yes, it's crazy, right?" I answered.

"That is crazy."

"This dinner tastes good."

"Yeah, it does. It's a good thing I didn't cook it."

That made me laugh a little.

"So how was your day?" I asked.

"Good, 'cause I knew I had this date tonight."

I just smiled at him. He winked at me. He is really sexy, I thought.

"The name of the snake we found is Lcarus."

"I like it."
"Me too."
"Eden."
"What?"
Tac put his hand on mine. "I want you, and I know you want me too."
"It doesn't matter." I pulled my hand away from him.
"It does to me."
"Tac, you know I love Ty."
"Well, he's a jerk, and he doesn't deserve you."
"What is it with you two? You guys use to be best friends."
"You wouldn't understand."
"You know he says the exact same thing when I ask him."
"Where did you tell him you were tonight?"
"I told him I was going to bed."
"You lied to him?"
"Well, I knew he would blow this out of proportion."
"Thought you told him everything?"
"I do, almost everything."
"Did you ever tell him about our kiss?"
"What kiss?"
"The one by the fountain."
"When I was thirteen?"
"Yes."
"No, I didn't tell him about that."
"Why not?"
"I guess it never came up."
"You know I had the biggest crush on you."
"You did?"
"Oh, yes."
"Why didn't you ever say anything?"
"I guess I was too scared."
"I had the biggest crush on you too."
Tacitus smiled at me.

"Then we should act on that now," he said.

"No, Tac, I can't."

"Give me one chance, E, please."

OK, one night with Tac wouldn't really be that bad. Ty was getting married to another woman. So why not? I was tempted. He is very sexy. But I love Ty so much, I didn't want to hurt him.

Tac picked my hand up again and then locked his fingers with mine. While he was doing that, I was imagining he was Ty.

"Tac, I'm so sorry, I can't do this."

I pulled my hand away from him again.

"Do what?" Ty interjected.

Of course, right when I do the right thing, I thought. I should have known I wouldn't get away with this.

Tac wasn't sweating at all, but I had a look of guilt all over my face. Ty was ready to kill me; I could see it in his eyes. I knew that look very well.

"Ty, it's not what it looks like," I explained.

"Well, let's see—candles, flowers, and wine," said Ty.

"You're right; it is what you think," Tac chimed in.

I said, "Tac, you're not helping, and in my defense, I'm drinking water."

"So how long has this affair been going on?" asked Ty.

"No, Ty, we've never done dinner before or anything else, for that matter," I explained.

Tac added, "Of course, the night was young, and if you hadn't interrupted, who knows."

I was really frustrated with Tac. I narrowed my eyes at him. These two love hurting each other and using me to do it, I thought.

Tac was sipping his wine like everything was just fine, without a care in the world.

Ty said, "You know, Tac, I have decided I want to kick your ass right now."

Tac put his wine down and stood up from the table.

"Let's do this," he said.

I got in between them. I was facing Ty, putting my hands on his chest, stopping him from charging Tac. Ty was pushing me up against Tac's front.

I said, "OK, OK, both of you clam down."

I forget sometimes how strong Ty really is.

Ty said, "Forget it. You two want to fuck each other, you go right head and do it. I don't care."

"Thanks. We appreciate that," Tac responded.

I added, "Ty, wait, it's not—"

Ty punched a hole in the wall on his way out. I followed him out; I didn't even say goodbye to Tac. I was really upset with him anyway. Tac had made it sound like I was cheating on Ty and had been doing it for a while.

"Ty, will you please talk to me," I said.

"Why should I do that?"

"Because I want to explain; it's not what you think."

"Really? So you didn't lie to me and tell me that you were going to bed?"

"OK, that part is what it is, but—"

"Just forget it. You wanna hurt me, go ahead."

"Ty, let me explain, please."

"There is nothing to explain. You find him attractive, and you want to fuck him, right?"

"OK, yes, I find him a little attractive, but—"

Ty got really upset and threw a glass at the wall. The shards of the glass fell all over the floor.

I knew that I should have taken this seriously, but I couldn't help how fucking gorgeous he was. When he's angry, I just get so turned on. My body was already screaming at me to get him to touch me. I was having a hard time focusing on why he was mad.

"Just go be with him, then," Ty continued.

"Ty, I went out to dinner with Tac for you."

Ty had a puzzled look on his face.

"What are you talking about?" he asked.

"How do you think I found out about Ba-lie?"
"I don't know. Never thought about it."
"Yes, of course you didn't."
"What the hell is that supposed to mean?"
"It means that I needed a map. I couldn't look at Father's maps because he didn't want me helping you. So the only person I knew other than Father with a map was Tac. He would only let me see his map if I had dinner with him, which I agreed to do because I knew how bad you needed to get that gold back."
"Is that right?"
"Yeah, that is right. Because everything I do, I do for you. No, I have never had sex with Tac, and I don't want to. Yes, I find him attractive. But you are so much sexier than he is. My heart belongs to you, and it always will. I love you, Ty, more than life itself."
"Then why didn't you tell me about the map in the first place?"
"Because I knew you wouldn't let me do it."
"You're damn right."
"Can we just forget this whole thing and go to bed?"
"You still lied to me."
"I know. I'm so sorry."
"I need air. I'm going to clear my mind."
"Ty."

And just like that, he left the room, leaving me all alone and feeling like shit. I put my hand on my belly. I told my unborn child it was going to be OK, that Daddy just needed some air.

I was tossing and turning in my bed, trying to sleep. I couldn't get comfortable. I was woken up by a nightmare. I realized Ty never made it to bed. I didn't bother putting clothes on; I grabbed a blanket and wrapped it around myself to cover up.

I went to my children's room to search for Ty. Sometimes he went there to watch our kids sleep. It helped him relax. But he wasn't there.

The only other place was the swimming pool, where he liked to swim at night. Ty is a vampire snake; he needs blood. So my dad built him a swimming pool and filled it with blood.

When I got there, I could see Ty swimming around. Of course he was in snake form. He is just as beautiful as a snake as he is as a man. The swimming pool is huge; this is necessary because when Ty is in snake form, he's bigger than Golden Rose.

I dropped my blanket as I walked down the stairs into the pool of blood. The blood was heated, making it so inviting as I stepped farther into it. It isn't deep. It went up to my hips. Ty slithered up to me. He raised his head out of the blood. He looked down at me, towering over me like a tall mountain. The warm blood was dripping from him down onto me like a shower, and it felt really good. He lowered his face to me, and I crested the top of his head with both hands. He felt so smooth and soft. He pushed the top of his nose gently against me as I wrapped both my arms around him, enveloping him further into my naked skin. His scales are warm like a blanket, keeping me safe. Snakes express love by rubbing their head against the object they are trying to be affectionate to.

We nuzzled each other for a while.

Ty went completely back down into the pool of blood and then came back up in human form.

I watched the blood drip down his broad, muscular shoulders as he was walking toward me.

He was making my heart beat go a million beats per second.

His six-pack, his arms. His everything is perfect.

I wanted him so bad. He's so yummy. It was like, Tac who?

Ty wrapped his big, strong arms around me, squeezing me into his body like I was painted onto him.

I could feel his erection up against me. If he could feel me down there, he would know how soaking wet I was. I knew the moment when he would do that was rapidly approaching.

"I love when you greet me naked," he said.

"Anything to make you happy."

He looked into my eyes. "E, I love you so very much."

"I love you too."

"I guess when I saw you with Tac, I was—"

"Shh, let's not talk about him."
"I can do that."
"Good!"
So do you want to fuck like humans or like snakes?"
"Let's do both. We can fuck like humans now and then fuck like snakes after."
"I love that idea."
"I knew you would."

He shoved his tongue in my mouth, and I took over his mouth like he was my source of air. Even the blood I was tasting on him was enticing.

Nothing or no one will ever change how I feel about my brother.

And together we will rule this kingdom.

No matter what level you are on, a snake will always appear in your life, whether you are in the garden or in the desert.

—Patience Johnson

Part III

The Fire Realm

Introduction

The Fire Realm is to the west, where it is always overcast in the sky. It is warm and dry; there is no vegetation.

The west is covered in red cliffs that are made up of brimstone and one gigantic volcano mountain called Agni. At the base of Agni mountain is a lava river called Ignis.

There is only one kingdom in the west; it is called Daktyloi, the kingdom of fire. The people who live in the west are called Pyrolatreia.

Pyrolatreia worship Vulcas the God of Fire. They all have red hair. The females have reddish-orange eyes, whereas the males have dragon eyes.

The Pyrolatreia women have the power of fire in their hands. The Pyrolatreia males have the power to turn into dragons.

Now when it comes to finding your mate or love partner, it all depends on a woman's flame.

A Pyrolatreia, or Pyro for short, male can turn into a dragon by their thirteenth birthday.

The women have the power to summon fire by their ninth birthday, and they learn to control it when they hit puberty.

It is very important that a Pyro woman can control her flame by her fifteenth birthday, or else she is considered ash.

Now, all of the girls' fires look the same, but they are all very different. Now, the one thing that is the same is that they are all very hot.

Each girl has their own unique and special way to deliver their flame because women's needs are diverse.

Every woman's desire inside her is different, and how she presents it and handles it is how she attracts her mate.

Now, usually a woman can attract a male by their sixteenth birthday.

Now, when a woman is ash, she is considered undesirable and will never attract a male.

Agni is a very important mountain to the Pyros because its temperature is what keeps them alive; it is key to their thermoregulation.

The king of the Pyrolatreia is King Helios Redrick. His wife is Hera, and their last hope for the future rests on the shoulders of their daughter Princess Pyra. Everyone calls her Pye.

The royal family lives in Novngarde Castle, which is right next to Daktyloi, the kingdom of fire.

Novngarde and Daktyloi are separated by a big bridge, and the Ignis river of lava flows under it.

The Draconem are three old wise dragons that determine law and justice in the Fire Realm. Only the oldest dragons get that honor.

The biggest problem the Fire Realm faces is that Agni Mountain is losing its heat.

Vulcas symbolizes survival and passion. Their religion is called Atar.

Chapter 15

Princess Pye Redrick

No matter how many times or how many different ways he showed me, I never understood it. It was something so simple, but I couldn't master it.

Blaze instructed, "Now a swish of the hand, a flick of the wrist."

I responded, "Blaze, I have done this a million times; it never works."

"Well, do it for me a million and one."

I did as he said, and, boom, a huge combustion of mass destruction. Once again I had managed to disintegrate the entire area. Like always. Thank goodness we weren't doing this in his office. Of course he learned that the hard way: when I was eleven, I managed to burn his classroom down.

"See, I told you," I said.

"OK, Pye, you're flame is very interesting."

"What's so interesting about it?"

"Well…it's strong."

"I'm getting worse, aren't I?"

"No, it's…"

I narrowed my eyes at him.

"OK, yes, you are getting worse," he admitted.

I put my head in my hands. Nothing but a failure.

"Have you been practicing the exercises I gave you?"

"Morning, noon, and night."

"OK, let's try this: What do you think about when you unleash your flame?"

"I don't know. Fear, I guess."

"OK, let's tackle that issue."

"Blaze."

"Just hear me out. What are you afraid of?"

"Of my father losing his throne because of me."

"That would never happen."

"It's going to happen if I don't manage my flame."

"You will."

"I'm nineteen years old. The only reason why they haven't marked me ash yet is because I'm the princess."

"Pye, I have been teaching girls to control their flame for twenty-seven years, and I have never met a girl I couldn't help."

"Well, there is a first for everything."

"You need to boost your confidence and stop being afraid all the time."

"You make it sound so easy."

"Once you find your happiness, everything is easy."

"What if I never find happiness?"

"Oh, I know you are going to find happiness."

"Really, how do you know?"

"Because, Pye, your flame is the most powerful flame I have ever seen."

"For real?"

"For real. That kind of strength is determined to get what it wants."

I smiled. He smiled back at me. I think if Blaze hadn't believed in me, I would have given up on trying to control my flame a long time ago. Blaze is probably the oldest dragon in Daktyloi. He has a long red beard to go with his long red hair. He once got asked to be a Draconem, but he turned it down, for teaching to him was more valuable.

"Thank you, Blaze."

"Anytime. Shall we try again?"

"We shall."

Chapter 16

Princess Pye Redrick

I was sitting on my parents' bed watching my mother brush her vibrant red hair. She was sitting at her vanity looking at herself in the mirror.

She's so beautiful. I wish I could have half of her beauty; then maybe I would be more confident in myself, and then maybe I could control my fire, I thought.

"What are you staring at?" my mother Hera asked.

"Just noticing how stunningly beautiful you are."

My mom got up and brought me over to her vanity. She pulled my hair off my face.

She said, "See how beautiful you are when you're not hiding your face in your hair?"

I looked at myself in the mirror, and I couldn't see it, what my mom was calling beautiful.

"Mom, do you really think I'm beautiful?"

"Oh yes, Pye. You have these eyes that are mesmerizing, beautiful pouty lips."

"Yeah, but I have red hair with orange streaks. No other girl has that."

"I know. That means you're perfect."

"If I were perfect, I would be able to control my flame."

"You will. Plus, have you asked the God of Fire for help?"
"All the time."
"What does he say?"
"Nothing, really, but I think if he were going to say something, he would say you should've had another kid."
"Ha ha. Not funny."
"Where's Father?" I asked.
"He went to go talk to the Draconem."
"Dad is going to lose his throne because of me."
"No, he's not; it's going to be fine."
"How can you be so sure?"
"Because you are too beautiful to not catch a man's eye."
"If Uncle Jupiter gets his hands on father's crown, I don't think I can live with myself."
"First of all, your uncle has to prove he's the better candidate, and we all know he's not."
"But I—"
"But nothing. Don't worry."
My mother gave me a big hug and continued to brush my hair.
She kept reassuring me that it was OK. I could feel that it was not.

Chapter 17

Princess Pye Redrick

I have lived a very sheltered life. I've never done a thing on my own. Never even left the castle grounds. Since the day I was born, I was told what to eat, how to dress. I've never even had a friend, except my cousin Heat. But we have nothing in common, and he's my mother's sister's child, so the fact that he's family means he may not be considered a friend.

I tried to commit suicide a couple months ago. As you can see, it didn't take. I just would rather die than deal with all the pressure and shame around the fact that my Uncle Jupiter may get my father's crown.

However, if I had died, he would have gotten it anyway. So I can't win either way.

From what I hear about my uncle, he's vicious and evil. He only cares about himself. He and my dad do not get along at all. My uncle just wants power by any means necessary. Uncle Jupiter has a small gang called the Jacowitz. These guys have no respect for human life. My father outlawed them when I was little because they caused a lot of problems in Daktyloi.

The good news is I have never met my uncle, and I hope I never have too. If I do not marry soon, my father will not have a successor to pass his crown to.

I like to sit in the castle's courtyard. There are no plants there, only a tree that never has any leaves on it. Just branches. I sit on the tallest branch. This is my favorite spot in the entire castle because it overlooks the Kingdom of Daktyloi. Watching all the families enjoy their lives. All the little boy dragons who are learning how to fly. Wishing I could fly with them.

I also like watching Agni Mountain 'cause the lava flowing from it is really peaceful to see.

It was nice and quiet until my cousin started climbing the tree. He's a few years older than me.

Heat's really nice to me. He and his father don't get along. Mostly because Heat thinks he knows what's best for him.

"Have you thought about jumping?" Heat asked me.

"Maybe once or twice."

"That's one heck of a fall."

"You don't think I can make the jump?"

"Definitely not."

"Well, if you come down after me, you can save me."

"That's true, but there is a chance I might not get there in time."

"Well, here's hoping, right?"

"You know I went with your dad to see the Draconem?"

"What did they say?"

"Not anything good."

"So bad news, then. It seems that's the way my life is these days."

"Then maybe it's best to not tell you."

"Oh, come on, Heat, please."

"Twelve men have become very sick, and they're getting worst."

"Do they know why?"

"They think it's because Agni's temperature has dropped another ten degrees."

"That's awful. How are they going to fix it?"

"The Draconem believe that the reason why the temperature is dropping is—"

Heat didn't want to tell me.

"Why?" I asked.

"Pye, don't worry about it. It's going to be OK. We will fix it. Your dad has a plan."

"If Agni mountain stops producing lava, then there is no heat. The males will die off, then soon the women."

"It won't come to that; your dad won't let them."

"How is he going to fix it?"

"He hasn't told me yet, but we may have bigger problems."

"How could we have bigger problems than surviving?"

"The Draconem have invited your uncle for a chat."

"Oh yeah, that is a problem. What do they want with him?"

"I'm not sure, but any way you look at it, it's not good."

"So that is it, then—my father loses his crown, and it's all my fault?"

"Pye, I don't think it's that simple."

"Why else would they want to talk to him? You said it yourself, any way you look at it, it's bad."

"Pye, you can't jump to conclusions, and what I meant was him being here is no good because of who he is."

"Maybe I can talk to my father, see if they can give him some more time."

"Are you close to controlling your flame?"

"No, but I would have more time to figure something out."

"Trust your dad; he can fix this."

Trust my dad? How could I do that? If he was looking at this the way I was looking at it, then there was no way to fix the situation.

Why couldn't I control my flame? It was a question I had asked Vulcas the Fire God so many times. My mother couldn't have any children after she had me. And I feel like it was all my fault. I can never do anything right.

At dinner that night, it was even more awkward. My father looked like he had the weight of the world on his shoulders. My mother acted as if everything were fine and great. Heat was looking at me across the table as if to say, "It's going to be OK."

I felt like I should speak, but unless I could control my flame, I didn't see the point in speaking.

Heat's father is my dad's torch, meaning his adviser. His second-in-command. My uncle Baskara has known my family for a long time. He even served my grandfather when he was king.

Baskara came into the dining room where we were eating dinner and started whispering something in my dad's ear. Then he took his seat next to his son and his wife, my aunt Rhea, Heat's mother.

I didn't know what Baskara said to my dad, but he looked even more worried now.

"Well, this dinner sure does look good," said my father.

"Yes, it smells good too," my mother added.

I thought, Way to go breaking the tension, I guess. Heat started making funny faces at me to get me to laugh. They were working. But he had to stop because he was getting in trouble with his dad.

I didn't feel much like eating; I just kept pushing the food around my plate. I kept my head down so I would go unnoticed. It didn't work.

My father asked, "Pye, what's wrong?"

Everyone looked at me.

"You have to ask?" I responded.

"Well, yes. You are hiding your face."

I felt so embarrassed. I was blushing. Thank Vulcas no one could see 'cause my hair was covering my face. I had to say something to get the attention off me.

"Nothing, Father. I guess I'm just tired."

My mother said, "Well, it has been along day for all of us. Maybe some sleep is what you need."

I decided to do whatever it took to get everyone to stop looking at me. I don't like being the center of attention. I would rather hide in the shadows. At least there no one can judge me or put pressure on me.

"You're right—sleep is what I need."

I got up to excuse myself.

"Wait, aren't you going to give us a kiss?" my father asked.

I went over and kissed my mother first. Then I kissed my father. He looked into my eyes. I wanted so badly to say, "I'm sorry, father. I'm sorry I'm not the daughter you wanted or deserved." I wanted to say that I should have been a boy instead.

But I didn't have the courage to say it.

"Good night, Father."

"Pye," he said. He grabbed my hand before I could leave.

"Yes?"

"I just wanted to say how much I love you."

It was kind of hard to believe when I had done nothing but be a complete disappointment to them.

The fact is that I love my father very much, and my mother. I would do anything for them. But the smallest task I can't do; it is infuriating.

So I simply reassured him.

"I love you too, Daddy."

He gave me a smile. And I could almost feel hope behind it. Like everything was going to be OK.

Chapter 18

Princess Pye Redrick

I lay in bed staring up at the celling. I felt like my walls were closing in. My parents are such good people, they don't deserve someone like me as their child, I thought.

I think it would make more sense if they just adopted Heat as their son. Then they wouldn't have to worry about me. Then I could just fade away and disappear.

I was so tired of being a burden in everyone's lives. I kept wondering why they hadn't gotten rid of me. I would have if I had been them.

I was starting to doze off when I overheard my parents arguing outside my door in the hall.

I overheard my mom saying it wasn't fair; she didn't know how much I agreed with her.

I put my pillow over my head to block out their argument. I was a blatant stain on their life, and I didn't want to be reminded of it.

I was completely asleep when my mother pushed open my door. I woke up abruptly.

She was shuffling around my room grabbing things and shoving them in a sack.

I was half-asleep, and a part of me was thinking this was a dream.

"Mom, what are you doing?"

"No time for that; you need to get dressed now."

"But it's still late. The sun isn't even up yet."

"Pye, please don't argue with me. Just get up and get dressed."

I did what she said, but I was being rushed. She then threw a cloak over me and bundled me up. Like I was going on an outing.

She grabbed my hand and led me out of my room and through the castle. Servants and guards were all scrambling around like the castle was coming down.

My mother was acting even more weird. Like we were playing a game of hide-and-seek. She kept ducking us low like we might get caught by someone.

"Mom, will you please explain what is going on?"

"Shh, they might hear you."

"Who!"

She didn't answer; she just kept pulling me. Then we finally made it to a spot in the castle I had never been to. She pushed a place on the wall, then it opened.

A hidden staircase led down. It was dark and musty.

"Stay close to me, and never let my hand go," my mother said.

I shook my head up and down; she was really scaring me. We made our way down the staircase to an iron gate that was closed.

My mom melted it with her fire. It was very gracefully done. It opened in no time.

Then I saw Blaze waiting for us at the entrance of what looked like a tunnel. My mom and I were out of breath when we reached him.

"Blaze, what are you doing here?" I asked.

"Keeping a promise to your mom."

My mom handed Blaze my bag, then she grabbed my face. I looked deep into her eyes.

"Pye, I need you to do me a favor," she said.

I looked at her with confusion, 'cause I was confused.

"Yes!"

"I need you to never come back here again."

"What are you talking about?"

"Pye, listen to what I'm saying to you. I need you to leave with Blaze and never come back."

"But how? Why? I don't understand."

"I know, and you will someday."

I seemed to understand that my mom was literally kicking me out of my home. Not likely.

"Mom, if this is about me controlling my fire, I promise that I will do better."

"Pye, it's got nothing to do with that."

"Then why are you doing this?"

"There is no time to explain."

"But I have never been outside the castle grounds; I don't know where to go."

"Blaze will help you."

I looked at Blaze and then looked back at my mother and started crying. I felt like nothing I said was going to change her mind. She obviously didn't want me anymore.

"If we are going to do this, then we need to go now," Blaze said.

My mother brushed a tear from my cheek with her hand.

"It won't be so bad, I promise," she said.

"You rejecting me actually feels really bad."

"Pye."

"No, it's fine. I actually knew this was going to happen."

I walked away from my mother and started down the tunnel without even looking back at her. Maybe this was for the best.

Blaze came up beside me.

"This way, Your Highness," he said.

"You don't have to come with me. I can figure it out myself."

"Thanks, but I made a promise to your parents."

Oh, I see, so they didn't want to feel completely guilty sending me away on my own, I thought.

"Well, I relieve you from your promise."

"Thanks, but only your dad can do that."

"Haven't you heard, I don't have any parents anymore."

"Did it ever occur to you that your parents are doing this to save you?"

"Wow, how much did my parents pay you to say that?"

Blaze laughed at me. He then shook his head.

I followed Blaze through the tunnel. Our only source of light was the lantern that Blaze was carrying.

I tried to hide my crying, but my sobbing was echoing through the tunnels. I knew Blaze was tired of hearing it because I was tired of hearing it. But for some reason, I couldn't stop myself from crying.

I had never seen that part of the castle before. If I had had to guess where we were, I would have said somewhere underneath the castle and behind it.

Finally we could see some light poking through. Good, 'cause I was ready to leave this place and be on my own.

Now that we were out of the tunnel, I could see I was right. The back of the castle.

"Well, we made it," said Blaze.

"You didn't answer my question," I responded.

"What's that?"

"How much are my parents paying you?"

"Nothing."

"Then why are you doing this?"

"I told you, I took a blood oath."

"OK, let me get this straight: You took a blood oath to get me through a tunnel?"

"Nope, I took a blood oath to take care of you."

"I don't need a babysitter."

"I know. Think of me more as a friend or a companion."

"I have never had a friend before."

"Sure, you have Heat."

"But he's my cousin."

"He still can be a friend."

"I guess."

I rolled my eyes. Why would he want to be my friend? I can't do anything right, I thought.

I didn't think I was a princess anymore, so why help me at all? This blood oath Blaze was staying true to must have been one hell of an oath.

I started walking away from where Blaze was standing.

"Wait, where are you going?"

"Daktyloi—it's this way."

"Yes, but the Cliffs of Tshy are this way."

"The Cliffs of Tshy!"

"Yes."

"Why would I go to the Cliffs of Tshy?"

"You said you have always wanted to go there."

"I said that hypothetically."

"Well, the hypothetical can now be a reality."

"But that's to the north."

"Yeah, so?"

"So that's a two-day journey."

"Not if we fly."

"You want me to fly on your back?"

"What's wrong with that?"

"That's a little out of my comfort zone."

"It will be fine. You might like it."

"What if I get airsick?"

"Pye, you have to learn how to live a little."

That was easy for him to say; he hadn't lived a sheltered life.

I had never seen Blaze in dragon form before. He told me that when men change into their dragon, they have to take off all their clothes first or they will rip their clothes when they transform.

Blaze told me to turn my head while he got undressed. I did.

Seeing Blaze as a dragon was impressive. He had green scales and huge wings. A massive tail. And he wanted me to ride him. Yeah, this isn't going to be fun, I thought. I gathered his clothes off the ground and mounted his back with great discomfort and nervousness.

Chapter 19

Princess Pye Redrick

As we landed in Tshy, I couldn't wait to get off Blaze's back. I had really bad whiplash. The whole time I was riding his back, I kept my eyes closed. I knew if I looked, I would puke my guts out.

While Blaze was getting dressed now that he was a human, I looked around.

There wasn't much to look at. There were cliffs and massive boulders. Then a tumbleweed just flew by.

"So this is the Cliffs of Tshy," I said.

"What do you think?"

"There's nothing here."

"Of course. That's the great part about it."

"Just great."

I let out a big sigh.

"While we are here, why don't you start a fire?" Blaze suggested.

"Me?"

"Why not, there's no one here, so you can't hurt anyone, and there's nothing for you to destroy. I can't think of a better place for you to learn."

I just looked at him with uncertainty on my face. But I agreed to do it.

"Wait, before you do this," Blaze said, then hid behind a giant boulder.

"What are you doing?" I asked.

"I don't want to get caught in the cross fire."

"OK. Do you feel safe now?"

"Yes, let it rip."

"Right!"

I did my flick of the wrist, and then, bam!

After it was done and the smoke had cleared, Blaze came around his boulder of protection.

"Very good. Instead of one fire, you made several and a divot in the ground."

"Sorry, but I got nervous, and then fear kicked in again."

"What do you have to fear at this point?"

He was right; I had nothing to be worried about. Now that my parents had disowned me, I should have been happy that the pressure was off. No worries about letting anyone down.

But I was not happy. I felt more like a failure than anything. I had felt failure before, but now it was like my failure was real. My parents had gotten rid of me because I was ash. I knew I was ash. I just didn't know why it had taken them so long to figure it out.

While Blaze was making dinner with one of the many fires I had made, I looked down at the view.

You could see Daktyloi in the distance, but you had to squint just to make everything out. It was so far away, kinda like the problems that I used to have. They seemed so small now. But now that I thought about it, they weren't really problems if they have no merit to them.

After dinner Blaze and I lay in our sleeping bags next to the fire. He was fast asleep. But not me; I just kept looking at the stars. Why did I miss my parents so much? I knew they were not missing me. I wanted to hate them, but I couldn't. I still loved them. How pathetic is that? I thought. I guess deep down I didn't blame them for how they felt. As I said before, I would have done the same thing if I were my daughter.

I hope I never have a daughter or any children, for that matter. The good thing is that it won't ever happen because I'm ash. I wondered what I should do now that my life was my own. I looked over to see Blaze snoring away. I wondered how long he would stick around.

I prayed to the God of Fire that he had something in store for me. I knew that women who were ash usually went into solitude. I guess that would be OK with me, I thought.

Love wasn't made for me. Everyone who loved me ended up disappointed. I wanted to find my own happiness now.

I started to toss and turn in my sleeping bag. I had never slept on the ground before. Being this close to the Winter Realm made me a little sluggish. The weather up here was very different than it was in Daktyloi. It was cooler. That's why a lot a people don't travel this far away from Agni Mountain. It makes us sick when we don't have heat.

Chapter 20

Princess Pye Redrick

I woke up with a stiff neck. Not the best sleep I have ever had. Still, this was the first official day of me being on my own. I would enjoy it no matter what.

I looked around and saw Blaze making breakfast.

"Good morning," he said.

"Morning."

I was still half-asleep and a little groggy.

"Breakfast is almost done."

"How long are we supposed to say up here for?"

"Oh, I don't know. Why do you ask?"

"Just wondering what is next for me."

"Sky is the limit."

He laughed. I just looked at him, not amused.

"Oh, come on, that was funny."

"Yeah, OK."

Blaze was always trying to get me to see the brighter side of things, and I never got it. But I should give him more credit, for at least he's trying, I thought.

"You know why they call this the Cliffs of Tshy?"

"After Vulcas the God of Fire's uncle."

"Yes, but it's also where Tshy met his maker."
"Well good, he deserved it."
"He was the worst dragon of them all."
"No, I would have to say Tshy's older brother Volos was the worst."
"OK, yes. Volos was pretty bad."
"But when you think about it, Apophis wasn't good either."
"Out of all the brothers, Apophis was the only dragon that was kind and gentle."
"If he was so kind and gentle, then he would have never done that awful thing to Leabella."
"True, but it wasn't his fault."
"How so?"
"He was a slave to his impulses."
"That still doesn't make it right."
"Yes, but if Apophis hadn't done what he did, the God of Fire would have never been born, nor would we have, for that matter."
"Have you ever thought that the God of Fire isn't really there?"
"Bite your tongue. Why would you ever say that?"
"He never answers any of my prayers."
"How do you know?"
"Trust me."
"Well, trust me when I tell you that he is very real and hears you more than you know."

Oh, I see, so he is just a cruel god who only cares about certain people, I thought.

After breakfast Blaze and I did some exploring on the Tshy Cliffs.

"What's that symbol up there mean?" I asked.

I noticed some drawings of triangles with an arrowhead in them.

"I'm not sure, really. I have seen them before but don't know what they mean."

"They look interesting."

"Yeah, there are a lot more of them in the Hallow Lands."

"The Hallow Lands?"

"Yes. You remember the map I showed you, the one with all the other realms?"

"Oh right, it's that dark, shadowy party in the middle of the map."

"That's right; that part is nothing but swampland."

"So it's not a realm?"

"Nope, it's not."

"Well, if it's not a realm, then what is it?"

"It's, um, nothing really, just uninhabited land."

"And how do you know that there are more of these symbols there?"

"'Cause I flew down there once."

"You mean you can go down there without getting sick?"

"Well, sure. I mean, it's not that far from the west. All the realms except the water realm share a border with the Hallow Land. And it's not a realm, so there you go."

"Right, but if it's uninhabited, then how did those symbols get there?"

"You ask a lot of questions."

"I'm just saying that maybe when you flew down there, you just didn't see anybody."

"Trust me, Pye, no one lives there; they couldn't."

"But—"

"But nothing. Let's go. We have other stuff to do today."

"Oh really? Like what?"

"We still need to practice controlling your flame."

"Blaze, I'm ash now; I don't need to control it anymore."

"First of all, the only ones who can say you are ash are the queen and king."

"Yeah, and they have."

"How so?"

"They kicked me out of my home. You were there."

"Pye, just because they sent you away doesn't mean they declared you ash."

"Then what do you call it?"

"A new beginning."

"I'm ash now; I know it."

"Did your mother actually say that you are ash?"

"Well, no, but..."

"Exactly. So I win—no argument. Let's go."

I was getting very frustrated with this. Why did he still want me to learn how to control my flame? There really was no reason for it. The point of controlling your flame was to get a husband and get married, which I didn't need or want to do. So this was moot.

Chapter 21

Princess Pye Redrick

He had been drilling me over and over, again and again. The more he pushed me to control my flame, the more agitated I became.

I was becoming so explosive that if we kept on, there wasn't going to be much of Tshy Cliffs left.

"Blaze, that's enough. I'm tired; we have been at this all day."

"OK, we can take a break for a minute. I think we are making real progress, don't you?"

I was so annoyed with him, I couldn't even give him an answer.

"Blaze, please, why do we have to keep on?"

"Because it's important for you to control your flame."

"But I don't want to anymore. I'm fine not being able to."

"Pye, I'm not fine with you not being able to."

"Just give up on me."

"Never!"

"Look, you are still a good teacher even if you can't get me to control my flame."

"Pye, it's going to happen wither you like it or not."

I saw there was no point in arguing with him. So I just looked in the other direction. If I looked at him any longer, I was going to erupt again.

After I calmed myself down and the smoke finally settled, I noticed something in the sky, way off in the distance, coming from the kingdom. It looked like a dragon, and it was flying fast.

"Hey, Blaze, what's that?"

"Oh no, they must have seen your flames while we were practicing."

"Who!"

Blaze grabbed me and brought me behind a bunch of boulders that were stuck together like a wall.

He grabbed both my arms and looked into my eyes. I could see the panic in them.

"Pye, no matter what happens, I need you to say hidden."

"But why? I don't under—"

"It doesn't matter. No matter what you hear or what you think you hear, do not come out of this spot until I tell you to."

He was scaring me. And the look on his face conveyed if I didn't agree, it might hurt both of us.

"OK, I won't move from this spot."

"No matter what?"

"No matter what."

There I was hiding again. It seemed this was really what I was good at—hiding. I could hear Blaze talking to someone, but I didn't recognize the voice.

"Blaze! Now this is turning out to be a good day," said the voice.

"Forneus, I take it that if you are here, then all shit has let loose in the kingdom."

"Cut the crap. Where is she?" Forneus responded.

"Whom are you talking about?"

"Don't insult my intelligence."

"Now why would I do that?"

"You remember the last time you messed with me?"

"Of course I remember."

"Then I'm going to only ask you one more time, Where is the princess?"

"Wasn't she in Novngarde Castle?"

"No, actually no one seems to know where she is. All we found were her mother and father."

"Well, I don't know what to tell you."

It sounded like this Forneus guy was not buying it at all. I wondered what he wanted with me; I had done nothing to him. I didn't even know him.

"So why are you here in the Cliffs of Tshy?" Forneus asked.

"I thought I would go and get some fresh air," responded Blaze.

"OK, I have no patience for this. I guess I'll have to get it out of you the old-fashioned way."

It went quiet, and then I felt the ground shake. Yep, it was safe to say they were fighting dragon-style. Rocks and debris were flying everywhere. The ground was now quaking, and I felt like I needed to hang on to something.

The cliffs were breaking apart, and I needed to move and get out of here. But I had told Blaze I wouldn't move from this spot. If I did move, then this Forneus would know that Blaze had lied to him. This guy sounded like he wanted to hurt me, so I was staying put no matter what.

It went quiet again. I peeked my head out to see what was going on. My eyes got wide when I saw Blaze lying there in a puddle of blood. Oh no, he looks really hurt, I thought.

Based on impulse, I ran to him. I didn't care who saw me at that point. He was my friend, and he needed me. I touched his green scales. And his dragon eyes opened, and he looked at me.

"Pye, I need you to do me one more favor."

His voice was shaky and weak.

"Anything."

Tears were boiling up inside me.

"You see to the right, those rocky mountains with the white powder on them?"

"You mean the Winter Realm?"

"Yes. I need you to go there and hide."

"I can't do that. I will die in the Winter Realm."

"Pye, you don't have a choice; you must go."

"But why can't I stay with you?"

"It looks like I, too, am going to meet my maker here, the same as Tshy."

"But he was a bad dragon; you are a good one."

"Pye, you must go to the Winter Realm and never come back to the Fire Realm."

"But it's too cold there, and if they find out who I am, they will surely kill me."

"You can do this, and you must."

"But I'm just me. I'm nothing special."

"Pye, you are the strongest person I have ever known. Your fire can move mountains. No girl has ever been able to do that."

I looked at the Winter Realm, and I didn't know what it is, but it felt like something was pulling me in that direction. Even though every bone in my body said, "No, not a good idea."

"OK, I'll go, Blaze."

But he said nothing; he was gone. I cried and laid my head down on him. The only friend I had ever had, and I had lost him.

"So sorry for your loss," said Forneus.

I jolted to my feet.

"Look, I don't know who you are, but you have the wrong person," I responded.

I had never seen a naked man before, and from what I could see, they were very ugly naked, but here he was walking slowly toward me with a dagger in his hand.

"You are King Helios Redrick's daughter, are you not?"

"Yes."

"Then I have the right person."

I slowly backed away from him as he was walking toward me.

"But I haven't done anything to you."

"You were born," Forneus said.

He swung at me with his dagger, and he missed as I ducked.

"Look, if you sit still, princess, I promise that this will be over quickly and will be painless; you won't feel a thing."

I was running now toward the Winter Realm. Then I got to the rocks and started climbing, but they were very steep. I slipped and lost my footing and stumbled down to where Forneus was.

I then felt a sharp pinch on my side. I let out a loud scream as he pulled his dagger out of me. He had gotten me on the side of my stomach. It hurt so bad; I grabbed my side, trying to keep the warm blood from spilling out of me. It hurt worse when he pulled the blade out of me than when he stabbed me with it.

That was it—he needed to go away. I closed my eyes and remembered what Blaze used to tell me, that I was very dangerous because I had no off switch. He was right. I had nothing to be afraid of anymore.

I ignited myself and let it all out. No holding back this time. Forneus was screaming in pain. He jumped up and changed into a dragon again and flew farther up into the sky to get away from my fire.

I looked up and saw that the red cliffs above me had started to crack and fracture as my fire had caused the stress fractures to become bigger. The cliffs couldn't take the tension anymore. An avalanche of rocks was coming my way.

I started to panic, and my flame got bigger. I didn't know what to do. Then I remembered what Blaze used to tell me when I got out of control: relax and be calm.

My flame went out in no time, but the rocks were still coming down, so I moved up them as fast as I could without slipping this time. It was hard now 'cause I only had one good hand, while the other was helping me keep the blood in from my stomach wound.

I heard Forneus flying back my way. He was growling. I was not going to let him get me, not this time.

Chapter 22

Princess Pye Redrick

I was almost at the Winter Realm. I could feel the coldness. The white powder was getting thicker the farther up I climbed.

My hands were getting numb. I still didn't understand how this was going to help me get away from Forneus. But I guess it's better than fighting him, I thought.

With him in his dragon form, I didn't stand a chance.

Before I knew it, I was in the Winter Realm. The white powder was up to my knees, and I was feeling really sick. I turned around, looking for Forneus to come out.

I spotted him flying in the distance; he was charging right at me. I was getting ready to close my eyes as he got closer to me.

But then as he was about to pass the Winter Realm border, it blocked him. Like an invisible fence. He swung back around to try it again. But the same thing happened. He was hitting a brick wall that wasn't really there. The Winter Realm would not let him in. He tried one more time, but he kept hitting himself in the face. Whatever this invisible shield was, I was so happy that it was there. Then he kept spitting out fire at the Winter Realm, but it only backfired on him.

Praise Vulcas. Forneus gave up and flew back down. I was so happy that I fell back into this white powder that felt like thousands of needles on my skin.

I didn't know why the Winter Realm would let me in and not Forneus, but I was just so glad it had.

I didn't know what to do then. I was feeling really yucky and not just because I was bleeding real bad but also because I could feel the separation of heat. Tiny white things started coming down from the sky and onto me. It was more of that white powder stuff. I opened my mouth, and it tasted so cold, something I was not used to.

For the first time in my life, I really was on my own, and I hadn't the slightest idea what to do.

And as always, I was scared.

When fire dose not destroy it hardens

—Oscar Wilde

Part IV

The Winter Realm

Introduction

The Winter Realm is to the north. It is always covered in snow. The North is negative sixty degrees Fahrenheit during the summer and in springtime. But during fall and winter, it gets to be negative ninety degrees Fahrenheit.

In these cold conditions, it is hard for animals to survive.

There are three kingdoms in the north. The biggest and oldest one is Polaris, the winter kingdom. The second kingdom is Pulse, the kingdom of snow. The third is Eria, the kingdom of snowflakes.

Now the people who live here are called Ice-Aidens. They have silver-white hair and white eyes. They worship Bormack the God of Winter.

Ice-Aidens have the power to endure freezing conditions and have the power to create ice in the palm of their hand. They can freeze anything they want to—not that they would since everything is already freezing.

Bormack the God of Winter has two brothers and one sister. His brothers are North the God of Ice and Egrass the God of Cold Wind. His sister is Zephira the Goddess of Snow. Bormack is the only one who can bring them together, making him the God of Winter.

Now, the Ice-Aidens are very honorable people; they believe family is very important.

Ice-Aidens do not trust outsiders. If an outsider does come into the Winter Realm, the punishment by law is death. If an outsider claims they are an Ice-Aiden, they must past a test. The test is called Fibrous. There are six snow temples in the Kingdom of Polaris. They are covered in ice. Inside these temples are statues of the four Gods of Winter. Each statue faces the middle of the temple; that is where the outsider will stand. Each statue will pour out a frozen fog of ice breath that eventually will reach a temperature of negative one hundred degrees. If you can stand that temperature, then you are a true Ice-Aiden. If you can't, you die. These snow temples are filled with frozen statues of imposters.

Ice-Aiden men hunt, while the women cook and take care of the children. Now, when Ice-Aiden men have an argument or a disagreement, they fight it out. The one who loses the argument will get a notch on his forearm made by the winner. The notch is a big cut that will leave a big scar. An Ice-Aiden that has a lot of notches is considered less than worthy of being a man and cannot marry or have a family. They call them runts, and they will never be good providers.

The winner of the fight is marked with blue tribal ink on the back of their neck, back, and arms. An Ice-Aiden who has a lot of blue ink is considered righteous. This is a high honor in their world. They can have their pick of any women they want, with the God of Winter's blessing, of course. And they are always picked to lead the Korm. This ritual is called Nix.

Now, Korm is a ritual they perform once every year. In it, the Ice-Aiden men go on a two- or sometimes three-month hunt for food before the great winter storm. The storm is called Leeaya. This storm usually lasts eight months out of the year, freezing everything to ice. After the eight months is up, the ice melts and the new world begins again. The storm typically leaves about forty-five feet of snow.

The Ice-Aidens take about forty five-men on the Korm. Women do not like being without their spouse for that long, so some like to go on the Korm with them.

The Ice-Aiden women are very faithful to their men. They serve their husband until they leave in spirit. A married Ice-Aiden woman will have their hair braided to show that they are taken and that they have consummated their marriage. A married Ice-Aiden man will have a necklace of his spouse's snowflake around his neck to show he's happily married.

Snow Junipers are holy men that worship the God of Winter. Their job is to help carry out the Ice-Aidens' rituals, such as births, weddings, and Fibrous. Snow Junipers only deal with religion, not law.

"Mammoth" is a word that describes two Ice-Aidens that have impeccable memory and are very knowledgeable in all the winter laws. The Mammoths help the king to come to a rational conclusion for his people within their religion. The Mammoths are the king's advisers, and they deal only in law.

The king of Polaris is King River Sleight. His son Winter is going to be married soon to the woman he loves. Her name is Fray. Fray's father is Bylur. He is captain of King River's army. King River's sister is Rain, who has looked after Winter since his mother died.

The biggest problem the Winter Realm faces now is starvation.

Bormack symbolizes kinship and devotion. Their religion is called Quiver.

Chapter 23

Fray Iceberg

I knew Brisk had told me that I had to wait a few days, but I couldn't anymore; I needed to know. But something deep down already told me that I knew already. It would be better to get it confirmed by him. Since he is the Snow Juniper.

The ice chapel was going to be dead this time of day. No one would be there, so this was a great time to ask him. I found him rummaging through some books; the minute he saw me, he shook his head.

"No, Fray, not now," said Brisk.

"Oh come on, Brisk, please."

"I told you that you have to wait."

"I don't want to wait."

"Look, I'm extremely busy right now."

He handed a bunch of scrolls to Fright. Fright was a Snow Spur, meaning that he was in training to be a Snow Juniper. He was about eleven and very smart.

"Look, I have a feeling you already know the answer," I said.

Brisk looked at me and smiled.

"Women's intuition, it never fails."

"Well…"

"What do you think?"

"That I am."

I couldn't help smiling about it.

"Then I think you should go with your gut."

I jumped up and down and squealed really loud. I was so happy.

"Brisk, thank you so much," I said.

I gave him a hug.

Brisk said, "Wait a minute. You know the penalty when you have a child without Bormack's blessing."

"Brisk, I'm marrying Winter very soon, so technically I already have the God of Winter's blessing."

"Fray, you still have to participate in Crystallum, and just 'cause you and Winter love each other isn't a guarantee you will end up together. The God of Winter decides, not you."

"Isn't this baby proof that he agrees?"

"Fray, that's not how it works, and you know that."

I couldn't listen to what he was saying; I was too happy. He wasn't going to rain on my parade. Winter and I were going to have a baby together. I couldn't tell anyone about that 'cause it was considered avorta. The last thing I wanted to do was bring shame to myself and my future husband. So I decided I was just going to tell Winter. I was too excited to keep this to myself. I knew Brisk wouldn't tell 'cause he was the one that told me to not even tell Winter. But I had to.

Chapter 24

Prince Winter Sleight

Bylur was training me in the snow yard like he did almost every day. Training with him was the reason why my entire back was covered in blue ink. I have one notch on my forearm that I will never talk about.

Bylur instructed, "Extend your arm like this when holding your sword."

I did as he said to get a feel of what he was talking about.

"I like that," I said.

"Good. That will help make blocking your assailant a lot easier."

Our swords are square-tipped and very heavy. When I was a young boy, it took me a whole year to get strong enough to hold one.

Now looking at me, you could never tell I struggled at all.

We went trough a couple more drills, then I saw Fray. She looked like she had something to say.

Her father looked at her and smiled.

"You want to take a break?" he asked.

"Sure," I said.

Fray came and hugged her dad.

"So how's the training going?" she asked.

"Good. I'm kicking your dad's butt," I responded.

"Yeah right, in his dreams," Bylur added.

Fray and I just stared at each other, kind of giving her dad the cue to leave. I love Fray very much; she's my best friend. We have known each other since birth. But around that time I had felt like our relationship had been lacking something, and I didn't know why. This feeling all started when I turned twenty and my dad said I was going to have to get married soon. I was not sure I wanted to get married. When I'm ready to get married, do I want it to be Fray? I thought. Maybe it was just wedding jitters.

After her dad left, we hugged each other.

"So I got some great news," she said.

"Oh yeah?"

"Yeah!"

She was smiling at me. Must be really good news, I thought.

"Are you going to tell me, or do I have to guess?" I asked.

"Brisk tells me that I'm going to have your child."

My face just went blank. I was not ready to be a dad. This was moving so fast.

I just looked at Fray with confusion and uncertainty.

"Are you sure?" I asked.

"Yes, pretty sure."

"Oh."

"Oh? I tell you I'm carrying your child and you say oh?"

"I'm sorry, Fray. I just wasn't ready for this; that's all."

"But don't you want to have kids?"

Truth be told I, I was not sure I wanted kids. But I hated upsetting her.

"Yeah, eventually."

"Well, now it's for sure going to happen."

I could tell by her face she was getting mad.

"I think it's great."

I lied. Then I reassured her that I was OK with this by giving her a kiss.

"You really are happy about this, right?" she asked.

"Yes of course. I can't wait to be a dad."

Even the words coming out of my mouth sounded flat.

Fray looked up at me with a big smile. I just didn't have it in me to break her heart.

"We should celebrate," she said.

"Fray, we are going to have to keep this between us for now. You know how my dad feels about this kind of thing before marriage."

"I know. I just want to celebrate between the two of us."

"That sounds good."

This was really bad. I didn't want to get married, and now that Fray was pregnant, I didn't have a choice. My father would have gone ballistic if he had found out about Fray's condition. The other thing was, How was she going to hide this? The Crystallum wasn't going to happen for a whole year. Maybe I should just tell my father and get it over with, I thought. Some king I'm going to turn out to be.

My uncle Arctodus came in and interrupted me and Fray. I was kind of glad; I needed to get my mind on something else. His pet, Rex, came up to me and Fray. I petted him. Rex is a white sabertooth tiger that loves attention.

Arctodus said, "I'm not interrupting anything, am I?"

"No not all," I responded.

"You haven't seen your aunt by any chance?"

"Earlier."

"Well, if you see her, tell her I'm looking for her."

"Yeah, sure. Is everything OK?"

"Yep, couldn't be better."

My uncle was acting very nervous. It got more awkward the longer we stood there in silence.

My uncle said, "OK, well it was good seeing you guys."

"Good seeing you too," I responded.

"Rex, let's go," he said.

Chapter 25

Princess Rain Natalis

I said, "There you are; I've been looking for you everywhere."

My husband Arctodus responded, "Rain, we have to talk."

"OK. Why are you whispering?"

"It's not safe here."

"What are you talking about? You we're supposed to help me with the furs this morning."

"Come with me."

My husband pulled me by the arm and shoved me into the house. He then shut the door and started inspecting the room. He really has gone out of his mind, I thought.

"Are you going to tell me what in Zephira you are doing?"

"Now that the room is secure, yes."

"Secure from what?"

"Please, just sit down. Let me explain."

I did as my husband asked and waited a minute for him to catch his breath.

"So this morning, I snuck out to go fishing instead of helping you with the furs."

"I knew it. You promised me."

"I know, and I'm really sorry about that, but—"

"Well, I don't forgive you."

"You're right, I deserve that, but something happened, Rain, something you couldn't possibly comprehend 'cause I don't understand it myself."

"Huh!"

"So there I was fishing, minding my own business, when all of a sudden a Yache came out of nowhere and attacked me."

"You were fishing at Sucker Pond, weren't you? That place is crawling with Yache."

"Yes, but they have the best fish there."

I had no choice but to hit my husband on his arm. To be so reckless. He never thinks anything through, I thought.

"How could you be so stupid?"

My husband sat me down.

"Will you please calm down? There is more to this story."

"You are so lucky you are not dead 'cause I'm going to kill you."

"Rain, please let me finish my story, then you can do whatever you want."

"Fine."

"Were was I?"

"Yache."

"Oh right, so there I was getting attacked when Rex came trying to help me, but it wasn't good. Just when I think this Yache is going to eat me, this red light came out of nowhere and killed it."

"Red light?"

"Yes. Completely destroyed it; there was nothing left of it."

"OK. I think you hit your head, or maybe you are in shock."

"No, Rain, I'm serious. This red light was like noting I have ever seen before."

I just stared at my husband in disbelief.

"Well, that is a story," I said.

"I went to investigate where this red light came from, and it was this."

He signaled me to the bedroom.

"I'm not going to have sex with you; I'm very upset with you," I said.
"Will you just look in there, please?"
"Fine."

I opened the bedroom door, and my eyes got wide as my mouth popped open. There was a young girl in our bed. An outsider not from this realm. I quickly shut the door and inspect the house again to make sure we had complete privacy.

"Are you out of your mind? Why did you bring her here?"
"I didn't have a choice."
"You know that the penalty for bringing her here is death, right?"
"I also know what the penalty is for not repaying someone when they save your life."
"I don't think that law applies to outsiders."
"She saved my life, Rain. I wouldn't be standing here with you—"
"That's your own fault. You shouldn't have been there in the first place."

My husband is begging. The obligation is sinking in.

"Please, Rain."
"What do you want me to do?"
"I don't know, but I think there is something wrong with her."
"Yeah, she's from another realm; that's what's wrong with her."
"Just take a look at her."
"How did she even get in here?"
"I'm not sure, but I think she's a fire demon."
"How do you know that?"
"She has a symbol behind her left ear of that red light she made."
"Great. So she will kill us all with her red light."
"I think if she was going to kill me, she would have done it already."
"OK, OK, I'll look at her."
"Thank you."

I was not happy about this at all. Of all the bad things my husband had done, this took the cake.

I opened my bedroom door again; I moved closer to the bed. Her eyes were closed. I then realized she was just a young girl. Couldn't have been more than eighteen or nineteen. I pulled the covers gently off her and saw the wound on her stomach. I looked back at her pale and empty face. My heart went out to this young girl. She reminded me of my daughter. I had lost her eight years before to sickness.

"Well, what do you think?" my husband asked.

"She's lost a lot of blood."

"Do you think you can save her?"

"I need hot water and surgical threads. Oh, and bring me lilac ointment."

"I'm on it."

This young girl lying half-dead in my bed was not going to die on my watch. I hadn't been able to save my daughter, but I would save this girl. While my husband was off getting me the stuff I needed, I took off her wet clothes. She didn't wake up once. That was probably a good thing. It was touch and go with her.

After I got the stuff I needed from him, my husband waited outside while I worked my magic. I cleaned up her wound, and I sewed it back together. The good thing was that the wound wasn't too deep; it had missed all her organs. I made her warm and comfortable. The best thing she could do now was rest.

After I was done, I came out to sit with my husband and share a drink with him.

"Well?" he asked.

"Well, that's all I can do; the rest is up to her."

"If we ever get out of this, I just want to tell you that I love you."

"If this ever gets out, my bother is going to kill me."

"You mean, he will kill both of us."

"Yes, but more me 'cause I'm his sister."

"Once she is better, we will sneak her out and take her back to the place she came from."

"It may not be that easy."

"Oh, I know it won't be, but together we have a better shot."

My husband and I looked at each other and clinked our glasses together. We were definitely going to need liquid confidence for this task.

Chapter 26

Princess Pye Redrick

I felt like my body had been turned inside out. I was not sure if I was dead or alive. If am dead, then why do I feel so weak? I thought. Every time I tried to open my eyes, I couldn't. I was just so tired. There was this constant cold feeling all over my body. It was causing me to shiver. I missed the heat, and most of all, I missed my family. Watching my mom brushing her hair. My dad telling me how much he loved me, even though they got rid of me.

Every now and then, I heard Blaze's voice telling me not to harbor my fear. That I must stay strong. If he and I are both dead, then why can't I see him? I thought.

I tried to move, and then I heard another voice saying, "Be still. The fever is on you." I had never heard that voice before. I thought it might have been the God of Fire telling me he was carefully watching over me. That he would soon welcome me into the Agni Mountain.

I thought it was interesting that I was not afraid of death. That I welcomed it. I was glad that it was over. After all, it hadn't been much of a life to begin with. Having to live in a world of fear is not really living. I could still see that dragon that wanted to kill me. Sometimes I saw him coming at me like he was going to finish the job.

I didn't know how long I'd been lying there, but it was better than sleeping on the ground. As time went on, my body felt like it was getting stronger. My strength was slowly coming back. The chill was gone, but I could still feel the numbness of the cold.

Then it happened. I finally felt strong enough to open my eyes. When I did, nothing looked like I thought it was going to. I thought the inside of Agni Mountain would be more fiery and warmer. Looking around the room, I was hoping to find the God of Fire, but the room was empty.

The room was pretty. White walls and floor. There was this fireplace, and what I thought was fire was white. A white flame—how can that be? I thought I sat up to try to get a better look at it, but my wound was still very sore. I put my hand on it. I felt the bandages. I took my blanket off to get a better look at it. It looked almost completely healed. No blood. The bed I was lying on was really pretty as well. White and silver sheets. I'd never seen such colors brought together like that. The blanket that was over me was so soft. It was made of a material I had never encountered before. So fuzzy. I pressed it up against my cheek. It was more than soft; it was relaxing.

Where am I? What is this place? Why does it feel so cozy? I thought. I fought the soreness and sat all the way up. I then realized I was completely naked. I grabbed the blanket and covered myself up again.

I heard some faint talking in the background. It was getting louder, along with the footsteps. I didn't know if I should go back and pretend to sleep or if I should try to get out of there. I was getting really scared. I could feel my flame warming up inside me. I was terrified and shaking as I could see the door handle moving. I closed my eyes. The door swung open.

"Well, I'm glad you are up," said a woman.

The calmness of her voice calmed me down. I opened my eyes. This lady was beautiful. She had white-silver hair. White eyes. And her dress was made of the same material as my blanket. She sat on the bed next to me and wanted to feel my head. I was hesitant to let her.

"It's OK, I'm not going to hurt you," she said.

I didn't really know what to say to her. I was very confused.

"Oh no! You don't speak the common tongue, do you?" she asked.

"Am I dead?" I asked in turn.

She laughed.

"No, far from it."

She leaned in again to touch my forehead, and this time I let her. Her hands were really warm and soft.

"Well, you don't have a fever anymore," she said.

So it was her voice I heard earlier. I knew it sounded familiar.

"Where am I?"

"Polaris."

"Polaris. What's that?"

"The snow kingdom."

"But how did I get here?"

"That's what I would like to ask you."

"I'm not sure."

"Well, it's not every day we get a fire demon in the Winter Realm."

The Winter Realm—now I remembered. But I was not sure what I should tell her. I had just met her. I wasn't sure I could trust her.

"Why did you call me a fire demon?"

"That's what you are."

"No, I'm not."

"So you aren't from the Fire Realm?"

"I am, but we aren't called fire demons."

"Oh, I'm so sorry. We just have always known your kind as the fire demons."

"And my kind has always known your kind as snow ghosts."

"OK. Well, clearly we have a lot to learn about each other's kind."

"Clearly."

"My name is Rain, and I'm an Ice-Aiden."

"My name is Pyra, but everyone calls me Pye. I'm a Pyrolatreia."

"Well, Pye, it's a pleasure to meet you."

"You too, Rain."

We smiled at each other. Then a man burst into the room and startled me.

"It's OK. It's just my husband Arctodus."

I remembered him; he was about to get eaten by this hideous gorilla-looking monster. Then I blew my flame at it. Then I passed out. He must have taken me in after I saved his life.

"Arctodus, this is Pye," Rain said.

He nodded his head at me as he stood at the foot of the bed.

"Thank you, Pye, for saving my life."

"Well, it looks like we are even now. So thank you."

"Rain, have you told her yet?"

"I was getting there."

"Tell me what?"

"You can't stay here, Pye," said Arctodus.

Rain added, "The law says that outsiders are to be killed immediately, no matter the situation."

"And anyone sheltering outsiders is subjected to death by beheading, no matter what," said Arctodus.

"I see."

Rain went on, "We are very sorry, but we have to sneak you out of here back to your home."

These people took me in and took care of me knowing that it was against the law. Maybe I can trust them, but I don't have a home to go back to, I thought. I didn't want to stay in the Winter Realm, but I knew if I went back to the Fire Realm, that dragon was going to come back looking for me. And this time he would succeed in killing me.

I didn't want anyone dying for me. That was how I had lost my good friend and teacher Blaze. His blood was on my hands. I wouldn't be responsible for these people either. Not after they had taken such good care of me.

Chapter 27

Princess Pye Redrick

I hid in the wagon. Rain said it was better this way, that no one would ask questions. They piled a whole bunch of stuff on top of me so it would look like they were just hauling the usual. Arctodus's pet Rex, an animal that looked funny to me, kept trying to dig me up out of the cart so that he could lick my face. He was really soft, like the material of my blanket and Rain's dress. Rex is an unusual animal. He has two teeth that are too big for his mouth. He looks scary, but he is really sweet.

I heard Arctodus tell Rex to get out of the wagon so that he wouldn't spoil the plan. Rain went with us so that nothing bad would happen; she wanted to make sure I got back home OK. The cart was cold and dirty. I lay on my back, peeping out of the cracks in the wagon.

The place was so white. Nothing like my home. My home. When I do get back, I wonder if my father will declare me ash, I thought. That way I won't have to bother with it anymore. Of course, my mother said never come back; I need to honor that. That is, if I don't die first. I should have let that dragon kill me. Then I wouldn't have been here getting these good people in trouble. As the wagon started to move, I got really scared. I was tensing up. Oh, I hope we get away with this, I thought.

I continued looking at the snow kingdom from the crack of the wagon. It was so beautiful. There were so many animals I had never seen before. At home all we have are horses and dogs, lots of birds; that's it. But here it was like they were everywhere. Big animals, small animals. Some looked really odd. And they were all white. They blended in with the snow.

I spotted some Ice-Aiden children, boys and girls, playing together. They were taking what looked like white powder in the palm of their hands and then throwing balls of it at each other. When one of the kids got hit with it, they just laughed. The white balls were soft enough that they dispersed on impact. It looked like fun. Some of the kids were sliding on the white powder. They were gliding, almost like they were dancing. It was so pretty to watch. Then I saw an Ice-Aiden man making ice sculptures with the palm of his hand. I found it fascinating.

Kids at home play games, but not like this. Usually they stay away from each other because of the fire that each kid gives off. Pyrolatreia children are separated. Girls play with girls and boys play with boys until they are ready to find their mate.

We were out of the kingdom after a while. Following a road. Rain came back and kept me company. She put more blankets on me since I was freezing. I don't think I can get use to this weather, I thought.

"What is your dress and these blankets made out of?" I asked.

"Fur," she explained.

"Fur, what's that?"

"It comes from an animal."

"It's so soft."

"Yes, very. Don't you have things like that where you are from?"

"No, we don't have anything with fur on it."

"Then I'm glad you got to see and feel what fur is about."

"Yes, I like it a lot."

"Me too."

"How much longer?"

"Not much. We should be there in a few hours or so."

"Good!"

"I bet you are happy to be going back home."
In a way I am, and in a way, I'm not.
"Yes, I guess I am."
"Sure your mom is worried sick about you."
"Oh, I don't have a mom anymore."
"Oh, I'm so sorry."
"It's OK. It was kind of a long time coming."
"Well, then your father must be missing you?"
"I don't have a father either."
"So who looks after you?"
"As of now, no one."
Rain has a sad look on her face.
"So you are all alone?" she asked.
"Yes, but it's better that way."
"How can it be better that way?"
"'Cause no one can hurt me and I can't hurt them."
"Pye, you know if someone hurt you, you could tell me?"

I could have told her, but what would have been the point? I was leaving, and I'd never see her again. It was not like she could come to the Fire Realm and help me.

"Thanks, but I'll be OK."
"You sound just like my daughter."
"You have daughter?"
"Had a daughter."
"I'm so sorry."
"No, it's OK. She died a long time ago. If she had lived, she would be your age now."
"I bet she was a great daughter."
"She was."

I felt the cart jolt to a stop. I sat up. Rain looked confused as she looked up ahead. I could feel something was wrong. The horses started to get restless. They were neighing so loudly. My fear was stepping in again.

Rain stepped out of the cart and told me to stay put. I did as she said, but I didn't like that feeling of being alone at that moment.

It was quiet for a minute, then I could hear Rex growling.

Had we gotten caught? Was I about to die? I was not sure what to do.

"Rain, are you there?" I asked. "Arctodus, are you there?"

Nothing.

OK, I'm really sacred now, I thought. My anxiety was building up. My hands were shaking. Then I heard someone running back to the cart. It was Rain, thank Vulcas.

"Sorry about that, but there was something in the road and we had to make sure it was safe to pass," she explained.

"You guys sacred me to death."

"It's OK. Nothing to be alarmed about."

The cart began to move again, and I began to calm down. As time went on, I got hungry and tired. I felt like I'd been in this cart for days.

"Is it much longer now?" I asked.

"We are nearly there," said Rain.

"OK, good."

"Why do you do that?"

"Do what?"

"Why do you hide your face with your hair?"

"I just feel more comfortable when people can't see my flaws."

"Pye, I don't see any flaws."

"Trust me, I have them."

"Can I tell you what I see?"

I don't answer her; I just look at her.

"I see that you are a very beautiful young woman."

"Uh no, not me."

"Oh yes, you. Your hair, for starters, is so beautifully bright red. It's such a nice change from the average hair color you see around here."

"If you think my hair is nice, then you should see my mother's."

"Well, then now I know where you got it from."

I bowed my head down so that I could hide my smile. But I had a feeling Rain saw it anyway.

Then the cart came to another stop.

"We are here," announced Arctodus.

"Oh great, any longer and I was going to fall asleep," I said.

"Well, we had to go another way," explained Rain.

Arctodus added, "Yeah, we took the scenic route just to be careful."

Arctodus helped me out of the cart. I kept the blankets around me; I was not taking them off till I got back to the Fire Realm. Rex stayed in the cart.

"The border is right down there," said Rain.

"Here, we will walk you to it," said Arctodus.

Rain and Arctodus started walking, and I followed behind them. The snow was so hard to walk in. They were having no trouble, but I was definitely struggling. Then Arctodus put his hand up, signaling us to stop.

"What is it?" Rain asked.

"Shh! Yache," responded Arctodus.

"A what?" I whispered.

Rain pointed to the ground. It was a footprint of what I thought to be an animal. It was just so hard to believe that an animal had made a footprint that big. The word "huge" didn't even describe how big this was. Dragons have big footprints, and this was almost as big as that.

A foul smell came over us from nowhere. We were all sniffing and then scrunching up our noses, the smell was so bad. Then a deep growl came from behind us.

I had never seen a gorilla in person before, only in books. The Yache are giant white gorillas with huge tusks coming from their mouths. It would be better for something like this to be going up against a dragon; that would be a fair fight, I thought. Even though the dragon would definitely win.

We all tensed up as we turned slowly around. White shaggy fur was in front of us. We followed it all the way up.

This monster was the ugliest and smelliest thing I had ever seen, and I live with dragons. Now my whole body was shaking, and I was getting ready to pee my pants when Rain grabbed my hand and told me to run.

As we were fleeing for our lives, this monster was catching up to us.

"We need to hide," said Arctodus.

"How are we going to hide from that?" I asked.

"You hide in there; I'll go and distract him."

There was an ice cave not far from where we were running. It had icicles hanging down at its entrance.

"No way. I'm not leaving you to fight that thing," said Rain.

"We don't have much of a choice, Rain," Arctodus responded.

As we were running toward the cave, the Yache pounded his fist on the ground. The vibrations caused all three of us to fall to our knees.

Arctodus got to his feet and charged at the Yache with his sword. Rain was screaming at him not to be a hero.

This was all my fault. I had to do something. This man was not going to die because of me. I let go of Rain's hand. I walked toward Arctodus and the Yache fighting it out. Rain was telling me to stop, but I didn't listen.

She then got in front of me.

She said, "Pye, stop. You're going to get yourself killed."

"Trust me," I said.

She looked very confused. But she stepped aside and let me continue walking toward them. The Yache had flung Arctodus across the snow. Rain went to him to see if he was OK.

The Yache saw me and came charging toward me.

It was time for me to let my flame go. No holding back. Like Blaze said: "Do not harbor your fear."

When I saw that Rain and Arctodus were out of the range of my flame, I closed my eyes, and then, kaboom!

I opened my eyes, and as the smoke cleared, I saw all that was left of the Yache was its burnt remains. Along with a good chunk of snow that was now missing from the ground.

I went to Rain and Arctodus to see if they were OK.

"Are you guys all right?"

"That was amazing!" exclaimed Rain.

"I told you, a red light like you have never seen before," added Arctodus.

"But how did you? Oh, wow!" said Rain.

"Thanks, Pye," said Arctodus.

"No problem."

"Pye, can you do that every time?" Rain asked.

"Sure. That's not the problem; it's taming it."

"Why would you ever want to tame something like that?"

"Because it causes mass destruction. Nobody wants that."

"I want that."

Arctodus and I just looked at each other. Both of us were bewildered.

"What do you mean?" I asked.

"I have a brilliant idea," responded Rain.

"OK."

"Pye, you can melt the snow."

"Uh-huh."

"That means you can help us with the Korm."

"With what?"

"Rain, what in Egrass are you talking about?" asked Arctodus.

"She can help us hunt for food," explained Rain.

"How can she do that?"

"By melting the snow."

"What are you getting at?"

"Pye, one of the problems we have in the Winter Realm is starvation. There is not enough food. The reason is that it's hard for us to hunt in these conditions."

"Rain, I still don't understand," I chimed in.

"If you help to melt the snow, then we can hunt for a longer period."

"Are you insane? That would never work," Arctodus interjected.

"Why not?" asked Rain.

"Well, for starters, she's not an Ice-Aiden."

"Then we will make her one."

"How do we do that?"

"Simple, by giving her a disguise."

"No, that's crazy. They will know she's not one of us."

"Arctodus, we have to help our people. She can do it."

"And how do we melt the snow without someone finding out who she is?"

"You are a tracker, aren't you?"

"Meaning?"

"Trackers scout ahead; we will go ahead and melt the snow."

"If we get caught, we won't have heads."

"It will work."

"And then what? Pye can't stay here forever."

"We will cross that bridge when we get there."

Chapter 28

Fray Iceberg

I was not feeling all that great today. I figured it was just the sickness that came with being with child, so I didn't think much of it. I was sitting next to Winter and his father at the dinner table. My father was on the other side of the table, facing me. They were going on about the Korm coming up.

Winter was telling his dad they hoped that they would have a better year in terms of finding food. Last year there was barely enough to go around. Everyone was rationing when Leeaya was about over.

My dad said, "If only there were a way to hunt longer," but with snow as thick as it was, it was very hard to catch anything.

I was feeling cramps in my stomach. I tried to ignore them, but they were getting stronger. I was now feeling them in my lower back.

I tried to ignore the pain until I couldn't anymore. I had to excuse myself.

I said good night to everyone. But I didn't go to my room; I had to find Brisk. Something was wrong. I went to the ice temple. When I walked in, I noticed there was blood all over my feet. I then saw my dress was stained with blood from my lower midsection all the way down.

I was freaking out. The pain was getting stronger. I was screaming, and then it went dark.

I woke up to someone kissing my cheek. It was my dad.

"What happened?" I asked.

He said, "Oh, honey, I'm so glad you are OK."

"Yes, I think I'm OK."

"Brisk said you got dizzy and passed out."

"I remember that."

Brisk walked in the room with a pitcher of water.

He said, "Glad you are feeling better."

He handed me a cup of water. I drank it really fast.

"Thank you."

I gave him back the cup.

"You are welcome. Come now, Bylur, let's give your daughter some time to rest."

After my dad and Brisk left the room, I put my hands on my belly. Something wasn't right.

Brisk came back into the room.

"Your dad said he will be back to check on you," he told me.

"Brisk, is my baby OK?"

"Fray, I'm sorry, but you lost the baby."

"What, no! That can't be right."

"I'm very sorry."

The tears just came all on their own. I didn't believe him, and yet I could feel he was telling the true.

"But why?"

"You know the penalty for having a child without the God of Winter's permission."

"You knew this was going to happen, didn't you?"

"Yes, I knew."

"Why didn't you tell me?"

"I tried, but you just looked so happy."

"You should have tried harder."

"Would you have listened?"

"Of course not."

Why did this have to happen? Did the God of Winter hate that I didn't ask him for his permission so much that he had to go and prove a point?

What am I going to tell Winter? Maybe I won't have to tell him, I thought. If I lie with him again, then I might be with child again. But what if the Gods of Winter take another baby from me? No, I guess I will have to wait till I marry the man I love.

The days went by, and I still didn't have it in me to tell Winter. Brisk told my father I just got winded and that it was nothing. Thank goodness for that.

Even though I never met my child, it still hurt losing it.

Everybody was getting ready for Korm. They were all packing up their wagons. I was watching the children play in the snow, wondering if I would ever have a child of my own.

I was walking through the kingdom trying to get my mind off of things when I got distracted by a young woman carrying furs. She was struggling with them. So I went over to help her.

"Hey, let me help you with those," I said.

Before I could reach her, she accidentally dropped the furs. We looked at each other. And I was a little stunned by how beautiful she was. Her eyes looked like they weren't from this realm.

We both bent down to pick them up.

"Here, let me take some of those; that way you can see where you're going," I suggested.

She just froze, looking at me. So I spoke in our native tongue, the ice language. But she said noting, just kept looking at me like she'd seen a Yache. I could tell she was terrified.

"I'm sorry, you must be mute," I said.

"Oh no, I, um…" she responded.

She went back down to get more furs off the ground, then she stood back up.

"So you can talk?" I asked.

"Yes, I can."

I didn't know why she seemed so nervous, but I couldn't help but laugh a little.

"Where are you taking these?"

"Oh, um, over there to that wagon."

"That is Arctodus's wagon."

"Uh, yeah, so it is."

"How do you know him?"

"Uh, well, I…"

She froze again. This time she was looking down at the ground, trying not to make eye contact, hiding her face in her hair.

I was getting ready to say something again when Rain came out and broke the awkwardness.

"Fray, good to see you," she said.

"You too, Rain."

She gave me a big hug.

"So what's up with you?"

"Oh, nothing. I was just helping."

"Oh, where are my manners?" said Rain. "Fray, this is Pye; Pye this is Fray."

We shook each other's hands.

"It's nice to meet you, Pye."

"You too."

She seemed not as nervous now that Rain was here.

"Correct me if I'm wrong, Pye, but I don't believe I have ever seen you before," I said.

"That's 'cause she is from Pulse," explained Rain.

"Pulse?"

"Yes."

"And how do you two know each other?"

"Well, her parents died, and I knew them, and they asked me to take her in if anything should happen."

"That's so nice of you," I said.

"Well, I didn't want her to be alone," Rain responded.

"I wonder why Winter never told me."

"Well, he might not have known about it; my brother might not have told him."

"Yeah, he has been distracted often."

"Well, we have a lot to do, so I guess we will see you on the Korm."

"Yes, you will."

"Great!"

I looked at Pye. She smiled at me. I couldn't help but feel a little intimidated by her beauty.

"Thank you, Fray, for helping me," she said.

I handed her the rest of the furs.

"You're welcome," I responded.

I walked away from them. Something about Pye was off. For one, her eyes were so different. Like an unusual different. Then there was the way she got nervous. As beautiful as she was, what could she possibly have been worried about? She was also wearing a lot of covering, almost like she was affected by the cold. That was odd.

I couldn't think about that right then; I needed to tell Winter about our baby. He was training with my dad again.

When he saw me, he knew I needed to speak with him. We sat down together.

"I'm glad you are feeling better," he commented.

"Yeah, me too."

"And the baby is OK, right?"

"Winter, I have something to tell you."

"What is it?"

I took a deep breath. I closed my eyes and then looked at the man I love. He is so perfect, I thought. I knew that the love we had for one another would never change. No matter what.

"Winter, I lost the baby."

His face became serious. Then he kissed my forehead. And hugged me tight.

"I love you." That was all he needed to say. I felt so much better. A rush of happiness overcame me.

We held each other for a good minute. Then I remembered meeting Pye.

"So did you hear that your aunt akinned a girl?" I asked.

"What are you talking about?"

"Yeah, I just met her. Apparently your dad allowed it."

"If my dad did something like that, he would tell me."

"Why would your aunt lie?"

"I'm not sure. I'll talk to my dad about it and see what he says."

Chapter 29

Princess Pye Redrick

I looked at myself in the mirror, and I didn't recognize myself. How did I let Rain talk me into this? I thought. She dyed my hair silvery white, and she gave me the lowdown on the laws and the religion of the Winter Realm.

If anyone asked, I was supposed to say I was from Pulse and I had no parents and try not to talk to anyone.

It wasn't my fault, the way I ran into Fray. I tried not saying anything, but she kept on. I felt bad, too, because she was helping me and I didn't want to come off as rude.

Fray is really pretty, I thought, and she has a lot of confidence, I could tell.

I hated how cold it was here. I just wanted to go back to the Fire Realm and forget this ever happened.

Arctodus was sitting in his chair smoking his pipe, while Rex was sprawled out on the floor.

Then Rain came bursting into the room.

"We have some very bad news," she declared.

"What is it?" Arctodus asked.

"I just had a very interesting talk with my brother."

"Oh no, he knows."

"No, but he found out, probably from Fray, that I akinned Pye without his consent."

"You akinned? Since when? Were you going to tell me that?"

"I wasn't going to do it, but now that everyone knows about Pye, I have no choice."

"I'm sorry, what does 'akin' mean?" I interjected.

"That we take you in and you become our daughter," Arctodus explained.

"No thanks. I was a daughter once, and I wasn't very good at it."

"Well, now we don't have a choice, Pye," said Rain.

Arctodus asks, "How did this even come up?"

"It's my fault. I ran into Fray, and she was asking all these questions. It just slipped out," Rain said.

"What did River say?"

"He wants to meet Pye."

"Well, this was a good try, but it's over."

"It's not over. We can still get away with this."

"Are you nuts? Wait, don't answer that question; I already know the answer."

"Look, he wants to meet her with me there."

"Pye, can you give me and Rain a moment alone?" Arctodus asked.

"Sure thing," I responded.

I went into the other room, and I could still hear them talking. I was not trying to eavesdrop, but I did want to hear what they had to say.

"What are you doing?" Arctodus said.

"What do you mean?"

"Are we really going to adopt her?"

"Yes, of course. It's for our people."

"Are you sure it's not for you?"

"What is that supposed to mean?"

"She's not Elsa."

"This has nothing to do with our daughter."

"Really? 'Cause I feel like this has everything to do with her."

"I cannot believe, with everything that is going on right now, you are bringing this up."

"Rain, I love Elsa too, and I miss her so much, but doing this isn't going to bring her back."

"Wow! You know, you sound just like my brother."

"Just tell me that you are doing this because of the food shortage."

"I am, I promise."

"Rain, Pye belongs in the Fire Realm. She needs to go back. This is only going to get worse."

"Will you please trust me? I know what I'm doing."

"Just promise me that you will pull the plug if it gets too deep."

"I promise."

I didn't want them to adopt me. I didn't want to disappoint them like I had disappointed my parents. I couldn't have that stress anymore. I knew these people needed help, but I was not sure I was the one that could help them.

Rain didn't understand that my fire is very unpredictable. When I let it go, I have no control over it. I was so afraid I was going to hurt someone. Then they would see what a failure I am.

Rain was drilling me about the questions I might get asked. I wanted to tell her to forget the whole thing and take me back home. But I had nothing to go back to. This way I could stay alive a little longer. Not that I cared. Maybe if I do a bad job, these people will kill me, I thought. But then they would kill Rain and Arctodus; I didn't want that. I just can never win.

"OK, I guess that's everything but your eyes," said Rain.

"What about them?" I asked.

"They are very distracting.?

"Oh, I'm very sorry. I can hide them behind my hair."

"No, you can't. Pye, Ice-Aiden women are pioneers; we forge ahead, OK? We hold our heads high."

"Well, if I were as pretty as you, I would hold my head high too."

"Pye, the only way you are going to see how beautiful you are is by believing it."

"You can't believe what isn't true."

"Come here."

She put me in front of the mirror again.

"Look at you. You are so beautiful. Your eyes are distracting because they are beautiful," she said.

"I just don't see it."

"How can you not? You have this hair and this body. I think you are the blind one."

"My mother used to say that to me."

"She was right."

"How is it that your brother can make this legal?"

"'Cause he is the king."

"What? You never told me that."

"I'm telling you now."

"Great. Now I just got even more nervous."

"You will be fine. I will be there."

"Tell me again who is going to be there."

"My bother the king and my nephew, his son Prince Winter, who is a little older than you."

"And you will be by my side?"

"All the way."

"There is one problem: the symbol on her neck, it's not like ours," Arctodus interjected.

"We can paint over it," replied Rain.

I didn't like the sound of that. Painting over it would make me feel like I was betraying the God of Fire.

Rain showed me their symbol. It was an Ice triangle . It was white. She made one in her hand. It looked similar to my symbol; it was so pretty.

Rain said that after we covered up my symbol, we would meet the king. No pressure.

I kept telling myself not to get nervous. If I get too sacred I will let out my fire, I thought.

I was listening to Blaze's voice in my head again. "There is no fear." He would tell me all the time, "Pye, you are in control of your fear, no one else."

Rain and I were walking in a hallway through a corridor.

I felt like I was going to puke I was so scared. She kept telling me not to say anything unless I was spoken too. Follow her lead and all would be good. Yeah right.

We stopped in front of two big doors made out of ice that had drawings etched in them.

I was starting to breathe heavy. Rain told me to try to relax. Yeah, easy for her to say, I thought.

"Would you calm down?"

"I'm trying to."

Rain grabbed the fur blanket I had wrapped around my shoulders. The fur dress I had on was warm, but it wasn't enough to keep me from shivering.

"Hey, give me that back," I said.

"No, it's too suspicious."

"But I'm freezing."

"It's only for a minute. You have to look and act like an Ice-Aiden."

Just great, now I'll be scared and cold, I thought.

"Would you stop shivering?"

"I can't help it."

"Try not to think about how cold it is."

Again, that was easy for her to say.

She took one last look at me. Straightened me up and dusted off my dress to make sure it wasn't showing any imperfections.

She could see the look of doubt in my face.

"It's going to be fine."

"Sorry if I don't believe you."

She let out a big sigh. She then opened the door a little so that we could peek our heads in.

"See, nothing to worry about," she said.

I saw her brother the king on his throne, and he had a kind face. That did calm my nerves a little. But then I saw her nephew, and my stomach turned into knots.

Winter was the handsomest man I had ever seen.

"See, my brother is a good man, and that person next to him is my nephew Winter, who is very good as well," Rain said.

I stopped listening to what she was saying. I was fixated on Winter. I had never had a psychical attraction to a man before. Not till then.

When I was learning to control my fire, I was doing it to help my father from losing his throne. I never took into consideration what the true meaning of controlling your fire really was.

Falling in love. The thought of that never crossed my mind. The thought of a man loving me was even further from my mind.

But now I wanted this man so much. My eyes were trailing down his physically fit, immaculate body, and I was getting warm all over. The cold suddenly didn't bother me anymore.

The knots in my stomach were getting stronger. My heart was pounding in my ears. What was I going to say to him? Do I smile? Maybe a nod, I thought.

"All right, it's time to go," announced Rain.

Oh no. I'm really not ready for this, I thought.

Rain opened the door, and I just stared at Winter. He is such a beautiful man. I was feeling breathless. My chest was getting tight.

Rain grabbed my hand and pulled me along.

I thought, Here we go.

Chapter 30

Prince Winter Sleight

I hate to say it, but I was glad Fray lost the baby. The God of Winter was really looking out for me. I was so not ready to be a dad, regardless of how she felt about it.

I was shocked when Fray told me what my aunt had done. Although it didn't surprise me. After my cousin Elsa died, she wasn't really the same.

When I told my father, he said he would have a talk with her, and now we were here ready to meet this young girl.

My aunt and the girl both walked in, and praise the God of Winter.

"Beautiful" would not describe how attractive this young girl beside my aunt was. Her eyes were like nothing I had ever seen in this world. Thick, beautiful, pouty lips that I wouldn't mind sinking my teeth into.

Then I looked down her body, and I couldn't help but get turned on. I was picturing this girl naked and in the seven different positions I could have her, and my dick was hard as ice.

I wasn't paying a bit of attention to what she and my dad were saying. I couldn't; I was too enchanted by her. I wanted this girl in ever which way.

"Hello, Winter," said my dad.

I just looked at him. I had no idea what he was talking about.

"Huh!" I said.

"I said, this is Pye," my father repeated.

I looked into her eyes, and she had me. I was stuck; there was no getting out.

"Hi."

My aunt pulled a strand of Pye's hair behind her ear to get it out of her face.

"Hello," she said.

We started at each other for a good minute. I didn't know if it was just me or both of us, but the sexual tension was building up inside me, and if it didn't break soon, I was going to ejaculate in my fur pelt.

Then my dad hugged Pye and told her, "Welcome to the family." I thought, Great, if she is one of the family members, then I should be looking at her as my sister and not someone I want to make love to. Maybe that's for the best. I have someone I'm supposed to be in love with. I won't hurt her; I can't hurt Fray. She's my best friend.

Then I heard my dad say that he would look forward to seeing them on the Korm. Now I had to see her on the hunt.

After they left the room, it was just my dad and I.

"That is by far the most beautiful young lady I have ever seen," he commented.

"I don't think 'beautiful' is a strong enough word," I responded.

"You're right; how about gorgeous?"

"You are getting close."

"Well, I'm glad it's not just me that sees it."

I couldn't even look at my dad. I was too afraid he would see how I had just dived in headfirst with a girl I didn't know anything about.

"Pye—that's unusual but very pretty name," my father continued.

"Dad, can you excuse me for a minute?"

"Is everything all right?"

"Yes, everything is fine."

My dick felt like it was going to shoot off if I didn't relieve myself soon.

I got into my room and slammed the door. I wasted no time, and I pulled my dick out. I gripped my hand around it. Two pumps is all it took, and I blew my load everywhere.

"Fuck me!"

If this was going to happen every time I saw her, then I was just going to have to stay away from her. I was so screwed.

Now that my aunt had gotten permission from the king to officially make Pye her new daughter, she was going around introducing her to everyone. It was getting really annoying.

I met up with my father outside; he was making sure we had everything for the hunt.

"Winter, my boy, are you all packed?" he asked.

"Yes, Dad, I'm ready."

"Good, 'cause Bylur wants to leave at first light."

"You aren't coming this time?"

"Not this time. It's time you lead one of these on your own."

"Do you think I'm ready?"

"Of course I do."

"Well, I won't let you down."

"I know that. I'm proud of you, son."

My dad and I gave each other a big hug. Then he looked at me with a smile. I could tell he was pleased by the way I turned out.

Then Fray came up behind me and gave me a big hug.

"Hey," she said.

"Hey," I responded.

"I'm not interrupting anything am I?" she asked.

My father responded, "Of course not. Besides, you are my future daughter-in-law; you're allowed to interrupt."

"Well, good, I'm glad to hear that."

My dad and Fray gave each other a big hug. Then he left us alone. I continued packing the cart.

"So what do you think about Pye?" she asked.

"Can we not talk about her, please."

"I'm sorry, I didn't know it was a touchy subject."

"It's not a touchy subject. I just don't want to talk about her."

"OK."

After dinner I was lying in the bed staring up at the ceiling. Fray was lying next to me asleep. We had just gotten done making love, and the whole time we were doing it, all I could think about was Pye. How she tasted. What her skin felt like. The sound she would make when I was inside her. Wonder what her face will look like when I'm the one making her body explode from the inside out, I thought.

Shit! I was way over my head. God of Winter, help me get rid of this obsession, I said to myself.

Chapter 31

Prince Winter Sleight

The next morning I was up and ready for the day. It was Korm Day, and I wasn't going to let anything get to me. My dad was counting on me to have a successful hunt.

After my dad said goodbye to me, he told me not to get discouraged if we didn't come back with enough meat. We would figure it out. He then told me that "Leeaya does not wait," so I had to have enough time to get back before the storm hit. This wasn't my first Korm; I knew what I was doing.

Bylur and I were going over the map one more time when Fray came up to us.

Bylur said, "Arctodus is going to scout up ahead; he and his family left last night, so we are going to follow his trail."

"That works out, and we should be back before Leeaya even gets close," I responded.

"According to the way he's going, we should."

"Great, let's get going then,"

"Wait, Winter, can I talk to you for a minute?" Fray asked.

"Sure. What's up?"

Fray looked at her father, and he got the hint and left us alone.

"You feel good about today?" she asked.

"Yeah, why wouldn't I?"

"Just making sure. I know it's your first Korm without your dad."

"Yeah, but I think I got this."

"I know you do, and I'm here if you need me."

"Thanks."

"You know, you were different with me last night."

"How so?"

"You were more passionate and endearing."

"I'm sorry."

"No, it was really good. You should be like that more often."

"OK, I will be."

We headed out on the Korm. I was leading on my horse with Bylur on my side. Fray was on her horse as well; she was a little far behind us but still with the pack. There were about thirty to forty families traveling with us, which was not unusual.

Now, the first day of Korm is usually just traveling to get to the hunting ground. The wild snow boar, or *ferox aper*, is the main meat source in the Winter Realm. But they don't like staying in one place too long; they move around all the time.

I was nine when I caught my first boar. My father said I had become a man that day. The ferox aper is nine to eleven feet tall, and they weigh around six tons. So I was pretty impressed with myself for having caught something that was ten times bigger than me.

A full-grown ferox aper can feed a family of twelve for fifteen days. That's a lot of meat, but they are getting harder to find. The snow doesn't help either.

We had been traveling for hours when I noticed some of the snow on our path was missing. You could see the ground as clear as day. I had never seen what the ground looked like without snow.

Bylur stopped the heard from going on. While they stopped, he and I went and checked out the road.

"You ever seen anything like this before?" I asked.

"Nope, never," Bylur responded.

We both kneeled down to touch the ground.

"What could do something like this?" I asked.

"I'm not sure, but this will definitely make it easier to hunt."

"Should we keep going?"

"I don't see why not; it's just the ground. The storm will put the snow back on it."

"That's true."

We continued on. But something about this was iffy. I could hear everyone in the back talking about how clear the path was without snow. It was very odd.

We sat down to rest for a while. Everyone went and filled up their buckets at a nearby stream. Then we were back on the trail. We finally caught up with my aunt and uncle. They were just as shocked about the snow being cleared off the road as we were.

We finally made camp.

After I got situated, I was going to go get feed for my horse when I saw Pye feeding the ice bears. Of course I would run into her. The Ice bears are very important when hunting because they are the only things big enough to flush out ferox aper.

"You aren't doing that right," I said.

I startled her.

"Oh, they didn't tell me how. They just said go feed them," she explained.

I yanked the bucket out of her hand and immediately regretted it, but I couldn't let her see that.

"You don't let them eat out of the bucket. You throw the food on the ground," I advised.

"Oh, I see now."

"That way the food gets dispersed evenly."

"I'm so sorry; they didn't show me."

"Well, now you know."

"Yeah, I'll do it better next time."

"You know, they don't like being fed at night; it's usually in the morning. So maybe you should find another job, one you can't fuck up."

She just looked at me like I had just spit in her face.

"OK," she said.

She walked away from me.

I thought, What is wrong with me? Why am I being such a prick to her? I should've never taken that bucket from her hands. Or make her feel stupid.

I felt like being mean to her was the only way I could keep myself from doing something I shouldn't.

I did my best to avoid her. I stayed clear away from her, but that wasn't enough because I would find myself staring at her all the time—from afar, of course, but staring at her nonetheless. It became a constant habit. The more I stared at her, the more I felt like there was something about her I just couldn't figure it out. I had noticed that she tried to hide her face with her hair. But my aunt kept pushing it out of her face. I could tell Pye found it annoying. I found it amusing.

Chapter 32

Prince Winter Sleight

The next day was good. The men and I caught a good kill. I caught two ferox aper. As I was dragging them into the campsite, I saw Pye talking to Zane. Zane is a good friend of mine; his dad is a guard in my father's army. He is the same age as me. We grew up together as well. He was telling Pye something, and she was laughing at it. I know Zane; he's not funny at all. Watching them together was making my blood boil. I was getting pissed. So I stormed over there to break it up.

"What's going on here?" I demanded.

"Just telling Pye a joke," responded Zane.

"Really, what joke?"

"What do ice bears have for—"

"Zane, your dad wants you."

I lied. I didn't care; I wanted him far away from her.

"Oh well, next time, right?" Zane said.

He winked at her. The way she smiled at him made me very upset. After Zane was gone, I narrowed my eyes at Pye.

"What exactly are you doing?" I asked.

"I'm helping your aunt clean the furs."

"Really? 'Cause that's not what it looks like."

"What do you mean?"

"It looks like you are laughing and goofing off."

"Well, I, um—"

"This is not a tea party. If that's what you wanted, you shouldn't have come, got it? Get back to work."

I stormed off back into my tent and started punching my bed. I was losing control. This girl was making my mind go crazy.

I stayed in my tent the whole night; I didn't want to talk to or see anyone. Just wanted to be left alone. Even when Fray came to bed, I didn't say one word to her. Just pretended like I was asleep.

The next morning I woke up refreshed. I'm going to push everything out of my mind and focus on the hunt, I thought. I sat down at the table and ate my breakfast. Everything was fine till Zane sat next to me.

He slapped my back.

"So you excited about getting married?" he asked.

"Thrilled."

I was so not in the mood for him right now.

"I'm thinking about settling down myself," he went on.

"Yeah right, since when?"

"Since I laid eyes on her."

He pointed his finger behind me. I turned my head. That motherfucker; I'm going to kill him, I thought.

"You don't even know her," I said.

"I know all I need to know."

"Meaning?"

"Meaning that Pye is the most beautiful woman I have ever seen. I know all I need to know."

I wanted this day to be a good day. I just wanted to go about it like I had never met her, but no, that couldn't be.

Zane was making me irate.

"I'm going to ask Arctodus about marrying her this afternoon," he announced.

That was it; I couldn't take it anymore. I drew my sword at Zane. He looked at me confused.

"What are we arguing about?" he asked.

"Just get your ass up now."

Everyone stopped what they were doing and watched us, but I didn't care. This was going to stop now.

When the fight was over, I put a notch on Zane's arm, and as I was walking away, he was screaming all kinds of unchoice words at me.

I didn't care; I needed to clear my head. The thought of Zane touching Pye made me want to destroy everything to the ground. She would never be his. Over my dead body.

I was in my tent racking my brain when my aunt burst in.

"You want to tell me what in the cold wind that was about?"

"I don't want to talk about it."

"You don't want to talk about the fact that you just put a notch on a good friend of yours over an argument he knows nothing about."

"Go away."

"What is going on with you, Winter?"

I let out a big sigh and stood up from my bed.

"I want you to get rid of Pye," I said.

"Excuse me!"

"Send her back to Pulse, now."

"I can't do that; she doesn't have anyone."

"I don't care. She doesn't fit in. I don't want her here. Get rid of her now."

My aunt scrunched up her face at me."

"So this argument is about Pye," she said.

"Just forget it."

I left my tent with my aunt in it. I couldn't talk to her; I couldn't talk to anyone.

I felt really bad about what I had done to Zane. It was not his fault.

Chapter 33

Prince Winter Sleight

The next day we all headed out to the next haunting ground. I rode up next to Zane.

"Zane," I said.

"What?" he responded.

I could tell he didn't want to talk to me.

"I'm really sorry about yesterday. When we get back home, I will tell Brisk to dispute the notch."

He smiled at me.

"Nah, I like it. I think I'm going to keep it."

"But why?"

"'Cause now we match."

He put his arm next to mine. We compared our notches together. I smiled at him.

"Are you sure?" I asked.

"Yes. Plus, girls love battle scars."

"Then are we cool?"

"Don't worry, Prince Winter, I still got your back. Plus, now I know what the argument was about."

I just looked at him. Did he really know?

"I get it, Winter—she's very pretty," he said.

"I have no idea what you are talking about."

"I should give you a heads-up there's at least a dozen guys I know that have their eye on her."

That didn't sit well with me. I wanted no one to touch her but me.

"It's not what you think," I explained.

"Yes, it is," he said.

Great. If he could see without me telling him, then I couldn't imagine what everyone else was saying.

"Have you told Fray?" Zane asked.

"There is nothing to say. I love Pye, and she's the one I'm going to be with."

Zane smiled at me again.

"You mean Fray."

"Huh!"

"You said Pye is the one you love and are going to be with."

"I said Fray."

"No, you didn't."

"Yes, I did!"

"OK, but you should know she's not going to be single for long."

I narrowed my eyes at him.

"You have nothing to worry about; I have renounced my claim on her," Zane said.

"I wasn't worried."

"But you better figure out what you want, 'cause I have a feeling you are going to end up in more arguments."

He rode off. I thought, He's right. I can't fight all of them for having feelings for Pye. What am I going to do?

Chapter 34

Princess Pye Redrick

I was getting tired of the cold air. I was getting used to it, but it was making my head hurt all the time. Rain gave me this hot medicine to drink that would help it go away from time to time, but it always came back.

I did like it here in the Winter Realm. Now that I was akinned, I felt like part of the family. Everyone was really nice to me. Well, almost everyone.

"He's staring at me again," I said.

"Who?" Rain asked.

"You know who—Prince Winter."

"He's not staring at you."

"Yes, he is. He hates me."

"Why would you think that?"

"He belittles me all the time."

Rain wasn't really listening to me. She was too busy spinning the food on the fire.

"Just the other day, he embarrassed me in front of everyone because I dropped the bucket of water everywhere."

"Maybe he thought you were being funny."

"I know everyone else did. They all laughed and pointed at me. No one bothered helping me up."

"Do you want me to go talk to him?"

"No, then it will look like I'm letting him get to me."

"Then what do you want me to do?"

"I don't know. You think he might suspect that I don't belong here?"

"You are overreacting, like always. It's going to be fine. Everything is working out. The roads are clearer than they have ever been."

"Yes, but people are starting to talk; they think it's got something to do with the gods being upset."

"It's just a bunch of superstitions, nothing more."

"I hope you are right."

"I am. Now trust me. I haven't steered you wrong, have I?"

"Well, no I guess not."

"OK then."

I still couldn't control my fire. When I cleared the roads, we did it at night with nobody watching. And everyone was at least a day's ride away from us. The plan was working. They were bringing in more meat than they could have possibly imagined. Rain and Arctodus were very happy.

I was happy for them and happy that I could help. It was a good change, seeing my fire as a miracle more than a disaster. But I had this feeling that we were going to get caught.

The fire here in the Winter Realm is different from the fire in my realm. The fire here is white, and it feels warm to me, not hot at all. But to the Ice-Aidens, it is extremely hot, and it heats everything up for them.

I'm adjusting to their customs. And even though Prince Winter is a jerk to me, I can't help but fantasize about him. Mostly at night. Rain told me that Winter was engaged to Fray. I had only been jealous of one woman my entire life, and that woman was my mother. I was jealous of how beautiful she was. And perfect. But now I envied Fray. I wished I were her more than anything. She got to be with Winter. He touched her all the time. I wished I could trade places with her. Imagined it was me he was in love with, not her. She was a very lucky girl. 'Cause I think I would give up my life to have him touch me or look at me the way he looks at her just once, I thought.

Fray was so pretty. So it made since that the most handsome man would be with the most beautiful woman. They made the relationship look so easy.

"What's love like?" I asked Rain.

"Why do you want to know?" she responded.

"Just curious."

"Did you ever ask your mom that question?"

"Yes."

"And what did she say?"

"That words can't describe it."

"She's not wrong."

"So you can't tell me."

"No, I can, but you will never understand until you feel it. The feeling is much stronger than words."

"It sounds exciting and terrifying at the same time."

"It is very much so. Why? Are you in love?"

"No. I was just wondering."

"Well, here, this will get your mind off it."

She handed me a bucket.

"What do you want me to do with this?"

"What do you think? Go fill it up with water."

As I was walking toward the river, I saw Zane."

"Hey, Zane!" I said.

"Hey, Pye."

"Any new jokes to tell me?"

"Not today."

Zane just walked away for me. I didn't know what was going on, but after that fight he had with Prince Winter, he wouldn't come near me. He used to come up and talk to me all the time and made me laugh. I thought he liked me there for a minute. It had been like that with all the young men here. They were all so sweet and kind to me. But now when they saw me coming, they turned the other way. I wasn't big on getting attention, but it was nice to have for a little while.

I didn't want to be paranoid, but maybe they knew I wasn't really an Ice-Aiden.

I got to the water and started filling the bucket. This water was so cold. I didn't know why it hadn't frozen over yet. I accidentally let go of the bucket in the river. The water was so cold it was hurting my hands.

Just great, I thought. The current was pushing it up river. It was a slow current. But the bucket was getting away from me. I put my feet in the river to catch it. Holy Fire, is this cold water, I thought. The water reached up to my knees. I could feel tiny stabs all over my feet and legs as I was pushing through this freezing-cold water. The bucket was snagged on some bushes that where in the middle of the river. I went down to get the bucket, and when I came up, I saw Winter standing there in the water behind the bush. He was taking a bath, so he was completely naked. His back was facing me. Oh wow, he is so beautiful, I thought. When I saw Forneus's body I got creeped out and disgusted. But Winter's body was so attractive that it got me excited.

I should have gone, but I couldn't look away. He's body was immaculate. Blue markings of ice symbols covered the entirety of his muscular back. They went down just a little on his left buttock. Rain told me that they are called Nix. They looked really good on him. My body was tingling all over, and it was not because of the cold water. I was getting really aroused, especially between my legs. I was not sure what that was about. But that was what he was making me do. I was burning up inside.

He got ready to turn around, and I ducked. I couldn't let him see me; that would have been so embarrassing. I had to get out of there before I got caught.

Lucky for me, more men came out to the river to wash as well. That distracted him so I could make a clean getaway.

I handed Rain the bucket. I couldn't help but smile.

"That took you a minute."

"Sorry."

After I handed her the bucket, I went in my tent and lay down. I closed my eyes and fantasized about Winter. In my dream I was naked with him. And he kissed my lips so sweetly that my body was covered in hot flashes.

"Pye!"

I rolled off my bed and hit my head. I looked up and saw Rain staring at me.

"Yes!" I responded.

"What are you doing?"

"Nothing."

"Well, I've been calling you."

"I must have dozed off."

"OK, well, dinner is ready."

"Oh right, coming."

As I said before, I can never win.

When I got to the table, I see a bunch of men cutting up a ferox aper. Their blood is blue. They were taking the blood and tattooing in on their backs.

"I thought you said Nix is for arguments," I said to Rain.

"It is; it's also for marking your kill."

"So how do you know which is which?"

"Here, I will show you."

Rain called Arctodus over. He showed us his arms first.

"See the ones with the blue claws," he said.

"Yes," I responded.

"Those are the marks of your kill."

Then he showed us his back; it was a lot like Prince Winter's.

"These ones that look like blue swirls of wind…"

"Yes, I do see them."

"Those are for winning arguments."

"Does it matter where they go?"

"Nope, just as long as they are on you."

From far away they looked the same 'cause they are connected. But up close you could see each one had meaning.

I was eating my dinner when I saw Prince Winter and Fray walk up to the table next to us. I stayed focused on my plate. Then a young man sat in front of me.

He was cute, but he didn't get my body humming like Prince Winter. I don't think there is anyone more attractive then Prince Winter.

He looked at me and smiled. I smiled back. I had the urge to hide my face in my hair, but I didn't."

"Hello," I said.

"Hi," he responded.

"My name is—"

"Pye. Yeah, I know who you are. My name is Snow."

"It's nice to meet you."

"It's really nice to meet you. Is this your first Korm?"

"Yes, it is."

"How do you like it so far?"

"It's going to take some getting used to."

"Well, if you need any help, just let me know."

Before I could thank him, Prince Winter came over. He grabbed my plate and dropped it in my lap. The food was warm, and it felt gross as it was seeping through my dress. I was so embarrassed again. Everybody was staring at me. This time I was trying to hide my face in my hair, but it wasn't working.

I looked up at Winter. I wanted so badly to say, "What is your problem?" But again I lacked the courage.

Winter and Snow just eyeballed each other.

"She's got to go clean that up now," commented Winter.

"Oh, Pye, let's go get you a new dress," said Rain.

As Rain was bringing me to my tent, I looked back and could see Snow and Winter continuing to stare each other down. Neither one of them bothered to help me. Why does he hate me so much? I asked myself.

Chapter 35

Prince Winter Sleight

I knew what Snow was doing. I had made it very clear that Pye was off-limits to everyone. I didn't need a reason. I'm a prince; my word is law.

"What are you doing, Snow?"

"Just making conversation."

"Yeah, I bet you are."

"I am."

"You know very well to stay away from Pye."

"I know that, but does she?"

He nodded behind me at Fray, who was staring right up at me.

"What do you want?" I asked.

"Just wondering if you have though about what I asked you."

Snow didn't have a lot of blue on his back. He started earning them a little late in life because his mother was worried he might hurt himself. He wanted to lead the hunt tomorrow to try to earn some respect. But his father didn't think he was ready. He didn't have any notches on his arm either; he usually kept his mouth shut. But if he thought blackmailing me was going to help him, he was wrong. I had no problem putting a notch on his arm.

"Getting in an argument with me is a good way to get a notch," I said.

"Oh, I'm not stupid. I know you would kick my ass. That's why there is no argument here."

"Then I will talk to your father, but as I said before, it's up to him."

Snow smiled at me and then walked away to his father, probably to get him to lead the hunt tomorrow.

I went back to my table, and I started to eat. Fray was staring at me.

"What was that about?" she asked.

"It's nothing."

"It didn't look like nothing."

"Well, that's what it is—nothing."

"It's about Pye, isn't it?"

I let out a big sigh.

"No, it's not."

"Winter, if there is something going on, please tell me."

I looked into her eyes. She looked very concerned; I could tell.

"Fray, I promise you there is nothing going on. Why would you think that?"

"You always stare at her, and it hurts me."

"I'm sorry. It's just that—"

I stopped myself as I looked at her.

"I won't do it anymore."

I kissed her on the forehead and went back to eating. That seemed to make her happy.

That night I couldn't help my dreams. Pye was on top of me. I was inside her and loving every minute of it. She was looking at me with those eyes of hers. I grabbed her and pulled her closer to me. Then she said, "Do you love me?" I wanted to say yes, but I couldn't; I just looked at her. She asked me again. And still nothing. Then I woke up in a puddle of sweat. My dick was rock-hard again.

"Hey, are you OK?" Fray asked.

"Yeah, I'm fine. Go back to sleep," I responded.

I think I am in love with Pye, I said to myself.

The next morning I was feeding my horse again when my aunt came up to me.

"We need to talk," she said.

"About what?"

"I saw what you did to Pye last night."

"Yeah, so?"

"So can you tell me why you are being such a bully?"

"I told you to get rid of her."

"That's why you are being this way?"

"I'm not being any way."

"Pye is a very sweet and kind girl. I'm sure if you took the time to get to know her—"

"I don't want to get to know her. I just want you to get rid of her, like I have been saying."

"I need a reason to get rid of her, and not fitting in is not one."

"OK. You want a good enough reason?"

"Yes."

"I want her."

My aunt scrunched up her face at me and took a step back.

"You what?"

"I want her. I find her very attractive."

"Oh, now I see. You have feelings for her."

I didn't answer her. I just stayed looking at my horse. I could tell she was smiling at me.

"But, Winter, having feelings for Pye is not a bad thing."

"Actually, it's a very bad thing."

"How so?"

"Are you forgetting about Fray?"

"What about Fray?"

"Me having feelings for Pye would break Fray's heart; I won't hurt her like that."

"But you don't love Fray."

"Who's to say I don't?"

"Well, I think your actions have spoken loud and clear."

"It doesn't matter. Fray is the one I want."

"So you are just going to spend the rest of your life in a relationship with a woman you don't love?"

"I'm in love with Fray. Pye is just an infatuation."

"Well, you better figure that out because the last thing Fray would want is for you to be in a relationship that you are not happy in."

"I will be happy with Fray."

"OK, but the heart wants what the heart wants."

In a way, she was right. But how do you tell your best friend, someone you have known your whole life, that you are in love with a woman you just met? I thought. I wasn't sure what the truth was anymore. Was I in love with Pye? When I looked at Fray, I felt safe and secure, familiar. When I looked at Pye, I felt desire and passion. With a hint of excitement.

The Korm was over, and we got home just in time for Leeaya to start. We had more than enough meat this time around. My father was very pleased. I told him about how the roads were completely cleared off. He thought it was also a sign from the God of Winter. That he was helping us to make it through the storm. I, on the other hand, was not sure how to trust it. It was not right for us to have snow missing like that.

After a few days of being home, I became more relaxed. After getting home, I didn't see Pye at all. I was very grateful for that. I spent this time making sure that Fray knew she was the one for me. I spent all my attention on her. Even though Pye and I were living in the castle, I never ran into her once. As the storm was going on, we stayed in. We wouldn't go out until the storm was over.

I wasn't sleeping very well. Every time I closed my eyes, I would think about Pye. So I would try to avoid sleep as much as I could. But it wasn't good when I was up 'cause I would still think about her. It became a constant habit. I had never wanted something so bad and not been able to have it.

My father and even Fray were getting really excited for Crystallum. I was doing my workout stretches when my dad came in all happy.

"This is going to be a great Crystallum," he said.

"Yeah, Dad, it's going to be good," I responded.

As I said before, I wasn't all that eager to get married. When Leeaya was up, I would be picking my new bride or should I say, Bormack the God of Winter would be picking for me.

"This is how I found your mother, you know?"

"Yeah, Dad, I know. This is how we all find the woman we're meant to fall in love with."

"And your aunt just asked if I could put Pye in the race."

I immediately sat up and looked at my dad.

"You told her no, right?"

"Well, no. I told her yes."

"Why would you do that?"

"Well, why not? She's eligible."

"Dad, she can't compete."

"Why not? The rules specifically say an eligible maiden between the ages of seventeen and twenty-two and with royal or noble blood."

"This can't be happening."

"What are you so worried about? It's only one more girl. Plus, the God of Winter knows were your heart lies."

I don't fucking believe this. My Aunt did this on purpose. How could she be so stupid? I thought. I went looking for her.

I found her in the kitchen cooking.

"Hello, dear nephew," she said.

"What do you think you are doing?" I shot back.

"I'm making something for Pye."

"Why did you tell my dad to put Pye in Crystallum?"

"Why not?"

"Are you trying to hurt me?"

"Of course not."

"Then you will tell my dad that Pye can't be in it."

"I'm not going to do that. Pye has the right to be in it. Plus, you have made it very clear that you are in love with Fray. So Pye isn't going to make a bit of difference."

"But why put her in?"

"I just wanted her to get the experience because, thanks to me and your uncle, she is now royalty. This is part of the perks of being royal."

"No, you did this because of what I told you."

"No, I didn't. I swear."

"Fine, let her be in it. You are right—it won't change a thing."

Chapter 36

Princess Pye Redrick

I was sitting on my bed watching the storm through my window. It was like a peaceful dream. Just white came out of the sky; it was like it was never going to stop. Being cooped up in this castle made me think of home. I wanted to unleash my fire, but I couldn't. I would have practiced in my room, but I was afraid I might burn the castle down.

The other thing was that I had feelings for Prince Winter. I shouldn't have because he disliked me. But I couldn't help it. I wanted him. I thought about him all the time. I wondered what he would do if he knew how I felt about him. He probably would laugh. This pent-up attraction had me on edge, and it was causing me to have the need to unleash my flame of desire.

Then I heard Rain enter the living room.

"Hey, Pye, can you come in here, please?" she said.

I came into the room to see Rex lying on the floor in his usual spot and Arctodus in his chair. Rain was sitting at the table. She signaled for me to sit next to her.

"Pye, what do you think of Prince Winter?" she asked.

When she said the words, my throat closed up. Was I talking in my sleep? Had she heard my dreams? I wasn't sure what to say.

"Um…"

"The only reason I ask is 'cause I have signed you up for the Crystallum."

Arctodus was choking all of a sudden. He finally cleared his throat."

"Why would you do something like that?" he asked.

"Well, because it would look even odder if I didn't."

"This is going way too far," he responded.

"How so? He's going to marry Fray."

"Would you bet your life on that?"

Rain smiled at Arctodus and then looked at me.

"Anyways, you were saying?" she prompted me.

"I'm not sure. Why do you ask that?"

"Well, Prince Winter is twenty; he has to get married."

"OK!"

"And you are nineteen, correct?"

"Yes."

I knew she didn't want me to marry Prince Winter. Right?

"Great. That means that you are eligible for Crystallum."

"But what is that?"

She said, "When two Ice-Aiden families want to get married, the family of the Brudguma, or groom, will offer the family of the Brudur, or bride, a dowry of fur, wood, or meat. If the bride's family feels that the offering is good and not lacking, then they ask for the king's approval to ask the God of Winter if they can marry. But the Brudguma has to have lots of blue on his back and not a lot of notches. Now, when asking the God of Winter, both Brudguma and Brudur draw blood into the answering bowl. This bowl is white and asymmetric. Ice-Aiden blood will form into red ice crystals when out of the body. When it is mixed with other Ice-Aiden blood, it will come together to from an ice prism snowflake. Now, when you have a very distinct color in your snowflake, that is Bormack saying yes, he approved. This is called Khione; it means you have the God of Winter's blessing.

"Now, royal weddings are different. All ice maidens that are between the ages of seventeen and twenty-two and have royal and noble blood are eligible to marry the prince. But he cannot choose his bride.

The God of Winter chooses for him. Each contestant has to be evaluated by the king. If he feels the girl is a good match, then she is to create her own snowflake. No two snowflakes are exactly the same.

"Each snowflake is presented to the snow priest. The prince will not know which snowflake belongs to which girl. The prince will bleed a few drops on each snowflake. After he spills his blood, he will tell Bormack in secret which girl he loves, hoping that the Gods of Winter hear his plea. The snow priest will then hang the snowflakes up and wait for the God of Winter to choose. The snowflake that changes more dramatically in color is the one that Bormack has chosen to be the Prince's Brudur. This process is called Crystallum."

"And you want me to be in this?"

"Well, yes. Why not?"

"I can't make a snowflake."

"I will make one for you."

"Isn't that cheating?"

"Of course not. No, as long as it represents you."

"How is it going to do that when I can't make it?"

"Trust me, it will work."

"But Prince Winter hates me."

"Then you have nothing to worry about."

Arctodus chimed in, "He loves Fray, anyway, so you are good."

But why didn't I feel good about this? Maybe 'cause it had to do with more lying. What if Prince Winter did choose my snowflake? I would die. But he wouldn't really be in love with me. He would be stuck with me. This whole process just felt very unsettling. The main thing was he was going to choose Fray. That's where his heart was, so maybe it wouldn't be too bad.

As time went by, I learned all I could about Crystallum, with Rain helping me all the way. Before I knew it, the time had come to speak to King River about how I would be a good wife for his son.

There were only three girls competing in the Crystallum: Fray and I, and Snow's sister Iceland. She was of noble blood, and she had just turned seventeen.

Fray went in and talked to the king first while Iceland and I awaited our turns.

She was really nice to me, and she kept saying that even though she was not going to be the one to marry Prince Winter, she thought he was so handsome. She wasn't wrong about any of that.

"I think that Fray should be the one to marry him," said Iceland.

"I agree," I responded.

"You know, Pye, you are really pretty."

"Thank you. I think you are really pretty as well."

I mean, Iceland was really cute. She was young, but I could see why boys would be attracted to her.

"Thanks."

"You are most welcome."

"You know, when this is all over, you should really think about getting to know my brother."

"Why is that?"

"Because he really likes you."

I couldn't help but blush at that. A boy liking me—I never though the day would come.

"Why do you think your bother likes me?"

"'Cause he talks about you all the time. And I don't think; I know."

"I wonder why I have only had one conversation with him."

That ended up in embarrassment.

"He said the moment he laid eyes on you, he knew you were the one."

"Well, I have never been 'the one' before."

We both laughed. Then Fray came out and said it was my turn. Ever since this whole thing started, Fray had been a little salty toward me. I had been telling her congratulations 'cause I knew she was going to win, but she kept rolling her eyes at me. I was trying to lighten up the mood with her, but it didn't seem to help.

I wasn't really nervous. I knew I wasn't going to win, so there was nothing to be frantic about.

I sat next to King River. He kind of reminded me of my dad. Always trying to show how much he cared about his son's future, showing that he would stop at nothing to give him the best.

"Are you nervous?" the king asked.

"No not at all," I responded.

"Good!"

We kind of sat there in silence for a minute. Then he smiled at me.

"Well, let's get this ice melting."

"OK!"

"Do you love my son?"

OK, that was a question I wasn't planning on hearing, but now that was out there, what could I say?

"Um, well, I hardly know him."

"If you did get to know him, could you love him?"

"Yes, I'd like to think I could."

I thought, Heck, I would do more than love him. I would let him do whatever he wanted to my body as long as he touched me.

"Do you want children?" King River asked.

I knew what Rain had told me to say.

"Yes!"

"And given the chance, do you think you could be a princess?"

"Yes, I could."

I thought, I have had practice in that area. After all, I am one.

"Now tell me in your own words why the Gods of Winter should choose you to marry my son."

They shouldn't, and they won't. This just felt wrong.

"The truth, King River, is that I don't think I'm worthy of marring your son."

"Oh, why is that?

"Well, your son deserves a woman who is strong and beautiful. Someone who will love him no matter what."

"And that's not you?"

"I'd like to say yes, but no, that's not me. I have never been in a relationship before, so I know I wouldn't be good at it, and I'm not very pretty, so he and I would look weird together."

"But, Pye—"

"No, it's OK. I have never stood up for myself, so he would get tired trying to bring up my confidence."

"But love—"

"I have never been in love before, but I know it's not for me. I'm sorry if I wasted your time."

"No, you didn't."

I left the room feeling good that I had told most of the truth. But he deserved to know. The good thing was I wouldn't need Rain to make me a snowflake. Now it wouldn't feel like I was cheating.

I was in my room again lying on the bed when Rain rushed in and said she had finished.

"Finished what?"

"Your snowflake, silly. Come look at it."

"Oh no, I won't be needing that."

"Why not?"

"'Cause I told King River that I wouldn't make a good wife."

"Well, he must have not listened 'cause he has told Brisk that you have his approval."

"What? Are you sure?"

"Yes, pretty sure."

"No. This can't be."

"Well, it is, so come look at it."

She showed it to me, and it was beautiful. She had carved my flames in it.

"Rain, this is perfect."

"I thought you might like this."

"And it won't matter 'cause he's going to choose Fray, right?"

"Right. You have nothing to worry about."

Rain sent my snowflake over to Brisk; now we just had to wait. Rain said it would take two days, but I wasn't worried; it wasn't going to be me.

"Who will announce the winner?"

"Brisk will come by if you are the bride-to-be."

"Oh! So he will be at Fray's door then."

"Yep."

I was happy for them both. As I said, before they deserved each other.

Chapter 37

Prince Winter Sleight

I walked up to the ice temple, and Brisk handed me a knife.
"Here, take the bowl so it will catch your blood," he instructed.
"You will tell me first, right?"
"Yes, I will tell you. But remember, tell Bormack through your heart who your love is."
"I got it."
After I spilled my blood in the bowl, Brisk wrapped my hand up in a bandage. Then I went over to the statue of Bormack and kneeled before him.
I wasn't sure what to say. "I love Fray," I guess. Then I looked at him. It felt like he didn't believe me. "Well, what do you want me to say?" I was getting frustrated. I stood up and then I told him, "Just do what you want." I was getting ready to leave, and then I stopped myself. I turned back around and faced him again. "I think we both know who my heart belongs to. So I'm leaving it up to you," I said.
I went to my room and tried to think about something else, anything else. I was sure that the outcome would be fine, that I had nothing to worry about. And yet I was freaking out.
I couldn't eat or sleep; I was too wound up. Then I imagined what my life would be like married to Fray. It looked good, not boring or dull

at all, and I was not unhappy. I just felt like I was missing something. Then I imagined being married to Pye. I smiled a little. It was interesting. Then I got a knock at my door. One of the guards said Brisk wanted to see me.

I hurried back to the ice temple. It had only been a day.

"Well, do we have an answer?" I asked.

"We do."

"Well!"

"What do you think?"

"Brisk, just tell me. It's Fray, right?"

Brisk narrowed his eyes at me.

"Sorry, but no, it's Pye."

"What!"

"Yes, it's Pye."

I should have been upset, but inside I was so happy. My heart was jumping up and down. I was trying to hide my smile.

"I'm very sorry, Your Highness," said Brisk.

"Uh, yeah. I mean, it is what it is."

I wasn't sure what to say. I got the girl I wanted. I was so happy. Thank you, God of Winter, for everything, I said to myself.

Brisk was watching me closely.

"I have a suspicious feeling you got what you wanted."

"As I said, it is what it is."

Now there was no holding back my smile.

What would I tell Fray? I thought that no matter what I was going to do, I was going to hurt someone. It was either me or her. I thought, I'm not going to tell her right this minute; I'm going to enjoy this feeling for a little while.

Brisk continued, "Well, then maybe a congratulations is more appropriate."

"I think that is the better word, yes."

When I told my dad, he was more surprised as I was. He asked if I was happy with Bormack's decision.

I smiled at him and said yes, I couldn't have been more happy.

But I had to tell Fray. I found her out back feeding the ice bears. She looked so beautiful. This was going to hurt so bad.

She stopped what she was doing as she saw me. She ran up and hugged me.

"I take it we have good news since you are here now," she said.

"Well, um—"

"So I was thinking we should have the wedding during the springtime."

"Fray, that—"

"I think outside would be best, don't you?"

"Fray, about that…"

"Don't worry—outside will be perfect."

"Fray, I'm not marrying you."

Fray looked hurt with bewilderment. I might as well have stabbed her in the heart.

"Winter, what's going on?"

"Bormack chose Pye, not you."

"But how can that be? We love each other."

I didn't look at her; I couldn't. I was losing my best friend; I could feel it.

"Don't we?"

"I do love you, Fray. I'm just not in love with you."

She pulled away from me.

"But you love Pye?"

"Yes, I do."

That felt so good coming out.

"You told me there was nothing there."

"I said that 'cause I didn't want to hurt you."

"Oh, I see, so you just decided to hurt me now."

"I'm sorry, Fray. I really am."

"Well, I wish you and Pye all the happiest."

"You don't really mean that."

"You're right, I don't."

"Fray, you're still my best friend. I don't want to lose you."

"I was your best friend, and you did lose me."

Before I could say anything to her, she walked away. That hurt more than I thought it would. I thought, How do I fix this now? I could go after her, but I would just make it worse.

Chapter 38

Princess Pye Redrick

"The God of Winter has spoken," said Rain.
"They have there Brudur?" I asked.
Rain smiled at me.
"Look at you, already speaking our language," she commented.
"I'm a fast learner when it comes to words."
"Yes, they have their Brudur."
"Well good, I know Fray and Winter will be happy together."
"Well, Fray might not be happy."
"Why is that?"
"Because you are the Brudur."
"What!"
"Yep, Bormack chose you."
"Oh no, I bet Winter is devastated."
"There is only one way to find out."
"I have to find him."
"I think he's in his room."
Rain showed me to Winter's room. Before she left, she smiled at me and said good luck. I wasn't sure what she meant by that, but I put it out of my head. I knocked on the door. He opened it. He didn't look upset. He was actually surprised to see me.

He didn't say a word; he just invited me in and closed the door. I looked over and saw his bed. I had imagined being in that bed a hundred times. I needed to focus, but it was hard when he was staring at me like that.

"Look, Winter, I know that you are in love with Fray, and I'm sorry about this outcome."

He still said nothing, just looked at me.

"But if you want to forget the whole thing and run off with Fray, I completely understand."

"Is that what you want?"

I wasn't sure what to say. Was that what I wanted? What I really wanted was for him to take me on his bed and show me what this thing called love was all about.

"I'm not sure I understand the question."

"Do you want me to run off and marry Fray?"

"I want you to be happy."

He moved in closer to me. He was so close I could feel his breath on me. He smelled so good. My body was tingling all over. I looked up into his eyes. Hot flashes covered my body again. I was becoming extremely moist between my legs. I kept telling my flame to stay calm.

"Then I'm happy with you."

I about choked.

"What!"

"I love you, Pye."

My entire body felt like it was going to melt. He pressed his forehead up against mine. And I closed my eyes. I couldn't believe what I was hearing. Is this a dream? I asked myself. Am I about to wake up at any minute now?

"Of course if you don't feel the same…" he continued.

"Winter, I think about you all the time. Mostly at night when I touch my—" I immediately cut myself off.

He smiled.

"I'm glad it's not just me then."

"You should know I have never done this before. I might not be good at it," I said.

Winter put both his arms around me, and I became mush in his hands. Our lips met, and then he stuck his tongue in my mouth. He was drinking me up. And my body eagerly wanted more. All of him.

I was so afraid this was a dream and I was going to wake up. So I told myself no matter what, I would not let anything distract me.

> *To appreciate the beauty of a snowflake, it*
> *is necessary to stand out in the cold.*
>
> —Aristotle

Part V

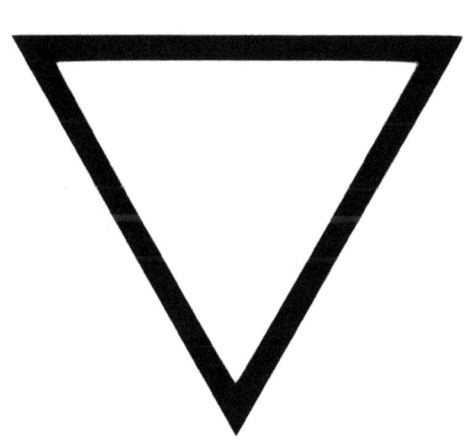

The Water Realm

Introduction

The Water Realm is everywhere; it surrounds the land realms. The Water Realm is divided between Scylla, the sea, and Orisa, the ocean. What separates them is that the sea people are called Nereus. The Nereus stay close to land because it stills holds an important resource for them even though they live on the water.

There are three kingdoms in the sea. The biggest one is called Thetis, the kingdom of the sea. Thetis rules all sea-animal life. The second one is called Pontus, the kingdom of tides. Pontus rules the currents and the waves. The third is called Orca, the kingdom of storms. Orca rules over sea weather.

Now, there is only one kingdom in the ocean. It is bigger than all the sea kingdoms put together. Nodons is the kingdom of the ocean. Nodons rules over the freshwater streams from the sea and is the protector of Armetha's Tears. The people who live in Nodons or on the ocean are called the Nijord. The Nijord have never set foot on land. They do not need land for anything.

The Nijord and the Nereus both believe in Armetha the Goddess of Water. They all have blue hair and blue eyes. They both have the power of water manipulation. The Nijord can shape and move small bodies of water with the palm of their hand. The Nereus also have this power, but theirs is different. The Nereus can extract water and move it with sound. The Nijord can breathe underwater, while the Nereus can walk on water. Both are excellent swimmers.

Under Nodons, submerged in water, is Nervia. The kingdom of mermaids. Nervia is under the rule and governance of Nodons.

Now the Nijord and Nereus are not enemies, but they are not acquaintances either. They generally like to keep to their own race. It is typically frowned upon when Nijord and Nereus mix, so they stay away from each other in that regard. When fresh water and salt water intertwine, they can become corrosive. Corrosion is feared because it is uncontrollable.

The problem in the Water Realm is flooding. This flooding to the sea has caused the ocean's pH balance to drop, making it very hard for the Nijord and the Nereus to sustain life.

And an ocean without life is no ocean at all.

Armetha symbolizes unity. Their religion is called LIR.

Chapter 39

Princess Niarea Runtassel

As I was kneeling over my father's open casket, I felt so guilty about his death. I kept wondering what I could have done differently to help prevent this from happening. I sat there alone letting my tears flow down my cheeks. I wiped them the minute I heard my younger brother Naxos enter the room.

He said, "Nia, you've got to stop blaming yourself."

"How can I when our father lies here dead?"

"He died from a heart attack; you heard Blue."

"I know, but as soon as I told father what Neptune was up to, he took a turn for the worse. The same with mother."

"Nia, Mom and Dad did not die because of you."

"I wish I could believe you."

"Well, you're going to have to, 'cause I need your help."

"With what?"

"With my coronation tomorrow."

"Oh, Nax, I'm so sorry I forgot. Congratulations. What can I help with?"

Now that my father was dead, Nax was the next one in line to take the throne.

I dried my eyes and gave him a big hug, but I could tell something was wrong.

"Nia I don't think I can do this," he said.

"What are you talking about? You're going to make a great king."

"I'm turning it down; I don't want to be king."

"Nax, I will support you in any decision you make, but—"

"Good, 'cause I think you should rule."

I thought my brother had gotten seasick.

"Me? But that's not a good idea."

"Why not?"

"The Pedestals will never go for it."

"Nia, you are more than qualified to rule. The only reason why they passed on you is because you're a woman."

"Yes, the reason why they don't want a woman is because of Great-Aunt Cora."

"Yes, but you are not Aunt Cora."

"That's the reason why the Pedestals won't go for it."

"Nia, given the chance to rule, would you?"

I though about it for a minute: I would love to have the crown and rule Nodons. I know I could do it. But can I?

"OK, yes, I would."

"Then you are getting that crown."

"As long as you are by my side."

"I wouldn't have it any other way."

Chapter 40

Princess Niarea Runtassel

The Pedestals are the legislation of Nodons. There are four of them. Elkhorn sits in the octopus chair. He is in charge of law. Atoll sits in the squid chair. He is in charge of currency. Capensis sits in the seahorse chair. He is in charge of religion. Chrysaor sits in the jellyfish chair. He is in charge of order.

Now, they decide what is best for Nodons, but the king or queen gets the final say to act out their decision. If the king or queen does not agree with their action, then they sit in a room and argue it out until they can all come to an agreement.

All the Pedestals are male. And before they can swear in the new King, they have what is called The Batoids. The Batoids is a gathering. It is a tradition to have it before a king's coronation. The Batoids is held in the pillar coral room, and the Pedestals host it. It is mandatory for all blood relatives to be present. The reason for this is so they can express how they feel about the new king. Whether they agree or disagree, this is the time to speak up.

The Batoids had started. All my relatives were there, except my older brother Neptune, who was now a fugitive on the run.

My heart was feeling heavy. I knew at any minute my brother Naxos was going to go in front of the Pedestals and tell them he was going to decline his crown.

A big part of me was hoping he would wimp out and just accept it.

Atoll spoke first. "Now that we are all here, let's get started."

Elkhorn added, "Lord Naxos, would you be so kind as to step forward?"

Nax did as he said. All eyes were on him.

Chrysaor spoke next. "If anyone disputes Naxos Caspian Runtassel as the next king of Nodons, now is the time."

Everyone looked around, but nobody was saying anything. Then my brother spoke.

"I stand here to tell you that I dispute it."

Everyone gasped.

Capensis said, "Are you saying that you have no legal claim to the throne?"

"No, that's not what I'm saying. I'm just refusing the crown," Nax responded.

More shock and aw filled the room.

The Pedestals were even more shocked. They huddled with each other to talk among themselves, keeping their voices down.

I just looked at Nax. He was smiling right at me. I was too nervous to smile back at him. I heard my uncle Cove behind my back saying, "Why would he do a stupid thing like that?"

Finally the Pedestals broke up their huddle and were now addressing the crowed.

Atoll said, "Order, order, I say."

The audience went silent.

Capensis spoke next. "Lord Nax, you have every right to decline the throne."

Atoll added, "After all, it is your choice."

Elkhorn chimed in, "And that law states that you have the power to pass down the crown to your next successor."

Chrysaor explained, "And that would be your cousin Bretzel."

"No, I will be passing the crown down to my sister Princess Niarea."

The crowd was in an uproar. Everyone was arguing and shouting. The Pedestals were all looking at me as if I had planned it.

I knew this was a bad idea.

Elkhorn said, "Settle down, everyone, please."

Atoll said, "Nax, I'm very sorry, but your sister is ineligible."

"Is she not genetically related to our late king Romulan Yosef Runtassel?"

Atoll responded, "Yes, but—"

"Is she not a full-blood Nijord?"

"Yes, she is," said Chrysaor.

"And her being the second born, she is old enough to rule."

"But you are forgetting one important detail," cautioned Capensis.

"And what is that?" asked Nax.

Atoll said, "She is a woman."

Elkhorn added, "And a woman will never rule Nodons."

"My lords, I understand why having me on the throne has put a bad taste in your mouth," I said.

Chrysaor responded, "Then you will understand why we have objections."

"Yes, but I'm not my great-aunt Cora," I added.

My cousin Bretzel started clapping as he was circling me and Nax.

He said, "Let's be honest here. Nia talks a good game. But she's not fit to rule."

"And why is that?" Nax asked.

Bretzel responded, "Well, for starters, she has no training, and let's be serious, no one will support her claim."

Atoll said, "Now, there is a way to settle this."

Capensis explained, "That's right; we can have a vote."

Chrysaor declared, "All those in favor of Niarea Runtassel for queen, raise your hands."

Only my brother Nax and I raised our hands.

Elkhorn chimed in, "All those for Bretzel for king."

Everyone raised their hand. Except for me and my brother, of course.

Bretzel was smiling and acting all smug.

Atoll said, "Well, there you have it."

"Wait! Now, you are forgetting one important detail," I shouted.

Bretzel asked, What's that?

"Bretzel is not a full-blooded Nijord; he's only half," I said.

"That's right, and one of our noblest and oldest traditions is that we have always had full-blooded Nijord on that throne," Nax said.

Bretzel protested, "My parents are full-blooded Nijord."

"Yes, but you have set foot on land, making you a Splake," said Nax.

I added, "Let me remind you that pure-blooded Nijord are the true rulers of the ocean.

All the hands that had gone up for Bretzel started to slowly come down.

Bretzel said, "So what? The fact that you are a woman outweighs that."

Atoll advised, "No, Princess Niarea is right."

Chrysaor confirmed, "We have never had a land lover sit on that throne, and we never will."

Atoll said, Then let's do this again. All those for Princess Niarea for queen, raise your hands."

This time everyone raised their hand, including me and my brother.

Elkhorn said, "Well, I think we have our winner."

Bretzel said, "Fine, you want to put a woman on the throne—I can't think of a better way to destroy this kingdom."

"Bretzel, get out of here," said Nax.

Bretzel responded, Oh, I will, but you will fail."

My entire family watched as Bretzel left the room. Then they all looked back at me. I could see they had their doubts.

Atoll said, "Your Highness, will you please step forward?"

I did as I was told.

Chrysaor explained, "Tomorrow we will be informing the nation that Niarea Nala Runtassel is Queen of Nodons."

Atoll said, "And if any one has any objections, now is the time."

Nobody said a word. Then my brother shouted out hail to the queen. And the crowed followed his lead.

Chapter 41

Queen Niarea Runtassel

It was my first day as queen. I was committed to being the best queen Nodons had ever seen. I would not let my people down. I would rule with amnesty and compassion. I would not let anything discourage me. Or get in my way. Now that I had the power, I would stay focused, driven to give my people the best. I would not let them regret having me as their queen.

Being a queen to me meant standing up and leading my people to a better future. And that was what I planned on doing.

I was stationed on my throne. The throne my father used to sit in. I looked at myself in the reflection of the walls. Seeing myself with the metallic blue crown on my head showed that this was not a dream. It was very real. I couldn't help but admire myself.

Then my brother burst through the doors, disrupting the silence.

"We have a problem," he said.

"It's my first day as queen. How can we already have a problem?"

"That's politics for you."

"OK, fine. What's the problem?"

"The Sea Realm has stopped all shipments coming out or going into the Ocean Realm."

"I see. Do we know why?"

"They are all claiming that they will not do business with a kingdom that has an unfit ruler."

"All shipments?"

"Yes, and they are no longer letting Nijord enter the Sea Realm."

"Well, Cousin Bretzel works fast."

"This isn't Bretzel's doing."

"Well, then who else?"

"King Dax."

"King Dax!"

"Yes, he's king now that his father has passed away."

Daximus Ivals. There is only one word that can describe this man—no, I take that back; there are many words. "Arrogant bully" is a good one. And there are other words, but I don't want to get myself worked up. He's not worth it.

I have known Dax most of my life. His father King Nerio Ivals has done business with my father for many years. They were just business partners, nothing more, and the two couldn't be more opposite.

So when he came to our kingdom, he would bring Dax, and when we went to his kingdom, my father would bring me and my brothers.

My oldest brother Neptune and Dax hit it off pretty well. But Dax and I, not so much. When I was nine, he called me an ugly cod fish that needed to be put back into the water so no one could see how heinously disgusting I was. He would also put knots in my hair.

It was so typical that he wouldn't support my reign. But it was OK; I didn't need him. And he was going to find out I was not a scared little girl anymore.

"I had know idea King Nerio died," I said.

"Yeah, right around the time Mother past away," Nax explained.

"So he's been king for a while?"

"Yes, he has and has proven to be a better king than his father."

"OK, so what should we do?"

"Maybe you could talk to King Dax, get him to side with you."

"Are you insane? I loathe that man, and I would rather drown a thousand times over than grovel at his feet."

"We need those shipments."

"Do we? They are luxuries, not necessities. We can do without."

"Nia, our people are counting on you to make sure that their resources stay the same. Uprooting them would not look good on are part."

"OK fine, then we hire Glaucus."

"Hiring ocean smugglers is illegal."

"Says who?"

"Our father."

"Yes, but he's not king anymore, is he?"

"You can't trust them, Nia. They are nothing more than vicious leeches."

"OK fine, then let's do business with Tentinium."

"You would do business with Drekums?"

"Of course not, but if I didn't have any choice, then I would."

"OK, I see your point. The Glaucus sounds like the better deal. So let me find some things out first."

"Thank you, Nax. That's why I love you."

"Yeah, so you tell me."

"It's true. I wouldn't be here if it wasn't for you."

"That's not true. You saw through Bretzel's crap. You did this on your own."

"Yeah, but you were there to see me through it."

"That's what brothers are supposed to do."

"Is that what a brother is supposed to do?"

He and I both laughed.

"Oh, I should tell you that you got a birthday invitation," he said.

"From whom?"

My brother handed it to me. As I was reading it, I was getting mad—no, furious.

"That bastard!" I shouted.

King Dax had the audacity to invite me to his birthday after he had just banned all Nijord from the Sea Realm.

"He's mocking you," said Nax.

"No shit!"

I was getting ready to rip up the invitation.

"No, wait," Nax interjected.

"For what?"

"We should go."

"Nax, has the ocean fried your brain cells? Why would we go?"

"To stand up against him, to show him that we don't need him."

My brother had a very good point.

"To gloat that we are standing strong and that he will never break us," I added.

"Exactly!"

"OK, I like it, but we are Nijord; he just forbade us from going in."

"Yes, but you have an invitation. Plus, we are royalty; it doesn't count for us."

Chapter 42

King Daximus Ivals

I was turning twenty-three today. I am not up for celebrations usually, but in this case, I was really excited because my good friend Neptune was coming to see me. We had remained friends over the years. And always had each other's back. He was there for me when my father died.

"Neptune, my friend," I said.

"Your Highness."

We gave each other a big hug.

"Will you be staying for the birthday party?" I asked.

"I can't; I have some other matters to attend to. But I will be giving the birthday boy this."

He handed me a small chest.

"OK, what is this?" I asked.

"Just open it,"

Inside it were Perls. Lots of them. Neptune was now the ruler of Amphitrite, thanks to me. But Amphitrite was not a kingdom. But it was very profitable and had a lot of resources. One of them being clams.

"What's this for?"

"Your birthday present, plus my contribution toward your kingship. And what I owe you for helping me get Amphitrite."

"Thanks, Tune."

"Don't thank me; it had been a long time coming. And happy birthday, by the way."

"Thank you, but it's just going to be another boring day; they always are."

"Well, then change it—you are the king."

"You're right, I should."

"By the way, thanks for boycotting the Nijord."

"Hey, no problem. Well, my Pedestals aren't too happy about it. Still, we rely on Nodons for a lot."

"Yes, I understand, but my sister is no ruler."

"Hey, you don't have to convince me. I still don't understand why they gave it to her in the first place."

"Well, my little brother coward, out and Bretzel was probably ineligible."

"But to give it to Nia—are they really that stupid?"

"That brings me to my next question."

"What's that?"

"I need to ask you for a favor."

"What's up?"

"I need you to seduce Nia."

"What for?"

"Dax, I need dirt on her so that I can get her discredited."

"She will do that all on her own. Just wait. Plus, there is no guarantee she will show up."

"I know, Dax, but I want her humiliated with shame. Oh, she will show, and if she is caught flirting with a Nereus…"

"I get it—then she loses all her credibility."

"You got it. So what do you say? Can you do it?"

"Please. I'll have her eating out of the palm of my hand."

The last time I saw Nia, she was twelve years old. And her body hadn't grown in yet. The only thing that had grown in was her teeth. They were too big for her mouth. Ugly kids are bound to grow up ugly. It's common sense.

Anyways, this was going to be fun. I did miss picking on her; that was loads of laughs. So maybe this would be a fun birthday. My plan was to butter her up, then embarrass her in front of everyone. She wouldn't be able to show her face. That would be great for everyone since she was not that great to look at.

The party was kicking off pretty well. Everyone who mattered was here. If Nia was here, it was probably a good thing that Neptune wasn't. He left about an hour before the party started.

Everyone was talking to me and wishing me happy birthday. Not that I cared. I was too busy looking for Nia. I didn't see her anywhere. How hard is it to find the ugliest woman in the world? I asked myself.

I was searching the room with my eyes when a young, beautiful woman caught my eye. Her long blue hair was sparking through the room. She was talking to King Tiber, ruler of Pontus. Tiber is married to my sister Celine.

I had never seen this woman before. She was absolutely the most stunningly gorgeous woman I had ever seen. I called to Cecil. He's my Shoal, also known as my second-in-command. He served my father.

"Cecil, who is that?" I asked.

"Who, Your Majesty?"

"The young lady talking to my brother-in-law."

"Oh, that is Queen Niarea."

"That is Queen Niarea!"

"Yes, Your Majesty."

"I think you are mistaken."

"No, Your Highness. That is Queen Niarea, and the younger boy next to her is her brother Naxos."

Holy Armetha, was she beautiful. I still couldn't comprehend it. She started out as such an ugly duckling and somehow had become an alluring swan.

"Wow, her body definitely filled out in all the right places."

"I beg your pardon, My Lord," Cecil said.

"Never mind."

OK, so I had a new plan. Seduce the Queen—that was a given. But go further than flirting.

Her smile was so beautiful, I couldn't wait to drink it up.

Chapter 43

Queen Niarea Runtassel

I had been at the party for a total of thirty minutes, and I still hadn't seen the king. I thought, I'm supposed to be here supporting my reign. And all I have done is talk to a bunch of people who have congratulated me on being Queen but have no complaints about the Nijord being banned from the Sea Realm.

"Here you go," said Nax.

"Thank you," I responded.

My brother handed me another drink. It was my favorite, blue champagne. It's called Aqua.

"You should really go easy on that; it will go straight to your head," he commented.

"Thanks, Nax. Are you my dad now?"

"No, I'm just trying to help you. Plus, I am your Shoal."

"I'm sorry, Nax. I'm just feeling agitated; everyone here thinks I'm a joke."

"No, they don't."

"Yes, they do, and what's even worse, I feel like we have been stood up. I don't think the king is even here."

A woman's voice from behind us said, "Yes, he's over there." She pointed to the corner, where a group of women were crowding around someone.

I couldn't see him. But I noticed she said she was Dax's sister.

"Hi. I'm—"

She interrupted, "Yeah, I know who you are. Queen Niarea. And may I say you are very beautiful?"

"You may."

I just looked at my brother. I hate schmoozing. It didn't seem like she really meant that.

"You must be Queen Celine?"

I shook her hand.

Celine said, "You are correct. It's great to finally meet you."

"And you as well. This is my brother Naxos."

They both shook hands.

I had not met Celine before today. There were rumors when I was younger that she and her father didn't get along very well. So they were never seen together.

"So you say that your brother Dax is really here?"

"Yes, he is. I know it's hard to see him, but he is here."

While we were talking to Queen Celine, she then pointed to the corner again; this time we could get a good look at Dax.

Our mouths stood open. And I would have said it, but my brother beat me to it.

"Oh my, is he the sexiest man I have ever seen."

I couldn't have said it better myself.

"OK, so he's very attractive. That doesn't mean he's not an arrogant prick," I said.

"You think he's into men as well?"

"I guess there is a possibility."

"I'm going over there."

Before I could stop my brother, he was already over there. The two were talking and laughing as if they were old chums. I hate being fake, and my brother wasn't playing it off very well. He looked like he was genuinely having a good time.

OK, so Dax is a very, devastatingly handsome man. So what? I would not drop my guard with him. I was very aware of King Daximus

199

Ivals's reputation. I knew he was a womanizer and a big flirt. He went through women like he was fishing. Caught one, then when he was done, threw them back in the water. I thought, And why wouldn't he be that way when women flock to him and throw themselves at his feet? His idea of a woman is a fish in a barrel. The only thing that man cares about is himself. Literally thinks that he is a gift from the Goddess of Water herself.

As I was watching the two of them, the chunks of betrayal were rising in my throat. Then the two of them were looking at me. Nax waved to me; I didn't wave back. Dax winked at me, and I narrowed my eyes at him. Then the two of them went back to laughing. I felt like they were laughing at me.

I went to the bar and pounded down a few more glasses of Aqua.

Then my brother came up behind me.

"Wow, he is amazing," he said.

"I see, and now you have joined the side of betrayal. And for what, a man who has blue spiky hair? And a body that is filled with nothing but muscles."

"Don't forget the thick lips."

"Are you kidding me right now?"

"What? I just went over to say hello."

"Yeah, it looked like you were doing a lot more."

"I wish. He's definitely not into men."

"How do you know?"

"Because he can't stop looking at you."

I don't know why I did it, but I did it. I looked at him, and he was staring right at me with a grin on his face that was making me shake all over.

I turned my head the other way as if I hadn't noticed.

"He wants to talk to you, Nia."

"Well, I don't want to talk to him."

"Fine, have it your way. I'm going to the bathroom."

"When you get back, we are leaving."

My brother shook his head and headed to the bathroom. I was ordering another drink when a voice from behind me said, "I think you have had enough, don't you?"

"Oh great, another father figure."

When our eyes met, I felt a spike of adrenaline all over. It was Dax.

"Not a father figure, just concerned, that's all."

"Oh, now you want to act like you care? How nice."

I turned my head again and pretend he wasn't there. I could see out of the corner of my eye he was smiling at me. Why do I have this strong pull of desire toward this man? I asked myself.

"It's good to see you, Nia."

"Well, I'd liked to say the feeling is mutual."

I was getting a little dizzy and flushed. I was trying to get away from Dax when I almost fell and he caught me.

"Here, come with me," he said.

Before I could respond, he was holding me up and pulling me in another direction. I was trying to push away from him, but he is really strong.

We entered a big bedroom. With a waterfall in it. Leading to a massive pool around the bed. Dax sat me on the bed. I wasn't clear on what was going on, but I knew I needed to get away from him.

He put a finger to my forehead. Then he extracted alcohol from my forehead, and I started feeling much better.

"How did you do that?" I asked.

"Magic."

I didn't want to thank him, but I felt I had to.

"Thank you, but I have to go now."

"How come?"

"Because I don't trust you."

"I should work on that, huh?"

"Yeah, good luck with that."

I headed for the door and put my hand on the handle.

"Why don't we stay here and talk for a minute?"

I stopped what I was doing and faced him.

"You want me to stay here in a bedroom with you alone?"

"Sure, why not?"

"'Cause you are trying to ruin me, and I'm not going to fall for that."

"Oh, I see, you're mad about the whole boycott thing, right?"

"Right."

"Then let me make it up to you."

Before I could say no, he had me pinned up against the door with both of his hands on each side of my face. He leaned in and kissed me, and I took every bit of it in. I wrapped my arms around him. He did the same to me. Our bodies were so close that I could feel his heart beat. I couldn't help but make a moaning sound. Then he gripped my waist tighter.

Then I came to my senses and pulled away from him. What is wrong with me? I asked myself. You would think that the way this man treated women would have been enough to make me feel grossed out about him.

"What are you doing?" I said.

"Kissing you."

"Why, when you are a big bully jerk who has always hurt my feelings since I was a little girl?"

"That's why I'm kissing you, to make up for the horrible way I treated you."

He started taking his clothes off.

"What are you doing?"

"I'm going for a swim; I want you to join me."

He was completely naked. I put my hand over my eyes.

"I know what you are doing," I said.

"Really? What am I doing?"

"You are trying to confuse me so that I will like you or worse, fall for you."

"You got all that from a simple swim?"

"No, it was from the kiss."

"You are reading way too much into this."

"I'm reading way too much into this!"

"If you weren't, then you would come for a swim with me. It's just a swim."

"No, it's much more."

"I have a strong feeling you can't swim."

"I'm a Nijord; of course I can swim."

"Then come on."

I heard a splash and put my hands down from my eyes. He was in the water. I thought, OK, I will show him I can swim, then I'm leaving no matter what he says.

"Fine. Turn around," I said.

He did as I said and looked the other way. I took all my clothes off and dove in. The water was cool and a little refreshing since my emotions were causing me to be hot all over, or was that the alcohol that was still lingering inside me?

"See, that wasn't so bad, was it?"

"You are trying to charm me."

"I think me and you both know I'm sending more than just charm."

He swam up closer to me.

"Dax, I—"

"Nia, what if we gave in to what our bodies really want to do to each other?"

"I think I would be in a lot of trouble if I was caught messing with you."

"Who's going to know? It would be our little secret."

"Guys like you don't keep secrets."

"Why not?"

"'Cause you would use it to hurt me."

"What would I want to hurt you for?"

"The same reason you won't let the Nijord into the Sea Realm; you think I'm not fit to rule."

"Then prove me wrong."

He got even closer to me. He had me pinned up against the pool wall. We stared at each other for a good minute.

"My brother might be wondering where I am."

"I'll take care of it."

Dax leaned in closer to me. But I pulled away and got out of the water. I grabbed my clothes off the bed. I didn't care if he could see me naked. I needed to get out of there. I reached the door, but he stopped me.

"You should get dressed before you storm out of here."

I realized that I was holding my clothes against my body. Dax grabbed me and pulled me closer. This time he was up against the door. And he was pinning me up against him.

"But I hate you."

"Then let me show you how not to."

Everything in my head was screaming, "Get out of there." But my body was yelling at me to let him keep going.

Dax took over my mouth like he was trying to stop a leak from getting out. He pulled the barrier of clothes I was holding down to the floor.

My body just seeped into him. He tasted so good. He picked me up with his big, strong arms and dropped me on the bed. There he was standing naked in front of me. His body was amazing.

Then I looked down and saw his erection. His penis was huge. He looked like he could satisfy a killer whale. There was no way I was going to get that whole thing inside me.

I looked back up at his face, and he smiled at me.

I just shook my head to indicate "no way."

"Yes, you are going to take it all."

"There is no way."

"We will go slow, OK?"

"OK."

Yeah, really slow.

Chapter 44

Queen Nia Runtassel

While Dax was sleeping, I slowly slid out of the bed. I put my clothes on quickly, trying to make as little noise as I could. The door squeaked a little as I closed it behind me. I was pretty sure he hadn't woken up.

I found my brother's room and woke him up.

"Nax, we have to go now," I whispered in his ear.

"Why? What happened?"

"Nothing. It's time to go. Wake the crew so we can get the boat running."

"Why are we whispering?"

"Just 'cause.

I felt comfortable whispering. Even though I was nowhere near Dax, he could still wake up.

I was soon on the boat, and I felt more comfortable since we had left without seeing Dax. As we were pulling away from Thetis, my heart started to calm down. I could feel more relaxed.

I was in my room down below in the ship. I knew my brother was going to burst through my door and demand I tell him what happened. The truth was I didn't even understand what happened.

Like I didn't understand why I missed Dax already. That I was crazy about him. Dax turned my body out. The first orgasm he gave me was so strong that I shook so hard I bit the inside of my lip; I could taste the blood in my mouth. Then he ate me out. I could feel that orgasm all the way to the tip of my ears, to the bottom of my toes. But I kept it cool. I masked my pleasure; I didn't let him know that he had just rocked my world. I had to. Guys like that will eat you up and spit you out when they're done. You can't let them in your heart; you'll only regret it.

It took my body a minute to get used to his huge appendage. It was really painful, but then pleasure came after that. Then it was mixture of pain and pleasure. That got me hooked. We fucked everywhere. On the bed numerous times. On the floor, in the water, up against the wall. And in every single position ever done. There wasn't an orifice on my body Dax didn't explore.

I was so numb. I felt like my body had been ridden hard and put away wet. I was sore, but a good sore. I wanted it again; I was fixated on him, and it scared me 'cause I couldn't tell him, not even if I wanted to.

Naxos burst through the door.

"So are you going to tell me what happened?" he asked.

"There is nothing to tell."

My brother looked at me like I had plankton coming out of my nose.

"You were in King Dax's bedroom for seven days, and you are telling me there is nothing to tell?"

I gasped.

"It doesn't matter because I'm never going to see him again."

"Nia, you've fallen for him, haven't you?"

I looked at my brother and started crying.

"Nia, it's OK."

"Ok! Do you realize if this ever got out, I could be in a lot of trouble? I have let everyone down."

"Nia, you haven't let anyone down. So you like Dax? Who can blame you? The guy is sexy. He puts the sex in sexy."

"I feel so ashamed. I let my guard down."

"Stop beating yourself up. It's going to be OK."

"Naxos, you have to promise me that you won't tell anyone about this."

"Tell what?"

I looked at my brother and smiled.

"What did you tell the Pedestals?"

"That we were experiencing boat trouble; they don't suspect a thing."

"Oh, thank goodness."

"I'm dying to know one thing."

"What's that?"

"Is he hung?

"Oh, Nax!"

"Please, Nia, I have to know."

"Let's just say the word 'hung' doesn't describe it."

My brother got really excited for me. I mean, it's not every day you get freshly fucked by a man who looks like he was handcrafted by the goddess herself and dipped in the holy grail.

"I knew it. You are so lucky."

"All right, can we talk about something else, like business?"

"Yes, we found Neptune."

"Really, where?"

"Apparently he is now the ruler of Amphitrite."

"I bet King Dax helped with that."

"There's more."

"Of course there is."

"He is trying to get his hands on every map of the water realm. And he's hired a lot of oceanographers."

"What's he looking for?"

"Not sure, but, Nia, he is up to something."

"Well, we will have to keep an eye on him."

I didn't know what my brother was after, but I knew it was something that he thought would make him powerful.

Chapter 45

King Daximus Ivals

My Pedestals were pissing me off. We had been arguing all day. Bardo sat in the octopus chair; he is the law. Deniz was in the squid chair; he deals with currency. And is the biggest tightwad you will ever see. He is always trying to cut corners. Fiji is on the seahorse. He's a Novacas, meaning a holy man that deals with religion. Then there is Nen. He's was the jellyfish chair and deals with order. Nen is better at ordering people around than keeping order.

Bardo said, "Your Majesty, you have to have a wife."

Fiji chimed in, "It worries us that you don't have anyone to pass down your legacy to."

I responded, "Gentlemen, I have told you that I will find a woman when the time comes."

Nen responded, "That was two years ago. No more waiting."

"What are you saying?" I asked.

Deniz said, "That if you don't find a bride and deliver an heir, then you forfeit your crown."

"You can't do that to me," I protested.

Bardo responded, "We can, and we will."

"There is no one to replace me."

Deniz said, "Your sister's son will take your place."

"Trent! He's only thirteen."

Fiji added, "And has a marriage proposal."

"If he can produce and heir before you," Bardo said.

Deniz completed his thought. "Then he is the next King of Thetis."

"OK fine, I will have a bride by the next full moon."

Very good, Your Highness," said Bardo.

Nen said, "Now there is the matter of the sea wall. It is causing a massive flood in the Sea Realm."

"Yes, I know, and I'm working on it."

Fiji added, "Finn was talking about moving the species that have been affected by this farther out to sea."

"We can't do that because of the tides," I responded.

Nen asked, "Then what is your suggestion, My King?"

"I'm working with Finn to find a better solution."

Bardo said, "Well, let's pray to Armetha that you fix it soon."

Nen announced, "Looks like that is all for today."

"We are adjourned," said Deniz.

I have only cared about and wanted one thing, and that is power. That right there is enough to get me hard and off for the rest of my life. There is no such thing as to much power. I crave it like I have a mad fucking disease. My idea of power is that everyone is sick and only I have the cure and you better bow down to me, kiss my feet, or suck my dick. Gives me chills just thinking about that. At least that was the case until I had Nia.

I was getting a massive headache. I told Cecil to get me a drink, which he did with haste. I was stressed. But most of all, I was missing Nia. It had been a minute since I had seen her. I couldn't stop thinking about her. She was the best lay I had ever had. She had ruined me for any other woman. I missed tasting her. Touching her. I loved that every time I got her off, she acted like it was no big deal. Like I hadn't just rocked her world. It was almost like a challenge that I couldn't get her to fall for me. But she was mine, and damn if the whole ocean didn't know it yet. I thought, I will have that woman worshipping the ground I walk on. 'Cause I'll be cursed if I go into this alone.

The other part was Neptune. He had just arrived.

"Tune!" I said.

"King Dax!"

We shook hands this time.

"So how are things going?" I asked.

"They are going. How was your birthday?"

"It was OK."

The best birthday I had ever had.

"And how did it work with my sister?"

"It didn't go to plan."

"She turned you down, huh?"

"Yep, I believe her exact words were 'I hate you.'"

"That's OK. There is always plan B."

"What's plan B?"

"You will see soon enough. But I was wondering if I could have your maps of Nebula."

"The western sea?"

"Yes!" exclaimed Neptune.

"What are you looking for?"

"Something that is going to make me a god."

"You are crazy," I said.

"And you look stressed."

"That's 'cause I am."

"What about?"

"My Pedestals want me to get married right now."

"That's not too bad."

"That's easy for you to say."

"Maybe I could help with that," said Neptune.

"How so?"

"Oh, I'll think of something."

Chapter 46

Queen Niarea Runtassel

"I don't know what you did to make King Dax let the Nijord back into the Sea Realm, but whatever it was, it worked," said Nax.

"A little louder, Naxos; I don't think they heard you."

"Oh, calm down. We are alone."

"Still, we need to forget it."

"Forgotten."

"Thank you."

My kingdom was doing much better now that we had our resources back. But I was not doing good at all. I was feeling very sick lately, and I couldn't seem to get myself to focus. I was just so tired all the time. But all I did was sleep. It made no sense.

I was puking again; it was my third time that day.

"You need to go see Blue," said Nax.

"What for?" I asked.

"Because, Nia, you have been feeling like crud for a while now, and you don't seem to be getting better."

"I assure you I'm fine."

"You don't look fine."

"You worry too much."

"Look, just see Blue for me."

"Fine, but I'm telling you he will say there is nothing wrong with me."

Blue came to my room an hour later. I knew that this was a complete waste of time. He spent thirty minutes looking me over.

"I'm good, right?"

"Yes, of course," said Blue.

"Great. Now will you tell my brother I'm fine?"

Nax narrowed his eyes at me.

"Yes, she is fine. In fact, she is pregnant," explained Blue.

My brother and I both shouted out, "What the fuck!"

Blue looked at us and then laughed.

"Oh, I get it. Very funny, Blue," I said.

"Nia, this isn't a joke," he responded. "You are about four weeks along."

"But that's not right; you have to be wrong."

"I'm not."

"And you said there is nothing wrong with you," interjected Nax.

"Will you please shut up?" I said.

"And there's the hormones," he responded.

"OK, let's just pull back the waves here," I said.

Blue said, "You can pull them back all you want to; it still doesn't change the fact that you are with child."

"Would you stop saying that? I'm not that thing you say," I protested.

"Your Majesty, lots of women get pregnant. That's one of the great things about being a woman."

"Yes, I know women have babies, but I'm not that woman."

"Well, now you are."

"Here, chew this, but don't eat it."

"What's it for?"

"Seagrass. Helps with the nausea."

"It looks gross."

"It taste better than It looks. I'm going to give you a whole jar of it take it with you at all times."

"I can't believe this is happening."

"You're going to need lots of sleep; this baby is going to take up all your energy."

"Sounds just like its father," Nax commented.

I hit my brother in the arm real hard.

"Ouch! That hurt," he said.

"You are not helping," I responded.

"Hey, doc, do you think you could give Nia something for her mood swings?" Nax asked.

Blue said, "You know, Nax, keeping the mouth shut never hurt anyone."

"Right!" exclaimed.

"Take care of your sister; she's going to need your help."

"Don't worry, doc, I got this."

"I'm a little worried," said Blue.

"She's going to be fine," Nax responded.

"I was talking about you. She may kill you before this is over."

"Ha ha. Very funny," said Nax.

After Blue left the room, I just stared out into the ocean. My world had been turned upside down in less than forty-five minutes.

I thought, What am I going to do? I can't have a baby. I'm no mother. I wouldn't even know where to begin to try.

"Nax, what am I going to do?"

"Looks like you are having a baby."

"Oh no, I'm carrying a Nereus in my belly. My kingdom will never accept this child."

"First of all, this child is only half, and it's actually more Nijord than Nereus."

"The Pedestals won't see it that way."

"Yes, they will. As long as the baby doesn't set foot on land, it's fine."

"And when they ask who the father is, what do I say?"

"You can't remember."

"Do you know how stupid that sounds? That makes me sound incompetent."

"When are you going to tell Dax?"

"Never!"

"Ni, you can't do that."

"Why not?"

"'Cause he's the father."

"So?"

"I can't believe you right now."

"Can we focus on the more important things right now, like what I'm going to tell the Pedestals."

"Fine. If you don't tell him, I will."

My brother crossed is arms and gave me that look. The look of seriousness.

"OK, I will tell him eventually."

"Good."

Chapter 47

Queen Nia Runtassel

It was the day I was going to tell the Pedestals I was with child. I still couldn't comprehend that word. Or the fact of me being a mother. I had always thought about being queen or gaining power of some kind. It was all I have ever wanted, and now that I had it, I didn't want to lose it. But after this day, I could lose it all.

I went looking for my brother and found him with the captain of my father's army and now my army. His name is Caption Noah Swimmer. Noah is a young captain; he's the same age as my brother. But he has had his fare share of battles.

I have always thought my brother and Captain Noah had something going on. But whenever I ask him about it, he denies it. My brother never did like the opposite sex. I have known since we were younger. My father said it was wrong. My mother said he would grow out of it. But I didn't care as long as he was happy.

"Gentlemen, I'm not interrupting anything?" I said.

"Nope, Noah here is just filling me in on some information about Thetis."

"Oh, what have you heard?" I asked.

Noah explained, "King Dax has to find a wife very soon."

"Why!" I exclaimed.

"'Cause the Pedestals what an heir," said Nax.

My brother looked at my belly, then looked at me.

"Well, I'm sure he will have no problem finding him a wife," I said.

"Or an heir," added Nax.

Noah said, "I'm sure you are both right. Lord Nax, Your Majesty, I have to run my rounds now."

I watched as my brother and Caption Noah looked at each other for a brief moment.

"Nia, stop looking at me like that," Nax said.

"Are you sure there is nothing going on between you two?"

"No, for the tenth time."

"Why not? He's cute; you are cute."

"I just don't think he likes me like that."

"Are you blind? Do you see the way he stares at you?"

My brother quickly changed the subject.

"Can we go tell the Pedestals and get this over with?" he said.

"Fine!"

I let out a big sigh.

When we got to the throne room, the Pedestals were waiting for us there. They were very eager.

Atoll said, "Your Majesty, the floor is yours."

"Gentlemen, I have just found out that I'm with child," I said.

Silence filled the room.

"I know this comes as a shock to everyone," I added.

The Pedestals were whispering into each other's ears. Yeah, this is not going to be good, I thought.

I looked and my brother. He smiled at me and squeezed my hand, letting me know it was going to be all right.

Elkhorn declared, "I'd like to say from all of us, congratulations!"

My eyes went wide.

Chrysaor added, "We were actually wondering how you were going to get an heir without getting married."

Capensis then said, "And it looks like you took care of that for us."

Atoll queried, "The father, of course, is Nijord?"

I looked at my brother. He shook his head up and down.

Elkhorn declared, "Then your reign is strong, Your Majesty."

"Thank you!"

I thought, Oh thank you, Armetha. Feeling so much better. Feeling even better about being a mother. Maybe I can be both.

Capensis said, "We hate to tarnish this good news with bad news."

Chrysaor added, "But unfortunately we do have bad news."

"Oh, what kind of bad news?" I asked.

The Pedestals told me that the mermaids had come forth with complaints about some of the water being toxic, causing the plants that they depend on to die.

They also told me that King Varuna, ruler of Orca, had just lost his wife; the funeral would be the next day. And it would be in my best interest to attend.

"Gentlemen, I want you to set up a meeting with the leader of the mermaids when I get back from the funeral," I said.

Atoll responded, "Yes, of course, My Queen."

"Have Blue look into the toxic water. I want answers when I get back," I added.

My Pedestals both bowed to me and told me that they would get on it immediately.

Now I had to go to a funeral. The other part was that I might run into Dax. I warned my brother not to mention anything about me being pregnant. Of course he agreed only if I told Dax soon.

Chapter 48

Queen Nia Runtassel

Orca is in the Sea Realm. It's the kingdom of the sea storms. King Varuna's wife had been sick for many months at this point.

When I got to Orca King Varuna's, Pedestals greeted me and my brother and showed us to our rooms. I had not met King Varuna, but I had heard he was a strong-willed man.

After we got settled in, we went down and met with the other guests. They announced our names when we entered the room, and everyone looked up. There were only a handful of people there. And only a few of them I knew or had met before. King Dax wasn't there yet; I knew 'cause I asked the dock workers and they said that King Daximus's boat wasn't docked yet.

I needed to avoid him at all costs. I was so afraid I might slip up and say something about the baby.

"Well, this is a very sad affair," commented Nax.

"Nax, it's a funeral; it's supposed to be sad."

"Isn't the funeral tomorrow, though?"

"Yes, this is just a little gathering before the grieving."

"Well, then where is King Varuna so we can give our condolences?"

"There. He is over there."

King Varuna was surrounded by people weeping. He himself looked very strong, like he was trying to hold it together.

Nax and I walked over to him.

"King Varuna, I'm very sorry about your loss," I said.

"Queen Niarea, thank you for sympathy."

"Of course, and if—"

Varuna interrupted, "I hear a lot of rumors about you."

"Oh!"

"None of them are true I assure you," Naxos interjected."

"This is my brother Naxos," I explained.

Varuna said, "It's a pleasure to meet you, Naxos."

"The pleasure is all mine," he responded.

"You know your older bother Neptune was here the other day."

"Neptune was here?" I asked.

"That's right. He's under the impression that the reason why the Sea Realm is flooding is because of you, Queen Niarea."

"But I have nothing to do with the Sea Realm flooding."

Varuna explained, "As I said before, it's just a rumor I heard. Although Neptune does make an interesting case."

"How so?"

"Well, he says that it wasn't until you became queen that the sea started to flood."

Celine interjected, "Oh, come now, Varuna. We both know that the sea has always had a flooding problem."

King Dax's sister had come out of nowhere to defend my honor.

Varuna said, "Queen Celine, hasn't anyone told you that it's rude to interrupt a conversation."

"No more than accusing people of something they have no control over."

Celine grabbed my arm and walked me away from King Varuna. Nax followed us.

She said, "I'm so sorry about King Varuna. Whenever he is feeling bad, he has to go out of his way to make other people feel bad."

"Thank you for coming to my rescue."

"Yes, of course!"

"It's really good to see you again, Queen Celine."

"You as well, Queen Nia!"

"This is my brother Naxos."

"Actually, your brother and I have met."

"That's right, at Dax's birthday party," said Nax.

"That's right. I forgot," I said.

Nax commented, "Well, you were a little inebriated at the time."

I was so embarrassed I was getting ready to tell Celine that I wasn't an alcoholic. But then the voice filled the room. "Announcing King Daximus Ivals."

Everyone in the room looked up, but not me; I stayed looking in the other direction.

Celine said, "Well, leave it to my brother to be fashionably late."

"That's kings for you," commented Nax.

"That's so true. Nia, if you ever need anything, I'm here for you."

"Thanks, Celine. You too."

She gave me a big hug and went to greet her brother.

"Well, here comes your baby daddy," Nax teased.

"Shhhh!"

"No one heard me."

"Don't leave me alone with him."

"Why not?"

"Because he is a manipulator."

My bother started laughing.

"I guess that explains how you got in the situation you are in right now," he said.

Dax was walking toward us. I couldn't talk to him; I had to get away. I quickly dashed away from my brother and, I could hear him say, "Wuss" in a low voice.

I didn't care. I was too nervous to be around Dax. I was also feeling nauseous. I was chewing on the seagrass Blue gave me. It was helping the morning sickness, but it wasn't calming down my nerves.

I was by the buffet table pounding down some water when a familiar scent overcame my nostrils. The smell was coming from behind me, causing the hairs on the back of my neck to stand up. Dax smelled like the ocean after a storm. When the fresh rainwater hits the salt water. An intoxicating smell that made you feel fresh and clean. Like brand-new.

"Hello, Queen Nia."

Shit.

I turned around and faced him. Still as handsome as ever.

"King Dax."

"How have you been?"

"Good. You?"

"Good."

"So glad to hear it."

"This is your first time in Orca, isn't it?

"Yes."

"Great. They have these amazing rose gardens I'd like to show you."

"Dax, I'm not going to be alone with you."

"Why not?"

"Do you not remember the last time I was alone with you?"

"Yes, I remember it vividly."

"Good, 'cause it's never going to happen again."

"Why not? Was it not good?"

"That's not the point."

"Then what is the point?"

"The point is that I'm not going to be alone with you."

"I'm just showing you the rose gardens."

"Yeah right. That's how it will start. Then—"

"Wait a minute."

"What?"

Dax was looking me over. His eyes kept going up and down my body slowly.

"Something is different about you."

My body tensed up. I thought, He can't tell, can he? I'm not that far along.

"I have no idea what you are talking about."

"Did you do something with your hair?"

"No."

"Yeah, there is definitely something different about you."

Then of course Naxos had to comment on the conversation.

"Yeah, she does have a glow of some sort to her," he said.

"You see it too?" Dax asked.

"How can you not?"

I looked at my brother, reminding myself that when this day was over, I was going to kill him.

"OK, this is the end of this conversation," I said.

"Nia, I would really love to show you the gardens."

"Oh, she would love that," Nax interjected.

"Nax, are you not forgetting that thing?"

"What thing?"

"You know, that thing I told you earlier."

"Oh right, well, you will be OK. After all, there are gardens."

I couldn't believe what my bother was doing. He was sending me up the stream without a paddle. Oh, he is so dead, I thought.

I was following Dax to the gardens. We weren't saying anything to each other. I thought, I'm not sleeping with him. No matter what he does, my clothes are not coming off. No kissing, no nothing.

We got to the gardens, and they were absolutely beautiful. The roses were all different colors, floating on the water. And there was a huge waterfall with a weeping willow on top of it.

"OK, you are right—these are amazing," I said.

"I told you I wouldn't lie."

"Yeah, but you would do whatever you could to get me alone."

"I always get what I want, Nia."

"Is that right?"

Well, I'm glad to burst his bubble, 'cause he's not getting me ever again, I said to myself.

"We should go swimming again," he proposed.

"Dax no I'm not fucking you,"

"Who said anything about fucking?"

"That's how it starts. We go swimming. Next thing we know, we are on top of each other."

"And what's wrong with that again?"

"Dax, I'm a Nijord, and you are a Nereus; that means we don't mix."

"We shall see."

"No, we shall not see."

"Nia, you can't predict the future."

"No, but I can predict this."

I needed to get to my room. I couldn't do anything stupid if I was in my room alone with a door that locked. And kept. him out.

"Oh, Nia, I love when we have are little arguments."

"Dax, there is no 'we.'"

"If you say so."

"OK, this is nice, but I'm going to my room now."

"Good. I will walk you."

"No, you won't."

"Why not?"

"'Cause I know where my room is. I don't need your help."

"Well, it just so happens that I also want to go to my room."

"Good. You should go to your room."

Dax followed me all the way to my door.

"Dax, I though you were going to your room."

"I am; it's right across from your room."

I couldn't believe it. Dax was literally right across the hall from my room.

"That's your room?"

"Yep, and it's a good thing you are going to your room. You look tired."

"I'm not tired."

"Oh, but you are. Now get some sleep."

"Dax, I'm not tired."

"Then prove it. Come to my room."

"Why would I do that?"

"Why not? You say you're not tired. Prove it."

"That's it, Dax. Nothing else."

"Nothing else."

Chapter 49

King Daximus Ivals

Nia has a tell. If you tell her she can't have it, she will take it. And she will go above and beyond to prove you wrong. No matter what.

I wasn't asleep when I felt Nia getting out of the bed. I then heard her getting her clothes on. This time she wasn't getting away without saying goodbye.

"So you are running off again?" I said.

I startled her a little.

"I'm not running."

"What do you call it?"

"Well, we spent most of two days fucking each other's brains out, so I would call it over."

"Nia, I want to see you again."

"That can't happen."

"Then I guess we should get married."

She looked at me, frozen.

"If I marry you, I forfeit my crown."

"So? You would still be a queen."

"But not of my people."

"You could be a queen of my people."

"No, Dax. I want my people to see I can do this. So many people doubt me right now."

"I don't doubt you."

"So now you think I'm worthy of ruling?"

"Yes, of course."

"OK, what about you? Are you willing to lose your crown to marry me?"

"Nia, I can't do that. I made a promise to my father before he died that I won't let him down."

"Then you know why I can't marry you."

"This is funny: two people who know what they want but aren't willing to submit to it."

"Goodbye, Dax."

"Goodbye, Nia."

After she left, I just stared at the bedroom door from the bed. Thinking she was going to come right back through that door. I had a vise around my heart; its name was Nia. I closed my eyes and thought about her all over me again. The way it felt when her mouth was on my dick. I was so sprung.

I thought fucking this woman one more time would get her out of my system, but no, I wanted more. I wanted her heart. I wished I could lock her up and keep her all to myself.

I looked over to the nightstand and saw a jar. I picked it up and opened it. I smelled it, and it had a very bland odor. I remembered seeing Nia with this. I wondered what she needed this for. I knew it was too late to go after her, so I figured when I saw her again, I'd give it to her. And I would see her again.

I got back to Thetis and went looking for Finn.

"Finn, I need to talk to you for a minute."

"Yes, of course, Your Majesty."

I handed him Nia's jar; the one she forgot.

"What's this for?" I asked.

Finn opened it up and pulled it out.

"This, My Lord, is seagrass," he explained.

"What is it used for?"

"Well, it's used for up set stomach aches but mostly given to women who are with child."

"Say that again!"

"When women are pregnant, they have nausea problems; this helps with that."

"Are you trying to tell me that this is for a woman who is having a baby?"

"Given the amount, I would say most likely."

"Yes!"

"Your Grace?"

"Finn, this is the best news I have heard in a very long time."

"Well, I'm very happy I could help, My Lord."

"You have been great."

I gave Finn a big kiss on the cheek. He looked at me like I was possessed.

This was fantastic. Nia was pregnant with my baby. That meant she was mine all mine. I felt like I could fly I was so happy. This was better than planning it myself.

Cecil came up and welcomed me back; he then said that Neptune had arrived.

"Neptune, sorry to keep you waiting. I didn't know you would be here," I said.

"Well, I wanted to surprise you. So what's the big excitement?"

"Big excitement?"

"Well, I heard you in the next room shouting with joy."

"I'm just so glad to be home, and I found out that you where here. Yay!"

"Well good, 'cause I have a solution to your problem."

"My problem?"

"With the marriage thing the Pedestals are forcing you to do."

"Oh right. What is your solution?"

"You can marry my daughter Cora."

"But isn't she, like, fifteen?"

"Seventeen, to be exact."
"Yeah, but does she want to marry or me, for that matter?"
"Dax, she is smitten with you."
"She is?"
"Of course. She has had the hugest crush on you for years."
"OK. Then I guess that sounds like a plan."
"Great. Then I will bring her in here so that you can talk it over."
"Wait, she's here?"
"Of course."

Neptune called his daughter into the room. Cora was pretty in a superior kind of way. She seemed very sweet and innocent.

Neptune left the room so that we could get reacquainted with each other.

"Cora, are you sure you want to do this?" I asked.
"Yes, of course. Why wouldn't I?"
"Well, I just don't want you to waste you life on an arranged marriage."
"Dax, it is my duty to help my king."
"OK, well then you should know I'm only doing this so I don't lose my crown."
I know that, and I would be happy to help with that."
"Well, then I think I should be completely honest with you: my heart already belongs to another."
"I understand."
"You do?"
"Yes, of course I do. Plus, there is still a chance I can win over your heart."

I really didn't know what to say to that. I wanted Nia, that was all, and if I couldn't have her, then I felt there really was no point. Cora can't win something that I don't have anymore, I thought.

I knew Cora and Nia didn't care for one another. I heard it had something to do with a love triangle. Never did find out the whole story.

Chapter 50

Queen Niarea Runtassel

It has been months since I last saw Dax. With each passing day, my belly was growing bigger. I was definitely showing now. I was about eight months along.

I was lying naked on my bed looking at the mirror next to me, analyzing my pregnant belly. I was pressing down a little on my stomach. It was causing the baby to kick me in the other direction. When it did that, my whole belly shook. It made me laugh. Then when I put both hands on my belly, I could feel the baby shift and then pop its butt out. I think its the butt could be the head, I said to myself.

I was getting more excited about being a mom. But I couldn't help but wonder about Dax. I missed him so much that there wasn't a day that went by that I don't think about him. What he was doing. I thought, Is he ever thinking about me? I would love to marry him. I really would. But I'm not sure I can trust him. His ego would have to go. But it didn't matter 'cause my crown was all I could see in front of me at that point. I was also feeling more guilty about having his baby and him not knowing about it. And the fact that he wouldn't be there when his child was born. Or even know his child.

A couple years ago, I was in love, or at least I thought I was in love. I gave him my virginity. In the water language, virginity is called *virgo*.

And once it's given up, you must bathe in the ocean for two whole days so that the Goddess of Water can bless your womb.

But he ended up breaking my heart; I felt so ashamed. My first time was sweet but nothing like what Dax does to me. No matter how much time we spent apart, I could still feel Dax's touch under my skin.

I got a knock on my door, and my ladies-in-waiting all came in and got me dressed in a hurry. After I was dressed, my brother came in.

"Good morning, Naxos."

"Morning, Queen Nia."

I grabbed my brother's hand and put it on my belly.

"Do you feel it kicking?"

"Wow! This baby is ready to come out."

"I know. Sometimes I feel like it's running in there."

"Nia, I need you to sit down for a minute."

"Why? What's going on?"

"Nothing. I just need you to sit down for a minute."

"OK, I'm sitting. Now what?"

"Dax is getting married."

"Is he really?"

"Yes."

"Well, good."

"You're not mad?"

"Well, um…no, I'm not."

"Really?"

"Yes, really. I mean, we all knew this day was going to come."

I just really hoped he wouldn't go through with it.

"Nia, that's a great attitude for you to have."

"Nax, give me some credit."

"Well, just keep that positive attitude in mind 'cause you are going to need it for what I'm going to tell you next."

"What do you mean next?"

"Dax in marrying Cora."

"Cora? As in, our niece Cora?"

"Um, yes."

I sat up from the chair

"How did you find out about this?" I asked.

"The wedding invitation was sent to us."

My brother handed me the wedding invitation, and the more I read, the more upset I got.

I was ripping up the invitation; I couldn't read it anymore.

"I take it we aren't going?" Nax joked.

"Of all the women in the water realm, he has to marry Cora."

"Nia, calm down. Remember what Blue said, stress isn't good for the baby."

"That bastard couldn't give us a heads-up before he sent out the wedding invitations?"

"I have a feeling this is more Neptune's doing."

"What!"

"With Dax marrying Cora, Neptune gets liquid immunity in the Sea Realm."

"You know what, fine, I don't care about him; let him marry Cora. I'm sure they will live happily ever after."

"Well, guess now you do have a real reason to hate him."

I started screaming. My brother was trying to calm me down. Then I started crying. I just felt like my heart had been rip out and thrown to the sharks.

Why did Dax have to marry Cora? She told me when we were younger that she was going to marry Dax. Guess she got her wish, I thought.

The next day was my Yemaya, and I was not going to let anyone mess it up for me. No Dax. No Cora. This was my day.

A Yemaya is a ceremony for your unborn child. Armetha will shower my child with life.

The party started out great. Wonderful gifts, good food, great company. And pleasant music. My ladies-in-waiting and some of my closest friends were all having a great time. Even me. Until my brother, Captain Noah, and a few other soldiers burst into my party.

"Nax, what are you doing?" I said.

"Nia, I'm so sorry to disturb your shower, but you have to come with us."

I looked at Noah; he had the look of dread on his face.

"I'm sorry, Your Majesty, but it's very important," he said.

My brother led me into the strategic defense room, where my Pedestals and a couple other soldiers were leaning over a table looking at the map of the Ocean Realm.

When I entered the room, they all bowed there heads and it got really quiet. Everyone was staring at me, but no one was telling me anything.

"Well, someone tell me what's going on," I insisted.

"Nia, the Temple of Oleen has just been destroyed," said Nax.

"What! But how?"

Noah said, "Neptune, My Queen."

"But why would he? How could he?" I exclaimed.

Nax said, "Nia, all we know is that there was some argument about maps that Neptune was requiring."

"Are there any survivors?" I asked.

"Not that we know of," said Nax.

"I want a group of solders out there right now."

"We already have a dozen out there right now."

"I want Neptune found right now."

"Nia, we are on that too."

"My God, Nax, there were children in that temple."

"I know, Nia, and we are going to find him."

"I want a bounty on his head right now, dead or alive. I don't care about the cost."

"Nia, we will take care of it."

"Where was he spotted last?" I asked.

"He was passing Red Rock, My Queen," responded Noah.

"Nia, we are already on his trail," Nax added.

I started crying. Nax grabbed me and held me in his arms.

"What is he after, Nax? What does Neptune want?"

"I'm not sure, but we better find it before he does, or I have a feeling this is the beginning."

"This is all my fault."

"Nia, don't go there."

"I'm the queen of the Ocean Realm. My job is to protect everyone in my realm, and I failed."

"Nia, how were you supposed to know about this? This blame is not good for you or the baby."

"Take me to Oleen Temple. I want to see it for myself."

"Nia, that's not a good idea."

"Why not?"

"'Cause there is nothing for you to do. You are just going to get yourself worked up."

"I don't care. Take me there now."

Chapter 51

King Daximus Ivals

"Neptune!" I screamed.

"Dax, how nice of you to drop by," he responded.

"Have you lost your goddamned mind? Blowing up Oleen Temple?"

"I don't think I like your tone, Dax."

"I don't give a shit what you don't like."

"You said you had my back in getting rid of my sister."

"Yeah, you said to discredit her. You never said anything about killing innocent people."

"After I discredit her, then what?"

"What?"

"Did you think we were just going to be all merry and sunshine about this?"

"For fuck's sake, Tune, you are going to start a war."

"Good, that's what I want."

"I'm not going to war with Nodons, do you hear me?"

"And why not?"

"Because we don't have an army big enough to beat them."

"As soon as I find what I'm looking for, we will beat them."

"Enough! I don't want to hear it anymore. The Ocean Realm has a huge bounty on your head. Every pirate, bounty water hunter, and sea urchin is coming after you. So I suggest you stay real close to home."

"I'm not afraid of any bounty."

"Tune, you are forbidden to enter the Ocean Realm."

"Is that right?"

"Yes, 'cause now I have to go and clean up the mess you just made."

"I think you have forgotten who you are talking to, Dax."

"No, Tune, I think it's you who have forgotten who you are talking to."

"Oleen was an unfortunate accident."

"An accident? There are no survivors. That's not an accident; that's a massacre."

"Sometime casualties are inevitable."

"What the fuck is wrong with you?"

"Did you know that my sister is with child?"

"Yeah, so?"

"Well, don't you think it's odd that nobody seems to know who the father is?

"And why would I care who the father of her baby is?"

"I just think it's odd that nobody knows who he is."

"Do you feel any remorse for what you have done?"

"Should I?"

"Un-fucking-believable!"

"Lighten up, Dax"

"Stay away from the Ocean Realm—I'm warning you."

"You are warning me?"

"Yes, I am. I'm king, and you're done."

I had to get the fuck away from him. He was pissing me off even more. I thought he might suspect me of being the father of Nia's baby. I had to steer him off that theory. Neptune had been hiring spies and buying up all kinds of information on Nia's pregnancy. I had to be careful.

Being married to Cora had been good to keep the Pedestals off my back. But I missed Nia still. I was having withdrawals, and it was starting to get to me. If I don't have her in my arms soon, I thought, I might just say fuck it and go to her. I was glad she didn't come to the wedding.

Now I was going to have to figure out how I was going to smooth things over with Nodons. Neptune fucked the Sea Realm over badly.

I was sitting on my throne when Finn came in. He told me that the flooding of the sea walls was coming from Gwyneth, the northern sea. So without hesitation, we headed up that way.

The northern sea is ruled by me. No one goes up here because it's too cold. There are icebergs everywhere or at least there were.

The sea wall here is completely covered in water. You can't even see it. The water was flowing over the sea wall and up into the Winter Realm, which seemed impossible because the sea wall is fifty feet tall at least.

Finn said, "See, My Lord, the icebergs are melting at an alarming rate, causing the flooding to travel down the coast."

"What's causing the icebergs to melt?" I asked.

"I'm not sure, but according to this, the northern sea is getting warmer."

Finn dropped his temperature gauge back into the water, hoping to get an accurate answer. The rest of my crew walked on water over to the sea wall to try to stop the flooding.

I went back into my ship and was pulling some maps out to find where I could put all this excess water when Cecil barged in.

"Yes?" I said.

"Your Highness, Queen Niarea is here," he responded.

"Really!"

"Yes."

"Show her in, then."

"Yes, Your Grace."

I suspected this was going to happen.

I sat down and tried to remain calm. I hadn't seen her in a while. I thought, I know what she looks like, but whenever I lay eyes on her, I'm reminded again just how beautiful she really is.

She stood there in the doorway looking mad as ever. She walked right in and stopped at the end of the table. I asked myself, How can a woman who is already flawless become even more gorgeous? I'll tell you. It's because she is carrying my child; that makes her even more sublime.

There was no denying she was with child. My child, I thought, and I couldn't help but smile at her when I looked into her eyes. Even though she had nothing but anger in hers.

"Queen Nia, what a pleasant surprise. And in such fine condition, I see."

"Quit the bullshit, Dax. You know why I'm here."

"Straight to the point. How I do love that about you."

"I will make this very simple: give me my brother, now."

"You know I can't do that."

"Why not?"

"Tune has liquid immunity."

"Which you gave him and have the power to take away."

"You know if I do that, my marriage is voided and I forfeit my crown."

"So that's it, then?"

"No, Nia. I'm very sorry about Oleen."

"Oh, you're sorry?"

"Yes, and I will pay to have it rebuilt."

"Oh, how nice. Of course that doesn't make up for all the dead bodies that I had pulled out of the ocean. You know, Dax, some of them were children."

"He will be punished for his crime."

"Not good enough. You will give him to me."

"It's not that simple."

"So you are just going to protect a murderer?"

"Nia, I won't let him get off."

"I'm not asking you; I'm telling you to give me my brother."

"I won't do that."

"Fine. Then you leave me no choice. Give me my brother, or we go to war."

"You can't be serious."

"Oh, I'm very serious."

"So you are willing to kill thousands of people all for the sake of one man?"

"No. You are choosing to let thousands of people die 'cause you won't do the right thing."

"Nia, think this through. You have no idea what you're getting yourself into."

"I know what I'm doing. My people demand justice; I will get it."

"Nia, you are not up for a war. You have no idea what that entails."

"Don't tell me what I'm up for."

"Look, you are angry; I get it. But this is not good for you or our baby."

"Let's get one thing straight: this is my baby, and don't act like you give a damn."

"I do care!"

"Ouch!"

Nia grabbed her side and scrunched up her face in pain.

"What's wrong!"

"Nothing. He's kicking me again. He does that when I get really mad."

"So it's a boy?"

"Yes, it is."

"How do you know that?"

"Armetha told me so. She's been telling me something else, but I'm too mad to understand."

I got up and helped her into a chair. Then I kneeled down in front of her.

"May I?"

She looked at me with worry and then grabbed my hand and put it on her belly.

"Wow! He's very strong, my son."

"And stubborn like you as well."

"Well, I can't take most of the blame; his mother has a lot of stubbornness herself."

She shook her head and smiled at me.

Feeling my son and seeing her smile in this moment made me feel so complete. It was the greatest feeling ever. Knowing that my son was going to be the most important thing in Nia's life. That gave me chills.

"I want to be apart of this really bad, Ni."

"I know you do, and a part of me wishes you could."

Before I could say something back, Neptune burst in the room, breaking up the moment. Nia pushed my hand away, and the two of us stood up immediately.

"Am I interrupting something?" Neptune asked.

"What the fuck are you doing here?" I shot back.

"I heard my sister was in town, so I thought I'd say hi."

"Tune, I have a bounty on your head," Nia announced.

"Yes, I have heard all about it, but you will have to excuse me as I'm not afraid of it."

"You should be 'cause you will pay for what you have done," declared Nia.

"I want to know who the father of your child is."

"None of your damn business."

"That's not very queen-like, is it?"

"Father was right about you. You are a coward."

Neptune was getting ready to slap Nia, but I intervened.

"Tune, that's enough," I declared.

"Oh, Dax, did you tell Nia that we are working together to discredit her as queen?"

"Now is not the time, Tune," I said.

"Oh really, and how are you going to do that?" Nia asked.

I responded, "Nia, it's—"

She interrupted, "No, I want to know."

"Well, Dax was going to seduce you and humiliate you."

Nia looked at me like she was ready to stab me. Then she looked at Neptune.

"Why did you blow up Oleen, Tune? What are you looking for?" Nia asked.

"Armetha's tears," Neptune responded.

Nia and I looked at each other. Then back at Neptune.

"Tune, you cannot be this stupid," I said.

Nia added, "If you contaminate that water, everything in the water realm will dry up; we will all die."

Neptune explained, "That's Armetha's version. But there is another one in which a person with a strong soul and heart will inherit the power of Armetha's tears. With them, I will wipe out all the kingdoms."

Nia said, "Tune, that is not true; that's just a fairy tale from a make-believe story."

"We shall see," said Neptune.

"That's it. I'm arresting you now," Nia insisted.

"Nia, you can't do that," I said.

"Yes, I can."

"You are in the Sea Realm; you have no authority here."

"You are mistaken; it is the sea that needs the ocean, not the other way around."

Chapter 52

Queen Nia Runtassel

I was getting ready to have my brother arrested when a sharp pain came up my back. Then the pain grew stronger. I called out for Naxos.

After Naxos entered the room, I couldn't get the words out to have Neptune arrested as a gush of water was leaking down my legs.

My baby was coming.

I was screaming at the top of my lungs; the pain was unbearable.

I could hear Neptune laughing. Dax picked me up, and as he was carrying me out of the room, I heard Neptune say, "Another time, then."

"Hurry, we got to get to the ship," said Nax.

I felt like my body was ready to be split open. I could feel the pain everywhere now.

Dax carried me to my room and gently put me down on my bed.

Blue was already waiting for me there. He insisted on coming because of how far along I was.

"Nia, it's going to be OK," said Dax.

"Dax, the next time I see you, it's going to be on a battlefield."

"That's just the hormones talking," Nax commented.

"No! I'm serious."

"Shh, you're in labor," said Blue.

"Dax, you have to go; you can't be here," said Nax.

"I know. I'm just worried about her."

"Don't worry. I will take good care of her."

"I know, but I really want to see my son being born into the world."

"I want that too, but Neptune is watching."

"You're right. Just please make sure she is taken care of."

"Don't worry, I got it. I won't let anything happen to her or your son."

"Thank you, Nax."

"Aaahhhhh!" I shouted.

Nax walked Dax out of the room. My ladies-in-waiting came in with hot water and towels. Then they pulled up my dress. Blue spread my legs apart to see what was going on.

He said, "OK, Nia, you are completely dilated; you are going to have to start pushing."

"No, I'm not pushing until this ship starts moving."

Blue responded, "Nia, the baby is coming."

"Ahhhhh! I know that, but I'm not going to have this baby in the Sea Realm; it will be born in the Ocean Realm."

"For crying out loud!"

"This hurts so bad. I can't do it."

"You can do it. Just breathe."

Blue told one of my ladies-in-waiting to tell the crew to get this ship going now. I could feel the rotors on the boat going as it shook the whole ship.

"Ahhh! I'm never giving birth again," I exclaimed.

Blue said, "Nia, I need you to push now."

"No. Not until we get to the Ocean Realm."

"Listen to me, this baby is coming whether or not you push, and we are not going to make it in time."

"We will make it. Just tell them to step on it."

"If you do not push, you are going to hurt yourself and the baby, so push."

"Noooooooo!"

Then they shouted from above that the ocean boarder was in sight.

"Did you hear that?" Blue asked.

"Yes!"

"Good. Now push."

I pushed with all my might. The pain felt like it was never going away.

"Ahh!" I shouted.

Blue said, "Good, Nia. I can see the head; it's coming."

My ladies were wiping down my head with water. It was nice, but it wasn't helping the pain at all.

I could feel the baby shifting, trying to leave my body, and before I knew it, they screamed again from above saying that we were now in the Ocean Realm.

I gave it my all again and pushed as hard as I could.

I felt a huge tug of relief as little tiny screams flooded the room.

"Praise Armetha, it's a boy," said Blue.

He handed him to me in my arms. He had blue fuzzy hair and blue eyelashes.

"He is perfect," I said.

"Congratulations, Your Majesty," said Blue.

"Ouch!" I exclaimed.

I could feel something wasn't right inside me. One of my ladies grabbed my son as I was in more pain. Blue pulled my legs farther apart to find out what was going on.

He said, "Oh wow, there is another."

"What? Another!" I shouted.

"Push, Your Majesty; you must push again."

I did as he said, and this one only took one big push. And then it went silent. I could feel no more pain so the baby was clearly out.

"Is everything OK?" I asked.

Blue responded, "Everything is fine, Your Grace. It's a girl."

Blue handed me the second baby; she wasn't screaming, but her eyes were wide open and she was looking right at me.

"So you are what Armetha was trying to tell me about," I said.

She started cooing at me like she knew I was her mother.

They brought over my son. I held both of them in my arms.

"I'll bring your brother in," said Blue.

"Thanks, Blue."

"You're welcome, Your Grace."

"No, Blue, I really mean it—thank you for everything."

Blue smiled at me and left the room.

When Nax came in, he couldn't believe it.

"Wow! Twins," he exclaimed.

"I know, right?"

My brother kissed them on their heads, and then he looked at me.

"So what are you going to name them?" he asked.

"I'm going to name him Apollo after the great whale and her Athena after the Druid ocean."

"I like both of those."

"Nax, I need you to write Dax a note."

"Of course, that you had twins."

"No, that I lost the baby at birth."

"What! Why?"

"Because he is working with Neptune to destroy me."

"Are you sure?"

"Trust me on this; he's the enemy."

"I don't know, Nia. I don't like this."

"Listen, we have to protect them."

"I know, but this has a way of coming back and biting us in the ass."

"I don't care. We will tell everyone that I lost the baby and only tell our Pedestals the truth."

"Nia, when you keep secrets like this, it's bad for everyone."

"Please, we must protect them."

"If Dax is working with Neptune, then how is it that Neptune still doesn't know who the father of your baby is?"

"For all I know, he does."

"Are you really doing this to protect them, or are you trying to hurt Dax for marrying Cora?"

"Maybe it's both."

"I don't like this ."
"I don't care. I'm doing what's right."
My brother looked at me with sadness.
"I got played again, Nax."
"Nia, Dax is not Octavius."
"It doesn't matter. He was using me just like Octavius did. I'm the fool once again."

*Because there's nothing more beautiful
than the way the ocean refuses to stop
kissing the shoreline, no matter how
many times its sent away.*

—Sarah Kay

Part VI

The Light Realm

Introduction

The Light Realm is in the sky. Beyond the clouds, there are two kingdoms. Dritan, the kingdom of illumination. And the second one is Elior, the kingdom of luminosity. The people that live in the Light Realm are called Lumentals.

Lumentals have gold-blond hair. White wings. Honey-brown eyes and golden skin. Their skin is very shiny.

Lumentals can't get sick or hurt. They age very slowly and have eternal youth, and they don't die—they are reborn with the knowledge of their past life. That is their everlasting immortality. This is called Hebe. Hebe allows a Lumental to go back to the age of puberty, and for Lumentals, puberty starts at age fourteen.

Three eons is only one year in Lumental time.

When two Lumentals are bound together in love, they will join, and when this happens, an aura of light will shine so bright between the two of them that a baby will form. This light will carry the child until it is ready to be born. That is how Lumentals reproduce.

When Lumentals are expecting, the light that the child is being developed in will only show around the woman's head like a halo. They call this Nimbus.

The Lumentals are always kind and never mean or rude. No one knows how to be evil as everybody is loved equally, and they are forbidden to cause harm to each other. Lumentals' feelings are always happy feelings. This causes their emotions to be positive about everything.

The Lumentals have the power to grant miracles. To make the impossible happen. They have this power as long as they stay pure and untainted.

The Dritan and Elior kingdoms are not divided but one.

Dritan creates the light, while Elior reflects the light to shine bright through the sky and the stars. Neither one can live without the other.

The king of Dritan is Odin Seraphim. The King of Elior is Metatron Aster. The two of them hope to join their families together in holy matrimony.

A Lumental girl can only become a woman when they graduate Juno. This is a test to prove if they have what it takes to be divine in womanhood. When this happens, their sole duty is to serve their partner and the God of Light with an infinity of everlasting love.

It is the same with Lumental boys; they have a graduation to become men. This is called Lito. It's a jousting tournament that proves a man's strength and courage. This will prove his divinity in manhood. To swear allegiance to their consort and the God of Light.

Everyone passes graduation; there are no losers here.

Lumentals worship Orifiel the God of Light. Their religion is called Uriel.

Orifiel symbolizes virtue, integrity.

The problem with the Light Realm is that there is no problem.

Chapter 53

Princess Odessa Seraphim

I looked down on the land realms and wondered what it would be like to worry like they did. I wanted to go on a journey away from my home so bad. Maybe even have an adventure with some excitement.

My mother tells me that there is nothing there and that I'm not missing anything. But how would she know? She has never left her home.

I sat on some clouds hoping that one would break and I would fall into the land realms and then the fun would begin. But unfortunately that was as close as I would get to the land of excitement.

I looked at my pet owl Una. How I envy her, I thought. She can go anywhere she wants, the Nature Realm, the Water Realm, and never have any problems. Why couldn't the God of Light have turned me into an owl?

Then I heard the grand clock ding from above. Just great, I missed class again. My mother was going to care that I missed class but she would not be concerned.

Una and I flew home as fast as we could, but it was no good. My mother Odette was there waiting for me along with all her chambermaids.

She looked strange, like she was angry. I think that's what being upset looks like, I thought.

"All right, out with it," she said.

"I'm really sorry, I responded.

"Why didn't you go to class again?"

"Because, Mom, it's so boring. Sit up straight, don't talk unless you are spoken to, sit still."

"Odessa, that is what Lumental women do. It's like a painting—we are to remain beautiful forever while being on display."

"But I don't want to be a painting when it's so dull."

"Well, I'm sorry, my dear, that is our lot in life; it's not much, but it's what we do."

"Then I want a redo."

"Oh, nonsense. Now get cleaned up and come downstairs. We have guests."

"Do I have to?"

"Yes, and no missing class. Is that understood?"

"Yes, ma'am."

"Thank you."

That was sort of weird. Was that an argument? I didn't have time to think about that right then.

My brother's future in-laws were here. King Metatron was marrying his daughter Alina to my brother. And my father wanted me to marry King Metatron's son Magnus. My father's plan was that my brother and his new wife would rule Dritan, while my future husband and I would rule Elior. But nothing was set in stone, not like my brother's marriage, which was definitely going to happen.

When I get downstairs, I noticed that all the women were wearing the same-color dress. How unoriginal.

My brother came up and gave me a hug. I love my brother; he is my best friend. He is the only thing that makes this place tolerable.

"I heard you missed class today," he commented.

"That I did."

"Watching the land dwellers, were we?"

"Can't help it."

"I love that you are an oddball."

"That's me!"

My mother saw me and immediately came toward me.

"Mom, will you please stop touching my feathers."

"I'm just making sure you're not molting," she said.

"I'm not; now leave my wings alone."

"Mother, she looks fine," added Oren.

"I just want to make sure she makes a good impression," my mother said.

"How can she not when you're here?" responded Oren.

"Odessa, there is Prince Magnus. You should invite him over," my mother said.

"Why?" I asked.

"Because it's time you two got to know each other."

"I already know who he is."

My mother gave me that look that said, "You better get over there." So I reluctantly walked toward him. On my way to Prince Magnus, I overheard my father having a conversation with King Metatron about the land Realms.

Metatron said, "What do you think about those land realms?"

My father Odin replied, "I hear three of them are on the verge of extinction."

"That's right. And the other three are facing deplorable conditions."

"Good riddance, I say."

"I say the same thing."

"After all, our race and culture are the only true way to obtain life."

"That's why we have no problems."

"Father, did it ever occur to you that maybe we should help them?" I interjected.

"Don't be absurd, daughter."

"No, Father, I'm serious. We have theses gifts to make the impossible happen, and yet we do nothing."

"King Metatron, I apologize for my daughter's outspokenness," my father said.

"That's OK, King Odin. Women's views on politics always seem to amuse me."

They both laughed at me and then continued talking as if I were not there.

I looked at my brother, who was shaking his head at me and mouthing the word "no," but I couldn't let it go. I knew I should have.

"Father, all I'm saying is what good are these gifts we have if we never use them?"

"Odessa, that is enough. Apologize to King Metatron for interrupting our conversation."

"Sorry, King Metatron."

"That's all right, princess, but you should really know your place."

"Yes, sir."

My father added, "Yes, a princess should definitely know her place."

My father looked at me with anger and resentment. I could tell my brother was disappointed in me too. I walked away from them. The feeling of shame overcame my mind. Whats wrong with me? Why am I so defiant? I asked myself.

I was in no mood to talk to Prince Magnus now and was definitely not in the mood for the party. But I did as my mother said. After all, a princess must know her place.

I find Prince Magnus uninteresting and very humorless. I think he is physically incapable of making a smile. He likes to talk about how he will make a good king when his father hands him the throne.

And as for me, I was trying not to look so bored.

Chapter 54

Princess Odessa Seraphim

As night fell, I waited in my room till everyone was asleep. Even though we don't need sleep, it is very relaxing to us. Then I headed down to the stable, quietly of course. With Una as my lookout. I do this ever night. Well, I try to do it every night.

When I got to the stables, I couldn't help but get excited to see my horse Twyla. She has wings. Every animal here in the Light Realm has wings. Twyla is brownish yellow, and her mane is white.

I was not supposed to be riding her. My mother says it's very unladylike to ride a horse.

I got on top of her and let her take me for a spin. I feel so alive when I'm riding her. I love to go fast 'cause the thrill of the excitement makes my heart do flips in my chest.

She does this trick I love. She takes me as high as she possibly can take me, then on the way down, she falls backward, making me fall off her; it looks like I'm falling. The thrill is not knowing what's going to happen on my way down. Then when I think I'm about to fall past the clouds, I let my wings catch me and I float back up again. Sometimes I wish I could not spread my wings and just let myself continue to fall and see where I end up.

My father says that the land dwellers must never see us because if they did, they would try to catch us and use us like their own private genies, casting wishes. He says land dwellers are all greedy and selfish and we must stay away from them. But I think, They can't all be like that, can they?

And if they are, shouldn't we help them to see that being selfish is not a kind way or right?

I do know that the Dark Realm is full of evil monsters and demons. I also know that the only way to get there is through the Hollow Land, which is in the middle of the land realms. The Dark Realm, like my realm, is something the land dwellers can't see or shouldn't see.

If we were going to help the land dwellers, the first thing I would do is start with the Dark Realm. It's because of that place the land dwellers are the way they are. I would eradicate all evilness in this world. I'm not afraid of it either. I have heard all the evil stories of the Dark Realm, and they don't frighten me at all.

Chapter 55

Princess Odessa Seraphim

I was still stewing about what my father and King Metatron had said earlier. That I should know my place. How can I know it when I feel so out of place? I asked myself.

After I put Twyla back in her stall, Una started making noises letting me know that someone was coming. So we both hid in Twyla's stall.

I heard two voices. It was my dad and Abner. Abner is a Sanctus. Sanctus are pure and virtuous men that only speak the word of Orifiel the God of Light.

"I thought you said that it was getting better," said my father.

"And for a moment, it was, but now it seems that the light is getting dimmer," Abner explained.

"What can we expect if the light goes completely out?"

Well, emotions, for starters, that we have never experienced before."

"Like what?"

"Confusion, a state of feeling lost and disoriented."

"That doesn't sound too bad."

"That's because you have never experienced it; no one has."

"Well, a little confusion is not something I feel is a threat."

"It's not just confusion. It can make a strong man feel weak and kindhearted people, which is what we are, become cruel and evil."

"Then you must find a way to fix the light; don't let it go out."

"Yes, Your Majesty, but I can't promise you anything."

After they left, I stood up from the stall. What light could they be talking about? Surely they couldn't be referring to the Heart of Orifiel. That light can't go out. It would be physically impossible. The Heart of Orifiel is a light that you can see in the Temple of Qiell. This light is so pure that you can feel its rectitude.

With this light, my people will never know heartache or pain. But yet I feel so unhappy here, and I'm not supposed to. I do believe I'm the only one that feels this way.

The Heart of Orifiel is the God of Light's heart encrusted in a white gemstone. When it shines so bright, you can't look directly at it. It is the reason all life is balanced.

Chapter 56

Princess Odessa Seraphim

Today I actually made it to grammar school, but I wasn't paying attention. What my father and Abner were talking about was all I could think about. What light, and what could possibly make something like that go out since everything is so perfect here? I asked myself.

Mrs. Hyper was writing something on the board.

She said, "All right, class, when does a lady raise her voice?"

Everyone was raising their hand but me. But of course she picked Caroline Right. She is such a teacher's pet.

Caroline said, "Never."

"Very good," Mrs. Hyper responded.

I was staring off into space when Mrs. Hyper called my name. Kinda woke me up to reality.

"I'm sorry, what was the question?" I asked.

"What are young ladies such as yourself meant to do in this life?"

I know this answer but I find it so stupid, I thought.

Caroline interjected, "I know, Mrs. Hyper. They are supposed to be graceful and elegant till the day they get reborn."

"Very good, Caroline."

"But don't you find that so boring?" I asked.

Everyone in the class looked at me like I had horns growing out of my head.

Mrs. Hyper responded, "Well, Odessa, maybe you should start behaving more like a lady and see how it is very hard work."

"Yes, ma'am," I said.

This all-girl school thing is not for me. I think if I could attend the all-boys school next door, I would have much more fun. They get to learn about fencing and protecting their people. Charging into battle when needed. And they get to learn about Lito. This is an entertainment tournament, not just a graduation, in which two strong boys or men from the Drite army joust on lions with wings.

My bother is the undefeated champ when it comes to Lito. But it doesn't really matter since everyone is a winner. I watch him from the crowd with my family, and I want so badly to participate in the game. But of course only boys are allowed to play that game. The Lumental men are meant to learn how to be strong, virile, independent protectors; that is what they are meant to do in life till the day they are reborn, and then they get to do it all over again. And of course fall in love and get married. Make babies.

Not me. I want so much more than that. I think I'm destined for much more. I feel like I should be somewhere else. I'm not sure where, just somewhere else.

The bell rang for break. But I didn't go back to class; instead, I watched the land dwellers again. The Water Realm is my favorite. Watching the mermaids swim. They look so free from up here. I wonder what it's like to swim. I'm sure it feels great.

Chapter 57

Princess Odessa Seraphim

I feel stuck sometimes, like I know I can fly but I can't go anywhere. I was sneaking back into the castle when my brother caught me.

"Getting in kind of late, aren't we?" he commented.

"I lost track of time again."

"You need to wear a watch."

"How much trouble am I in?"

"Mom sent almost the entire army after you."

"Of course she did."

"Don't worry, she will calm down; she always does."

"Oren, when is the last time you went to Qiell?"

"Not in a while. Why?"

"'Cause I overheard father talking to Abner about a light going out."

"You were eavesdropping?"

"Not exactly."

"OK. Well, what not exactly did you hear?"

"Father was talking about a light going out, and Abner was saying that this light is very important. That if it goes out, we could be in danger."

"And you think it's the Heart of Orifiel."

"Yes!"

"Oh that's impossible; that light can never go out."
"Well, I'm thinking about going to Qiell to find out."
"You can't. Father has it closed down right now."
"What? Why?"
"He says they're remodeling the building."
"What for?"
"Well, he says that they are making it bigger for more people to attend services at the temple."
"That doesn't make any sense."
"The light is fine. If it were going out, we would know 'cause something dramatic would happen."
"Maybe something dramatic has happened but we can't see it."
"Nothing has happened; you are letting your imagination run wild."
"Still, I think we should take a look at it."
"O you are worrying about nothing. Besides, shouldn't you be getting ready for Juno?"
"That's today!"
"Why do you think Mom has the entire army looking after you?"
"Just great!"

I flew into my room and without hesitation put my dress on. The one my mother picked out for me. She had it laid out on my bed.

Of all the days to be late, this shouldn't be one of them, I thought.

I brushed my hair till it looked presentable. I don't like dresses, and they don't like me. For some reason, I always feel so vulnerable in them. And I always trip in them; it's inevitable.

I snuck down the main hall; all the girls from my class were standing neatly in a line wearing their best dresses and looking amazing.

I crept into the line like I had been there this whole time. Phew, I said to myself, that was a close one. No one noticed I had just come into the line.

All the guards were looking frantic. Probably wondering where I was. Then my mother walked into the hall and locked eyes with me. Immediately I could tell she was not her usual self.

Chapter 58

Princess Odessa Seraphim

"Where have you been?" she asked.
"I'm sorry, Mother. I lost track of time."
"To be late on Juno, of all days."
"I know, Mom, and I'm sorry."
"Odessa, do you know how important it is for me and your father that you are worthy of marriage?"
"I promise I won't let you down."
"Be sure that you don't."
"Why isn't Juno being held in Qiell?"
"It's under construction. Now remember to be efficient and poise. And above all—"
I interrupted, "Mother, I know. Flawless and elegant; that is the Lumental women's endeavor."
"Good. Then you are ready."
My mother took one last look at me and fixed any imperfections she saw. This day is supposed to be exciting, but I don't feel it, I thought. I do want so badly for my parents to be proud of me. And I'm going to try really hard not to let them down.
Most of my family made up the judges. It was my mother and my aunt, also my grandmother and Mrs. Hyper. My Aunt Mira, who is my

mother's sister, was expecting. The halo around her head was extremely bright, meaning her child was due very soon. They say expecting mothers are extremely generous. So I should have this in the bag, I said to myself.

They called my name first to be judged. I knew they were going to do that. I am the princess.

In Juno the first test is seeing how long your hair is. The longer it is, the higher the score. Long hair is considered perfection in my world.

Mrs. Hyper took out her measuring stick. She put it up to the base of my head and then said, "Forty-two inches long." The judges wrote it down.

The next topic was the color of your hair. It had to shine like the sun. Then it was your figure. I have never cared about my looks. What is the point, when everyone here looks the same?

I was holding my arms up while Mrs. Hyper was measuring my bust when I noticed she had bloody tears coming from her eyes.

"Mrs. Hyper, are you OK?" I asked.

"Of course I'm OK."

"Well, there are tears coming down your cheeks."

Mrs. Hyper touched her face, and then she looked at how bloody her hands were. Then all of a sudden, she grabbed her chest.

She got down on her knees and started screaming out in pain; I had never heard anything like it before. Everyone rushed to her aid to find out what was going on. Then she floated off the floor with her wings spread out.

Then her chest burst open and blood went everywhere. Even all over me. Everyone was shocked. My grandmother was screaming. I grabbed my aunt Mira before she fainted.

Mrs. Hyper drop to the floor, dead, I thought.

Chapter 59

Princess Odessa Seraphim

I had never seen blood before. Or death. I had only read about it in books. I was in my room washing off the blood. Watching it flow down my body. This blood belonged to my teacher, who had just been standing before me alive and well.

I got dressed and heard a knock on the door. I answered it.

"Are you OK?" It was my brother.

"I think so."

"Father just filled me in on what happened."

"And what does he plan on doing to fix it?"

"There is nothing to do. Mrs. Hyper just fell, but she is fine."

"Oren, she didn't fall; she died."

"Dessa, Lumentals don't die; they are reborn."

"Oren, I know what I saw. Her chest was being ripped open from the inside out. I think she was even experiencing pain."

"But that can't be. We don't feel pain unless we are tainted."

"Then maybe Mrs. Hyper was tainted."

"How, when there is nothing here to corrupt us?"

"I'm telling you, there is something else going on here."

"There is nothing going on here."

"Yes, there is, and I know where to start."

"Where?"
"Qiell—to see the Heart of Orifiel."
"You can't go there; it's sealed off."
"Oren, you can either help me or get out of my way."
My brother let out a big sigh.
"You aren't going to let this go, are you?" he asked.
"No."
"OK, let's go."

Chapter 60

Princess Odessa Seraphim

My brother and I got to Qiell, and it was sealed up really tight. The weird thing was that the temple looked so depressing.

"There are guards at every entrance; we won't get in," my brother said.

"Oren, you are the captain of the army. Just tell them you want to get in."

"OK."

When my brother and I entered the temple, there was no construction, but instead all the windows were covered. In the middle of the temple was Orifiel's Heart. But it wasn't shining bright. The light was dim, just like Abner had said, and it was turning into a gray color.

"See, I told you something is going on," I said.

My brother's face looked horrible, just like how I felt when I saw Mrs. Hyper dying.

"I'm going to talk to Father right now," Oren said.

"Good. I'm going with you."

"No. I'm going to talk to him alone."

"But!"

"Odessa, don't forget Lito is tomorrow and King Magnus is playing for your hand."

"There is no guarantee he is going to choose me."

"Yes, there is."

"I don't even know if I passed Juno."

"Trust me, if you didn't, Mom would be devastated."

"Oren, I'm feeling scared and worried."

"I know; I'm feeling that too."

"So how are we going to fix this?"

"Don't worry about it. I'm taking care of it."

These feelings were all new to us. I could feel my world shifting, and not knowing how to fix it was causing fear. Was the fate of my people going to follow the way Mrs. Hyper ended up? I asked myself. That horrible scream she made and the way her face looked like she was suffering. I could not bear it.

I lay up in my room, looking down out my window. Una was looking right at me. Like she could also feel a change in me. It was getting stronger, this emotion of doubt. Something we Lumentals had never experience. It was making me feel so uncomfortable.

My grandmother Dawn came into my room. She calls me Lumina, which means brilliant light in the light language.

"Lumina, I wanted to see how you are doing," she said.

"I'm fine, Nana."

"That was a terrible thing for you to witness."

"Nana, Mrs. Hyper, she did die, didn't she?"

"Of course not. She's fine and very much alive."

"How do you know that? Have you seen her?"

"Well, no, but your father assures us that she is fine."

"What if he's lying?"

"Lumentals can't lie, so how could he?"

"To cover up what's really going on."

"And what is really going on here?"

"I don't know. I just know that something is very wrong."

"Lumina, I, too, feel a change in our feelings and the way we think and behave."

"So then you know we should do something about it."

"How can we when we don't even know what's wrong and panicking isn't going to help us?"

"Then what should we do?"

"Stay calm and try to remember that your family loves you and is there for you."

"Nana, do you think we will be OK?"

"Well, of course I do. I mean, I'm feeling the depression, but I just pray to the God of Light and he lifts me up again."

My grandmother hugged me, and that made me feel a lot better. But I knew that this was only the beginning. In order for this to get better, it was going to have to get worse.

Chapter 61

Princess Odessa Seraphim

It was Lito day. Prince Magnus was jousting for the right to choose his bride. Everyone was getting ready for the celebration. He was going up against Vega, who is second-in-command of my fathers army. And is in love with my cousin Zita. So I knew who Vega would choose for his bride.

I was coming down the stairs when I overheard my father and brother arguing. They never argue or shout, for that matter. It was a very heated argument. I could tell because my father's and brother's faces were bright red. Lumentals don't get mad, and seeing it for the first time made me want to cry—another emotion I had never experienced. I couldn't make out what they were saying since they were shouting so loud. Then my father stormed off. I went up to my brother.

"Are you OK?" I asked.

"I'm fine."

My brother was getting ready to walk away from me when I grabbed his hand.

"Wait, what was that about?"

"Nothing, Dessa, just stay out of it."

"How can I when you guys looked like you were going to tear each other apart?"

"Isn't there somewhere you should be, like in the crowd cheering on your future husband?"

"I don't want to get married, and I'm not going to."

"Oh, yes you are. That's what you are supposed to do."

"Not me!"

"Look, you are feeling like this because the Heart of Orifiel isn't shining bright; that's why you have mixed feelings."

Was that why I didn't want to marry Prince Magnus? Was the whole reason why I felt like I didn't belong the fact that the light was going out?

Then Beacon came running up to us, out of breath. Beacon is a soldier, like Vega, in the Dritan Army.

"Beacon, what's wrong with you?" Oren asked.

"Your Majesty, it's Vega; he's not feeling very good."

"What's wrong with him?" my brother said.

"I'm not sure, but he's saying things uncontrollably."

"Is he grabbing his chest?" I asked.

"Yeah. How did you know about that?"

My brother and I looked at each other. And we all three hurried down to the armory room.

When we got there, Vega was on the floor. Everyone was huddled over him. He was crying blood from his eyes. My brother went to his side and grabbed his hand. Vega squeezed it hard. My brother squeezed it back even harder since we don't feel pain.

"Vega, tell me what's wrong," my brother said.

"It's too much and not enough."

"What are you talking about?"

"Oren, this is it, the end."

"Vega, tell me, are you in pain?"

"There is no pain in life."

"Quick, someone send for the light healers!" my brother shouted.

"What's Abner going to do?" I asked.

"I don't know—help him."

"Oren, light healers help improve light; they are not doctors."

"I'm aware of that. Plus, there is no such thing as doctors. Why would there be?"

"Wait, Oren, look."

Vega was now spitting up blood. My brother and I took his armor off to make him feel more comfortable. But it didn't help. He then floated off the ground, his wings sprawled out. This was just like what Mrs. Hyper went through. I knew what was going to happen next. I grabbed my brother and the rest of the guards and pulled them back. Then Vega shouted out, "Quae finitur." Then his chest burst open and blood went everywhere. He dropped to the ground.

The guards were all shaking and standing still. They were so scared. They didn't like feeling like this. It caused some of them to fall to their knees and pray to the God of Light.

I went over to check and see if Vega was still alive. His eyes were white, and his body looked limp. I touched his arm. It was cold. I examined the big hole in his chest.

"His heart is gone!" I shouted.

My brother came over to me to see for himself.

"Where could it have gone?" he asked.

"It looks like something or someone took it."

"No, it just exploded when it burst. I can't believe I just said that. What is going on?"

"I told you, it happened just like it did to Mrs. Hyper."

"We don't die!"

"Then how do you explain this?"

"I'm not sure, but he's not dead."

"Well, he's not alive."

"Is he really dead?" Beacon interjected.

"Of course not; he's just resting," said Oren.

I just looked at my brother and shook my head. I thought, He's in such denial.

Beacon said, "I'm not sure how to feel about this. I want to feel upset, and yet all I feel is boredom."

"I feel the same thing, like I don't care that a good friend of mine has just died," responded Oren.

"So then you agree he is dead?" I asked.

"No, I don't agree, and I don't believe it."

"Oren, how much proof do you need?"

"It isn't happening."

Beacon added, "Oh no, what about Lito. Vega is supposed to be in the game in less than half an hour."

"Someone will just have to take his place," Oren responded.

"What about Vega?" I asked.

"There is nothing we can do about that now. We will hide this till Lito is over and then figure it out," said Oren.

"And who will take his place?" I asked again.

"Beacon can do It," Oren suggested.

Beacon said, "I'm sorry, Your Majesty, but I haven't finished training yet."

"OK, Faro, you take Vega's place," Oren said.

Faro responded, "I haven't finished either, My Lord."

"OK, has anyone finished their training?" Oren asked.

"I raised my hand."

"Oh no, you can't participate," Oren said.

"Why not? I passed Juno, which means I'm eligible."

"The rules state that no girl can play the game."

"What about a woman?"

"Especially not a woman. Plus, our parents will be very upset."

I started picking up Vega's armor to see what size it was.

"Then do you have another plan?" I asked.

"Elijah, surely you have finished all your training," my brother said.

Elijah responded, "Actually, I still have another month of training to go."

"I don't believe this," said Oren.

"That seems to be going around," I added.

"Oh well, even if you haven't completely finished your training, one of you will have to go out there," Oren said.

Beacon said, "No offense, My Lord, but if we do that, we could lose our eligibility to become a man and never get marred."

"I won't let that happen. The king will understand," Oren assured him.

"Will he, though? I wouldn't count on it, with the way things are going," I chimed in.

"Odessa, you can't go out there."

"Why not? I know how to joust; you have been teaching me since I was eight."

"Practicing and the real thing are totally different."

"You said it before—I'm better at jousting than half the Drite army."

"Yes, but—"

"And I'm better at fencing than you."

"But you are a woman. Plus, you're going to get into trouble not just with Father but with Prince Magnus as well."

"I will be fine, and no one will know that I'm a woman with the armor on."

"You are also breaking the rules of Lito."

"What are they going to do to me? Send me to my room?"

I got done putting on my own armor 'cause Vega's wasn't going to fit. I came out, and my brother was not happy.

"You take that armor off right now, before Mom sees you," he said.

"I thought we went over this; there is no other way."

"Just give me a minute."

"We don't have time."

Beacon handed me my helmet.

He said, "She does look good in the armor."

Beacon started laughing, and we both looked at him confused.

He continued, "I'm sorry, I don't know why I did that. For some reason, I have no control over my emotions."

"Maybe you should let me go," Oren said.

"No, they know how you joust. They will figure out it's you in a heartbeat and stop the game," I responded

"OK, but let him win. Just fake it; that way we won't get into trouble."

"I got this. Don't worry."

I climbed on Vega's winged lion Hiero. He didn't seem to mind that I wasn't his owner. Prince Magnus is strong, and his winged lion is ferocious. He's a worthy opponent and very good at jousting, but he's not unbeatable and I'm not just going to let him win. He also has a weakness. When he jousts, he pulls to the left too much, making his right vulnerable. If he's going to win my hand, then I should have something to say about it. And I say my hand is not for sale, I told myself.

Chapter 62

Princess Odessa Seraphim

It all happened so fast. I was having so much fun, I didn't realize why I was there in the first place. I shouldn't have taken my helmet off after it was done.

My brother and I were outside the throne room waiting for my father to call us in. He would most likely be concerned.

"You were supposed to let him win," said Oren.

"Well, I didn't want to make it too easy for him," I responded.

"And why did you take your helmet off afterward?"

"I'm sorry, I just got so caught up with the crowd cheering me on."

"You were supposed to let him win and then leave like nothing happened."

"I'm sorry, but at least it was quite a show."

"This isn't funny."

"I know it isn't. Did you tell Father about Vega?"

"Yes!"

"And what did he say?"

My brother looked at me with worry in his eyes.

"That he has already taken care of it," said Oren.

"His idea of taking care of it is sweeping it under the rug," I said.

"What happened to Vega is still unsolved; we need answers before we can tell people."

"And how do you suppose we get those answers?"

"I'm not sure, but what happened is awful, just unspeakable."

"That's how I felt when I saw Mrs. Hyper die."

"But why can't I feel sad about it?" Oren asked.

"I don't know; I feel the same way."

"I have never wanted to stay alive more than I do right now."

"Oren, I will not let you die."

"I'm sorry, I didn't believe you before."

"Hey, I don't blame you. Death is not something that happens to us."

"Just promise me that whatever happens to us, you never stop fighting."

"As if you could stop me."

My brother hugged me tight. The door opened, and my father was ready to see us. Time to face the music, I thought.

"How dare you. What were you thinking?" my father said.

"Father, it's my fault. I—" Oren began.

"Oren, I will get to you later."

"But, Father, if—" I said.

"No, you have brought shame to this entire kingdom," my father said.

"Not to mention embarrassed Prince Magnus and his family," added my mother.

"You will write a formal apology and pray to the God of Light that he takes you as his wife," my father said.

"I don't want him to take me as his bride," I said.

"Why would you say something like that?" my mother asked.

"Because it's true; I don't want to get married."

"Odessa, how can you have such a disregard for our beliefs?" asked my father.

"I just don't think the God of Light wants me to get married."

"How can you question him?" my father said.

"How can you not with the way things are going?"

"Odessa, you should be grateful for all you have," offered my mother.

"I'm grateful, Mother. I just feel like there is something else I should be doing."

"There is—writing an apology to your future husband. And no more of this blind foolishness," my father said.

"What about your blind foolishness, Father?"

"Don't talk back to me, young lady. I'm your father."

"How can you have such disregard for our people dying?"

"Enough! You will go to your room, and I will never hear you say that word again."

"But, Father—"

"Is that clear!" shouted my father.

There was no point in arguing with my father. So I just ran to my room. He has changed. Seeing my father raise his voice made me doubt our survival. He also used to listen to me. I could see in his eyes that he was slipping. Where is the God of light? I asked myself. Why won't he help us now, when we need him so much?

It's said in the Book of Light that the God of Light will love you no matter what, so be true to your heart and he will be true to you. My truth is that I'm not a bride. I felt different even when I was a little girl. I never found pleasure in being pretty. Instead, I want to make a difference.

My mom came into my room. She was trying to comfort me, but it didn't matter. Because the truth was clear: I did not belong here.

"I'm sorry for the way your father talked to you," she said.

"It doesn't matter."

"Yes, it does."

"Mother, I'm fine. You don't have to check on me."

"Odessa, don't you know why it's important to get married?"

"You said to look pretty."

"No, looking pretty is like our hobby, but getting married is for true love."

"Mother, I don't want to fall in love."

"Falling in love is the most incredible experience ever. It unites you to the God of Light."

"That's great, but it's not for me. I will never fall in love."

"Don't be so sure."

"Mother, I feel nothing when I look at Prince Magnus."

"Maybe you should look a little harder."

"I don't want to look anymore; I want to fly."

"You will see that love will make you fly so high you won't be able to come down."

Chapter 63

Princess Odessa Seraphim

What my mother said didn't change how I felt. I had to leave this place and go where I could do something other than look pretty. No more wishing about it. I just needed to do it.

I petted Una. I think she knew I was leaving 'cause she looked sad. I told her that it was going to be OK. That I would never forget her and she needed to keep my brother safe while I was gone.

I was starting to pack when I heard screaming down the hall. I rushed out to see what was the matter. I came across Zita, who was screaming her head off as she was witnessing Beacon floating in the air just like Vega and Mrs. Hyper. But this was different. I saw a shadow figure from behind him. Whatever this was, it wasn't from our realm. It placed its hand inside Beacon's chest and ripped its heart out. Then it looked at me, confused. I think it was terrified that I could see it. From what I could make out, the shadowy figure was a skeletal, solemn man cloaked in black.

It took off in a dash with Beacon's heart. I knew I had to go after it. I had to stop it and get Beacon's heart back.

"Zita, I need you to pull yourself together," I said.

"That was the most horrific thing I have ever seen," she responded.

"I know it was bad, but—"

"Odessa, what is going on?"

I wasn't sure what to tell her, especially since no one knew what was going on.

"Zita, listen to me. You have to go and find my brother and father, tell them what happened."

"Wait a minute. Is this what happened to Vega?"

"Zita, please go tell my father now."

"What are you going to do?"

"I'm going after it."

"After what!"

I didn't have time to explain. I had to catch this thing, whatever it was. It was making a screeching sound. I flew after it as fast as I could all the way to the Temple of Qiell.

Then It disappeared into the boarded-up temple, I busted the door down. But it was too late. The shadow went into the Heart of Orifiel, taking Beacon's heart with it. I went up to the dim light and put my hand in it, and it disappeared just like the shadow figure.

I wanted to go after it. But before I could do that, a voice told me to stop.

"It went this way," I said.

"Stop right now," responded Oren.

He got in front of me and pulled me away from the dim light.

"I have to get Beacon's heart back and possibly Vega's, Mrs. Hyper's."

"You have no idea where that leads, and how would you get back?"

"I will figure it out later. Did you not hear me? It went this way."

"What went this way?"

"I'm not sure what it was, but, Oren, I'm telling you that it is not from this realm, and I saw it pull Beacon's heart out of his chest."

"You mean like Vega's heart?"

"Yes, but this time I actually saw what was causing it."

"Well, did you see it when Vega was getting his heart ripped out?"

"Well, no, but this time—"

"Dessa, maybe you thought you saw something but the truth is your eyes were playing tricks on you."

"No, Oren, I saw it."

"I didn't see anything or anybody when Vega was killed."

"Well, neither did I, but it—"

"Look, we have to get back to help Father hide the dead body before we cause a panic."

"But that's just it. You and Father are right: they aren't dead, just frozen in time."

"What are you talking about?"

"They appear dead, but they aren't because Lumentals can't die."

"OK, stop. Let's go."

"Put your hand in the light; see for yourself."

"Dessa, we are going now."

My brother was pulling me by the arm. I didn't want to go, but he wasn't listening.

"Oren, can't you see that's why we can't cry, 'cause they aren't dead?"

"I don't want to hear it anymore."

"Oren, why won't you hear me out?"

"OK, then why did you see something now? Why didn't you see it with Mrs. Hyper, Vega?"

"I'm not sure. I haven't figured that out yet."

"OK, this is what I want: for you to stop talking about it."

"Oren!"

"No!"

Chapter 64

Princess Odessa Seraphim

My father was pacing back and forth and of course didn't believe me either. He then told me that nothing from other realms could come into our realm. He said that anything impure wouldn't be able to survive in our world. But with the Light of Orifiel's heart going out, the very thing that kept my people who they were was no longer working properly, and I believed that anything was possible. I just had to figure out what realm that thing was from, and I knew it would be back again.

"Father, listen to me. I saw that thing take Bacon's heart right out of his chest," I said.

"Odessa, didn't I send you to your room? This doesn't concern you."

"He's right. Father and I will take care of it," Oren added.

I looked at my brother. After everything that happened, I would have thought he would know I was telling the truth about what I saw.

What do I have to do to get people to hear me out? I went to get my brother's sword. I decided not to go to my room but instead go back to the temple. I looked into the light, but I didn't see anything. This thing that attacked my people went inside there and was still hiding inside. So I was going, regardless of what my brother said.

I jumped inside the light. It was surprisingly big, and in the center was the Heart of Orifiel. I looked around and saw the shadow figure cowering in the corner. I drew my sword on it.

"Who are you?" I asked.

The shadow came alive and stood above me. I wasn't scared that this thing was bigger than me and maybe even evil.

"My name is Aether," it said.

"Where are you from?"

"I come from Daemonium."

"The Dark Realm."

"Yes, I got stuck here."

"How can that be?"

"I'm the Liminal, the gatekeeper between the living and the dead. I stumbled into your realm by accident, and I have been trying to get back to my realm."

"So then why don't you?"

The figure moved to the other side of me. I quickly turned around with my sword up to protect myself.

"Your realm is full of love, goodness, and happiness; it makes my power too weak to open up a door to get back to my realm, so I have been trying to inflict hate and depression."

"So you are the reason the Heart of Orifiel is going out."

"No, actually the light was already going out; that's why I stumbled here by mistake."

"No, that can't be."

"It is. Changing your emotions is harder in this realm, causing me to get sicker the longer I'm stuck here, so I thought the best way to speed things up would be to cause severe pain. And what better way to do that than lose someone you love? But you can't kill Lumentals."

"That's why you took the hearts—to make my people sad with grief and pain."

"But it's not working; I'm still here."

"Why is it I can see you and no one else can?"

"Because you broke your tradition and questioned your own religion."

"Making me what? Tainted?"

The shadow laughed at me.

"That's not enough to make you tainted. The fact that you broke your tradition to help your brother seal the truth so that it won't cause panic to your people makes you still pure."

"Give me back the hearts you stole."

"Gladly."

"Just like that?"

"Well, it's not doing me any good."

I held out my hand, and the shadow handed me the hearts.

"Now what is to come of you?" I asked.

"Oh, Odessa, one swipe of your sword will end me, but that won't help the Light of Orifiel from going out."

"And you know what will?"

"Actually, I do."

"OK, then what will?"

"The reason why the light is going out is you aren't using your powers for those who need it."

"I don't understand."

"In our world, there is an equilibrium, a push and pull. Without balance, there is no structure. After all, the light needs the darkness in order to be seen."

"So you want me to go to the dark world and slay all the monsters?"

"Ha ha! Oh, Odessa, you are so funny. Of all the worlds within our world, the Dark Realm is the last place I would recommend you go. However, the Dark Realm does have its fair share of problems, and now that I know Lumentals really do exist, they could solve a lot of problems down there."

"What kind of problems could I help with?"

"I think it's better you go and find out for yourself."

"I'm just supposed to go to the Dark Realm? They would eat me alive down there, and how do I know you aren't just sending me down there to be savagely ripped apart?

"You're right. You have no reason to trust me, so don't go, but your light will surely go out in time and your people will disappear one by one."

I thought for a minute. Looking at this evil entity that was slowly deteriorating. He can't be trusted and yet I feel that he might be telling the truth, I thought. And another thing, once I was in the Dark Realm, how was I going to help anyone by killing everything? How was that going to make it better? I had always thought that I was a strong and brave person, but the thought of going to the Dark World caused doubt in me. But I needed to save my people, and going on a quest to bring righteousness to my people made me feel invincible.

"How could you be stuck here when you could go through the Hollow Land to get to the Dark Realm? It lies within the middle of the realms. I could take you there."

"You're right. That is one way to enter the Dark World, but it leads into a very bad part of the Dark Realm that I would rather not go to."

"All parts of the Dark Realm are bad. What makes this one any different?"

"The only thing that can enter the Hollow Land is death. Once they enter it, they sit in purgatory, then are judged, then claimed by the King of Death. And since I am not dead, nor do I want to be judged, I would rather choose the other alternative."

"And what's that?"

"For you to end me with your sword."

"And you are OK with that?

"I don't really have a choice. Whether you kill me or I slowly die here, either way, I'm doomed."

"What will happen when you're dead?"

"Well, since I'm dying in your world and not my own, I will disappear."

"But aren't you already dead since you came from the Dark World?"

"No. Right now I'm very much alive. Well, I have had better days; as you can see, I'm getting very weak."

"But don't you have a life you want to get back to?"

Why do you care? I thought you wanted to end my life."

"Well, that was before you gave up the hearts of the people I care about."

"Oh well, so glad I could persuade you."

"I'm a Lumental. It is in my nature to care, no persuading necessary."

"Well, if you get to the Dark Realm, you are going to have to button it up, or they really will eat you up."

I could hear my brother calling me from up above. Aether and I looked at each other.

"That's Oren; he probably saw that I wasn't in my room," I explained.

"Look, just end me now. There is nothing you can do for me."

"I can't just end your life. And how am I going to get to the Dark Realm?"

"Look, would you rather I suffer and die slowly?"

"No, I don't want that, but if I'm being honest with you, I have never killed anything before."

"Think of it more as a mercy killing. Besides, you can get to the Dark Realm on your own. If I got here by mistake, then you can get there."

Chapter 65

Princess Odessa Seraphim

My father started yelling at me. Telling me that going to the Dark Realm was the stupidest idea he had ever heard and that saving our people to do it was even more ridiculous.

After I gave my brother the hearts to bring Vega, Beacon, and Mrs. Hyper back to normal, my brother got the credit for saving their lives. My father was praising him for it. In fact my father was so proud of my brother he was throwing him a celebration. Everyone was calling him the savior of our people.

But the light was getting worse. People were still getting emotionally sick. I was sitting in my room overlooking the balcony, watching everyone get ready for this party. Una was looking at me like, "I thought you were leaving." I looked back at her as if to say, "Yeah, I know I'm pathetic."

Then my mother walked into my room.

"I had a special dress made for you for the party," she said.

"I'm not going to the party."

"Oh yes you are, and you're going to see this party as an opportunity to apologize to Prince Magnus."

"Apologize for what? I did nothing wrong."

"Odessa, I don't want to fight with you; this is a time to be celebrating."

"What exactly are we celebrating? The Light of Orifiel is still going out."

"Your brother has fixed that problem."

"No, he hasn't, Mom. Is everyone in this world so naïve?"

"Look, I know that this is very hard for you to believe, but you are helping your people by getting married."

"Mother, I don't want to get married. Can't you see that's the last thing I want?"

"OK, then tell me, what do you want?"

"I want…"

I had to think for a minute about what I wanted. I was living in a world where I didn't belong, and the only way I could contribute to my race was by getting married. I knew I didn't want that. Also, killing was not really for me either. When I killed that thing from the Dark Realm, there wasn't any pleasure in watching it disappear.

"Well, what is it that you want?"

"I have already told you: I want to fly without any restrictions. I want to show this world that I'm just as strong as any man here. I want to make a difference without getting married."

"That's quite the tall order you have."

"Well, it's what I want, to be independent."

"What about love?"

"Mom, not this again. I told you, I don't care for it."

"But it's a wonderful dream come true."

"That is a dream I don't care for. I will never fall in love because I will be too busy defending what's right."

My mom looked at me and smiled.

"It's a shame you feel that way."

"Mother, can you understand that I feel like I'm in a cage? I'm only worth anything as long as I stay beautiful, get married, and have a few babies."

"That's not true; you are very special. Plus, you might not go looking for love, but it will find you whether you want it or not."

"Well, then I will just shove it away."

"If only it were that simple. The God of Light is everywhere and in everything."

My mother kissed me on the forehead and then left. I told myself, She does not get it; I think no one will. After some time passed, I got dress and went out. As I came down the stairs, I ran into my brother.

"Hey, I'm so sorry, Dessa. I told Father that you were the one who got those hearts back, but he didn't want to hear it," Oren explained.

"It's OK; I know."

"This party is a fake to me."

"I'm going to the Dark Realm."

My bother's eyes got wide.

"Are you crazy? Why would you do something like that?" he asked.

"I need to help our people."

"Dessa, listen to yourself. If you go there, you can never come back home. Think about what you are saying."

"I am, and for the first time, I know this feels right."

"I will never see you again, and Father will clearly declare you fallen."

I grabbed my brother's hand and pulled it up to me.

"I love you, Oren, very much, but I feel so wrong here. The feeling of being a caged bird makes me suffer inside, and we will see each other again, I promise."

"How?"

"When the Light of Orifiel shines bigger and brighter than it ever has, then you will know it's because I fixed it, and then you will know that I'm still here with you."

My brother gave me a big hug.

"Do not let anyone catch you. Stay free, please," he advised.

"I won't."

"I mean, demons and monsters cant be trusted."

"I will stay free, I promise."

"I don't know what to tell Mom. She will lose her mind."
"Tell her I'm free."
"I feel like I'm losing a big part of my life."
"You will never lose me, no matter how far away I am."
"And I will always be here for you, no matter what."
My brother hugged me again tightly.
"Take care of Una for me, will you?"
"Like she is my child."

I got dressed in my armor. My brother gave me his sword. He told me that it was always meant for my hand, not his.

Chapter 66

Princess Odessa Seraphim

I had no idea how to get to the Dark Realm. The Hollow Land seemed like a harder way to get in. But the evil entity told me that if he got here, then there was another way.

My brother kept my parents busy while I escaped. I got Twyla, and the two of us headed for Qiell. I felt like that was the way to get into the Dark Realm. Also, something was calling me to it, some kind of feeling. I took one last look at my home and gave my memory little details it wouldn't forget.

While I was in the Heart of Orifiel, I looked around. I couldn't see much; the light was dimming by the second. I was about to give up when I noticed a crack in the far left corner. It was not a very big crack, merely a little bigger than my foot. I pulled out my sword to see if I could open it more. While I was doing this, my sword went in the crack completely. I pulled it back out. I was starting to open the crack farther when the whole bottom fell out and Twyla and I fell downward without control. I tried spreading my wings to catch myself, but the wind just kept pulling us down. There was no light, and I couldn't see anything.

I opened my eyes very slowly. I must have passed out. I was lying on the ground. It felt weird, rough, and not comfortable. I couldn't see a thing because it was so dark. It was darker than the night sky that came at night. I could barely see what was in front of me; it was pitch-black. I could see my hands, and that was only because my skin apparently glowed in this kind of dark.

I sat up trying to get a better view but again nothing but darkness. Then I heard noises coming from behind me. I couldn't make out what they were saying. The voices were raspy and spooky. I walked toward the sounds. Then I came across a small hill. The voices were coming from behind it. I peeked my head around it. They had torches lit up by them. And then I saw the two ugliest things I had ever seen. They had horns coming out of their backs and black wings and tails. I could only see their backs. They were fighting over something, but I couldn't make out what it was, so I went in a little farther. And when I saw what they were fighting over, I gasped; they heard me. It was Twyla. They were eating her. She was already dead. There was nothing I could do.

They started grunting at me. And as they were smiling at me, black saliva was coming from their misshaped mouths. Yuck.

They had this look in their eyes; they wanted to eat me. They started talking again, but I couldn't understand what they were saying. As they came closer, I drew my sword at them. One charged at me, but I cut off his head. The other one came at me. He was fast. He grabbed my arm and then turned into stone. I pulled my arm from the stone monster, and there were scratches on my arm, but they healed immediately. I had never had injuries on me before.

We must have made a lot of sound with that commotion because a group of more torches came my way and I could make out more monsters; some were flying toward me. This was it—what I had come for. I wasn't afraid. I knew I could handle myself.

There is a crack in everything, that's how the light gets in.

—Leonard Cohen

Part VII

The Dark Realm

Introduction

The Dark Realm is in the underground below all the realms. Where the light never shows. Just an endless darkness. The dead fill the air with a stench, and souls are what keep this realm alive. All the dead godless souls come to the Dark Realm, whether they are good or bad. After they reach purgatory, they come to the Kingdom of Despair, where they wait in a continuously long line, awaiting there fate.

The are two kingdoms in the Dark Realm, the biggest one is the Kingdom of Despair, and King Draven is the ruler of it. He is said to be the Demon God Balor's son. But that is not why Draven is king of this world; he is king because he has the power to consume souls and the one who can do that is ruler of the underworld.

King Draven has two bulbous black horns coming out of his head. He is pale but built. He is over a hundred feet tall. His eyes are black, and so are his nails. He has sharp fangs and black wings. With each soul he consumes, he gets stronger and stronger. And because Draven has the dark power of immortally, he will live forever. When a soul is presented to Draven, it is usually a bad soul. Corrupt souls can be consumed by him, making him tyrannical. A good soul is usually put into slavery since they can't be consumed but instead act out the King of Death's every command.

King Draven is in control of the Arattus. The Arattus will only serve King Draven as long as he holds the dark power to consume the dead. The Arattus are demons, born evil savages with no regard for human life. They eat everything and anything. The Arattus are about twelve feet tall. They have black wings. Their eyes are solid black, and they have two black horns coming out of their heads. They are pale like King Draven. but they are very strong.

The second kingdom is the Kingdom of Sorrows, and it is ruled by Kings Draven's oldest son Aceifer. Aceifer is also the ruler of the most powerful army in the dark realm. The Arathagore are the first army of Balor the Demon God. The Arathagore's will not bow to King Draven. They are at war with him and his Arattus. The Arathagore's believe that King Draven is the son of Balor the Demon God but that his mother was not a demon, making him a half-breed and unworthy to possess the Dark Realm.

The Arathagore's are not born evil; they have a choice to be good or bad. The Arathagore's are the same size and height as the Arattus; the only difference is that the Arathagore are all red and they have a tail. Their skin and horns are red as well, along with their eyes and wings.

King Draven's younger son is Slymael. He and his brother Aceifer have a very powerful bond that can never be broken. Aceifer was meant to lead and rule, while Slymael is a powerful warrior meant to fight. Slymael is the captain of the Arathagore. Together they have been trying to overthrow there father. King Draven has no care for his sons, and he doesn't need them; since he will live forever, he doesn't need an heir.

There are thousands of different kinds of demons in this world, and they all believe in the Demon God Balor.

Balor symbolizes death and sin.

Their religion is called Orcus

The problem in the Dark Realm is that there are too many souls and nowhere to put them. They are over crowding the Dark Realm, causing the Dark Realm to flood in black tar that is a harmful substance of poison that eats through anything it touches. It is called the Vile.

Chapter 67

Princess Odessa Seraphim

I was fighting the demons left and right. They are as smelly as they are ugly; I had never seen or smelled something so foul.

Then a whistle was blown and they all stop and looked at me. A white, pale-faced man with black eyes came up toward me; they all looked at him as if they were waiting for his command.

He looked at me up and down, then walked around me like he was studying me. I wasn't worried because if he touched me, he would turn to stone like the other monsters that had come at me.

He started speaking, but I couldn't understand what he was saying. It was a language I had never heard before.

Ludo said, "Ut eam sed non tangere." (Get her, but don't touch her)

Lazare responded, "Quid est?" (What is it?)

"Quae est aurum fodiuntur." (She is a goldmine.)

"Quae est lucida." (She's so shiny.)

"Quod est." (That she is.)

"Quomodo eam sine tactu capmius?" (How do we catch her without touching her?)

"I habere ideam." (I have an idea.)

I kept my sword drawn on the pale-faced man. I wasn't going to let him surprise me. He pulled something out of his pocket. A small glass like object. He looked at me with a smile. His black eyes told me that he could not be trusted. He dropped the glass box onto the floor, and the box started burrowing into the ground. Before I realized what it was doing, a huge oversize glass box came from out of the ground and swallowed me. It jolted me, and I dropped my sword. The glass was see-through, so I was pounding on it and screaming, "Let me out."

The pale-faced man came right to the box and smiled at me. I picked up my sword and started slashing at he box, but it was no use; it would not break.

Ludo said, "Quae est una vivet, non est illa." (She's a live one, isn't she?)

All the monsters laugh at me.

Lazare said, "Adhuc haven't indicavit mihi quid est." (You still haven't told me what she is.)

Ludo responded, "Rara occiso miraculi." (Rare opportunity of a miracle.)

Two big-winged monsters came out of nowhere and picked up my box with me in it, using their feet, and flew me off the ground.

I was still pounding. I didn't know where they were taking me. My brother told me not to get captured, and here I was in another cage.

I continued to hit the box as I was flying in the air with those disgusting monsters. I think I annoyed one of them, 'cause they hit the box, causing me to fall backward. Then they both started laughing.

When I get out of this box, I'm going to kill every last one of them, I thought.

I was coming across a town-like village filled with all kinds of monsters and demons. They were looking up at me in the air.

Great, they are probably going to eat me, I said to myself.

Chapter 68

Prince Slymael Arius
Kingdom of Sorrows

My brother Ace and I were going over the Book of Death trying to finds ways to trick my father into giving up his power. But of course he was not stupid enough for that. If only it were that easy. My bother should have been the one ruling this kingdom; his reign would have been far better than my father's.

My brother asked, "How many times have we read this book from cover to cover?"

I responded, "A million and one."

"There has to be a loophole somewhere."

"If there was, we would have found it by now."

"So how do we solve an impossible task?"

"If we made him weak, that would be a start."

"How can we do that? As long as the dead keep coming, he will never be weak."

"If there was a way to convert the dead to go to you instead of father…"

"But there isn't one. As soon as they are dead, they come to him automatically, and then he puts his mark on them."

"Maybe if you came up with your own mark…"

"It won't have any power to it."

"Then maybe we should just block the portal to the dead and the living."

"That would not only hurt father but us as well."

"It's worth a shot. What do we have to lose?"

"Only our sanity."

My brother and I looked at each other and started laughing. Our sanity had been gone a long time. In fact, we were never sane.

Then a reaper came up to us. He passed me an envelope.

"Who's it for?" Ace asked.

"You!" I responded.

"Who's it from?"

I open the letter and read to myself.

"It's from Ludo. He says he has something for us. Something that will solve all our problems."

I handed the letter to my brother and let him continue reading on.

"It says here that if we do not come and get it, he will give it to father."

"It's probably some more worthless trinket or some hybrid demon he's trying to sell us."

"Yeah, but when has he ever dealt with father?"

"You know vampires can't be trusted; they are very shifty. He probably said that so that you would come."

"Yeah, but you know that Ludo would rather cut off his arms than deal with father."

"If I had a pint of blood for every time Ludo tried to sell us something worthless, I would have my own blood bank."

"It can't hurt to check it out. I mean, Hecate isn't that far from here."

"OK, but I'm telling you it's going to be a waste of our time."

Hecate slave market

Ludo said, "Your Majesty, I'm so glad you came. I knew you would."

"Ludo why are we here?" Ace asked.

"I have something for you. I think you will be very happy. No, I know you will."

"More of your so-called junk that you want to pawn on us."

"No, this is far from junk."

Ludo told one of his minions to go get it. After a while, we where getting really impatient. My bother looked at me, and I shook my head. Then the minion came back and whispered in his ear, and he had to excuse himself for a minute.

"I told you—a waste of time," I said.

Then he came back out with a big smile on his face.

"I'm so sorry, Your Majesties, I was just making sure everything was perfect."

"Ludo, our patience is wearing thin," Ace responded.

"Yes, of course."

Ludo signaled his demons to bring it in. Then a huge box covered in a red velvet curtain appeared.

"That is very nice, Ludo, but a curtain that covers a box isn't going to help us," Ace commented.

"Oh, Your Majesty, you slay me. It's what's under the curtain that will get your blood going."

"Whatever you say," I responded.

"I give you the most amazing, the most incredible—"

"Ludo, just take off the curtain and hurry up," Ace interrupted.

Without delay Ludo released the curtain.

My brother and I were a lost of words. For what we saw in the box was astonishing. We got closer to get a better look at it.

"Ludo, do have any idea what this is?" Ace asked.

"Of course. It's a—"

"Lumental." I finished his sentence.

"That's right," said Ludo.

"Where did you find her?" Ace asked.

"She was wandering around in Duat."

I got so close to the box you could see my breath on the glass. I couldn't believe she was real. I had never seen beauty before, at least not like this. She was absolutely stunning, and the feeling she gave me made me feel like I wanted to repent for my sins. Her skin was so shiny. We looked into each other's eyes. I was hypnotized. I didn't like this feeling in which I had no control of my emotions, and it caused me to be very skeptical.

"How do we know she is real?" I asked.

Ludo brought out one of his demons. It was turned to stone.

"She did this?" Ace asked.

"Yes, and you know the saying: anything that touches a Lumental that is impure turns—"

"To stone. Yeah, we know the story," I interrupted.

"All right, Ludo, what do want for her?"

Ludo put his hands together and smiled devilishly.

"You know me; I'm not a greedy man."

"Hold it, can I talk to my brother for a minute?" I asked.

"Of course, talk among yourselves. I can wait."

I pulled my brother into the other room so we could have privacy.

"Don't you think we should think about this before you buy her?" I asked.

"Sly, do have any idea what that is? She could help us."

"OK, this is incredible; I get that. Finding this is like finding a alive human down here."

"Exactly!"

"But that is my point. Don't you find this all suspicious?"

"Sly, we have been trying to overpower Father. The only thing that can come close to that is her. She has a very powerful ability to overthrow him, and I want it."

"But you're forgetting something: the only way to obtain power from a Lumental is by falling in love with them, and they have to fall in love with you or you turn to stone."

"No problem. I can fall in love."

"Since when have you ever cared about love? And I don't think it's possible since our hearts are black."

"I can get her to fall in love with me. Hell, I'm almost there; you felt that attractive pull when you laid eyes on her."

"Being attached is only half the equation."

"See, I told you I'm almost there."

"I still don't like it I want to know how in the hell she got down here."

"Maybe we should ask her."

"Do you know how to speak the light language?"

"No, do you?"

"Yeah, actually I do," I said.

"Wait, how do you know that?" Ace asked.

"Remember, Mom taught us when we were younger. I just stuck with it while you chose to ignore it."

"You kept up with a language from a civilization that was thought to be a myth?"

"Well, Mom said it would come in handy."

"She is a very smart woman."

I let out a big sigh. My brother could see I was very uncomfortable with this. My gut told me that this was going to be a bad idea.

"Maybe we should think about this for a few days," I suggested.

"Would you relax? Would you rather Dad take her?"

"No, that would be the worst thing."

"OK, then don't worry; nothing is going to happen."

My brother made the deal with Ludo and bought the Lumental for what the vampires call liquid gold. It's virgin blood that is completely pure and untouched. My brother gave him eighteen pints to keep his mouth shut about it.

Chapter 69

Princess Odessa Seraphim

I woke up this time in a bed. I looked up and saw a mirror above me. I almost didn't recognize myself. I was in a black sexy dress. My hair was pinned up, and my makeup was dark but pretty, if you like that sort of thing. My lipstick was so black. Definitely not something I would have chosen for myself.

I sat up, and the room was covered in candles that lit up the room. There was a chain attached to my ankle, and the other end was attached to the wall.

I thought, So I'm out of the box but still a prisoner. What a warrior I turned out to be. I wonder what my brother is doing. I miss him so much. I know if he saw me right now, he wouldn't judge me.

I scooted to the edge of the bed. Then I walked over to the table. And sat down at the chair. Then the door opened up, and I immediately stood up.

A woman with purple hair and dark makeup came toward me. She was beautiful in a dark, spooky kind of way.

She said, "Ethinka euflora supbrim." (I'm so sorry, I didn't mean to startle you.)

"You speak my language," I replied.

"You speak the common tongue; that's impressive for a Lumental."

"Not really. Where I come from, everything is common."
"I'm sorry to hear that."
"How do you know the light language?"
"I learned it from my mother and so forth."
"What are you?"
"My name is Morgana, and I'm a witch."
"What is a witch?"
"A witch is someone who can conjure up spells," Morgana explained.
"A spell?"
"Spells: a collaboration of hocus and pocus."
"What does that mean?"
"It is the optical illusion of fantasy alternating with reality."
She snapped her fingers, and my horse Twyla was there.
"Twyla," I said.
I went over and hugged her. Then Morgana snapped her fingers again and Twyla turned into a long, limbless reptile that slithered toward me. It was about to attack me when she snapped her fingers again and the creature turned into a glass of wine.

"See, it is the swift elixir of charm," said Morgana.
"I don't understand."
"Word of advice, sweet pea: don't try to understand the power of voodoo; it will only confuse you."

Something was not right about this woman. She had the power to turn truth into lies, or vice versa. I must keep my eye on her; she can't be trusted, I thought.

"How did you get me dress? Wouldn't you turn to stone?" I asked.
"That's the power of magic."
"So are you going to eat me now?"
"Ha ha! You are so funny. Why would we eat you?"
"Isn't that what they do down here? 'Cause that's all I have seen."
"You see, I would be queen of this world if the father of my children would marry me."
"The father of your children?"

"Yes, he's the king of this world, and I was his favorite at one point, but every time we laid together, I would give him a child, so he found me annoying."

"That's awful, for him to treat you that way. It's not like it's your fault."

"Yes, but you will find that women are desired but not needed in this world."

"That's horrid."

"Unfortunately that's the Dark Realm for you. But enough about me. Do you have a name?"

"Odessa!"

"That's very pretty."

"Only my mother can make it sound awful when she's upset with me."

"Mothers, right?"

"So if you aren't going to eat me, what are you going to do?"

"You are going to marry my son."

"No. I didn't come to this world to get married."

"Then why did you come here?"

"I wanted to help."

"You wanted to help the dark Realm?"

"In a way."

"Look, Odessa, in order for you to be safe in this world, someone must claim you, and who better than my son? Marrying him is for your protection."

"I don't need his protection; I can defend myself."

"Not against King Draven, you can't. He can corrupt you. He will do it by torture. He will get off on it by slowly watching you fold into misery."

"I'm not scared of him. If he touches me, he will turn into stone."

"You may be immortal in our world, but you aren't invincible. He can hurt you without even touching you."

"I find you mischievous."

"That is a great way of describing a witch."

"Power's like yours have great consequences."

"More than you know."

"What's your son's name?"

"Aceifer. He's the oldest, and my second son is Slymael."

"So who will I be marrying if I choose to do this?"

"Aceifer. You already met them today at the slave market; they are the ones who bought you."

I remembered them. They were both very good-looking considering they were demons. Both were physically fit, and even though they had two horns coming out of their heads, they both had great facial features, good jawlines.

The one that locked eyes with me had something about him that I didn't expect to see in a demon. Based on what I have seen, they are all hungry for blood. Nothing but evil. But not him; he had a warmth in his eyes, like he was kind and good. I couldn't understand why I felt that way toward him. A desire I had never experienced until I looked into his eyes.

Chapter 70

Prince Slymael Arius

My brother and I were waiting patiently for my mother to get done with the Lumental.

"So what gives? She's been in there for a while," Ace said.

"Maybe she is realizing that she's a fake," I responded.

"I'm telling you, she's not a fake."

Before I could answer my brother, my mother burst through the room and immediately made herself a drink.

"Well, did she say she would do it?" Ace asked.

"She didn't say no," my mother responded.

"So she said yes?"

"Well, she didn't say yes either."

"I don't think marriage is good idea," I interjected.

"I agree. I mean, no one even knows how to perform a marriage ceremony down here," Ace added.

"Son, that's not the point. Listen to me. It's safe to say that your father already knows about her, which means that he will send every spy or assassin to collect her. We have no time to waste; you must inveigle her. You have got to entice her heart if you are going to get her power."

"I have never had to chase the opposite sex before. They usually come to me," Ace declared.

"I still think she is a fake," I said.

"Oh, she is real all right," our mother responded.

"And what makes you so sure? Just because you had a conversation with her?" I asked.

"No, there's other stuff."

"Like what?"

"I put three love spells on her, and they didn't work."

"That doesn't mean anything."

"Sly, when you were near her, did you feel some kind of warm feeling in your body? It starts in the chest, then spreads all through your veins. That and the fact that she gives you a very good and righteous feeling."

"Yeah, so?"

"Lumentals are said to give off a good and pure vibes. They make you want to do good. That's why it's so hard to be bad around them. All you want to do is be honest and kind."

"I knew she was the real thing," Ace said.

I watched my brother as he smiled while my mother was telling us about the Lumental. It made me mad, bitter even.

"And she is absolutely gorgeous; her skin is flawless," said my mother.

"Did She say how she came down here?" Ace asked.

"Get this—she chose to come down here."

"She chose to come down here? Why?" I asked.

"She wanted to help the Dark Realm," she responded.

Ace said, "This is great. She will help us. This is going to work, but I don't know the first thing about how to woo her."

"You leave this to me. I will find out about her likes and dislikes; that will help you," my mother responded.

"Good. That will work."

My mother kissed my brother on the cheek and told him he had to go and look his best before she introduced him to her and he had to learn her language, even though she spoke the common tongue, it would be good to have something they could build on. After he left, my face turned red.

"I say we get rid of her, Mother," I suggested.

"Oh my love, we need her; your brother needs her to annihilate your father. Don't you want your brother to rule this world?"

"You know I do, but he's going to fall in love with her, and she will fall in love with him, and then what happens to me? He will forget all about me."

"That could never happen. He is just trying to use her, that's all."

"I will not let her come between us."

"Nothing could come between you two. You two have the most incredibly strong bond, one that will never break."

"You know, I have read that Lumentals can read people. How long do you think it will take her to figure out what we are doing?"

"By then she will be head over heels for your brother."

"Let's get one thing straight, Mother: I'm the only love in his life, no one else."

"Of course you are, my love. No one else. This is only an illusion of love. You and your brother have the real thing."

My mother started kissing my ear, and it wasn't making me feel any better about this situation.

"Stop. I'm not in the mood," I said.

"Oh come on, sweetheart. You are so angry; let me do that thing you like to relive that tension."

My mother started kissing my neck, and then she wrapped both her arms around my waist, pulling me into her body. This was only fueling my tension. It was like she was trying to persuade me to not worry about it. I continued to act like she wasn't there. She started taking off my clothes, and I was annoyed so I snapped. I grabbed her by the throat and squeezed. I looked into her eyes as she was gasping for air.

"I'm not in the mood!"

I let her go with a shove, and she fell to the floor. I slammed the door as I left the room. My mother has always favored my brother over me. Our relationship would be so much better if she weren't around anymore.

Chapter 71

Princess Odessa Seraphim

I have been in this room, from what I gather, for three days. The chain on my ankle was really annoying me. So this would make me a prisoner. So how can I help my people if I'm a prisoner? I ask myself. I have gone over my room many times, and there was no way I was getting out without some help.

Then the door opened.

"Sorry to have kept you waiting; I have been busy. I would bring you food and something to drink, but since Lumentals do not get hungry or thirsty, nor do they need sleep, what's the point?" Morgana said.

"Since I'm your prisoner, how long do plan on keeping me here?"

"You are not a prisoner."

I picked up the chain that was attached to my ankle.

"Then what do you call this?" I asked.

"That was for your protection, but there is no need for that."

She snapped her fingers, and the chain went away.

"Thank you."

"No problem. Now, would you like to get out of this room?"

"Yes, please."

She opened the door and led me out. She showed me to the grand throne room, where the man I saw when I was in a box was sitting in a big chair.

"Odessa, this is my son King Aceifer Arius. Ace, this is Odessa."

He sat up from his chair. And walked down the staircase. He had no top covering, revealing that he was very built. He was handsome in an odd, terrifying kind of way. He had two black horns coming out of the top of his head. His black hair went down to his shoulders. His eyes were black. And when I looked into them, I saw lifelessness, no remorse for feelings.

"Listen, Your Majesty, whatever you think I will do for you, you are—" I began.

"I thought you came here to help," Ace interrupted.

"I did come here to help."

"Well, then this is perfect because we could use your help."

"You could?"

He walked around me, admiring his view.

"You see, my father is a very bad man. There are too many dead people in this world, and there is nowhere to put them. If we don't do something about it, then my world is over. My father does not care about this problem."

"So how can I help?"

"By helping me take down my father."

"How can I do that?"

"You will see in time. Now, since you are not a prisoner, please feel free to roam the castle. As long as you don't leave the castle, I can guarantee your safety."

"So I can go anywhere in the castle?"

"That's right, my second-in-command Goliath will accompany you so you don't get lost."

Goliath is a demon. He's huge; at least twelve feet tall. His skin is red, along with his wings and horns. But his eyes are black, like Sly's and Ace's.

Goliath showed me the grounds. From the mess hall to the towers of the castle. He never said anything to me; I had a feeling that if he did, I wouldn't understand him.

This place was like a maze, a very spooky maze. I couldn't help but wonder how I could help King Aceifer. I really wasn't here to help him. I was here to help my people.

Finally we reached a long corridor with big, heavy doors. Goliath pushed the doors open, and inside were demons that looked just like him everywhere. They were sharpening their weapons, and some were arguing; I couldn't make out about what. There were a couple of them shooting off arrows for practice. Some were flying around. I followed Goliath in. There was a small arena; a bunch of them were sitting around it taking bets. Inside the arena there were three demons surrounding another demon in the middle. But this demon in the middle was different; I had seen him before, that day I was in the box.

I had a feeling that this must have been Slymael, Aceifer's younger bother. He did look a lot like him. And the way Morgana talked about them, it was a safe assumption.

The three demons charged at Sly with weapons, but it didn't faze him. Took them down without difficulty. The way he brought them down was fascinating. It was a neat and cool way of fighting.

"Wow! He's amazing," I said.

Goliath looked at me and grunted, then he walked away from me. I didn't know what I had said to make him mad. I followed him.

When the fight was over, all the demons congratulated Sly for winning. Goliath went up to Sly, whispered something in his ear; while he was doing this, he turned around, looked right at me. When Sly saw me, he rolled his eyes at me.

I had never met this man before, and yet somehow I had already offended him.

As the two of them walked toward me, my heart begin to flutter. Sly was much more attractive then his brother. His hair was shaved on one side, showing more of his left horn, and the other side of his hair was longer; it went to his jawline. And he was much more built than his brother Aceifer. Even though Sly's eyes were black, they had a hint of color to them. They showed a feeling of compassion and warmth. It was actually very refreshing since all the black eyes here were the same.

I was getting very nervous as they were staring at me.

"I'm—" I began.

Sly interrupted, "Menim onipa woye." (I know who you are.)

When he spoke my language, it was a big turn-on, and I didn't know why.

"That was very impressive fighting. Never saw anything like that."

"I think you should be in your room. Fragile things like you can get broken very easily."

"I'm not fragile. I can take care of myself."

"Yeah, I'm sure you can. Do me a favor: don't annoy me."

"I'm sorry, how did I annoy you?"

"Your very presence annoys me, so go back to your room now!"

While Sly was walking away from me, I picked up a bow and shot an arrow right at a bull's-eye target that was right in front of him. The whole room got quite, and everyone was staring at me.

Sly charged at me like he was going to hit me but grabbed the bow from my hand instead.

I could tell he was mad, but then he smiled at me. His smile made me a little light-headed.

"Aren't Lumental women supposed to be pristine and dainty?"

"I'm not your average Lumental."

"Maybe you're not a real Lumental."

After he said that, he told Goliath something, and before I knew it, I was sent back to my room. I was in my room trying to figure out why I had such a strong infatuation with Sly. He was a demon, and Lumentals fell for each other, not villains. The other thing that made me mad was that he said I wasn't a real Lumental. How would he know what real Lumentals were?

Chapter 72

Prince Sly Arius

"So she can shoot an arrow—so what?" Ace said.

"So Lumental women don't do that," I responded.

"Meaning?"

"That she is a fake."

"Sly, what is it with you and this girl? Why are you so determined to out her?"

"Because I don't like her and I want her dead."

"Well, she's one hell of a fake. Besides, we have bigger problems right now."

"Like what?"

"This came today."

My brother handed me a note. It was from Father. After I read it, I looked up at my brother.

"He wants you to come to the Kingdom of Despair."

"Mother is right. Our father knows about our rare find."

"This could be a trap."

"That's exactly what Mother said."

"All the more reason not to go."

"I'm having dinner with Odessa tonight. I will decide then."

"You are having dinner with someone who doesn't eat dinner?"

"I have to romance her someway."

"Romance? Do you have any idea what that word means?"

"Of course I do. Plus, it will be much easier once Mother finds her likes and dislikes."

"And if she is a fake?"

"Then we will deal with it."

"And Father?"

"We will deal with it. Together, we are unstoppable."

The next couple of days, my brother was all about his Lumental. Taking her on walks, sending her flowers and gifts—he was making a damn fool of himself. It was making me sick just watching it.

A virile king becoming a soft pushover—it was like he was forgetting who he was. You will never find me falling, I thought.

I stood on the high balcony watching my brother and his new pet watching the demons fight it out.

He was making her laugh. The two looked like they were the only two people in the world.

"You know, if you stare at them any longer, they may drop dead," my mother said.

"Maybe that would be for the best since my bother is acting like an idiot," I responded.

"Oh, your jealousy is something else, son."

"What, do I got to be jealous about? She is nothing to him."

"She is very beautiful."

"So? What difference does that make?"

"So then you will admit that you are attracted to her."

"So what if I find her attractive? What's that got to do with anything?"

"Just trying to figure out whether you are jealous of her getting your brother's attention or the other way around."

I looked at my mother; she could tell she had struck a nerve with me. My blood was boiling from her comment. I walked away from her. I had to before I unleashed my anger on her.

I went to the fighting pit to let out my anger. When it was over and done I felt a little less steamed. I lay on my bed and injected myself with Pterolycus blood. It gives you a high like anything else. I needed to fell numb. I closed my eyes and let it take effect on my body.

I was in a trance when I saw all of the faces of the demons I have killed. I couldn't help but feel guilty about it. Then I saw Odessa's face and I woke up. Of all the faces, why hers?

I went to look for my bother and found him walking out of my mother's bedroom.

"Sly, I was just getting ready to come find you," he said.

"Yeah, I bet," I responded.

"What's that supposed to mean?"

"Nothing. What's going on?"

"I'm leaning toward visiting Father."

"What? Are you crazy? It's a trap."

"Maybe, but I'm too close to getting what I want."

"Oh, so she's fallen in love with you?"

"I think so, but what's more is that I have fallen in love with her."

"Wow, so fast. Are you sure you're in love?"

"She's all I think about."

"Have you been able to touch her yet?"

"No, not yet."

"Well, that will be the only way to tell."

"I have her convinced that if she marries me, we can help her people."

"Her people?"

"Yes. She told me that her people are in trouble; some light that they depend on is going out."

"Are you really going to help her people?"

"Of course not."

"I thought you said you are in love with her."

"I am in love with her power. Her power is all I think about."

"So you get her power and then you visit Father?"

"Something like that."

"Ace, I've been thinking maybe we should get rid of your pet."

"Mother has told me about your jealousy toward Odessa, and you have nothing to worry about; it will always be us, little brother."

"Could never have guessed by the way you two have been acting."

"Sly, trust me, she means nothing to me. I just want her power; that's it."

"And once you get her power, then what happens to her?"

"Well, she will be mortal then, so we can do whatever we want to her."

I liked the sound of that. I wanted her dead. She was a distraction that we could not afford.

After I left my bother, I went to the mess hall. On my way there, I found Odessa roaming the halls.

"What are you doing here?" I asked.

"Just looking around," she said.

"Go back to your room."

"Believe it or not, I'm not a prisoner."

"So you're not a prisoner or a Lumental. So what are you?"

"I am a Lumental."

"You know what, I think you are a fake. Let's see if I have this right. Wherever you came from, you didn't fit in; that's the only reason I can think of as to why you would end up in the Dark Realm."

"But I—"

"I'm not finished. I think the real reason you didn't fit in was you didn't fall in-line very well. Probably think that you could be a hero somewhere else, maybe even wished you could see other worlds 'cause you got bored with your own home. You knew you would never be special in your world. How am I doing so far?"

I could tell I had gotten her mad; she let out a big sigh. And I cocked a smile at her. That last thing I said was to see how she would react, and it was worth it.

"You're not the only one who can read people. I can do it too," she said.

"Is that right?"

"You are a demon with your black wings and black horns but are far from evil. Oh, you may look the part, but you have something they don't have."

"And what's that?"

"You have a heart. I noticed that day you were fighting, you were very hesitant when it came to hurting the demons. They were charging at you, but you didn't really want to hurt them.

"Were you not watching that fight? I did hurt them."

"Yes, but you didn't kill them. Practice or no practice, you aren't evil."

"Let's get one thing straight: I have killed, raped, lied, and stolen things. I have also deceived people, all in the name of helping my brother, so don't tell me I'm not evil."

"You're not. It's in your eyes; they give you way. I notice you try very hard to conceal your remorse, but it's there."

"Go to your room!"

After she left, I punched a hole in the wall. I thought, I can't stand her, and what's worst she thinks she can see right through me.

Chapter 73

Princess Odessa Seraphim

I ran back into my room and slammed the door. I thought, He is the most infuriating person I have ever met. He makes my blood boil. Why am I so determined to prove myself to him? It's like he challenges me on purpose.

He had rattled my nervous so much that when Morgana came in, I couldn't calm down.

"Darling, are we OK?" she asked.

"I'm fine, thank you."

"Well, something has got you all in a huff."

"Morgana, what exactly is Ace king of?"

"He is King of the Sorrows."

"What does that mean exactly?"

"The dead have three choices granted. They are all bad choices; they only have three. One is being judged, and after that, they stand in a long line where they are consumed by the King of Death, or he puts them into a life of pain where they become slaves. They can escape here to the Kingdom of Sorrows. Now, here they can hide, but they will never be free from the King of Death.

"And if they don't want to be judged, they come here?"

"Yes, but the dead have an expiration date. If they aren't judged or put into their place, they dissolve into a poisons goo called the Vile. Those are there only options."

"That's awful."

"That's life. Quae finitur."

"I have heard that saying before. What's it mean?"

"Everything comes to an end."

"And Ace can't give the dead a better option?"

"All the dead are automatically marked with King Draven's symbol, so he owns them whether they are judged or not."

"And King Draven needs the dead in order to survive?"

"That's right. He who holds the dead in the palm of their hand seals their fate."

If only there were a better alternative for the dead. Somewhere they could go where they would never have to worry about pain. If only I could heal this world by using my power, that would have to help the Light of Orifiel shine brighter than ever.

"If I marry Ace, my power will help him to take over the King of Death, and then he will help these souls, right?"

"That's his plan."

"Then I will do it. I will marry him."

"Well, that's one hell of a good deed."

"You will find I'm not selfish."

"Most Lumentals aren't."

I knew what Ace wanted—he wanted my heart. But I was not in love with him. As hard as he tried, it was no use. I wasn't looking for love, nor was I giving any up. But maybe there was another way I could help by using my power. Being Ace's partner could help him cause fear in his father. Knowing that he was married to a Lumental—maybe that would be enough to cause the King of Death to reason with his son about the problems of the dead. It was worth a shot.

After I got married to Ace, it all happened so fast. It wasn't much of a wedding since no one really knew how a marriage ceremony was performed down here, but the word traveled fast. The next thing I knew,

King Draven had sent an invitation for his son to come to the Kingdom of Despair so he could congratulate him.

I felt like Sly, given the opportunity, would kill me in my sleep if he could. He had this hatred for me that I couldn't seem to shake off. The more I tried to make peace with him, the worse I made it.

I was walking back from my date with Ace when I ran into Sly coming up the stairs. The minute he saw me, he let out a big sigh and walked right past me like I didn't exist. I wanted to say something, but what was the point? As he slammed the door behind him, I shook. I thought, I don't really fit in anywhere no matter where I go.

Chapter 74

Prince Sly Arius

"Do you really think Father is going to congratulate you once you are there?" I asked.

"Depends. This could go either way. Especially now that he knows I'm married, he assumes I have the power to rule over him," Ace said.

"But you don't have her power."

"Yeah, but he doesn't know that, so he's going to try to make a deal with me."

"I still don't like it, but if we are gong to go, then we better take more guards with us."

"Sly, you're not coming with me this time."

"What are you talking about? I've got to cover your back; I always cover your back."

"Sly, as long as father thinks I'm in love, he thinks I have a weakness, and he will send his ghouls after Odessa to use her to get to me."

"So leave Goliath and Gabriel to protect her."

"No, I need someone I can trust; I need you. You're the only one I know who can pull this job off. You are the best fighter in the world."

"I don't want to protect her; I want to protect you."

"Listen, if Father gets his hands on her, he will find that I don't have the power and then he will use her against us and then everything we have worked so hard for will be all for nothing."

"I swear, if anything happens to you and I wasn't there to protect you, I will find a way to dismember your pretty pet."

"If anything happens to me, then it's up to you, little brother."

"I really don't like this."

"I know, but we don't have a choice. I will see what father wants, and I won't be long."

"If you are not back in two days, I'm coming after you."

"Three days."

"Fine, three days. Not a day more."

"Relax, it's going to be all right."

After my brother left, I despised Odessa even more. If anything happened to him, I would never forgive her for it.

I was teaching the younger Arathagore how to fight and properly hold their sword. They were getting a kick out of it when I could feel a pair of eyes on me that were making me agitated.

"You know, you would have a better stance if you spread your legs a little more," said Odessa.

"You're giving me fighting tips?" I said.

"Um, well, I was just giving you an idea."

"I don't need anything from you."

"I know you don't, but I was just—"

"Go to your room now!"

"I'm not a prisoner; I can go where I want."

"Well, I'm in charge, and I say you are a prisoner that stays in her room."

"But my room is very boring."

"OK, perhaps you prefer the dungeons underneath the castle."

She didn't say anything; she just looked at me, then walked away. I told Goliath to keep an eye on her.

I found my mother. She was sitting on my brother's throne and acting out my brother's wishes.

"You shouldn't get too comfortable in that seat," I said.

"And why not? I'm good at it," my mother responded.

"The only thing women are good for doesn't require a seat."

"And yet you haven't been in my bed for quite some time now."

"I think you know the reason for that, Mother."

"I love both my boys the same. I have told you that since you were babies."

"You know, it's funny, but I don't believe you when you say it."

"If you want me to say that out of the two of you, you are the strongest, then fine, you are the strongest."

"Forget it. It sounds even more like bullshit."

My mother laughed, and then she got up from the seat and walked away from me.

Once my mother was gone, Goliath rushed in and told me some irritating news.

Chapter 75

Princess Odessa Seraphim

On my way back to my room, I got lost. Everything started looking the same. I kept going down another corridor, then another corridor. I was getting dizzy. I stopped for a minute when I heard some growling, but I couldn't figure out where it was coming form. I felt I was in danger. Nothing around me looked familiar.

I finally came across some stairs that led me to a door. It opened up to a tower with nothing inside. Just when I thought I had seen everything the tower had to offer, a black figure appeared; I saw its sharp teeth. I ran toward the door. It swung open, and Sly appeared with a dagger in his hand. He flung it at me. I ducked, and the knife killed the black figure. It dropped dead.

"How many times do I have to tell you to stay in your room?" he said.

"You threw a knife at me," I responded.

"Actually, I was aiming for the monster behind you."

Sly walked over to the dead demon and pulled his dagger out of its head. The black blood squirted everywhere.

"You know, that could have hit me," I said.

"So what if it did? It wouldn't have done anything to you."

"That's not the point."

"Look, I don't have time to argue with you."

"What is that thing?"

"It's a ghoul. They work for my father. Most likely sent by him."

"They're hideous, and they smell horrible."

"That's the Dark Realm for you."

"But why are they after me?"

"It doesn't matter. What matters is that it's hard to protect you if you don't stay in your room."

"I can protect myself; I don't need you."

"Is that right?"

"Yes, it is."

"OK, fine."

Sly took out his sword and handed it to me.

"I will make a deal with you: if you can cut me once with the sword, then I will let you roam the castle whenever you like."

"And if I can't?"

"Then you stay in your room and you do what I tell you to do without any crap. Do we have a deal?"

"OK, deal."

I heaved the sword at him, but no matter how fast I was, he was one step faster than me. I couldn't hit him, not once.

"Looks like I won," he said.

"You cheated."

"Sore loser, are we? What were you doing up here anyway?"

"I got lost."

"More reason to stay in your room."

"Hey, Sly."

"What!"

"Thank you for back there."

"I didn't do it for you."

"Well, thanks anyways."

He put his sword back in its sheave, and we walked out of the tower together. I was following behind him, letting him lead me to my room.

"Where did you learn to fight like that?" he asked.

"My bother taught me."

"I take it he's older?"

"Yes, he's my best friend."

"I bet he is very upset you ran away."

"You and your brother are very close, aren't you?" I asked.

"Thick as thieves."

"How would Ace feel if you ran away?"

"He would probably feel the same way your brother does."

Sly opened the door to my room. I went inside. Before he shut the door, he looked at me.

"Can I ask you one more question?" I said.

"What?"

"I know you don't like me, but you should know that I'm not going to get in your way or make trouble."

"You already are."

Sly slammed the door, and I let out a big sigh. I guess that wasn't so bad. The next day I did as Sly said: I stayed in my room. It was driving me crazy. There was nothing to do. I thought about home. I wondered what Una was doing and if my brother was taking care of her. I missed the sun. It was always so dark here. What I would give to see one star in the sky.

I was getting ready to close my curtains to the balcony when I heard claw marks on the wall outside. I looked down and saw more of the ghoul things climbing outside of my balcony. I quickly panicked and picked up a candlestick. I waited for it to come through my window, and then I hit it over the head. I went over to make sure that it was dead. And another one grabbed me, but it turned to stone instantly. The other one that saw it looked at me and then dashed for the window. It was about to jump from my balcony when a sword went through its neck.

Sly landed on my balcony. Then he took his sword back out of the dead ghoul. Sly looked incredible with his wings arched out.

"How did you know they were here?" I asked.

"I have lookouts everywhere."

"What do they want with me?"

"My father wants you to himself, and he won't stop till he gets you."

"So then what do we do now?"

"Well, I think it's safer for you to change rooms, and whatever happens, you can't let any of them survive, so kill them as soon as you see them."

"I can do that."

Goliath came through the door. He was saying something to Sly. Then next thing I knew, Sly handed me another sword.

Chapter 76

Prince Sly Arius

We headed out to the corridor to put Odessa in another room. Goliath told me that they got all the ghouls but they would be back with more.

I told Odessa to keep that sword by her at all times. I know my father, and he won't stop at anything till he gets what he wants. It was day two; one more day left till my brother got back.

I told Goliath to up security around the castle and for everyone to keep a lookout.

After I left Odessa, I headed back to my room. I was getting ready to get high again when my mother burst through my doors.

"I'm taking Odessa for a walk tomorrow," she said.

"No, she needs to stay in her room," I countered.

"She can't stay in her room all day; she needs to get out."

"It's easier to protect her when she's in her room."

"Then you take her for a walk."

"Fine, I will!" I shouted.

My mom slammed the door. I could feel the pain in my head. I wasted no time; I shot up again. I wasn't going to let my mother ruin my high.

The next day I was in a much better mood 'cause my brother was coming home soon. I wanted this day to go by fast.

Letting Odessa out of her room made her think that I cared about her, and I didn't. I walked a little behind her.

"Are you done walking yet?" I asked.

"We've only been walking for a minute."

"Yeah, so?"

"Just a little bit longer. Thanks for letting me out of my room."

"Wasn't really my idea."

"Hey, Sly, what do you really want in this life?"

"I want my bother to be ruler of this world."

"Then what?"

"Excuse me?"

"Well, once your bother takes down your father and becomes king, then what?"

"I guess I will leave here and go somewhere else."

"Really, where would you go?"

"I'm not sure, just anywhere but here."

"I know how you feel we have a lot in common," she said.

"Let's get one thing straight: we have nothing in common, OK? Now hurry up and finish your walk."

"You know, you're not as tough as you think you are."

I got up right in her face and squinted my eyes at her.

"And how the hell would you know?" I challenged.

She was breathing very heavily. I could feel her breath on my skin; that's how close I got to her without touching her.

She looked at me square in the eye.

"What if I kissed you?" she asked.

I back up from her in confusion.

"I don't want to turn to stone."

"If you were as tough as you say you are, then you would kiss me right now, and who knows, you might not turn to stone.

I couldn't believe it. She was challenging me in a seductive way.

"The walk is over now," I said.

"See, not as tough as you say you are."
"Don't tempt me."
"What, don't you fine me attractive?"
"Are you trying to seduce me?"
"I just want you to know I'm not afraid of you."
"It's easy to not be afraid of me when your immortality is staring at me in the face."
"You didn't answer my question."
"You didn't answer mine either."
"I'll answer your question if you answer mine."
"Fine, I'll go first. Are you trying to seduce me?"
"Would you be mad if I said yes?"
"Don't play games with me. Yes or no?"
"Do you find me attractive?"
"Go to your room."

She was trying to get a rise out of me. That pissed me off. And answering my question with another question made me even more mad. I wished my brother would get here already. She was driving me insane. I couldn't decide what was pissing me off more, the fact that I wanted her or that she was trying to get under my skin. Either way, I wouldn't give in. She belonged to my bother, and I would not let her come between us.

Chapter 77

Princess Odessa Seraphim

I had never wanted someone to touch me so badly before. I would have given anything to have Sly stay right next to me. That right there sent my skin into an electrical uproar. If he were to touch me with just a finger, it would be enough to send my body over board. I screamed it in my head when he got real close to me to touch him first so I could endure the sensation I craved. My head and my heart went crazy when I was near him. I remembered what my mom used to say about love, and it got me thinking, Is this love that I'm feeling? I desire him so much; he's all I think about now. But today proved he doesn't feel the same. I prayed that the shivers on my skin didn't expose how I truly felt about him. My core felt like it was going to explode whenever he looked at me, making it difficult to breath.

I was in my room lying on my bed, thinking of ways I could get him to fall for me. Then I snapped out of it because that was not what I had come here for. I needed to help my people. I had to pay attention to the task. Not to mention, Ace was going to be here in a few days. It was only a matter of time. I thought, It's funny—I'm married to him, but I don't feel married.

I was tired of being in my room, so I decided to get some fresh air. I opened the door to find Goliath waiting outside, watching my door.

"Let me guess—you are here to keep an eye on me?"

He didn't say anything; he just looked at me with a grunt. I walked into the hallway, and he followed me. He didn't say a word, just continued to shadow me. With him behind me, I would never get lost.

I came across a room with lots of books and all kinds of papers. Goliath leaned up against the entrance wall as he just watched me looking around. I thought for sure he was going to stop me, but he didn't. I scrolled through all the papers on the desk, but I couldn't make out the language. From what I could make out in the drawings, there were two types of demons that seemed to be feuding, and for a long time too. In my realm there is no fighting. I wonder what they could possibly be fighting, I thought. It never seems to have a resolution. I looked closely at the drawings and saw one of the demons looked a lot like Goliath. Red Demon versus Black Demon. I looked up from the paper and saw on a podium nearby a really big book with all kinds of skulls embedded in it. I walked up to it. Orcus was written on it, along with the Dark Realm symbol. I got ready to open it when Goliath slammed his hand down on top of it, keeping me from prying into it. I looked at him, and he shook his head.

I stepped back from the book.

"You know, you are a demon of very few words," I said.

He rolled his eyes at me and hinted it was time to go.

"It's just a book, you know?"

He started growling at me. So I took the hint not to say anymore. Goliath didn't know what I was saying, but I felt that he understood me.

Morgana came around the corner; she looked worried.

"Oh, Odessa, there you are," she said.

"Is everything OK?" I asked.

"No. Sly seems to be in a terrible mood right now."

"How come?"

"He got a letter this evening. Apparently Ace is going to be a few more days. So I came to warn you to watch out. He is not at his finest. Maybe stay in your room and try not to annoy him."

"Thank you for telling me."

"It's my pleasure."

"They are really close, aren't they?"

"Thick as thieves. You couldn't pry them apart, even if your life depended on it. Believe me. I know their father has tried countless times to pin them up against each other, but in the end, they will only serve one another till the end of time."

"An unshakable bond."

"You know I have a daughter," Morgana said.

"No, I didn't know that. Where is she?"

"She was taken from me. She has a different father then Ace and Sly. When King Draven found out about my infidelities, he sold her off in a marriage that I didn't agree with."

"I'm so sorry."

"Don't be. I feel sometimes she's better off. Besides, you are now my new daughter."

Morgana's words did not give me comfort.

"Morgana, what is this feud that is going on between the Red Demons and the Black Demons?"

"Oh, that. Well, that was going on long before King Draven was king."

"But why fight at all when there is never any outcome?"

"I don't know. I'm not even sure what the fight is about, there are so many theories.

"Like what?"

"Well, some believe that the reason they fight is Balor the Demon God started it."

"Really? How?"

"Balor got jealous of some mortal and caused a big scene that started a war."

"But that's not what you believe."

"Well, a lot of people such as myself think that the real reason is that King Draven is not worthy to rule. He only came into power because he claimed to be the Demon God's son."

"Claims? You mean no one can prove it?"

Morgana looked at me kind of funny.

"What's this got to do with anything? Why are you so interested?" she asked.

"Nothing. Just curious."

"The only thing you have to worry your pretty little head about is getting my son on his rightful throne."

"Yeah, right!"

Then another demon, who looked like Goliath, came running up to us. He whispered something in Morgana's ear. She looked at me.

"Come with me. Sly has gotten out of control."

In the fighting pit, Sly was beating a troll to death. Black blood was spewing everywhere as he continued to pound him to a pulp. Goliath came over and grabbed him off the troll.

I never knew Sly could be so cruel and vicious. He hides it well with his eyes, I thought.

I watched as they removed the half-dead troll from the pit.

Sly was still clawing and pushing Goliath to get him to release him, but he wouldn't budge.

Morgana went over and slapped Sly in the face to get him to calm down.

"What did you do that for?" Morgana asked.

"He was in my way," Sly responded.

"Are you done acting like a fool?" Morgana said.

Goliath finally let Sly go. He was covered in the troll's blood, and he was all out of breath.

"I'm fine. You can leave now!"

Morgana threw up her hands and was getting ready to leave when she stopped at me.

"Careful, he might bite your head off," she said.

After she left the room, everyone went back to doing what they were doing, as if nothing happened. They started cleaning the pit, washing away all the blood.

Sly wasn't wearing anything on his torso. He went over to a bucket of water and poured it all over himself. I watched as the water came cascading down his body, washing the blood away.

I couldn't help but get enticed by this. He shook his head to get the water droplets out of his face. Then he saw me.

My heart was racing, but I didn't let him know that he had gotten to me.

"What the hell are you looking at?" he said.

"Who knew you could be so cruel."

"In case you haven't noticed, I am a demon."

"You know, that much hostility is not good for you."

"I wouldn't have this hostility if you weren't here."

"Why are you so mean to me when your brother is so kind to me?"

"Don't talk about my brother."

"It's true, your brother always has something nice to say to me."

"That's only 'cause you have something he wants, but whenever that changes, you will see he's not all peaches and cream."

"I'm sure your brother will be back soon."

"No. My brother was supposed to be back today, but because of you, he now has to sleep with one eye open, hoping that he doesn't make a mistake that will cause his father to eat him."

"Your father would eat his own son?"

"Wake up. Look around you. Do you think you are in dreamland? This is the Dark Realm, the realm of the dead. Everyone here is only out for themselves. It's survival of the fittest, sweetheart, and without your immortality, you would have already been eaten up."

"This realm and you don't scare me at all."

"You are so simple-minded."

"I am not. I can fight my way out of anything."

"Let me show you something."

Sly brought me outside of the castle terrace, where it was completely dark, no sunlight or moon of any kind. Just candles that were lit up in the kingdom.

"Look down there."

I looked down, and there was this black oozing substance surrounding the castle. And dead bodies that were floating around in it. Like a big soup mix of the dead. You cloud hear their cries if you got close enough.

I had never felt sympathy before, but I wanted to feel it for them. I wanted to cry for them, but I couldn't; Lumentals don't cry.

"It's called the Vile. It starts from the Kingdom of Despair, where my father rules, and flows down here and then spreads everywhere else like an infectious disease. You see, this is what comes from a king who doesn't give a shit."

I continued to watch and saw children floating in there and babies all just mangled together.

"But your bother is going to fix this when he becomes King of the Dead."

"There is no fixing this. This stuff is flooding my world. Every day the Vile gets bigger and bigger 'cause the dead would rather float in this than be judged by the King of Death. When a soul is separated from its body, it means it has been judged."

"So the dead have a choice?"

"Not really. All the dead become my father's, whether they are judged or not. Good souls are slaves who wander this world alone and depressed, whereas bad souls get eaten, as if they never existed."

"So if they are floating in the Vile, does that mean your father doesn't want them anymore?"

"No, what it means is that my father has a job that he can't do well. Instead of finding a safe haven for these souls, he lets them pile up like this. As long as the dead come to our world, he gets stronger. So you still think that there can be good and kindness in my world?"

"There is good in everyone, including you."

"Stop acting like you know me; you don't."

"You said you wanted to find a safe haven for the dead; that's kindness if I ever saw it."

"Do you know how annoying you are? Go to your room now."

After Sly pointed in the direction of my room, I went.

Chapter 78

Prince Slymael Arius

My brother told me in the note not to worry for a few more days. I wanted him back right then; I didn't like being a babysitter. On top of everything, his pet was annoying the fuck out of me. I had never met a more vexatious woman. Standing there all righteous and pure. It was enough to make me wanna puke. And yet she was all I thought about.

I was standing patrolling the castle. I had nothing better to do. It would help me get my mind off things. I was getting ready to call it quits when Goliath came to me and told me that they had spotted some ghouls coming up the east wall. Do they ever give up? I thought.

We went to Odessa's room to make sure she was safe. I burst through her door.

"What is it? What's going on?" she asked.

"Get your sword. The ghouls are back."

"So soon."

"Stay in here. Don't move."

"Where was I going to go?"

"Oh great, sarcasm to add to the annoyance you give."

"I'm just trying to lighten up the mood."

"Don't let anyone in unless it's me or Goliath."

"What about your mother?"

"Fine! You can let her in too."

"Sir, yes, sir."

"I cannot wait till my brother gets back."

"You are such a crybaby when it comes to your brother."

"Really? Is that what you think of me? Let me show you how much of a crybaby I can be."

Before she could say something, I left her room to kill some ghouls. When I came back, I brought her back the head of a ghoul.

"That's disgusting," she said.

"Do you still think I'm a crybaby?"

"I didn't mean it like that."

"I don't care how you meant it."

"Look, I'm sorry. I wasn't trying—"

"Shut up. It's so much better when you don't speak."

"There is just no pleasing you, is there?"

"You wanna please me?

"I don't even think that's possible.

"For you it isn't."

"Ugh!"

She picked up the severed head. While it was in her hands, it turned to stone. She threw it out her window.

"What's wrong, you don't like my gift?" I asked.

"No, actually I find it repulsive."

"Oh, too bad. Maybe next time I'll bring you something more grotesque."

She squinted her eyes at me.

"That's OK; I think I'll pass," she responded.

"Suit yourself."

I was getting ready to leave.

"Hey, Sly."

"Yeah…"

Before she could say something, another ghoul came through her window. I acted fast; I grabbed her wrist and pulled her to the side and stabbed the ghoul in the neck. When I jerked my sword out of its neck, it fell to the floor.

"Sly."

I turned around and look at her.

"Are you all right?" I asked.

"Yes, I'm fine."

"Good."

"Sly, you're holding my wrist."

She was right. I looked down and saw I was touching her. And I wasn't turning to stone. Her skin felt so warm and soft. I let her wrist go immediately. Then we both looked at each other. That warm feeling was happening again, the one I feel every time I'm around her, only this time it was in my soul.

It was getting really awkward, so I left immediately.

I was quickly walking down the hall when my mother came up to me.

"Mother, not now."

"What's with you?"

"Nothing. I just don't want to talk right now."

"So sorry, I just wanted to know if you got all the ghouls and Odessa is fine."

"Yes, she is fine. You can go talk to her."

"Great, I will go see her."

"Wait, Mother—is there a chance that you can touch a Lumental without turning to stone?"

"The only way I know is if both are in love."

I was starting to freak out. I'm not in love with her, I thought.

"Is there any way you could be wrong?"

"Of course I could be wrong. Everything I'm telling you I learned from a book.

I started to calm down a bit. For all I knew, this could just be an accident. Yes, this was nothing more than a huge misunderstanding.

"Thank you, Mother."

"Sure. I don't know what I did, but you're welcome."

I went into my room and shut the door. I needed to breathe. Who was I kidding? I needed to get high and fast. I wanted to forget everything that happened.

After I shot up, I forgot all my problems. I lay there and let it take over me once again. With my eyes closed, I drifted off. I saw Odessa from afar; she was flying toward me. The closer she got, the more excited I got she was near. I tried to ignore the feeling, but I couldn't. Then she reached out and said, "You are the one with the heart."

Then I heard a pounding in my head. It got louder and louder. I came to and woke up with a giant headache. I sat up in my bed and realized that someone was pounding on my door. "Yeah, yeah, I hear you."

I opened the door to Goliath. He told me that a letter had come; he handed it to me. It said that my brother was coming home; he would leave first thing tomorrow.

I was very overcome by this. But first I had to fix something or make sure something wasn't what I thought it was.

I headed to Odessa's room. I slammed open the door.

"Don't you knock?" she asked.

"There is no time for that."

"What are you talking about?"

"Touch this."

"What is it?"

"It's a dead goblin. Now touch it."

"Can I ask why?"

"Will you just touch it?"

She reached out her finger and touched it, and it immediately went to stone.

"Good so far."

Then I had a jar of my blood in it."

"Now touch this."

"Does this have anything to do with last night?"

"Just touch this, please."

She did, and the glass and my blood turned to stone.

I was so relieved. She didn't love me, and I didn't love her. Whew, that was a huge relief. Now my brother would return and everything would be just how he left it.

I was getting ready to walk out.

"Sly, are you all right?" she asked.

"Yes. Everything is perfect."

"Really, perfect?"

"Oh yes."

"I found a better way for you to prove that you are not a crybaby."

"I'm listening."

"I want you to kiss me right now."

Oh no, not this again, I thought.

"I told you, I don't want to turn to stone."

"But last night shows that you won't."

"But today clearly shows that I will, and yesterday was just a fluke accident."

"Then prove it; kiss me now."

"No! I'm not turning to stone."

"Show me that you are as tough as you say you are."

"I don't have to prove anything to you."

"You are right. So you are exactly what I thought you were."

"Look, I know what you are doing, and it's not going to work."

"What am I doing?"

"You are trying to tempt me."

"I've been hearing from your mother and your bother that you are this great and powerful warrior, and I'm just not seeing it. Oh, you can fight and you talk a big game, but in the end, you are just a coward."

Without even thinking about it, I went up to her. I was in her face.

"You want to see a coward?" I challenged.

I grabbed her, pulled her in, and took over her mouth. I couldn't stop there. I had to have her all the way. Every part of her was like a warm high that was better than the blood that I injected myself with. I was hooked on her body. Her skin was shiny, but it felt even better touching it. Like a packaged gift that is made up so nice and pretty and you just have to open up to see what's inside. I wouldn't stop myself even if my life depended on it, and I wasn't thinking about anything else. Because clearly enough, this gift wasn't mine to open.

Chapter 79

Princess Odessa Seraphim

Sly was forceful but gentle, which was surprising given his nature. He took me over and over again. There was no stopping him, and I indulged in every minute of it. I had no idea that my body could give and receive this pleasure I couldn't describe in any words.

I woke up and stretched. I felt like my body was not my own. I sat up. Sly was sleeping next to me. I was careful not to wake him. I slid out of bed and walked up to the mirror. I was observing my naked body.

I didn't recognize myself. I kneeled down on my knees and touched the mirror. It felt cold; I felt cold. I wasn't shiny anymore. My skin felt so sensitive. My stomach started to rumble. My body was completely sore all over the place. I thought I was dying. I was so overwhelmed that I was shaking all over. I didn't understand why I felt this way. What was wrong with me? Even my wings felt so fragile.

Sly was rustling in the bed. He woke up and sat up. He saw me shivering. He came up and wrapped both his arms around me.

"I don't understand what's going on with me," I said.

"It's OK. Your power of immortality is gone."

"You mean I'm—"

"Yes, you are mortal now."

He pressed his forehead against mine.

"I'm so scared."

"Don't be. I will take care of everything now."

Sly grabbed a blanket off the bed and wrapped it around me. It felt so nice, and it helped calm me down.

"What do we do now?" I asked.

Sly heard my stomach grumbling.

"Well, I guess I should get you something to eat."

"I'm also feeling a little light-headed."

"You probably need some water as well."

"Do you think I can survive as a mortal?"

"Sure you can. I'll help you."

"I feel better already."

"Let me go get you some food and water. Don't leave this room for anything."

"Sly, I have this pressure down below. What do I do?"

"You probably have to go pee."

"What's pee?"

"Oh, this is going to be interesting," Sly said.

After he explained to me what pee was, I couldn't help but feel grossed out.

"You mean you sit on a bucket and release?"

"That's pretty much it."

"That's so strange."

"Yeah, it is. Here is the bucket. You sit down and give it a try."

"You mean I just go?"

"Yep, it's pretty self-explanatory."

I was having a little trouble; Sly could see that. So after he got dressed, he kissed me on the forehead and told me that he would be back. He left so I could try it without his presence.

After I relieved myself, it felt so good. Who could have known something so gross could feel so great? I wasn't having pain down there anymore.

I quickly got dressed. The clothes on me felt different, smoother. Like this was the first time I had ever worn them. I was getting ready to sit down when the door burst open.

It was Morgana. She looked at me with strain in her eyes.

I stood up. Morgana didn't say a word; she just kept looking at me with confusion.

"Hello, Morgana."

"You look very different today," she said.

"I do?"

She massaged her chin for a minute, staring very hard at me.

"Yeah, you're not as shiny as you usually are. In fact, you're not shiny at all."

"Maybe it's bad lighting."

"No, no, I can see it—you seem more vulnerable."

"I assure you that I'm not. I'm just as always I have been."

"I saw my son come out of your room just now."

"Did you?"

"You know I saw him enter your room twelve hours ago."

"Really, twelve hours ago?"

"Yes, and now I see him leave your room."

"I think you're mistaken."

She squinted her eyes at me. I felt like she could see right through me. I had this wet stuff coming down from my head. The more nervous I got, the more of it leaked out.

"You know you are sweating?"

"Is that what that is?"

She came up and grabbed my arm. I immediately pulled away from her. Her eyes got wide. She shook her head at me.

"Sly, he's a great fuck, isn't he? I would know."

"You have had sex with your own son?"

"Oh yes! Him and Ace. I have even slept with both of them at the same time, and sometimes it was just the two of them and I wasn't one of the two."

"I don't believe you."

"Well, believe it! Because now that you are no longer indestructible, there is no need for you. I can't wait to see what happens when Ace comes back."

"Sly will protect me."

"I don't think so. If he has to choose between you and his brother, who do you think he will choose?"

Oh no, was I going to get eaten? Was Sly going to let me get killed? I was afraid of what Ace would do now. I couldn't face him.

"If I die, then I'm ready."

"Good, 'cause that is rapidly approaching as we speak."

She slammed the door in my face. I dropped to the floor. I was breathing heavily. What do I do now? I asked myself.

Chapter 80

Prince Slymael Arius

I was freaking out. What the hell did I just do? I thought. I was still contemplating it over and over in my mind: How could I have been so carless? What is Ace going to think? I was in the kitchen gathering stuff for Odessa to eat.

Was this my fault? I thought, She tempted me, right, so how can I be at fault? But secretly I wanted her, so it is my fault. Shit, what the fuck do I do?

I was getting ready to leave the kitchen when my mother came out of nowhere and slapped me across the face; it didn't hurt, but I got the message.

"Are you out of your fucking mind? You realize you just fucked your brother's wife," she said."

"I know, and I'm so sorry. Oh God, I'm so sorry."

I got down on my knees. I had never been so terrified in my whole life. And I see terrible things every day.

"We are going to have to figure out something. Ace is going to go ballistic," she said.

"I know. I will figure it out."

"You are going to have to kill her, and when Ace gets here, you tell him that she was a fake."

I got up from my knees and looked at my mother.

"I can't kill her," I said."

"Oh yes, you can, and you will do it now."

"I can't do that."

"Yes, you can, for you don't have a choice."

"I won't kill her."

"Oh God, don't tell me you are in love with her."

"I…I don't know. I'm so confused."

"Look at me, Sly. It's either you or her. Ace will not show you mercy. Listen to me: You love your bother, right?"

"Yes, I do."

"Then don't let her come between you two."

"OK, I will do it."

"There you go. And if your brother asks, we tell him that she wasn't who she said she was."

"Right."

"I will take her this food. You will wait till I leave her room, then you will go and end her."

"I can do that."

"I know you can."

After my mother left. I went to my room and grabbed my sword. I said to myself, I kill lots of things ever day. It would be hypocritical of me to not do this. She is nothing to me. So why do I feel so disgusted inside? We don't love each other, but then why didn't I turn to stone? Why did I make love to her for so long? I would never hurt my brother like that. I care more about him than anything in this world. So why does my heart feel like it's shifting? Could it be a hint of feeling ashamed?

I got to her door. My mother came out; she told me it was time. I went in there. I saw her looking at me with those golden-brown eyes, and all my worries were gone. Her smile made me forget everything again.

"Sly, I just tried food, and it is so good," she said.

"Oh yeah, food can be great."

I was getting nervous; I never get nervous. This woman was changing me, I didn't think for the better. And yet I was yearning to embrace it.

"When the food hits my tongue, it makes my stomach feel good. Now I get why the monsters in this world love to eat so much."

"Odessa, we need to talk about what happened between the two of us."

"It was amazing."

"My bother is going to be home any minute."

She just looked at me, waiting for me to explain further, but I couldn't. She walked up to me, put her hands in my hands. I lost control again.

I picked her up and dropped her on the bed. I took her body again right then and there. I was impulsive, without a care. That was what she did to me. She made it impossible for me to deny her. I now had the biggest weakness of all: I had given my heart up. But how could I have done that when it already belonged to my brother?

After we were done, she fell asleep. I covered her with a blanket, and I left. I went to my room to think. I had to think about what I was going to do next.

My mom burst through my door again.

"You did it, right?" she asked.

"Can you leave? I have to think."

"Right, but you did do it, right?"

"Not now."

"Oh no, you didn't kill her!"

"Just let me think."

"What's there to think about?"

"Look, Ace loves me; he's my brother. We have been through a lot of shit together. He will understand when I tell him."

"No, Sly, he won't. You took something that belongs to him."

"He only wanted Odessa for her power, but I haven't inherited any power. Therefore he won't care."

"How do you know you haven't possessed her power?"

"Because I don't feel like I have immortality."

"There is only one way to test out that theory. When Ace is here, you will tell him everything, and if he understands, then you will be fine. If he doesn't, then he will kill you, and at that time you will either survive or die."

"He will not harm me. I feel it, Mother."

"I cannot believe you are throwing everything away for that pretty face."

"I'm not throwing anything away. My loyalty is to my brother. I'm glad I can show him that there is no power to inherit from a Lumental."

"Let's just hope he sees it that way."

"That is the only way to see it."

"Sly, you have fallen in love, and you can't even acknowledge it."

"Shut up! I know what I'm doing."

"Really? 'Cause I don't think you have a clue what you are doing."

"Just stay out of it, Mother."

"No, I'm not going to let you do this. If you can't kill her, I will."

I grabbed my mother's arm and slammed her up against the wall.

"If you go anywhere near her, I will cut you head off and feed it to the werewolves."

A knock came at the door.

"Come in," I yelled.

It was Goliath. He told me that my bother had arrived.

Chapter 81

Princess Odessa Seraphim

I woke up to find Sly wasn't next to me. I sat up. I heard a lot of commotion outside my bedroom window. I got dressed and looked out. I saw Ace had arrived. I had mixed feelings about him being back. I was happy 'cause I knew Sly had missed him, but what would he do to Sly when he learned that he and I had been intimate?

I was getting ready to walk out when Morgana rushed in front of me. She slapped me across the face.

"Ouch!" I exclaimed.

"That's called pain, and you better get used to it 'cause there is a lot of it coming your way," she said.

"I haven't done anything wrong."

"I should slap you again just for saying that. I will not let you come between my boys. You better hope, for your sake, that their relationship goes on without tarnish 'cause if it doesn't, there will be nobody to save you.

She slammed the door. I touched my cheek and caressed the pain. I had to talk to Ace to let him know that it's my fault, not Sly's. That he should be angry with me, not Sly.

I ran into the throne room. Ace and Sly both looked at me. By their faces, I could tell they were in a very heated conversation. Ace's face was red; he was upset. Sly looked sympathetic and sad. Sly smiled at me. I smiled back. While Sly and I were staring at each other as if we were the only two people in the room, Ace grabbed his brother's sword from his hand and plunged it into his chest.

"Noooooooo!" I shouted.

I went to Sly as he fell into my arms. The look on his face made it look as though everything that he had grown up to know and believe had just been ripped to shreds.

He looked up at me and then closed his eyes. And like that, he was gone. The tears welled up in my eyes and flowed down my cheeks. The numbing pain of sorrow and hurt crept up into my body. I was experiencing heartache. And for the first time, my body gave out the right emotion.

Ace threw the sword down. I looked up at him from the floor as I was holding Sly in my arms.

He grinned.

"Guess he was right—you have no power to inherit," he said.

"How could you kill your own brother?"

"I didn't kill him; you did."

I was sobbing and moaning in torment as I was squeezing onto Sly's lifeless body.

"But I never meant…"

I couldn't get the words out. I was crying so hard and shaking everywhere."

"I take it this is the first time you have experienced tears? They can be real annoying."

Morgana came in once she heard the screaming.

"Ace, what did you do?" she asked.

"I will not let my brother choose her over me," Ace responded.

"So you killed him for it?"

"What would you have had me do? He betrayed me."

Morgana shoved Ace hard. He stepped back.

"If I can't have him, no one can!" Ace shouted.

"Do you know what this will do? The Arathagore will divide, making us weak," said Morgana.

"Then we will blame it on her."

They both looked at me.

Ace came up to me.

"Now that you are not immortal anymore, I will enjoy taking out my frustration on you."

Some of the Arathagore came in and carried Sly's body away. Ace told them to give him a proper burial.

I was lying naked on the cold slab of the dungeon floor, surrounded by skeleton bones all around me. The smell of my blood filling the air. My wings had been rip out of their sockets. My back was bleeding out, not just from the lost of my wings but also from the cuts I had endured from Ace's whippings and beatings. His torture methods went on forever.

I was in so much pain, but the thing that hurt the most was my heart. It was my fault Sly was dead. I caused the rift between him and his brother. With the family he loved so much.

My brother was right: I should have never come here. I thought, I'm so stupid. Here I am lying on my side curled up like a ball with nothing and no one to lose. And to have thought I could make a difference was just me lying to myself. My father was also right: I should have known my place. The tears did not stop from the moment Sly lay dead in my arms, and they would continue to flow undeniably; I had no will to stop them. I always wanted to know what tears felt like, and now I knew. My crying got so loud that I woke up something in the next cell.

"Never known a demon to cry. In fact, monsters don't cry either," it said.

I said nothing; I just kept sobbing.

"Come on, tell me—what demon are you?" it continued.

"I'm a nothing," I responded.

"What nothing cries like that?"

"Does it matter?"

"Let me get a better look at you, nothing."

I couldn't move; I was in too much pain. So she moved from one side of her cell to the other to get a better look at me.

"Well, from what I can see, you're not a demon. I would say human, but you look a little more special than that, or at least you did. Plus, humans can't come down here unless they are dead, so that's out."

"I told you, nothing matters, so just leave me alone."

"Well, that's not true, or you wouldn't be crying."

"The only thing that matters is that I'm dying, and I'm more than OK with it. It's fitting, considering I deserve to die."

"What if I told you that you weren't going to die?"

I mustered all the strength I had in me to sit up. I did it very slowly as it hurt to move. I was taking deep breaths to endure the pain. I could feel the warm blood dripping down my back from my wounds to the back of my legs and then to the floor. I grabbed the prison bars and used them to help pull myself the rest of the way.

"Well, there you are. I can't see all of you, but from what I can see, you're definitely not a monster. Do you have a symbol on your neck?"

"Everyone has a symbol on their neck, even if they aren't from this realm."

"I knew you weren't from this realm."

"You said I wasn't going to die. What are you?" I asked.

"I'm a witch, and my name is Empusa!"

I responded, "I have already met your kind, and since you are masters of manipulation, you will have to forgive me If I don't believe you when you say I won't die."

"I take it you have met Morgana," she went on.

I nodded.

"Well, then let me tell you that there are all kinds of witches. While she is powerful in spells and hexes, my power is more in fortune-telling, reading of the signs, and predicting the cosmos. Seeing the past present and future."

"I don't understand you, and I didn't understand her, but I knew one thing: she could not be trusted."

"That is true. How is Morgan? Still favoring the oldest son, is she?"

"Yeah. Why does she do that?"

"Even though Ace is the oldest and the natural-born leader, he is also the weakest. You see, Morgana can manipulate and twist Ace to do anything she wants, but Sly is of a different breed. He's not so easy to convince. Do know why that is?"

"Because Sly has a heart."

Empusa responded, "Very good! You see, Sly thinks for himself because he can feel, whereas Ace has no heart, so he will do whatever his mother tells him to do. Morgana fears Sly."

I couldn't stand up anymore. I was losing to much blood, getting weaker by the minute, so I sat down. I turned my head for a minute, and Empusa got all excited. She got a glimpse of the symbol on my neck.

"You're from the Light Realm, which would make you a Lumental."

"Not anymore," I said.

"Sure you are. Lumentals are the only ones from the Light Realm."

"Since I have no wings and no immortality, that would mean I'm not anymore."

"Fall in love, did you?"

"And now I'm paying for it. Now that Sly is dead, I hope to find him when I die and beg for his forgiveness."

"That will be kind of hard since he's not dead."

"You know, for someone who can supposedly read the present, you're not very good."

She laughed very hard.

"Actually, I'm very good," she said.

"If you're so good, then how did you end up here. Surely you must have seen this coming?"

"I told the oldest Prince of Darkness that he was going to die a horrible death, so he threw me down here to persuade me to change my verdict."

"And has it?"

"No, of course not. I don't make the future; I just read it like it is. And I saw that I was going to be imprisoned with Lumental and found it fascinating. To meet one would be a real honor."

"I have no honor. As I told you before, I'm nothing."

"I have heard that Lumentals have the power of miracles, to see things that no one can see."

"None of that is true, at least not for me."

"Listen, fallen angel, just because your immortality is gone does not mean you have no power left."

"I killed Sly; he is dead because of me."

"How many times must I tell you? He's not dead."

"Can you stop talking and leave me alone? You have no idea what you are talking about."

"If I told you something about yourself that you didn't tell me, would you believe me then?

"I don't care."

"I know that your name is Odessa and that you are King Odin Seraphim's daughter."

My eyes got wide. She had my attention. But so what that she knew that? It didn't change the fact that I was either going to die in this cell from loss of blood or be executed tomorrow.

"Very good, you got something right. Now please leave me alone," I said.

"I have another secret for you."

"I really don't care."

"You are going to have a baby—or should I say, babies."

The place where light and dark begin
to touch is where miracles arise.

—Robert A. Johnson

Part VIII

THE NATURE REALM

Introduction

The Nature Realm is in the south, where it is very warm. Not as warm as the east and much more humid than the west. The south is an immeasurable jungle and forest that flourishes with extreme plant life. The animals here are plentiful.

There are three kingdoms in the Nature Realm. The biggest kingdom is called Viniues, the kingdom of leaves. Viniues is smack-dab in the middle of the Nature Realm. The second biggest kingdom is called Photinia, the kingdom of flowers. It is farther south. The third kingdom is called Dahlia, the kingdom of the withered.

All who live in the nature Realm are called Viridis. They all have green hair and forest-green eyes. The Viridis have the power to grow all plant and vegetation life. They can also change into any animal of their realm. Except one girl who cannot change into animals but has the power to heal.

The Viridis believe in Hermia the Goddess of Nature. All that live here worship her. There are three spirit trees. One is a Methuselah tree that ensures growth. The second one is an olive tree that represents peace. The third one is an oak tree that ensures strength. The three spirt trees guard the Arbor Vitae, the tree of life. The Arbor Vitae is a willow tree. Hermia's eyes, they say, are in the willow tree. Without these trees, the Viridis would cease to exist and the vegetation would be no more.

Now, only King Midas Rupert Blumenthal, king of Viniues, and his queen Naomi are allowed to talk to the spirit trees. The tree spirits give them insight into how to rule through Hermia's way. There is nothing in the south that the spirit trees don't know about. They are the eyes and ears of the jungle and forest. Their roots are connected to all plant life and animals in their realm.

Queen Sarabi is King Midas's half sister. They have the same dad but different mothers. She is an enemy to King Midas and all of the Viridis. Sarabi is a Datura. Datura are the bringers of poison. She has the power to kill the oxygen in all the plants and flowers. Sarabi is Queen of Dahlia and has the Maikoa doing her bidding. She controls them. The Maikoa are as tall as a nine-year-old child, are covered in green hair, and have long, pointed ears and long, sharp nails and teeth. They have a taste for meat, so they eat animals. They are savage creatures that smell really bad. Then there are the Gux. Gux are giant rocks that look like big, burly men. They can roll themselves into boulders. The Gux are Sarabi's army; they protect the Kingdom of the Withered.

The A Gate army is King Midas's army and is the most powerful army in the south. They are now coming back from the Kingdom of the Withered. They were there to get Sarabi to sign a peace treaty stating that she and her Gux and Maikoa would stay in the Kingdom of the Withered.

The problem in the Nature Realm is plants keeping dying because of Sarabi, making the Nature Realm smaller and smaller.

Hermia symbolizes strong will and uniqueness.

The Viridis religion is called Terran.

Chapter 82

Princess Jade Blumenthal

The jungle was hot, as always. This is my favorite place to be, in the jungle. My mother tells me that I won't be able to enjoy it much longer since I'm a princess and have duties to my kingdom. My best friend Feed is a lot like me: he's very adventurous, and that's what I want to be.

We were sitting deep in the jungle, waiting patiently. I hunt; that's what I do, and it's what I'm great at.

"Why are we hunting for Maikoa?" Feed asked.

"'Cause they are a threat to are way of life," I explained.

"But your dad got Sarabi to sign a treaty that said they won't be coming this way."

"And he is stupid to think that Sarabi would honor that treaty."

"I'm so hungry."

"You are always hungry."

"I can't help it."

"You know you are very lucky to be as thin as you are and not gain a pound."

"I'm only twelve. They say weight catches up with you when you get older."

"Whatever you say."

"Come on, J, let's go back to the palace and get some food."

"Shhh! You will give away are position."

The bushes started to move. I got my arrow ready as I was waiting for whatever it was to show itself.

Before I knew it, an elk appeared eating some leaves on the ground. But I still was ready to fire my arrow.

"Well, this was a waste of time," said Feed.

"I said, Shhh!"

"What's the big deal; it's just an elk."

"Look closer."

As I was scoping it out, I smiled as I could see what I was looking for. A Maikoa was creeping up on the elk, but it is hard to see them; their green fur helps them blend into the jungle.

I shot my arrow and scared the Elk. But I wounded the Maikoa—I got his hand. But it took off, and I ran after it.

"No, I'm not running; I hate physical activity," said Fee.

"Come on, Feed, hurry. It's getting away!"

As I was running after it, I shot a couple arrows. One arrow scared it into another direction.

It was running out of time, with me gaining on it. It was easy to chase since it was leaving a blood trail from its hand. I stopped when I saw the blood trail had ended. This Maikoa was hiding somewhere.

I laced up another bow. I could feel it was near. I was startled by a black crow that flew down next to me. It was Feed. The crow looked right at me.

"I told you I don't run," he said.

"Flying is much faster anyway," I added.

"So where is it?"

"It's hiding."

"So how are you going find it?"

"Well, we could use some bait."

"Where are we going to get that?"

I looked right at Feed and smiled.

"No way!" he said.

"Oh, come on, I won't let him get you. I promise."

I could tell he wasn't up for it, but he didn't argue. He turned into an elk like the one we scared off earlier.

"I'm not happy about this," he said.

"Stop talking. Try to look the part."

"I am!"

I waited behind a tree. It took a minute, but the Maikoa finally showed itself. When Feed saw him, his eyes got big.

"OK, J, now would be a good time. Shoot!"

"Not yet. Wait till he gets closer."

"Jade, he is close enough. Shoot."

"Not yet."

Feed screamed as the Maikoa jump at him. But I let my arrow fly, and I hit it dead in the head. It fell to the ground, blood everywhere.

"Are you out of your mind? He almost got me."

"I told you, I won't let anything get you."

"Next time you become the bait."

"How can I when I'm the hunter? And I can't change into animals like you can."

"Well, I'm never going to do that again."

"Whatever you say."

"Pugh, they stink. What are they even doing on this side? They are not supposed to be here."

"Did you really think that a piece of paper was going to stop them?"

"That was the whole point, wasn't it? Otherwise, why did Sarabi sign it?"

I pulled my arrow out of the Maikoa.

"Because she is just pretending to play ball."

"Why?"

"Because she want's the Arbor Vitae."

"The tree of life? She's dreaming."

"Maybe so, but that's what she wants."

"You need to tell your father about this."

"Do you think he's going to listen to me?"

"But we have proof."

"Are you going to carry this thing to the kingdom? 'Cause I'm not."

"Well, how else are we going to convince your father?"

Before I could answer Feed, we heard bells ringing in the distance. Feed and I looked at each other.

"Oh no, the welcome home festival!"

"That's today?"

"Yes!"

The A Gate army was coming home today, and we were supposed to be there to greet them. Feed and I hurried to the kingdom without delay.

Chapter 83

*Prince Aries Fidem
Kingdom of the Withered*

"Why are you sulking?" my mother asked.
"How could you sign that treaty?" I responded.
"That's what you are upset about."
"How could you do it, Mother?"
"Its all part of my plan."
"To look weak is part of your plan?"
"I told you that I have to agree in order to keep doing what I'm doing."
"Enough! I want to go home. I miss father and Areos."
"I miss your father and brother too, but I can't go back unless I find what I'm looking for."
"If you would just tell me what you're looking for, I would be happy to help you."
"We have been over this. I can't tell you for your safety."
"I'm so tired of you telling me that."
"Look, a mother's duty is to protect her son."
"Yeah, but from what? They should fear us, not the other way around."

"Look, as soon as I find—"

"I don't want to hear it anymore. If you haven't found it by now, chances are you're not going to find it."

"I must find it; not finding it is not an option."

I got up from my chair. I was so tired of the same song and dance. My mother was hiding something, and it was becoming more and more clear she was afraid. She should know that I will protect her; she should not doubt my strength, I thought.

"Wait, where are you going?" she asked.

"To get some air," I responded.

"Well, don't go to far."

"Mother, if I want to go far, I will."

I slammed the door behind me. I went out to the courtyard. I'm a Drekum. We absorb power and strength. Everyone who knows that should stay away from us. So why was my mother cowering in her castle?

I hate this place, I said to myself. Of all the places we should be, this is not one of them. I was watching two Maikoa fighting over a dead animal. Is this what my mother has reduced herself to? I asked.

Somehow I couldn't help but feel that my mother had been forced here. By whom, I don't know, but when I find that person, I would show them suffering. I would show them pain like they had never felt before.

I wondered what my brother would have done in this situation. I thought, He's strong and smart; he would find away to help our mother.

I pulled my gun out and started practicing shooting. There was nothing to do here, and my mother wouldn't let me explore the forest.

I saw my mother out of the corner of my eye. She was coming toward me. She can't stand it when I'm mad. I got to love her for that.

"I was thinking, why don't we do some mind-reading practice? That always seems to cheer you up," she proposed.

"No, Mother, I'm not feeling that today," I responded.

"Oh come on, you love it when you get into someone's head."

"Fine. Who do we what to be the target?"

My mother put her hand on my shoulder and smiled.

"Look around you there are lots to choose from."

"How about that guard by the gate?"

"No that's too easy. Let's try an animal."

"I have never done animals before. Can it be done?"

"Of course it can be done. You can control anything you want; after all, you are half Drekum and half me."

"Mother, there are no animals around for miles."

She pulled out a birdcage with a falcon in it.

"Here, let this falcon be your eyes; control it to go where you want it to go. Let it show you what it can see."

"What good is controlling a bird?"

"You would be surprised how powerful birds can be."

"So you want me to take over its brain?"

"Concentrate. Close your eyes. Drown out all the sounds of distraction."

I did what mother said. I took over the bird's mind, and in doing so, I could see what it saw. I took over its wings and flew. I could see as far as the Kingdom of Viniues with the falcon. Taking over its mind, I could feel there neurons, the electrical impulses. When doing this, my eyes change to whatever mind I'm taking over. But I was losing the bird the farther it was getting from me.

"I'm losing control of the bird," I said.

"Then pull it back," she responded.

As I was pulling the bird closer to me, my Drekum senses where kicking in. It was taking over me. I pulled the bird's life into me. The bird dropped dead and fell right out of the sky, and it's body landed right in front us.

My eyes came to. I looked at my mother.

"I'm sorry. I will try hared next time."

"You did good, but you really have to control that part of you."

"I can't help it, Mother; it is what I am."

"I understand that, but not everything needs its life taken away."

My mother picked up the dead bird and threw it to the Maikoa to feed on.

"If that's the case, then what is a Drekum's purpose?" I asked.

"You know, it's just too bad that you can't put life back into what you take out."

"Now that's something I would love to learn. To bring things back from the dead."

"Even I can't do that one. No matter how many spells I conjure."

"Who taught you how to take over minds?"

"Well, no one taught me; it's in my blood. I get that from my mother as you got it from me."

"So your mother had the power of mind reading?"

"No, my mother had the power of magic; she could make anything she wanted happen."

"How long has it been since you last saw her?"

"It's been a while."

"Do you miss her?" I asked.

"Sometimes, but enough about that; let's try again."

My mother pulled another bird out of the cage.

Chapter 84

Princess Jade Blumenthal

Feed and I made it just in time. The army was just arriving. I was really looking forward to seeing my best friend Skylar Gladiolus. His father is Captain Dryad, the best fighter in the whole kingdom. I grew up with Sky, so I know everything about him.

The entire kingdom is celebrating their arrival. As the drawbridge opened up, the A Gate Army marched its way down the path of the kingdom, and everyone watched them on the side of the road, waving and throwing confetti on them. Everyone couldn't help but smile at them since they had done a good job.

Before I could go out to greet them, my mother grabbed my arm.

"Whoa, whoa! Where have you been?" she asked.

"Out!" I responded.

"Your father has something he wants to tell you."

"Does he have to tell me now?"

"It's about Lord Sky."

"What about him?"

"I'll leave it up to your father to tell you."

I couldn't have cared less what my father had to say; I was to excited to see Sky. The minute I saw him come up the stairs, I ran down to hug him tight.

"J, it's so good to see you," he said.

"Well, did you bring me anything?" I said.

"Business first, huh!"

"Hey, you did say you would bring be back something so that I wouldn't be sad that you were gone."

"That's true. I did."

Sky reached into his bag and pulled out a smooth brown rock. I had never seen anything like it. It had a dragonfly stuck inside it.

"What it is?" I asked.

"They call it amber dragonfly."

"It's beautiful."

"I thought you would like it."

Feed came over and grabbed my gift right out of my hands.

"How neat!" he said.

"Hey, Feed. How's it going?" Sky asked.

"It's going."

"Did you keep Jade busy while I was gone?" Sky said.

"Yes, I think I did a great job filling in your shoes."

We all laughed.

"Sky, tell me everything. What's the Kingdom of Withered like?" I asked.

"It's nothing but a dry and dead kingdom. There's nothing around it but black vines with thorns that are very poisonous. It's also hard to breathe there since there is no plant life."

"It sounds awful," I said.

"Why do you think I'm so happy to be home?"

"Sky, do you believe that Sarabi will honor the treaty?"

"Yeah. Why wouldn't she?"

"I found a Maikoa today in the jungle."

"Are you sure?"

"Yes, I killed it myself."

"It's true. I saw it," Feed interjected.

"Have you told your father about this?" Sky asked.

"You think he listens to me?" I asked in turn.

"You need not worry. The tree of life will show him the truth."

"I'm not sure why father trusts Sarabi; I wouldn't."

"Your father has sympathy for Sarabi since she is his half sister."

"What my father should have done is kicked her out of the Nature Realm. She doesn't belong here anyways."

"Sarabi has taken up most of the forest, causing the fairies and dwarfs to retaliate against her. Your father is trying to prevent a war. He doesn't want to see anyone get hurt."

"But if she is forcing people out of their homes, they will have no choice but war."

"That's why this treaty is necessary—to prevent her from spreading her poison."

I was watching Feed become fascinated with the gift Sky gave me when a messenger told me my father wanted to see me.

I looked at Sky.

"Don't worry, we will catch up later," he said.

Chapter 85

Princess Jade Blumenthal

On my way into the throne room, I ran into Sky's father Captain Dryad.

"Capitan Gladiolus," I said.

He responded, "Princess, please call me Dryad."

We gave each other a big hug.

"Congratulations on your successful task," I said.

"It was a real honor, Your Majesty."

"And thank you for bringing your son back to me in one piece."

"You care that much about him, don't you?"

"Of course. He is my best friend, and I think of you as a second father to me."

"Well, what a coincidence. I have always thought of you as a daughter. Maybe someday you will get to call me father."

He smiled at me, and for some reason I didn't like the way he made that sound.

"Well, you better not keep your father waiting," he continued.

I was walking in the throne room. My mother came and gave me a big hug. She was very excited about something. My father was sitting down in his chair. He also had a big smile on his face.

"This is wonderful news," my mother Naomi said.

She kissed me on both cheeks.

"Will someone please tell me what's going on?" I responded.

"Naomi, would you calm down and let me explain what's going on?" my father Midas said.

"I'm sorry, Midas. I'm just so happy for her," my mother explained.

"Happy for what?" I asked.

"Jade, my daughter, Caption Dryad has just informed me that he wishes for you and his son to be bound in holy union," my father explained.

The words made me feel like someone had picked me up and shaken me hard. I couldn't believe what I was hearing.

"Marry Sky?" I said.

"I know; it's wonderful news. You will be so happy," said my mother.

"Wait a minute, who's idea was this? Was it Sky's?" I asked.

"No, it was Caption Dryad's idea," responded my father.

"So Sky doesn't know anything about this?"

"No, nothing. His father is going to tell him soon," my father explained.

"Father, there has been a big misunderstanding. You see, Sky and I don't feel that way about each other. Sky only looks at me like a little sister."

"But you two are perfect for each other," my mother interjected.

"Mother, Sky is not in the least interested in me that way, and I'm not going to force him to marry me when he doesn't want to."

"How do you know he's not interested in you? Have you asked him?" my father said.

"Well, no, but he's never said anything."

"Before we decided what to do, I think you should go and ask him directly what he wants," my father advised.

"OK, I will."

"Jade, remember, ask him with your heart, OK?" my mother said.

"What does that even mean?"

"It means that no matter what answer he gives, you expect it openly," she responded.

"Of course I will, Mother. I always tell Sky the truth."

Chapter 86

Princess Jade Blumenthal

I found Sky in in the training yard. He was trying to shoot a bow and arrow. He's not very good at it, though he tires. He's better with a sword. But I encourage him no matter what weapon he chooses.

He fired the arrow, but he missed the target.

"I told you that when you release, you breathe out," I said.

He responded, "Why is it that you are so much better at this than me?"

"Because you breath too heavy, causing you to miss the target."

"Well, maybe it's because you make me nervous when I'm around you."

"Sky, have you talked to your father?"

"Yes, he just told me."

"About us getting married?"

"Yes. That's crazy, right?"

"Oh! I'm so glad you feel that way."

"Really, you mean that?"

"Yes, of course I do."

"OK, so tell me, when was the first time?" Sky asked.

"The first time what?"

"The first time you realized you were in love with me?"

"Uh, um, I…"

"I will tell you mine. It was when you were nine—I was eleven—and you were hanging upside down from the Saxon tree. I was watching you swing. You were so high up. Then the branch broke and you fell but grabbed another branch preventing you from falling farther. But that branch was getting ready to break too. I was freaking out."

"Yeah, I remember. You were crying."

"I was, and the whole time I was climbing that tree, I was thinking, I've got to save her; I got to get to her as soon as possible. I kept calling out your name, telling you not to worry, I was coming. Then when I got to you and our eyes met, your face was completely calm and serene. It was like you knew I was going to save you and you had no worries; you were so relaxed.

"That's because you were going to save me."

"Yes, but so many things could have gone wrong. The branch could have broken before I got there. The confidence you had in me made me realize how much you believed in me and gave me courage. It made me feel invincible. I knew right then and there that you were the one."

"But, Sky, we were just children."

"I know, so tell me when you first fell in love with me."

I had to lie.

"That was the same time I fell for you."

"I knew it; I knew we had a connection. J, I promise that I will make you so happy."

Sky gave me a kiss on the lips. It was just a peck. Then he hugged me. It was nice yet sweet, but it didn't get my vines going.

I couldn't tell Sky the truth. That would have hurt his feelings, and I couldn't do that. I care about him so much, but I just don't see him as the man who can make my flower bloom.

I had to change the topic; it was getting really weird.

"So what's Sarabi like?" I asked.

"She's OK. She kind of gives me the creeps. She has purple hair and green eyes."

"Oh, is that right?"

"Yeah, but her son he's really out there."
"Sarabi has a son?"
"Yeah, his name is Aries."
"What's he like?"
"Not really friendly. He kept trying to get us to leave."
"Is he older or younger than us?"
"Same age as me, I believe."
"Well, maybe he's the one controlling her?"
"Could be. J, when do want to get married? Spring is when all the flowers are in bloom."
"Yes, but autumn is when all the leaves change colors."
"Do you want to wait that long?"
"It's not that long!"

I told Sky that I had something I needed to do. I was lying, but I had to get out of this conversation before it got even more confusing.

I was running down the stairs when I saw Feed coming up them. He had fright written on his face.

"Jade, there you are. I've been looking everywhere for you," he said.
"What's wrong?"
"An animal has been hurt badly."
"Take me to it."
"Its in the jungle, outside the kingdom walls," he explained.
"Well, how did you find out about it?"
"Marigold. She told me just now."

Marigold is a lynx. She and Feed can communicate with each other; they have a language that no one else understands.

When Feed was just a baby, Marigold saved him. He lived in the forest happily until Sarabi came to the Nature Realm. When she killed most of the forest, a lot of the Viridis that lived in there died, including Feed's parents. Marigold found him, and she brought him to the kingdom, to our doorstep. My parents took him in and loved him like he was one of our own. So really, I have two brothers. Sky and Feed.

Chapter 87

Prince Aries Fidem

"Mom, I'm getting really sick of the Maikoa fighting 'cause there is not enough food," I said.

"So what would you have me do?" she asked.

"Send them out to feed."

"I can't do that right now. I signed a treaty."

"So what? We have the Gux army; we can do anything."

"The Gux army is powerful, but it's not a match for the A Gate army."

"The A Gate army is no threat."

"Look, just humor me for a little while."

"But you're not going to honor the treaty, are you?"

"Of course not. I just need things to clam down so I can search freely."

I didn't sign a peace treaty, so I'm not bound to anything.

I took two of the Maikoa with me and my gun. I put my armor on and sealed my helmet. The thrill is in the hunt.

Where I come from, we hunt all the time.

I had never been that far out of my mother's kingdom. What was left of the forest, what my mother hadn't destroyed yet, was thick and so green. I looked up to see my mother's castles getting farther and farther away.

My helmet is special; it can read body heat. So nothing can hide from me.

The soon-to-be-dead forest was getting ready to end. The jungle started to present itself. The Maikoa looked at me to go on. So I nodded to proceed.

Once in the jungle, I could smell a lot of things and feel so much that was going on. This jungle, much like the forest, is alive. I felt eyes everywhere on me but saw no one.

We came across some tracks. The animal, judging by its footprints, was a big animal. Probably something they call a bear. My mother made me read all about this realm, so I knew all the creatures in it. Especially the Viridis. I find them to be very ugly creatures that have no real power.

As we followed the tracks, we came across a rhinoceros. It was perfect. An animal like that would feed a lot of the Maikoa. I could see the Maikoa were drooling. I nodded at them. That gave them the heads-up to take the animal down any way they wanted.

The rhinoceros heard us rustling around and took off. I went after it. As I was chasing this animal, all the plants seemed to die where I went. I guess I really do take the life out of things when I'm not trying to, I thought.

I got tired of chasing the rhino, so I shot at it with my gun. Once it hit the ground, the Maikoa started feasting on it. While they were eating, I went and searched for more food.

I came across a river with a waterfall. I counted at least eight elephants. I drew my gun and aimed it at one of the elephants. I leaned up against a tree to steady my position. Then the tree bumped me, and I misfired my gun. The sound scared the elephants, and they went running. I hurt one of them, but it wasn't enough to kill it.

I grabbed my gun from the ground and looked at the tree. I wanted to take the tree's life away. That stupid tree had done that on purpose. But I ran after the elephant that I hit. It was leaving a blood trail.

As I continued through the jungle, I stopped. The blood trial ended, but there was no elephant in sight. Even my helmet wasn't picking up any body heat. How do you lose a whole elephant? They're huge and can't be missed. As I was looking around, I was getting disoriented. Even the way I had came looked different. I turned around, and the trees seemed to be changing in all directions. What once was a path was now cut off to a dead end. This jungle was leading me away from the elephant. It was hiding it from me.

I wasn't afraid. If I have to, I will kill this jungle to get where I need to get to, I said to myself. I was getting ready to kill the trees around me when a rock came out of nowhere and hit me on the right side of my helmet."

"All right, who threw that?" I said.

It was completely silent. When I was going down to pick up the rock, another one was thrown at me and knocked me completely down.

I stood up immediately with my gun drawn. I heard giggling.

"Come out right now," I said.

I had my hand on the trigger; I was ready to fire at whatever to get whatever it was to come out when I heard it say, "Pick on someone your own size."

I was looking around, and there was nothing there. Was this the trees? Could they talk? Was I going crazy? I was getting things thrown at me; that was not imaginary. But I wasn't seeing any body heat anywhere.

I was going to have to lure it out someway.

Chapter 88

Princess Jade Blumenthal

Feed led me deep in the jungle. I could hear the animal grunting in pain the closer we got to it. The animal was a teenage elephant. I knew this elephant very well.

"Sadie!" I shouted.

I kneeled down next to her to give her some comfort and examine the injury on her leg.

"The Maikoa did this!" Feed suggested.

"No, this was done by something else," I responded.

"What?"

"I have never seen a burn like this."

"Jade can you help her?"

"I'm not sure. Look, her wound is already starting to fester."

I leaned in to smell the wound, and it about knock the breath out of me it was so foul.

"What is it?" Feed asked.

"Whatever did this seared her skin."

"What do we do?"

"Feed, you talk to the trees find out what happened to her. I'm going to try and heal the injury."

Before Feed could get up, we heard laughing from above. We both looked up.

"Georgie!" I shouted.

"What are you doing here, elf? Your kind lives in Photinia," Feed added.

Georgie responded, I know where I belong, Viridis; you don't have to tell me."

Georgie slid down the tree trunk and came next to Sadie. He looked at Sadie, then looked up at me.

"Well, don't just stand there; heal her," Georgie said.

I put my hand on her injury, and I closed my eyes. The gash on her leg was deep; it took all my strength, but I was able to stop it. Her leg was all better. She stood up, and I could tell by her face she wasn't in any more pain.

She thanked me in her way. I smiled at her. After she left, I kneeled down to Georgie.

"All right, Georgie, why are you here?" I asked.

"I must speak to your father, Your Majesty."

"Why? What's going on?"

"I have a feeling that King James is going to make a deal with Sarabi."

"You're certain?"

"Yes, very!"

"What kind of deal?" Feed asked.

"That I'm not sure, but Algar has sent me to alert your father," responded Georgie.

Algar is the head elf and is very loyal to my father.

"Well, then I guess you haven't a moment to lose," Feed said.

Georgie responded, "I know the way. Plus, don't you have an elephant to avenge?"

"You know what happened to Sadie?" I asked.

Georgie responded, Some metal-looking creature was running after her."

"Metal-looking creature?" Feed said.

"That's what I saw. I was throwing rocks at it to get it away from her, but I only angered it."

"Where did you see it last?" I asked.

"Last time I saw it, it was going in that direction."

He pointed to the left of me. I looked at the way he was pointing, then I looked at him.

"Should we be worried?" Feed asked.

"No way. With Jade here, it doesn't stand a chance," Georgie responded.

I wasn't afraid. I picked up my bow and arrows, and I headed in the direction he was pointing.

Feed stopped for a minute and looked back at Georgie.

"This way, you say?" he asked.

"Hmm, just follow the dead plants," said Georgie.

"Dead plants!"

"Yes!"

I could tell Feed was afraid.

Chapter 89

Princess Jade Blumenthal

"Do you think that Georgie is not normal?" Feed asked.

"Why do you say that?" I said.

"A metal creature?"

"That was no normal injury on Sadie's leg."

"Well, he is an elf; they should not be allowed here."

"Just because the elves chose to live in Photinia does not mean they are not welcome in Viniues."

"But after everything your family lineage has done for them."

"Feed, you have to understand that Photinia has more to offer the elves' way of life than Viniues. They moved there 'cause it was best for their people, not because they were trying to upset anyone."

"What does Photinia have that we don't have?"

"Well, for starters, it has more flowers species than we do, and elves use flowers for everything."

"So? They have more flowers."

"They also have meadows, and we don't have them. Plus red maple trees grow only in the forest, not in the jungle. Elves live in the maple trees. You see my point?"

"Yeah, yeah, I get it."

I stopped dead in my tracks. Feed bumped into me from behind.

"Hey, why did you stop?" he asked.

"Look!" I said.

The plants and trees were all wilted and dried up. Like something had literally taken the life out of them.

Feed picked up a dead flower; it crumbled in his hand.

"This is Sarabi. She did this, right?"

Sarabi couldn't have done this alone because if she could have, she would have taken over my father's kingdom along time ago. Whatever did this was just sick and wrong. I could hear all the plants crying out for help; I could feel their pain. Their screams were getting louder.

Feed put his hands over his ears. Tears fell from his eyes.

"Jade, make it stop. Make them stop suffering," he said.

I fell down to my knees and balled up my fist. I dug deep down from the bottom of my lugs and breathed out my power. The green smoke from my lungs saturated the plants, bringing them back to life.

Feed was so happy that he jumped up and down. The flower Feed picked up bloomed in its natural form.

There would be no more suffering, not on my watch.

"Wow! I wish I could do that," Feed said.

"You can you make things grow," I responded.

"But I can't bring things back from the dead. That is truly a gift."

"Making life grow is just as important as saving it. Heck, I can't even change into an animal."

"Who needs to change into an animal when you have a gift like yours?"

I smiled at Feed.

"Come on, let's find this thing before it causes more harm to the jungle."

Feed and I found more of the jungle dead. We followed the trail, and while doing so, I brought it back to life. Then beyond some hedges, we heard a noise. We crept through the bushes and saw it.

Feed whispered, "Georgie was right; it is a metal thing."

This thing was hard to make out. It was covered in an unusual black metal armor. It had something in its hands. From the way he was holding it, I assumed it was a weapon of some sort.

"It is odd," I said.

"Odd, this thing looks like a metal statue."

The odd metal-looking thing was moving away from us.

"Wait, where are you going?" Feed asked.

"To follow it," I responded.

"Why would you do that?"

"Don't you want to see what it is?"

"No!"

"Feed, come on."

I was so intrigued. I had to know what this thing was and why it hurt Sadie and to stop it.

"What if that thing kills us?" Feed asked.

"Would you stop being a *Coleus canina*?"

"I'm not a scaredy cat."

Feed and I continued to follow it. We stayed hidden in the bushes so it couldn't see us. We crept up along side of it incognito.

Then it stopped. It turned around and looked in are direction. I had a feeling it could see us through the bushes. It was walking our way.

I whispered to Feed, "Feed, hurry, turn into an animal."

"What? Are you crazy?"

"You have to get it away from us."

"But I…I…I…"

"Do it!"

Feed turned into a crow, and soon, as the metal thing tried to open up the bush, Feed flew in its face and pecked at its metal head.

As it was trying to swat at Feed, it dropped its gun, then it spoke.

"Stupid bird," it said.

The voice sounded human and male-like.

It started going after Feed and was no longer interested in the bush I was in. I breathed out of relief. That was a close one, I thought.

Once it looked clear, I came out of the bush and looked over the weapon it dropped. It was so strange-looking. I was going to touch it when I heard footsteps coming back this way, so I hid in another bush that was a little farther away from it. But I still had a good view of what was going on.

The metal thing came back and picked up its weapon. He looked around his surroundings. Then he looked in my direction again. He pointed his weapon in my direction. Could he see? But how? I was completely covered in this bush. Oh no, it was getting closer.

I was freaking out about what to do. Then a loud growl came from behind him. He turned around, and it was Feed as a tiger.

I calmed my breathing. "Thank you, Feed," I said.

I watching as Feed and the metal thing were circling each other. Deep down inside I was rooting for Feed to get him and bring him down. But I was also freaking out, praying to Hermia to not let Feed get hurt.

Feed lunged at it, but the metal figure thing had Feed pinned down with the weapon to its head. Then it looked in my direction.

"Come out now, or the tiger gets it," it said.

Oh no! This is bad, I thought. I put my hands up and slowly came out of the bush. The moment it saw me, it stood up straight but still had Feed pinned down.

"Just calm down," I said.

"What are you?"

"I could ask you the same question."

"Don't play games with me."

"All right, I'm a Viridis," I said.

"I've seen pictures of Viridis; they don't look like you."

"Maybe you should get out more."

"Uh, hello from down here," Feed interjected.

We both looked down at Feed; he had changed back into his human form. The metal thing took his weapon off him and let him get up. Feed stood by me. We were both staring at the weapon pointed at us.

"If you're going to kill us, just get it over with," Feed said.

"Who says I'm going to kill you?"

"Well, whatever that thing is you got pointed at us says something different," I added.

He put his weapon down, and that gave me the opportunity to grab my bow. I quickly had an arrow pointed at him.

"You really think an arrow is going to get through this?"

He patted his chest of metal.

"What in all creation are you?" I asked.

"I'm a Drekum."

Feed and I looked at each other.

"What is a Drekum?" Feed asked.

"We strive to take power and bring order to chaos."

"That doesn't sound very dignified," I said.

"Thank you."

"So why are you here?" Feed asked.

"'Cause I am."

"OK, well, you need to go back to wherever it is you came from," I said.

"Do you have a name?" it asked.

"Doesn't everyone have a name?" I responded.

"Doesn't mean I want to know everyone's name," it said.

"What's your name?"

"Aries."

"Wait, are you Sarabi's son?"

"Sarabi has a son?" Feed chimed in.

"So you have heard of me?"

"Don't flatter yourself; it was a passing mention," I said.

"Are you going to put your arrow down?" Aries asked.

"Why should I do that?" I responded.

"I think we have established that I'm not going to kill you."

"Yeah, for now right," I said.

"If I wanted to kill you, I would have done it already."

"You know that's not making me trust you."

"OK, how about this?"

Aries dropped his weapon and twisted off his helmet.

What was underneath his helmet was not what I expected at all. I had never seen eyes with no white in them. Aries had solid forest-green eyes with no pupils or irises. And purple hair that was shaved on the sides but long on the top. I also noticed he had black markings all over his neck that went up behind both ears and continued into his shaved-nape hairline. He was very handsome. Took me completely by surprise. Now his metal armor made sense. I could tell he was very built under that metal exterior.

"You're just a boy," said Feed.

"Hardly. I'm nineteen," responded Aries.

"Jade is seventeen," Feed said.

Aries looked at me and smiled. I put my arrow down.

OK, so he has a good-looking smile; let's not lose our composure, I thought.

"So you enjoy hurting elephants?" I asked.

"I have to feed the Maikoa somehow," Aries responded.

"You can't do that. We have laws here. When you take a life, you must pay for it. The Maikoa are not allowed in here, so take them and leave, and I better not catch you here again."

"Jade—that's your name, right? I like that."

"Did you not hear what I said?"

"You know, you're really cute when you get mad."

"I'm warning you, stay out of—"

"You're warning me?"

"Yes, I'm warning you."

We were about to get into a fight when Feed came in between us to break it up.

"Well, my name is Feed," he said.

"Feed, huh? How did you get that name?" Aries asked.

"It's 'cause I'm very hungry all the time. I'm so hungry now."

"Here, have this."

"What is it?" Feed asked.

"It's called a biscuit."

Feed took it from Aries and bit into it.

"Feed!"

"What? I'm hungry."

"He attacked an elephant."

"So if I come back here and start killing animals, I will get punished, right?"

"That's right."

"Who's going to give me my punishment, you?"

This arrogant jerk, I thought. He wasn't taking what I said into consideration. He wasn't taking me seriously at all.

"Has anyone ever told you that you are an overbearing asshole?" I asked.

"Maybe once or twice," Aries responded.

"Let's go, Feed. We are leaving."

"Wait! I have to see you again," Aries said.

"I don't see how that's possible since you are not allowed here."

"Meet me here tomorrow, same time."

"No!"

"Why not?"

"'Cause I don't want to meet you."

"OK, then I guess I will have to kill more animals."

"No! You can't do that."

"Then I guess you better meet me here."

"And if I don't show up?"

"Then I will come find you."

"OK fine, I will meet you here tomorrow."

Aries smiled at me.

"I knew you would see it my way," he said.

"Whatever!" I said.

"Feed, always a pleasure," added Aries.

"Uh, yeah, you too, Aries."

While Feed and I were walking away from Aries, he called out to me.

"See you tomorrow, Jade!"

I didn't say anything back, just kept on walking.

"You really going to meet him tomorrow?" Feed asked.
"What choice do I have?"
"Well, I'll tell you one thing, he's definitely got eyes for you."
"OK, no more talking about this."

Chapter 90

Prince Aries Fidem

I caught back up with the two Maikoa and headed back to the Kingdom of the Withered.

As I entered my mother's castle's yard, I saw a centaur coming out of the castle.

"Where have you been?" she asked.

"Out!" I responded.

"Out where?"

"Just out!"

"Aries, did you leave the kingdom?"

"Its no big deal."

"Aries, what if something were to happen to you?"

"Nothing happened. Would you calm down?"

"Aries, listen to me: you can't leave my kingdom; it's not safe right now."

"Mother, there is nothing to worry about. I just went out for some fresh air."

"Don't do it again, do you hear me?"

"I'm nineteen years old. I can take care of myself."

"There are things in this realm you would not understand."

"Speaking of not understanding, wasn't that a centaur I just saw leaving here?" I said.

"Yes, it was."

"Aren't centaurs loyal to King James?"

"Yes!"

"So why is it here?"

"King James has offered me a proposal that is really good."

"What's the catch?"

"If he gives me what I want, I will give him what he wants."

"And what is that?"

"To find what I'm looking for, I need Arbor Vitae, the tree of life."

"You need a tree?"

"This isn't just any ordinary tree. The tree of life is linked to everything in the Nature Realm; it sees everything. It will help me find what I seek."

"And where does King James fit in all this?"

"King James has agreed to let me have his army under one condition."

"And that is?"

"Marriage!"

I couldn't help but laugh.

"You're going to marry King James?" I asked.

"No, but you are going to marry his daughter Princess Raven."

"What! Why would I do that?"

"Aries, with King James's army by my side, I can get the tree of life."

"What does King James get out of this?"

"He wants Viniues, and you will rule Photinia. It's a win-win either way."

"What if I don't want to marry her?"

"Why not? She's very pretty."

"So what, and how can we trust King James?"

"Why would he lie? He has no reason to."

"I don't like it."

"You don't like it 'cause you don't want to get married."

"Yeah, so no deal!"

"Aries!"

"It's not going to happen. I thought we were going home once we found what you were looking for."

"We can still go home. I just thought it would be a good idea for you to get married."

"Why would you think I would want that?"

"Because I want to see you happy."

"Thanks, Mom, but I'm good."

I got up in my room and lay on my bed. All I could think about was Jade. The moment I saw her, I felt like I would be missing something until I laid eyes on her again. She was perfect. I had to have her. I would have her.

I was getting excited and nervous about tomorrow when I see her. I couldn't sleep at all. The morning came fast. I went down the stairs to see my mother eating at the table.

"You seem to be in a good mood," she said.

"I am, actually," I said.

"I thought you would be mad at me."

"Why?"

"'Cause of are argument yesterday."

"Mom, it was just a disagreement, that's all. I'm not mad."

"Well, good. I was thinking we could practice more mind tricks. What do you think?"

"Not today. I have plans."

I picked up my cup of milk, and as I was drinking, I could feel my mother's eyes on me.

"What kind of plans?"

"Just stuff."

"Aries, you are not leaving this kingdom."

"Mother, stop. Calm down. I'm only going for a walk, OK?"

"No, it's not safe."

"It's fine. Just trust me."

I got up, kissed my mom on the cheek, and headed out. It was a little early to meet Jade, but I didn't care. I was too excited.

Chapter 91

Princess Jade Blumenthal

I was in the throne room. My father had a big announcement to make to everyone. Feed was standing right next to me.

"I can't believe you are going to marry Sky," he said.

"It wasn't my idea," I responded.

"So you don't want to marry him?"

"Of courses not!"

"Well, did you tell him that?"

"I tried to."

"You tried to?"

"It's a long story."

"If you don't want to marry Sky, then you better tell him."

"I can't, Feed; it will break his heart."

"But you are lying to him."

"Oh well. Being Sky's wife isn't so bad, I guess."

"Yeah, I guess!"

My father called me to the center of the room, where Sky, my mother, and his father were standing.

My dad grabbed my hand and put it into Sky's.

Sky was so happy he was smiling from ear to ear. At least one of us was happy.

Then my father announced to the whole congregation that Sky and I were to be wed. Then he said that the wedding was going to be in spring.

"Sky, spring! That's awfully fast. I thought we agreed on autumn," I said.

"I know. It's just that—"

"That's my fault, Jade. I wanted a spring wedding," my mother said.

"Well, that's nice, Mother, but it's not your wedding; it's mine. And I want autumn."

"Jade, the flowers will be better picking in spring, OK?" she said.

"Mother, this is my wedding, and—"

"And this is not up for discussion. Spring wedding it is, my love."

"Fine, spring it is."

"Great. Now we have a lot to do, so we need to get you fitted for a dress; we have to decide on tablecloths and table toppers. Oh, the invitations will have to have both royal seals on them."

"You know what, Mother I'm not feeling well at the moment, so I'm just going to lie down."

"What do you mean you're not feeling well? We have so much to do. Spring is right around—"

"Yes, I know, but I have a headache, so just give me a few hours, OK?"

"Just a few. We have a lot to do."

I hugged my mother tight.

"Thank you, Mother, I love you," I said.

I grabbed Feed and headed toward my bedroom.

"What are you doing?" Feed asked.

"I need you to lie in my bed and pretend that you're me."

"Wait, why? You're going to meet Aries?"

"Yes, OK!"

"But why?"

"You know why—I don't have a choice. Now get in the bed."

"Do you think it's safe for you to go alone?"

"I'll be fine, and I won't be long, but whatever you do, don't answer that door."

"Yeah, yeah, I got it."

I crept out my window and headed for the jungle. After some time I finally made it. Aries was leaning up against a tree. Looking bored.

"Well, I'm here," I said.

He stood up from the tree and looked at me with a smile.

"You're late!" he said.

"Oh. Well, I can leave."

"No, no, late is better than not showing at all."

"OK. Well, now that I'm here, what do you want?"

"I want to get to know you."

"You want to get to know me?"

"Yeah. What's wrong with that?"

"Well, for starters, you kill animals and destroy plant life."

"Then I will stop killing animals, and as far as taking plant life, I will try harder not to do that."

"Just like that?"

"Yeah, just like that."

"What is that thing in your hand?"

"Oh, this? It's a gun," he explained.

"What's it do?"

"It shoots a hot light out."

"Why would you have something like that?"

"'Cause where I come from, this is what we hunt with."

"Where do you come from?"

"A faraway place."

"Will you be going back anytime soon?"

"You don't like me very much, do you?"

"Is it that obvious?"

Aries was smiling as he was looking away for me.

"What if I got you to change your mind?" he asked.

"I don't think so!"

"Oh, come on, give me a chance."

"And why would I do that?"

"'Cause you find me attractive."

"No, I don't."

Aries got up in my face; I could feel his breath on me. It was warm and smelled like cinnamon. It made my skin break out into shivers.

"Let's test that theory."

I was slowly turning my head away from him, but he grabbed my chin softly.

"I can get into most people's heads, but I can't get into yours," he said.

"Why would you want to get into my head?"

"To get you to make the first move."

"What move do want me to make?"

"This one."

Aries took over my lips, and as he was doing that, he gripped my waist and pulled me in closer. This man didn't just get my juices flowing; they were dripping.

Chapter 92

Princess Jade Blumenthal

It was really late. I was climbing the wall back up to my window. I fell on to my bed and scared the life out of Feed.

"Do you have any idea what time it is?" he asked.

"Feed, I'm so sorry."

"You said you were only going to be a moment."

"I know. I lost track of time."

"Your mother keeps checking on you every forty-five minutes. I had to pretend like I was snoring."

"Well, thank you for not blowing my cover."

"No problem. So did you tell Aries so long and to hit the road?"

"Well, not exactly."

"What do you mean?"

"Well, you see, um, we kind of, well, I…it's complicated."

"How so?"

"Feed, just—"

"Oh no!"

"What!"

"You kissed him!"

"Um, well, you see, I—"

"Jade, you are engaged. You're getting married in less than a fortnight."

"I know; it was so stupid of me. I don't know what I was thinking."

"It's OK. You just have to never see him again."

"You are absolutely right. Never again."

"Good, I'm glad you agree with me. Now, you better cover up those bite marks on your neck before your mother sees."

"Wait, how did you become all grown up all of sudden?" I asked.

"I don't know but I like it."

"Yeah, well I don't."

The next morning my mother got me out of bed bright and early. We were going over wedding stuff. My mother told me that she wanted a three-layer cake. Of course I couldn't care less. All I could think about was Aries. Feed was right: I couldn't see him again. And yet I want to see him.

Just then I saw Georgie leaving my father's study.

"Georgie!" I said.

"Your Majesty," he responded.

"How did it go talking to my father?"

"Very Good!"

"Does he know what Sarabi is planning?"

"He says he has an idea."

"Oh, well that's good."

"Did you find the thing that hurt Sadie?"

"Um, yes I did."

"Good, I knew you would show that thing what it deserves."

"Yes!"

"Well, I'm off back to Photinia."

"Well, you take care of yourself."

"Thank you, Your Highness, and congratulations on your engagement."

"Oh yes, thank you."

After Georgie left I went to find Feed; he was in the kitchen eating, like always.

"Feed, I—"

I was startled to see all the food on the table. There was so much of it.

"Wait, Feed, are you going to eat all this?" I continued.

"Of course. Why wouldn't I?"

"Because you have enough here to feed a whole village."

"Trust me, I'm very hungry."

"Oh never mind that. Now, I need your help."

"What's up!"

"I need you to keep my mother busy while I'm out."

"Out? Where are you going?"

"I'm going into the jungle to—"

"You're going to see Aries?"

"OK, yes, I'm going to see him."

"I thought we agreed to not see him again."

"You're right, and that's why I have to see him this one last time."

"Or you could just stay away from him."

"Feed, please!"

"Fine, but don't take all day like you did last time."

"I promise I won't."

I left the kingdom and had made it farther into the jungle when I ran into two dwarfs. Cotton and Lucky."

They both bowed their heads and said, "Your Majesty" at the same time.

"Cotton, Lucky, what are you doing here?" I asked.

Cotton responded, "We have come to see your father. It's a very important matter."

They were dragging something big behind them, wrapped in cloth.

"May I ask what's so important?" I said.

Lucky responded, "This."

Lucky pulled back the cloth. It was a rhinoceros or what was left of it. I put my hand on my mouth and nose to stop from breathing in the terrible smell. It had flies all over it.

"That's awful!" I shouted.

Cotton explained, "The Maikoa did this."

Lucky added, "So we are going to your father to demand justice for this animal."

Cotton said, "If Sarabi can't honor the peace treaty, then neither can we."

"That's very understandable. You haven't a moment to lose," I responded.

"Wait, why are you out here?" Cotton asked.

"Oh, me? I was just hunting Maikoa."

"Well, good, but by yourself?" Lucky said.

"Oh, don't worry about me. I can handle it," I said.

Chapter 93

Prince Aries Fidem

I was sitting at the table when my mother burst into the room with excitement.

"Why so happy, Mother?" I said.

"King Midas's daughter is getting married."

"And that's good news because?"

"The wedding is a perfect opportunity for me to get into the kingdom to find Arbor Vitae."

"If he invites you."

"Of course he will invite me; I am his sister."

"Half sister."

"So what? We may not be on the best of terms, but we are family, after all."

"So whom is she getting marred to?"

"Skyler Gladiolus. He's Captain Dryadalis's son."

"They're the assholes that made you sign that ridiculous treaty."

"Technically it was my half bother, but yes, those are the ones."

"So his son will be King of Viniues, then?"

"That's the plan. To think Princess Jade would choose a warrior for a husband."

"I'm sorry, did you just say Jade?"

"That's right. Princess Jade Blumenthal."

What was the likelihood that Princess Jade and the Jade I was seeing were the same person?

"You sure they are really getting married?" I asked.

"My dear boy, the innovations are being written up as we speak."

"How misleading."

"How so?"

"Oh nothing, Mother, just talking out loud, that's all."

"Well, speaking of weddings, I need to give King James an answer about his daughter."

"Give me till tomorrow. I will give you my answers then, but first I have to find out some things."

"What things do you have to find?"

"Don't worry about it, Mother."

I got up from my seat and headed toward the front door.

"Wait, where are you going now?" she asked.

"Out."

"No, not this time."

"Mother, it's fine; I will be back."

"It's not safe out there. What if you meet someone you're not supposed to?"

"Like who?"

"It's just not safe."

"Mom, I love you, but you worry too much."

I got to the spot where I usually go to meet Jade. She was already there waiting for me. But she didn't look too happy to see me.

I was going to say something first, but she beat me to it.

"Did you kill a rhinoceros?" she asked.

"No, but the Maikoa did."

"And you knew about this?"

"It happened before I met you."

"So?"

"So what do you want me to do?"

"You have to pay for that's animals life."

"OK, fine. How do I do that?"

"You serve up the Maikoa that are responsible so that they can face justice."

"Yeah, my mother might have a problem with that."

"I don't care. You broke the law, and now you have to pay."

"Are you a princess?"

"What does that have to do with anything?"

"'Cause I want to know."

"I can't see you anymore."

"Oh, and why not?"

"'Cause I can't see someone who has no regard for animal life."

"I care about animals."

"You are such a liar."

"I'm a liar? You never told me you were a princess."

"You didn't ask; that's not lying."

"You still could have told me," I said.

"I have to go."

I grabbed her wrist before she could leave, and I pinned her up against a tree. She is so beautiful, I thought. We stared into each other's eyes.

"Aries, let go of me," she said.

"Never."

She was pushing my chest off of her.

"I said let me go!"

She then started hitting me. I grabbed both her hands and pinned them up above her, and I took her body, uncaring about how she felt. I would have stopped if she wanted me to. But she gave in to me. I could tell by the way she stuck her tongue in my ear. That and the scratches she left on my back.

Chapter 94

Princess Jade Blumenthal

I was lying next to Aries. We were both completely naked in the jungle. My body was so sore but satisfied from making love to him all day. I hated that I couldn't say no to him and that I wanted him. I felt like the *Dionaea muscipula*. Every time you touch it, it can't help but open itself up.

He was lying on his back with one arm behind his head. I was lying on my side with my back facing him. Nether one of us could sleep. Even though I should have, as tired as I was.

I sat up and started putting my clothes on. As I was doing that, I could feel his eyes on me, but I pretended like I didn't notice.

"Are you leaving so soon?" he asked.

"Aries, I have been with you since this morning, and it's now dinnertime."

"Yeah, so?"

"So it's time for me to go home. I should have been home hours ago."

"I hear you're getting married."

I stopped what I was doing and looked right at him.

"Where did you hear that?"

"I have my sources."

"Is that right?"
"Well?"
"Well, what?"
"Are you getting married?"
"So what if I am?"
"Do you love him?"
"Does it matter?"
"Yes, it does."
"Why?"
"'Cause I want to know why you are marring him if you are here with me."
"If I said I was in love with him, what then?"
"Are you trying to piss me off?"
"Aries, what did you think was going to happen? That we would go off somewhere over the rainbow and live happily ever after?"
"Is that what you want to happen?"
"I don't know what I want, OK?"
I was getting ready to walk away.
"Jade," he said.
"What?"
"I want to see you tomorrow."
"No!"
"I'm not asking."
I didn't say anything. I just continued walking.

The rest of the two weeks went by fast. We were now at the end of week three. With my wedding right around the corner. I would sneak out, spending the whole day with Aries. My mother was getting very fed up with my absence. She really didn't need me. She was planning the whole wedding; my opinion didn't matter.

I had my wedding dress on; it was getting fitted. The seamstress and my mother were arguing about how long the train should be. But I didn't care. I was lost in my thoughts. Aries never brought up the marriage thing, and I never said anything about it. But I knew he was thinking about it.

"Mother, I have a question."

"Shoot."

"Let's say you have two flowers. One you are fond of, and one you desire. Which one would you choose to keep by you at all times?"

"Well, that depends on what kind of flowers we are talking about."

"That's not really the point."

"Yes, it is 'cause if you are talking about orchids as a flower to desire—"

"OK fine, orchids are the flower you desire."

"Yuck! I would never choose orchids for desire."

"OK, whatever flower you want it to be; it really doesn't matter."

"Is this your way of saying that you don't like the flowers I have chosen for your wedding?"

"No, Mother. Just forget it. Doesn't matter."

"You look really sleepy. Have you been getting any sleep?" my mother asked.

"I'm fine, Mother, just nervous, I guess."

"Well, of course you're nervous; your wedding is coming up."

"Are we done with this? I want to go lie down."

"Yes, of course. You go get some rest."

I was heading out of the room when I ran into Feed. He was chewing on deviled eggs, and the smell hit me hard. I got so nauseous that I grabbed the nearest wastebasket and heaved all my breakfast out.

My mother ran out and put her hand on my back as she helped me up.

"Jade, are you all right?" she asked.

"Yeah, I guess my stomach didn't really like that smell."

"You know, that's the second time you have done that. You did that last night at dinnertime."

"I just have a lot on my mind, that's all."

My mother put her hand on my forehead.

"Well, you don't have a fever," she said.

"I just need to get some rest. You will see, I will be better tomorrow."

I got into my room and closed the door. I wasn't going to bed; I was going to sneak out to see Aries again. I just hope I don't puke along the way, I thought.

Chapter 95

Prince Aries Fidem

It was late. The sun had gone down. I had just gotten back to my mother's kingdom from spending the whole day with Jade again. I knew at this time she would be asleep, so I wasn't worried about running into her. Or so I thought.

"Where have you been?" she shouted.

"Mom, what are you doing up?"

"I want to know where you have gone all day every day for the past three weeks."

"I told you—out."

I could feel my head starting to tingle.

"Mother, would you stop trying to get into my head?" I said.

"Well, my son won't tell me what is going on, so how else can I find out?"

"Nothing is going on."

"Aries, you have been acting so weird lately."

"How so?"

"Well, last week you beheaded two of my Maikoa and would not give me an explanation as to why."

"Trust me, they had it coming."

"Also, you have been very distant lately. I never see you except in the mornings and late at night."

"I come back home, though, don't I, just like I said I would?"

"Aries, we can't keep secrets from each other."

"OK, Mother, you tell me why we can't go home. Tell me what you are looking for, and I'll tell you what I do all day."

"Aries, it's better that you don't know for your own protection."

"I'm so sick of you saying that."

"But it's the truth."

"Enough! You want to stop having secrets, then tell me what is going on."

"You wouldn't understand."

"You know what I do understand? I see you getting more and more stressed trying to find whatever it is you are looking for. You try to hide it, but I can see it and hear lately you've been double agitated. I though a big part of it was that I turned down King James's offer to marry his daughter, but no, there is something else going on here. You are drowning, Mother, and there is not a thing I can do to help you because you won't talk to me."

My mother looked at me. She let out a sigh and slumped her shoulders.

"You're right, and since neither one of us is going to tell the other what is going on, let me tell you what I think is going on with you."

My mother sat down. She put her head in her hand and looked up at me.

"I think you have fallen in love. I don't know with whom or even why, but I can feel it on you. It gets stronger and stronger on you ever day."

I turned around; my back was facing her. I closed my eyes.

"Good night, Mother. It's late."

When I opened my eyes, she was now standing in front of me, tears rolling down her cheeks.

I kissed her on the forehead. I headed to my room.

I lay on my bed thinking how bad that conversation with her had gone. How much I hated seeing her in trouble and being powerless to help her. When my mom is sad; I'm sad. I don't like or want to fight with her. But lately all we do is butt heads.

The more I though about it, the more guilty I felt. She was right: I was in love. And she was upset 'cause I couldn't share it with her.

I couldn't take it anymore, so I went down to find her to apologize. I got to her door and was going to knock but stopped. I slowly opened the door and stuck my head inside. My mother's back was facing me. I was getting ready to walk in when the mirror on the wall shined bright and a figure came out. A figure I was familiar with.

It was my grandmother.

"Revaya!" said my mother.

"Sarabi, you do know what day it is, right?"

"Is it the end of the seasons already?"

"Yes, it is, and you know what that means."

"Revaya, I want to ask you a question."

"Yes!"

"The real reason why you banished me was not that you thought I wasn't Drekum enough, was it?"

"Sure it was."

"Oh come on, let's put down our cards and stop with the false pretenses. After all, your son isn't here."

"Tell me, Sarabi, why do you think I sent you into exile?"

"Oh, I don't think I know it was because your son fell in love with me and that wouldn't be good for Mommy Dearest, especially when she was trying to rule the kingdom through her son."

"You know what, you're right—no need to mask the situation. Yes, my son might have fallen for you, but you see, there is a difference between falling in love and actually being in love."

"Oh, I see, and how exactly did you break his heart? Did you tell him I cheated on him, that I ran away with someone else?"

"I told him that you were trying to kill him and steal his throne."

"I bet he didn't believe you at first. I bet he was having a hard time accepting your words. That right there shows that he was in love with me."

"You know, Sarabi, I don't know why we can't get along. I've been very generous to you."

"Is that a joke? When have you ever been kind to me?"

"I kicked you out into the Nature Realm; that is a very nice place to be banished to."

"No, you kicked me out of my new home, away from my husband and sons, to the Dark Realm. It wasn't until I decided to make a deal with you that you let me go to the Nature Realm. Then it wasn't until I showed you some proof of what I was looking for that you allowed one of my sons to go with me; you weren't going to let me have both of them 'cause Areos is next in line to be king."

"And how is my grandson doing?"

"Good. He misses his father and brother, but I'm sure you have poisoned Areos against me."

"Why would I do that?" Revaya asked.

"Why not? You have bad-mouthed me to your son, why not mine?"

"All right, enough. I want what I came here for."

"I still don't have it, but I'm close; I can feel it."

"Nope. That is not the answer I want to hear."

"I'm sorry, but that is what it is."

"Then you know the penalty."

"Oh please, Revaya, just stop. You need me."

"Why do I need you, Sarabi?"

"Because I'm the only one who can find this thing. I know all about the Prevail power. I've studied it, and I have the ability to search for the crown faster than you can."

"You know, my patience is growing thin."

"I know, so the sooner you let me get to my job, the sooner I can find it."

"You have one month, Sarabi. If I don't have what I want, you will be changing your residence."

After my grandmother left, I walked into the room. It startled my mother when she saw me.

Chapter 96

Prince Aries Fidem

"Aries, have you been here the whole time?" My mother asked.
"Yes, Mother, and I heard everything."
"Wait, let me explain."
"She cannot do this to you, Mother."
"Well, she has done it."
"Then I will go back; I will tell Father everything, the truth."
"Listen to me. If Revaya finds out that you are against her, she will kill you."
"I don't care. How can Father believe her?"
"She's the queen mother. She can do whatever she wants, and no matter what I say, it won't matter."
"What about Areos? Does he believe her too?"
"I don't know what your grandmother has told your brother."
"This isn't right. I'm not afraid of her."
"Listen to me, I'm handling it."
"Yeah, I can see that."
"Aries, don't worry about it."
"What is this Prevail power she is talking about?"
"Aries, no. It's better if you don't know."
"Mother, you better tell me now."

"You know about the other realms, right?" she asked.

"Yeah. What about them?"

"OK, a long time ago—and I mean a really long time ago, before the realms were created—the gods came together to help mankind, and in doing this they created a religion; it was called Prevail. Now, to ensure that Prevail would succeed and get followers, the gods gave a mortal their powers. They called him the King of the World, but it all backfired. When the mortal king was killed, the gods disappeared, never to be seen or heard from again, and seven different species were created instead."

"I don't understand. Where is the power in this?"

"The King of the World had a crown, a very special crown that will unite the powers again."

"So the crown is what you're looking for, with its godlike powers?"

"No, the crown is just a key. You see, there is a foretelling, a prediction that a superior Prevail being will have all the powers of the realms and will become the next King of the World, bringing the gods back."

"Wait, so how do you even know this Prevail being exists, and if he does, how will you find him?"

"That's why I need to find the crown. It belongs to the King of the World, and with it I will find the next King of the World who will have Prevail power. The eternal one will come forward!"

"But, Mother, what if you find this crown and it shows you nothing? This power may not be real."

"It says in the Prevail Book that the superior being will come forth during the era when all the realms are facing deplorable consequences of extinction. That a set of twins will be born from each realm with powers unlike anything they have ever seen. As far as I know, three realms have given birth or are about to give birth to a set of twins. And all the realms are suffering somehow; that can't be a coincidence."

"And once you find this superior being, you just give it up to grandmother, who will most likely harness the power for herself, being a Drekum and all, and wipe out the world."

"That's her plan. Mine is to find it before she does and use it to destroy her."

"But you said you were going to help her get it?"

"I just said that so she would send me here instead of the Dark Realm."

"Why here?"

"Because this was the last place anyone saw it."

"So it could be anywhere now."

"No, the elves had it last, but they didn't know what it was, and then less than a century later, they moved to Photinia, and that's where my sight loses it."

"I see. So if you tap into the tree of life, you will be able to find it."

"Yes, 'cause the Tree of Life sees everything in the Nature Realm."

Oh great, everything in the Nature Realm—that can't be good, I thought.

"Then we can go home," I said.

"You can go home. Revaya will never let me set foot in Tentinium."

"But if you get the crown, you can stop her."

"Aries, I have my own reasons for getting the crown. One is getting your brother back so we can be together."

"Then I'm going to help you."

"Aries, we have to keep this a secret. If anyone finds out about this, they will be searching for it too. It's best that you stay out of it. The less you know, the better."

"Mom, I'm going to help you whether you want it or not. Besides, I'm having trouble believing this is real."

"Trust me, son, it's more real than you think. My mother believed in this."

"I just don't want to see you get your hopes up."

"Now that the cat is out of the bag, are you going to tell me about your new love?" my mother asked.

"Not yet, but I will."

Chapter 97

Queen Sarabi Fidem

I wasn't happy that my son knew about this. I only told him enough to keep him from asking more questions. I left out a few things. I didn't want him involved.

Revaya could not be trusted, and she would kill anyone who knew about the Prevail power.

My mother used to tell me that it's best to stay in the dark until it's time to make a move, no matter how long it takes, that the opportunity to reveal your enemies' weaknesses is always worth the wait.

I was now more worried about Aries than I had ever been. I had been keeping him close to me and making sure that he didn't wander off into the jungle. But the last three weeks has had me scared. He had found a new love. And maybe this new love would keep him from falling in love with Jade Blumenthal. I have been secretly keeping them away from each other, hoping that they never meet. 'Cause if they do, he will fall in love with her, and it will cause a war between me and my half brother. I can't have a war right now, not when I'm so close to finding what I'm looking for. And without King James by my side, I have had to play by Midas's rules.

I was walking in my courtyard and decided to go farther out. I wanted to measure how much my kingdom had spread.

I got to the point where my kingdom ended and the forest began. I saw a shadowy figure, so I went farther into the forest. As I got closer, I saw big black wings. Wait, I know these wings, I thought. This figure was squatting down, so I could only see its back. But its profile was known to me. I knew this figure.

"Sly!" I shouted.

The figure stood up and turned around to face me.

I was in utter shock. Holy God of Death!

"Sarabi," he responded.

"How are you in the land of the living?"

"Where am I?"

"You're in the Nature Realm."

He looked around.

"Aren't you supposed to be in Tentinium?" he asked.

"I was, but I grew fond of my husband."

"You fell in love, didn't you?"

"Yes! But it looks like I'm not the only one who's changed."

"What are you talking about?"

"Sly, you are different; something about you is not the same."

"I feel great better than I have ever felt."

I was reading him. Something was very off. I could feel it some kind of power that was not from our realm. It was radiating off him.

"Sly, you don't look like you know what's going on."

Sly looked down at his hands, and then he looked at me confused.

"I don't remember."

"What do you remember?"

"I was in a heavy conversation with Ace."

"Aceifer! Is he here too?"

"No, he's…I can't…everything is black. I just remember talking to Ace, then it all goes dark."

"Does anyone know where you are?"

"No, I don't think so."

"Maybe we should contact Mother."

He laughed.

"Mother is no longer speaking; I cut out her tongue," he said.

"What? Why would you do that?"

"You know why. She was always favoring Ace. Well, not anymore; now she suffers in silence."

"You sound just like your father."

Sly's eyes got wide.

"I'm above him; I'm above all of them. I no longer take orders from my brother. I have outgrown the Dark Realm."

"Sly, this is not you. What has happened to you? You're so dark and cold."

"The best thing, baby sister. I'm free, and I'm going to take over this world and everything in it."

Shit, I do not need this right now, I thought.

"Yes, of course you are."

"There is just one thing that remains."

"What's that?

"Are you with me or against me?"

"I'm with you, dear brother. Always with you."

Sly smiled, and then he looked in the direction of the Kingdom of Viniues.

"Good, we can start with that kingdom first," he said.

I just smiled at him. I thought, This is going to be the biggest shitstorm anyone has ever seen.

> *The forest is a mystery, a pocket of soul, a*
> *breath of the unending, a love grown old.*
>
> —Angie Welland-Crosby

The End

KYLA GALINDO is a lifelong fan of epic tales. As a mother of three children, she stays busy at home, but when she has a little spare time, she spends it reading her favorite novels. Kyla decided to write this book to inject new life into the fantasy genre. In doing so, she has created a never-before-seen world infused with her own storytelling prowess. She wishes to share her passion for women everywhere to know that they can rise up together against the obstacles that stand in their way.

Printed in the USA
CPSIA information can be obtained
at www.ICGtesting.com
LVHW050359040324
773409LV00003B/4